OATH OF DESTRUCTION

REIGN OF SECRETS, BOOK 5

JENNIFER ANNE DAVIS

REIGN PUBLISHING

Published by Reign Publishing

Cover Design by KimG-Design
Editing by Cynthia Shepp

ISBN (paperback): 978-1-7323661-3-8
ISBN (hardback): 978-1-7323661-4-5
eISBN: 978-1-7323661-2-1
Library of Congress Control Number: 1-7151369921

OTHER BOOKS BY JENNIFER ANNE DAVIS

The True Reign Series:
The Key
Red
War

Reign of Secrets Series:
Cage of Deceit
Cage of Darkness
Cage of Destiny
Oath of Deception
Oath of Destruction

The Order of the Krigers Series:
Rise
Burning Shadows
Conquering Fate

Single Titles:
The Voice

PRAISE FOR CAGE OF DECEIT

Mundie Moms

"Jennifer Anne Davis's CAGE OF DECEIT has a new home on my coveted all-time favorite bookshelves. Not many books make the cut; this is a book I want more of. I need this book's sequel like now!"

Cameo Renae, Bestselling Author of the Hidden Wings Series and After Light Saga

"I was completely captured by this story. An outstanding and riveting read."

Damaris Cardinali from Good Choice Reading

"I thought Jennifer Anne Davis's *True Reign* series was one to rave about, but *Cage of Deceit* has topped it, and has completely blown me away! I love this book! I cannot wait for the sequel! Davis will forever be on my MUST-READ list."

Liza Wiemer, author of Hello?

"*Cage of Deceit* is a wonderful blend of fairy tale and fast-paced, thrilling adventure. With a kick-ass heroine princess, this novel will not only get your heart racing, but leave you clamoring for book two."

Grace from Books of Love

"An amazing fantasy that is a thrilling adventure from start to finish. I totally found myself loving the world that Jennifer Anne Davis has written in *Cage of Deceit*. This was a real gem to read."

Melanie Newton from Nerd Girl Official

"Twists and turns, danger and drama—this book has it all! Heart-dropping moments that literally had me holding my breath and an ending that demands book two be available NOW!"

Jan Farnworth from J.R.'s Book Reviews

"Jennifer Anne Davis knows how to weave a story that pulls at your heartstrings. She makes you want to take the sword and run it through the evil characters. Davis is an outstanding storyteller and on my *must read right now* list."

Leah Alvord from Vitality Reviews

"We have flawed, judgmental characters who feel truly human. There's political intrigue and deceit so thick you can disappear inside of it. And threats that gleam like a blade in the night. Welcome to the *Cage of Deceit*, where even a princess isn't all she's cracked up to be."

For Sarah
Thank you for the motivation.

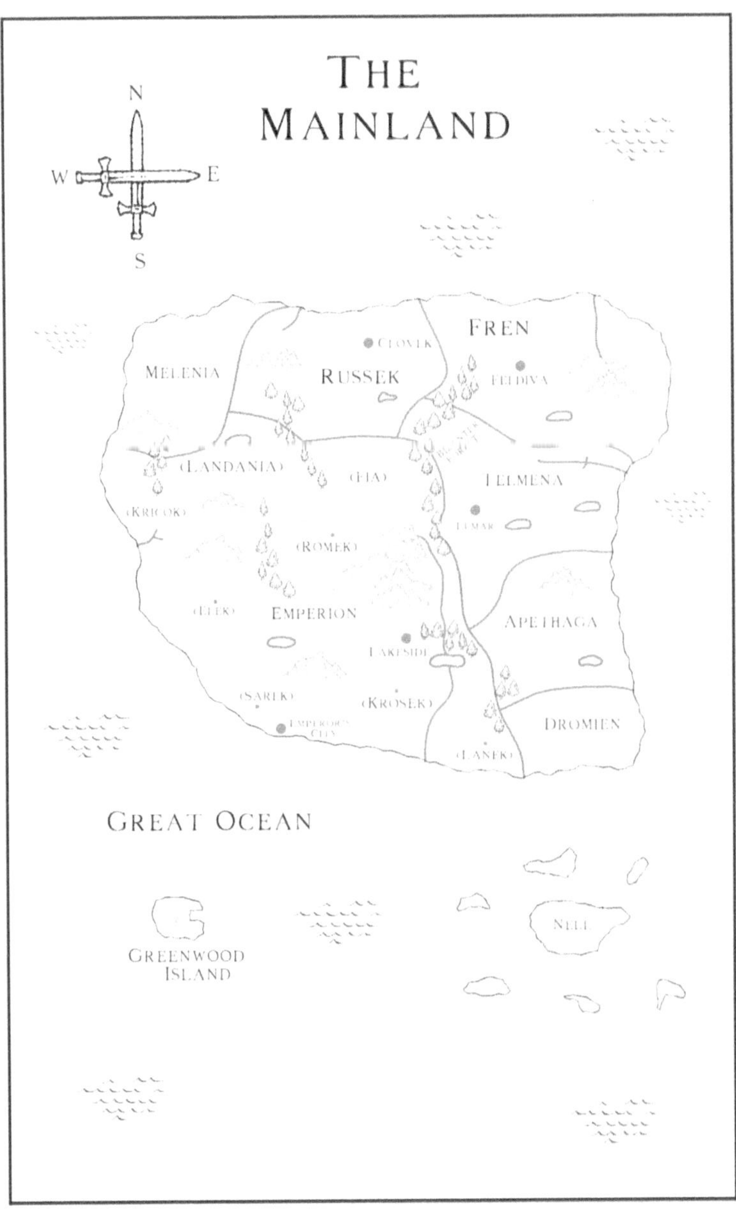
THE
MAINLAND

N
W   E
S

FREN
CLOVEK
MELENIA   RUSSEK   FELDIVA
(LANDANIA)   (FIA)   TELMENA
(KRICOK)   LEMAR
(ROMEK)
(ELEK)   EMPERION   APETHAGA
LAKESIDE
(SAREK)   (KROSEK)   DROMIEN
EMPEROR'S CITY   (LANEK)

GREAT OCEAN

NELI

GREENWOOD
ISLAND

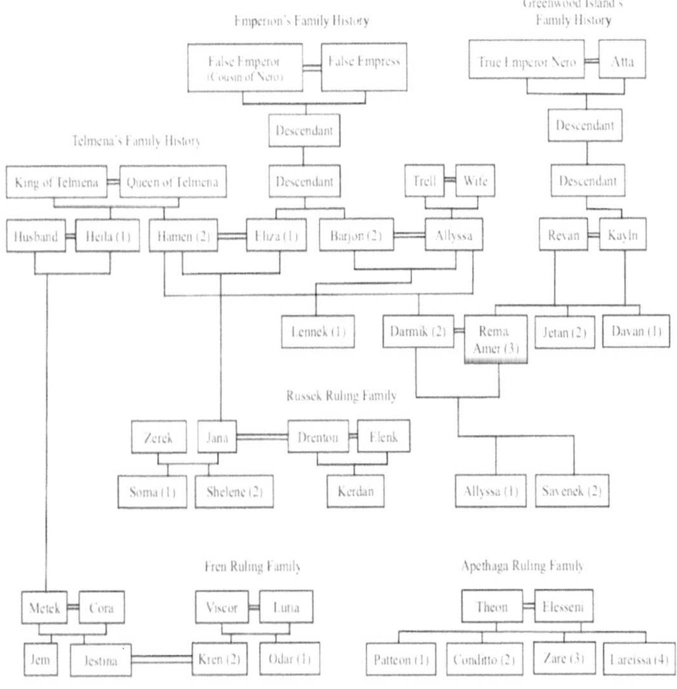

A number indicates the birth order in that family.
Indicates a marriage.

Oath of Destruction is the last book in the
REIGN OF SECRETS
series. Therefore, if you expect a happily ever after,
you may encounter such an ending.
Even though I enjoy leaving people hanging from cliffs,
this is the end of my beloved characters' story.
If you have the spirit of an adventurer, flip this page.
I DARE YOU!
After all, embarking on a tumultuous journey
is far more rewarding.
By turning the page, you understand that you are entering the fifth
book of the series
REIGN OF SECRETS.
After all the
laughs,
tears,
and heartaches,
we have finally come to the end.
Enjoy.

CHAPTER 1

Savenek didn't say a word to Rema or Darmik as the three of them made their way to the palace in Emperor's City. He wanted to be alone so he could think about everything they'd told him. However, time was of the essence. Allyssa, his sister, was dead. Savenek was now the crown heir.

Bullocks.

He was a bloody prince. It didn't seem real. He ran his hands through his tousled hair. Nathenek wasn't his father. In fact, Nathenek—the one person Savenek trusted and loved more than anyone else—had lied to him his entire life. Savenek wasn't even sure what he wanted to say to Nathenek right now. He'd probably start with one simple question: *Why?* Rema—his mother—had explained her reasoning. Not that he understood it or was okay with her justification, but at least she'd provided one.

Savenek glanced at the moon. It had to be past midnight by now. The cool air blew off the sea, coating Emperor's City with a light mist.

At the gate to the palace, a soldier granted them entrance. While their surroundings had been sandy, drab, and hardly anything green in the vicinity, the palace grounds were a different story. Instead of taking the main walkway as Savenek assumed they would, they veered to the left. For over a hundred years, this opulent palace had been standing amidst the desert city. Short green grass lined the pathway while perfectly manicured hedges grew next to it. In the distance, he could see a rose garden.

After fifty feet, the two guards traveling with them stopped and looked around. One knelt on the ground and opened a section of the grass, which ended up being a wooden door. It had blended in so well that not even Savenek had spotted it. He tried not to be too impressed.

Darmik gripped Rema's hand, helping her descend into the ground. He waved Savenek forward while scanning the area.

Savenek peered into the square hole, able to see a narrow staircase leading downward. He'd already decided to go with his *parents* to try to understand what was happening. First and foremost, Emperion was in danger and needed protecting. Even if he didn't fully comprehend everything, he had a duty to protect his kingdom—whether that was as a member of the Brotherhood or as a member of the royal family.

Savenek quickly descended the stairs. At the bottom, Rema reached out, taking his hand. He flinched. He barely knew this woman, his mother, who'd abandoned him for her kingdom. He didn't know if he admired her commitment or hated her priorities.

"This way," she whispered, still clutching his hand, refusing to let go. They moved a few feet away from the stairs, making room for Darmik.

After he descended, the door above them closed. The guards hadn't joined them. "Hang on," Darmik mumbled. There was a shuffling noise, and then a torch flared to life. Darmik held the torch out before him, revealing a squared tunnel. "Follow me."

They made their way along the tunnel, no one saying a word. The walls appeared to be dirt, chiseled by hand. Every ten feet or so, there were wooden beams that covered the sides and the ceiling, forming a "U" shape. They had to be for reinforcement. Savenek estimated they were twenty feet underground. After about a mile, they came to another set of stairs. Rema released

Savenek's hand, then rushed up them. At the top, she knocked on the ceiling twice, and a wooden door opened.

Savenek went up after her, stepping into a small room where half-a-dozen guards stood at attention. When Darmik entered behind him, the guards stood a little straighter. His presence filled the entire space, intimidating even Savenek.

"I want you," Darmik pointed at the guard closest to the door, "to escort my son to the Royal Chambers. You will remain with him until further notice."

Everyone's eyes widened in surprise at this news. Savenek took a deep breath and stepped around Darmik, wanting to get to his room so he could be alone for a few minutes. He needed to sort through everything. Right now, in the presence of the empress and emperor, he felt overwhelmed and was unable to think clearly. He wished Nathenek had come with him.

"I'm sorry, Your Majesty," one of the guards said. "Did you say *your son?*"

"Yes," Rema replied, her voice clear and articulate in the small room. "This is our son, Savenek, Allyssa's twin brother. He has been in hiding these past sixteen years."

The six guards dropped to their knees, bowing their heads. The move stunned Savenek. He scratched behind his ear, uncomfortable with the attention. Technically, he wasn't a prince, was he? Didn't there have to be a ceremony? Maybe the empress and emperor already had one when he was a baby. He shrugged. Was he supposed to tell the men to stand? Be at ease?

"You can declare your fealty to Prince Savenek tomorrow," Darmik said.

The men stood.

So Savenek was a prince then. He sure as heck didn't feel like a prince. Or look like one for that matter.

"This way, Your Highness," a guard said, opening the door for him.

Rema reached out, gently touching Savenek's shoulder.

Of all the times he'd wanted a mother, missed his mother, she'd been within reach. Profound anger and sadness overwhelmed him. Instead of saying something he'd regret, he ignored her and followed the guard out of the room.

When Savenek caught up to him, the guard took a huge step forward. Savenek tried to match the guard's strides, but the man increased his pace. Savenek was about to grab the guy and throw him up against the wall, demanding to know what his problem was, when the guard abruptly stopped.

"Your Highness," he said. "I am not permitted to walk alongside you."

"Why not?" Was this a subtle way of saying Savenek smelled? He'd been traveling for days and knew he needed a bath. Discretely angling his head, he sniffed himself. Yup, the stench of sweat was strong.

"Normally, I walk a step or two behind a member of the royal family. However, since you do not know the way, I am allowed to be in front of you. But not beside you."

Savenek didn't sense any deception in the guard's voice or words. He must be telling the truth. After rubbing a hand over his tired face, he nodded.

The guard started walking again, Savenek following at a reasonable distance.

"Are you allowed to talk to me?" Savenek asked.

"I am permitted to respond to your questions."

Excellent. "What's your name?"

The guard glanced over his shoulder. "The name's Brenek, Your Highness."

Savenek eyed Brenek's longsword. It appeared to be of a fine craftsmanship. The guard had to be decent in a fight to serve the royal family. "Do you enjoy your job?" Did Brenek see any action? He appeared about twenty-three years old.

"I do, Your Highness."

Savenek wished he'd stop calling him *Your Highness*. It was disconcerting.

They turned a corner. Large sconces with lit candles hung on the walls, casting the hallway in a soft glow. Savenek glanced at the pictures between the sconces. Each had an ornate gold frame encasing a portrait of someone he didn't know or recognize.

Savenek's footsteps echoed on the marble flooring. He lightened his steps so he didn't make a sound. Brenek glanced back and smiled.

When they came to a wide staircase, Brenek lifted a chamberstick from a side table and ascended.

"What's with all the keys?" Savenek asked as he went up the stairs. He'd seen keys carved into the doors, on handles, and even in some of the pictures.

The guard shrugged. "It has something to do with the royal family. The empress can answer your questions about the palace and its history."

They came to a landing and went up a second staircase.

"Are you usually stationed here? Or do you travel with the royal family?"

"I go wherever His Majesty tells me to."

At the top of the staircase, Brenek led the way down a carpeted corridor, dim candles barely lighting the area. There were a lot of shadows to hide in up here. They came to a set of double doors, soldiers standing on either side.

"This is His Highness, Prince Savenek," Brenek announced to the soldiers. "He will be staying in the Royal Chambers with the empress and emperor."

Both soldiers remained still, staring straight ahead like statues. If they were surprised by the information, neither showed it. Brenek opened the door.

Savenek stepped inside a posh sitting room. Four sofas, a low table made of gold, and several plush chairs were situated on thick carpet. Long drapes hung next to the windows. Several vases filled with flowers adorned side tables around the perimeter of the room.

Brenek headed toward the corner where an archway was located. Savenek followed him through it and down the dark hallway.

At the third door on the right, the guard stopped. "You can sleep in here." He positioned himself inside the room, next to the door, as if he planned to stand there all night.

Savenek stepped inside, scratching his head. "Okay, thanks." He went over to the bed and plopped onto it. The mattress was so soft he practically melted into it. He glanced around the room. A tall armoire stood in one corner, there was a dresser along the wall opposite the bed, a fireplace on the other wall, and a settee at the end of the bed. Half a dozen windows lined the wall behind his bed, none of which had the drapes pulled closed, so the moonlight shone brightly into the room.

Brenek still stood next to the door.

"Uh, you can go now." Savenek wasn't sure what the proper protocol was for dismissing someone.

"I've been assigned as your guard. I am not allowed to let you out of my sight."

Savenek snorted. He wasn't a soft prince who needed to be protected. "I have spent my entire life training with the Brotherhood of the Crown." He was certain he could take Brenek down in less than thirty seconds.

"Regardless, I have my orders." Brenek remained standing there with his feet shoulder-width apart, his hands hanging casually at his sides, as if he could stay in that stance for several hours.

"Can you at least stand outside my room?" Having Brenek in there was creepy. Savenek didn't want someone watching him sleep. Besides, quite frankly, it was insulting. He didn't need a babysitter.

"You'll have to discuss the issue with the emperor."

Not wanting to argue, Savenek pulled off his boots and fluffed a pillow. The mattress was too soft, the covers too luxurious. Staying in his clothes, he stretched out on top of the blankets, not wanting to get comfortable in this room. He half thought that when he woke up, he'd find himself back home, in his bed, and this would have been some sort of nightmarish dream.

SAVENEK FLEW UPRIGHT. SOMETHING SHATTERED IN the other room. Then someone screamed—the rage and grief clear. He rubbed his eyes, trying to get his bearings.

Brenek still stood next to the door, giving no sign he'd heard the commotion. Savenek slid out of bed and yawned. It was still dark out. He stood there for a minute, listening to two voices arguing—one male, one female. Unable to understand any of the words, he went over to the door and opened it an inch. Brenek didn't say anything.

"I understand you're upset," Rema said, her voice nasally. "I am, too. But that doesn't mean you can go on your own into Russek to kill Drenton."

"He'll never expect me," Darmik replied. "I can sneak in, slit his throat, and get out before anyone realizes what has happened."

It sounded like they were in the sitting room, just down the hallway from where Savenek stood.

"I have no doubt you can do it," Rema said, her voice shaking as if she was crying. "But we can't risk it."

"Then I'll be leading my entire army into Russek," Darmik replied, fury filling each clipped word. "We will destroy everything in our path."

Savenek shivered. He had no doubt Darmik would do just that. "I'm going to talk to the empress and emperor," he whispered. "Stay here."

Brenek nodded.

Savenek exited his room, closing the door behind him. Now that he'd ditched his guard, he needed to find a way out of the Royal Chambers. He wanted some time alone. He couldn't face Rema and Darmik right now, and he didn't want to be stuck in his room with someone watching his every move.

Heading away from the sitting room, Savenek crept along the hallway to the adjacent bedchamber. After pushing the door open, he went inside. Going over to the window, he saw he was on the third floor. He reached out, about to push the window open.

"What are you doing?" Darmik demanded.

Savenek cursed. He was never taken by surprise like that. How had he not heard Darmik approach?

"Did you think you could sneak out of the window?" Darmik asked. "Go traipsing around the palace and no one would notice?"

Well, yes, that was exactly what Savenek had thought. "I need to be alone."

Darmik stepped into the room, closing the door behind him.

"I don't like having someone watch me while I'm trying to sleep," Savenek added. He'd spent his life learning to hide in the shadows and avoid detection.

Darmik sighed. "Not this again."

"What?"

"Your sister would argue this very point with me all the time." He folded his arms across his chest. "I'll make the same deal with you that I made with her. There will be two guards posted outside your room at all times. However, you will not exit via the window. Ever. Understood?"

Savenek cocked his head to the side. Was Darmik trying to parent him? The thought nettled his nerves. His biological father hadn't been around during his entire life. Darmik couldn't just show up now, when he needed Savenek, and expect Savenek to jump and do his bidding.

Instead of answering, he changed the subject. "How'd you know

I was in here?" The room appeared to be similar to Savenek's. While it was grand, it wasn't opulent enough for an empress and emperor. If this wasn't Darmik's room, then had Brenek tattled on Savenek?

"Intuition. It's something your sister would have done."

Again, a reminder of the twin sister Savenek would never know. Would he spend his life trying to live up to her legacy? Would he constantly be in her shadow?

"Considering everything I've learned tonight, all I'm asking is for some time alone to process my new reality." Without someone staring at him. He didn't think it was too much to ask.

Darmik glanced over his shoulder at the closed door. Lowering his voice, he said, "Promise me you won't leave the palace grounds. I'm certain Russek has spies all over this city. It's not safe for you out there—no matter how talented you are. Now that you're a prince, you have to understand your safety is the priority. Emperion must have an heir."

What was Darmik trying to say? "I can leave the Royal Chambers?"

"If you leave through the doors, you will have a royal guard."

Which meant there had to be another exit. "Servants' passageways?"

"No. Too obvious. I'm sure you can find something a little more discreet. Your sister's preferred method is over there." He pointed to the corner of the room. "If anyone catches you, I'll claim to know nothing about it."

"My...sister would sneak out?"

Darmik smiled, the act softening his face. "All the time. She used to sneak into Lakeside."

"Did she not care for life at the palace?"

"She loved Emperion and wanted to make a difference. She'd track criminals, arrest them, and put them in jail."

His sister did that? A pain blossomed in Savenek's chest. He would never know Allyssa. All those years he'd felt like something was missing and when he'd finally figured out what it was, he couldn't even meet her.

"I need to get back to your mother. She's…well, as you can imagine, she's having a tough time. I'll see you at sunrise for a run." He left the room.

Savenek blinked. The man he'd just spoken to was not only his real father, but also the emperor of Emperion and the commander of the Emperion army. Undoubtedly the most powerful and important man in the entire mainland—not just Emperion. Savenek couldn't fathom the idea they were related.

Shaking his head in disbelief, he went over to the corner Darmik had pointed to. There was a square wooden door about two feet in diameter. He opened it. It must be the laundry chute. He eyed it suspiciously, pretty sure he wouldn't fit inside. Reaching in, he felt around and determined the chute was larger inside than the door indicated. It was worth a shot. If he got stuck, well, he'd worry about that if it happened.

He squeezed his body through the opening and into the chute. His feet found purchase against the walls, and he eased his head and arms in. It was a little tight, his shoulders touching each side. Taking a deep breath, he forced himself to remain calm as he lowered his body. With any luck, the chute wouldn't narrow. It was slow going, but he eventually felt another door against his left shoulder. Pushing the door open, he peered into the room. There was a large desk, and the walls were lined with books. He climbed into the office.

He wondered why an office would have a laundry chute. Unless this used to be a bedchamber at one time. When he stepped farther into the room, movement came from one of the corners. He froze, realizing he didn't have a weapon on him. Not that he needed one. However, a knife was nice to have in a fight.

A tall man appeared from the shadows. His tunic was pulled taut across his shoulders, his light brown hair was cropped close to his head, and there was a sword strapped to the man's waist. "I was wondering how long it would take you to show up."

Bullocks. It was Neco. Ari's father and Darmik's right-hand man.

Neco pulled the chair away from the desk and patted it. "Have a seat."

Savenek swallowed. He felt like he'd entered an interrogation room—and he was the one going to be interrogated. Unsure how to address this infamous man, Savenek decided not to speak and to just do what Neco had asked.

When he sat on the chair, Neco took hold of the back of it and leaned down next to him. "Technically, you aren't a prince yet, so I can address you informally."

Since Savenek had been trained in the art of interrogation, he knew he shouldn't say anything. However, his desire to make sure Ari was okay outweighed common sense. "How's Mayra?" He hadn't seen her since they escaped from Apethaga. Back when he didn't know she was Mayra, Neco's daughter. Back when he thought she was too far above his social class.

Neco's eyes narrowed. He released the chair, then slowly moved to Savenek's other side. He sat on the edge of the desk, assessing him. "I'll be the one asking the questions tonight."

Years of training with the Brotherhood and growing up with Nathenek had taught Savenek to keep his mouth shut. Not only that, but he also respected Neco. Not to mention Neco was Ari's father. He patiently waited for the man to speak.

"My daughter told me how loyal you are to the crown."

Savenek nodded. He believed there was nothing more important than protecting the royal family and Emperion. Strange to think the royal family now included him.

"I am here to make sure you really are as loyal as she claims." Neco slid his large hand onto Savenek's shoulder, squeezing it lightly.

Savenek forced himself not to flinch.

"Tell me, where do your loyalties lie?"

What was that supposed to mean? Was Neco questioning Savenek's dedication to the kingdom? To the royal family? To Ari? Savenek had the urge to scoot away from Neco, but he refrained from doing so. Sweat beaded on his forehead. *Blasted.* He never got this nervous during his training exercises.

"Answer the question." Neco released Savenek's shoulder, then casually folded his hands together on his lap.

The gesture didn't fool Savenek. Neco was trying to intimidate him. It wouldn't be so bad if the guy wasn't Ari's father. There was a reason he was doing this tonight, before Savenek was crowned prince and outranked him. He could respect that.

"My loyalty is to the rightful heir, Empress Rema."

"And the royal family?"

"Are second to her."

"Why?"

"Because she is the crown." He thanked his lucky stars that Nathenek had hounded Emperion's history into him.

Neco stood and moved to the other side of the desk, placing his palms on the surface so he now faced Savenek. "And tell me, since you are part of the royal family, does your loyalty change?"

Savenek wasn't sure what Neco was getting at, so he decided to be honest. "I won't pretend I'm not upset right now. I've been lied to my entire life. Rema and Darmik just showed up, told me I'm a prince, that I have a twin sister who was murdered, and they brought me here before I could even talk to Nathenek about everything." He ran a hand through his hair. "I've been trained my entire life to protect Emperion. I hope I can still put some of my skills to use." That he wouldn't be expected to be some court fop now that he was a prince.

Prince.

It felt like he'd been knocked off his feet in a sparring match. As the crown prince of Emperion, he would become the emperor when he turned thirty.

"I understand this is a surprise to you. It is to me as well. However, I need to make sure you are here willingly, that you plan to be a part of this family, and that you will do your duty."

Family. Savenek had a mother and a father now. "I will."

Neco leaned across the desk. "Even if that means you marry a princess from another kingdom?"

Savenek swallowed. He hadn't considered that. But Neco expected an answer. "Yes." Although, he wasn't sure he meant it. Regardless, he'd worry about that later. *Bloody hell.* His body prickled with heat, sweat dripping down his cheeks.

Nodding, Neco stood upright. "Rema and Darmik have just lost their daughter. You're all they have. I need you to be strong for them. Emperion won't survive otherwise."

"I understand."

Neco unlocked the door. "I'll escort you back to your bedchamber."

Savenek didn't want to go back to his confining room, but he dared not argue with Neco.

Out in the hallway, Brenek stood alongside another guard Savenek didn't recognize. The two men fell in step behind Neco and Savenek, not saying a word.

"You'll get used to it," Neco said softly.

Savenek eyed him sidelong. "Used to what?"

"Having guards with you at all times."

"Given my upbringing, I thought I'd be given more leeway."

Neco chuckled. "I've had this conversation with Allyssa many times. She hated to be followed around. However, she understood the necessity. In fact, my son is—was—the head of her guard."

Savenek remembered Nathenek saying something along those lines.

They went up a narrow stairwell and exited it just outside the Royal Chambers.

Neco stopped before the closed doors. "I will see you tomorrow after your run with your father." He turned and left.

Savenek went inside, thankful neither Darmik nor Rema were still in the sitting room. He went down the hallway. When he reached his door, the two guards took up position on either side of it.

Savenek went in and stretched out on his bed, thinking over everything that had happened tonight. Rema had told him that sixteen years ago, someone tried to murder him and his twin sister Allyssa, so she separated them to ensure the royal line persevered. She had told the kingdom that Savenek died while she secretly smuggled him out of the castle. Her good friend, Nathenek, had just lost his wife and baby in childbirth, so it made for the perfect cover. Nathenek had raised Savenek like a son. Treated him like a son. Loved him like a son. And Nathenek had never breathed a word of Savenek's true identity to him.

However, now that Russek's King Drenton had murdered Allyssa, Savenek was expected to step in and fulfill his duty, becoming the crown prince of Emperion. A duty he hadn't known existed until a few hours ago.

Savenek sat up in bed. He didn't have to be here. He could leave, go back to his old life. Be an assassin. Live with Nathenek. Was that what he wanted? Rubbing his eyes, he tried to think clearly. His number one goal was to protect Emperion. Right now, the best way to help the kingdom was to step into his role as the prince. And, as much as it pained him to admit it, he liked the idea of having a mother. He wanted to get to know Rema better— if only to understand her decision. Did she really put Emperion above all else? Not only herself, but also her family? Was that what it meant to be the ruler of this great kingdom?

He flopped back on the bed. For now, he'd see what this life had to offer. In the back of his mind, he couldn't stop thinking that maybe, just maybe, he was finally worthy of Ari.

CHAPTER 2

Savenek made his way out of his bedchamber. Two new guards stood posted on either side of the door. Trying not to let their presence bother him, he ignored them and headed to the sitting room.

He found Rema lying on the sofa, asleep. He stopped, not wanting to wake her. Her face was blotchy, as if she'd spent the night crying. She probably had. When he looked at her, he didn't think of her as the empress or as his mother. She was just a woman who'd lost her daughter.

A shuffling noise came from behind him. Savenek turned and saw Darmik exiting a bedchamber farther down the hall. Darmik joined him, and they quietly left the Royal Chambers. They descended the staircase with half-a-dozen guards trailing them.

"You'll get used to it," Darmik said.

Savenek wasn't sure he ever wanted to get used to people following him everywhere he went.

In the early morning light, Savenek was able to get a better view of the palace. Detailed paintings covered the ceiling, the doors appeared as if they were made from solid gold, and there were ornate vases filled with flowers everywhere. The palace felt... opulent and cold.

On the bottom floor, Darmik said, "We prefer to live at the castle in Lakeside. The only reason we are here is because this is farther from Russek, and this place has stronger fortifications than our other homes."

After exiting the palace, they entered a lavish garden filled with roses and trimmed hedges. A group of two dozen soldiers stood at attention.

"At ease," Darmik said to his men. "We're going for a short five-mile run to the dunes and back." He put his hand on Savenek's shoulder. "This is my son Savenek. He will be officially crowned later today."

Savenek didn't know if he was supposed to say anything.

One of the soldiers cleared his throat. "Commander," he said, "if I may, I'd like to speak on my squad's behalf."

Darmik nodded.

"We're sorry for your loss," the soldier said. "The princess will be missed."

As one, the squad of soldiers lowered their heads. Each put his fist over his heart—a sign of respect and an oath. Savenek had a feeling these men were silently promising retribution for Allyssa's death.

Darmik took a deep breath, slowly letting it out. "Thank you."

"If we go to war with Russek," the soldier said, "we'd like nothing more than to fight at your side."

Darmik nodded. "After my son is crowned, I'll go over the plan of attack." He balled his hands into fists. "Drenton will pay for murdering my daughter."

"When will the funeral be held?" the soldier asked.

"Immediately. I can't leave until after my son is crowned and my daughter is buried. And I am eager to seek justice."

Savenek wondered if Allyssa's body had been recovered. Then he decided that was something he'd rather not think about.

"Let's go." Darmik started jogging.

Savenek ran next to him as they headed northward. The soldiers followed close behind, running in two straight lines.

As Savenek ran, he wondered what to say to Darmik. Savenek

didn't think of Darmik as his father. But running side by side, Savenek couldn't help but notice the physical similarities. While Darmik was taller than Savenek, they each had the same build and facial structure.

"This is something Allyssa and I did together," Darmik mumbled. "She loved to run through the forest behind the castle back home with me."

"Is that one of the reasons you're still here? Are there too many memories in Lakeside?"

Darmik shook his head. "I want to get Rema back to Lakeside as soon as possible. She enjoys that location far more than this one. It's hard for her here. When we return home, though, I'm not sure how she's going to handle going through Allyssa's things." He choked up, not offering anything else.

"I'm sorry," Savenek said, because he didn't know what else to say to someone who had just lost his child.

"You don't need to be sorry," Darmik said. "What I need is for you to be there for your mother."

"I can do that." At least, Savenek thought he could.

"And I need for you to help me get revenge."

Savenek almost stumbled. He was going to be included in the plans to invade Russek? "I'll do whatever you need me to," he answered. Since Nathenek had sheltered him from anything even remotely dangerous, he thought he'd be excluded from any sort of combat with Russek. Maybe being a prince would have its perks.

"I was hoping you'd say that." They ran out through the gate in the wall and continued northward, heading parallel to the city. The sun started to crest the mountain range in the distance, making the air hot and dry.

"I've been trained with the Brotherhood," Savenek said. He wasn't sure how much Darmik knew about his upbringing.

"I know. And I'm going to count on you to handle a few things for me. However, we will discuss the details later. With Neco present."

Savenek wondered how much time he'd be spending with Neco now that he was going to be the prince. And he vaguely wondered if he liked that idea, or if the mere thought of it scared him.

"If anything happens to me," Darmik said, "you will take my place as the commander of the army. You will need Neco by your side in order to be brought up to speed with the inner workings and intricacies of the mainland."

Savenek knew plenty—Nathenek had made sure his students were well educated with politics.

"There is so much I need to tell you," Darmik said, almost to himself. "I still don't know whether your mother and I did the right thing by giving you up."

The turn of topics surprised Savenek. It was what he'd been wanting to ask, but he had been afraid to.

"After Rema decided we had to preserve the royal line and handed you over to Nathenek, she wasn't the same. It took months until she seemed even halfway back to normal. However, not a day has gone by where she hasn't thought about you. Every night before we went to sleep, we always imagined where you were and what you were doing."

They rounded the abandoned military compound and started heading south, back toward the palace.

Darmik said, "I'm telling you this because I'm leaving later today. I'm concerned about your mother. I don't know what Allyssa's death will do to her. Normally, she is the pillar of strength. She makes the decisions, and she's always steadfast in her purpose and goals. Now, I'm not so sure." His focus remained on the dirt road in front of them. "I need you to help fill Allyssa's void. I need you to be there for Rema while I'm gone."

Neco had basically said as much last night when they'd briefly spoken. "You plan to leave me here to babysit Rema while you're off fighting Russek?" The brief hope Savenek felt earlier was gone. He didn't know why he'd expected things to be any different now.

He would always be coddled and protected. Because he was a prince.

Darmik glanced over his shoulder at his soldiers. "We'll discuss what you'll be doing later. I have plans for you." His voice was deep and filled with determination.

"You're not going to lock me in the palace? Make sure I'm safe?"

They ran in silence for several minutes. Perhaps Savenek shouldn't have said that. It had probably been too harsh.

"I limited what Allyssa could do with the intention of keeping her safe," Darmik replied. "And she's dead."

A whisper of fear shot through Savenek. He couldn't pinpoint what the emotion was based on, but it was there nonetheless.

"On the other hand, Rema has always run headfirst into danger and succeeded in all she's done. I'm going to have a little more faith with you than I did with your sister, especially given your background. To the world, you will appear as a doting son and prince. You will be carefree, easygoing, and you will be nonthreatening. In reality, you will be the dagger no one sees coming. You will be my arrow. We will make everyone pay for what they've done to Allyssa." Darmik finally raised determined eyes to Savenek. "That is…if you agree to this plan."

Savenek's heart pounded. "You mean I'm not going to be stuck sitting on some throne looking pretty?"

Darmik smiled. "That will be the appearance. But no, I intend to put you in the thick of things. We are family. And there's no one else I trust more—or who deserves to be involved more —than you."

Savenek couldn't contain his smile. Finally, he was going to be a part of something. He was going to fight for Emperion. "Then I agree. I'll be whatever weapon you need me to be."

SAVENEK STOOD OUTSIDE THE CLOSED DOORS, wondering what awaited him. The darn cape was so heavy it pulled against his neck, practically choking him. He tugged it away, but it didn't help much.

The clothes he had on also bothered him. The seamstress had been waiting for him when he returned from his run. She'd pounced on him, measuring and cutting fabric to get his outfit ready for the ceremony.

The doors swung open, and trumpets sounded. This was it then. Savenek stepped forward, the heavy cape trailing behind him as he walked down the center aisle.

There were a ton of people present. He hadn't expected so many to be there on such short notice. Everyone stood and watched him as he passed by. He tried not to focus on the people. Most were dressed in army uniforms. They had probably been close, and that was why they attended the ceremony.

When Savenek reached the dais, he knelt. Rema and Darmik stood side by side, both wearing capes similar to his. Each also wore a golden crown with rubies.

An elderly gentleman stepped forward, standing before Savenek. He started his speech about tradition and sacrifice. He spoke about how great the kingdom of Emperion was.

Kneeling, Savenek realized he would never take the oath and enter the Brotherhood. He'd trained his entire life for that, but now everything had changed.

Sweat dripped down the back of his neck. The elderly man kept droning on and on about duty and sacrifice. Finally, he lifted a gold crown encrusted with rubies and placed it upon Savenek's head. The thing was heavy. Hopefully, he wouldn't have to wear it often.

Rema motioned for Savenek to stand. He complied.

"Repeat after me," the man said. "I, Savenek, do hereby promise to uphold the laws and values of our great kingdom Emperion."

Savenek repeated the words, not really paying attention to what he was saying. The realization he was being crowned —*crowned*—was almost too great to comprehend. When he was finished saying his oath, one he never in his wildest dreams envisioned saying, he was given a longsword. He took it, strapping it to his waist. It vaguely matched his crown.

Rema stepped forward. "I now present to you, Crown Prince Savenek of Emperion, my son."

Savenek turned to face the crowd. Everyone dropped to one knee, bowing their heads.

"Rise," Rema commanded.

As one, they stood, smiling and clapping. Rema and Darmik moved to stand on either side of Savenek.

"Let's go," Darmik said. "The three of us can't afford to be seen in public together. With Russek scheming to take over Emperion, we must be extra vigilant and assume assassins are always nearby."

With that enlightening thought, they headed down the aisle and out of the hall. Savenek reached up, feeling the crown atop his head. As he walked between the emperor and empress, his cape dragged on the ground behind him. *Blasted*. He was a prince. And not just any prince. But the prince of Emperion.

"We are going to introduce you to the city," Rema said. "Once that is done, we will go to the funeral for Allyssa." Her voice cracked, and tears welled in her eyes. "We must bring closure to this tragic event so we can move forward."

The only reason Savenek had been officially crowned was because his sister had been killed. He couldn't celebrate his position knowing what it cost Rema and Darmik. "Am I supposed to attend the funeral?" It seemed strange to go to a funeral for someone he'd never met—even if that someone was his twin sister.

"Yes," Darmik replied. "You won't need to say anything, but you should be there to show solidarity."

Savenek's entire body began sweating from the cape. The thing had to weigh fifty pounds. He unlatched it and tossed it to one of the guards, who deftly caught it. He felt like he could breathe again. Thankfully, neither Darmik nor Rema commented or chided him for removing the cape.

They continued to the entrance of the palace where a carriage waited for them. Savenek climbed inside, sitting across from Rema and Darmik. Mounted soldiers surrounded the carriage and they took off, leaving the palace grounds and entering the main part of Emperor's City.

While Savenek had known the royal family spoke to the citizens, he'd never attended one of their speeches. As a result, he wasn't sure what to expect. The carriage stopped before a tall building. The door swung open, and they exited. Savenek had seen this building before—it was one of the tallest ones in the city. He thought it used to be some sort of prison back in the day.

The soldiers ushered them inside. There weren't any visible windows. Only one torch had been lit, casting the room in a dark glow.

"I always hate coming here," Rema mumbled.

"I know," Darmik replied. Placing his hand on her lower back, he escorted her to a narrow staircase. They started climbing. Savenek followed them, smelling the dank air of the building.

After five flights, they came to an open floor with several windows, the sun spilling through. There was a single closed door on the west wall. Savenek assumed the balcony was on the other side. A dozen sentries stood guard on this floor, half watching outside, the other half focused inside the room. These sentries were different from the ones Savenek had seen throughout the palace. They were a little more muscular, their faces stern. Focusing on their uniforms, Savenek noticed a black stripe down the left arm of each man. General sentries wore black pants and red tunics with the royal crest embroidered on the front, while members of the royal guard wore solid red pants and a black tunic with the royal crest on the back. "Are these men part of an elite squad?" Savenek asked. City Guards wore solid black.

"These are men from my army who handle high-risk situations," Darmik answered. "I sent them here last night to prepare for today."

"Your Majesties," a soldier said, bowing. "Everyone is in position."

"Let's proceed," Darmik said.

The soldier opened the door. "Empress Rema and Emperor Darmik."

The crowd exploded in a roar of applause.

"Wait here," Rema instructed Savenek before stepping onto the balcony with Darmik at her side.

The door remained open so Savenek could see the crowded courtyard below. He couldn't believe how many people were crammed in there to hear the empress speak. Considering the princess was murdered and the kingdom about to go to war, he could understand why.

Rema raised her arms, and everyone quieted down. "My fellow Emperions," she bellowed, "these are troubling times. As you heard in the announcement yesterday, Princess Allyssa," Rema's voice wobbled, "my daughter, was murdered by King Drenton of Russek." An eerie silence descended over the courtyard. "Sixteen years ago, I gave birth to twins. When someone tried to kill my babies in their cribs, I took my son and hid him. To protect him and ensure the royal line would carry on, I told everyone he was dead. Now that the princess of Emperion has been viciously murdered, I have brought my son back to assume his place at my side."

The crowd murmured. Turning, Rema waved Savenek forward.

Darmik addressed the people, "We want to introduce you to Prince Savenek."

Savenek stepped onto the balcony between Rema and Darmik. The crowd responded with applause, probably not sure what to think of this startling news. Knowing it was imperative the crowd accept him as the heir, Savenek raised his right arm and waved. Rema and Darmik each placed a hand on Savenek's shoulders, linking the three of them. Savenek bowed his head and held his right fist over his heart, sealing his promise to protect the people of Emperion. The crowd erupted in cheers.

Darmik raised his right arm, and everyone became silent once more. "As the commander of the Emperion army, I am ready to lead our mighty soldiers into Russek and wage war against the murderous king. We must avenge Princess Allyssa's death."

Everyone screamed in agreement.

"Let's go," Darmik said under his breath.

They quickly left the balcony.

"That was brief," Rema said once they were inside the room and the door was firmly closed. "You didn't care to say anything else?"

"No. I didn't want to risk being out there any longer," Darmik replied. "Even with tight security, the balcony is too exposed."

"He's right," Savenek added. "I found a ship from Russek docked in the harbor a couple of months back. It was filled with poison from Apethaga." Nathenek had managed to sink the ship, thus destroying the poison. "I'm sure more Russeks have gotten past our spies."

Blinking, Rema swiveled her gaze from Savenek to Darmik and back again. "You two are so alike." She shook her head before descending the staircase.

Darmik patted Savenek's back. "Let's go, son. We have a funeral to attend."

BACK AT THE PALACE, REMA, DARMIK, AND SAVENEK were led to a room in the east wing. Since Allyssa's body hadn't been recovered from Russek, Rema had arranged dozens of flowers on a table that stood at the end of a long room filled with people. Unlike the last hall where hundreds of uniformed soldiers had been present, this room contained mostly people dressed in fancy clothing. They had to be courtiers then.

The royal family headed slowly down the aisle, approaching the table together. Now that Savenek was closer, he could see two daggers and a crown had been placed in the middle, resting atop a bouquet. He didn't know what he was supposed to feel. While Rema had tears streaming down her cheeks, she kept her head high and her shoulders back, managing to seem regal and a bit intimidating in the process. Darmik, on the other hand, had a stern face with dark eyes. Savenek shivered. If he'd met his father at a tavern, he would think Darmik was an assassin. But maybe that was what Darmik had on his mind—killing those responsible for murdering his daughter. Savenek hadn't even known the princess, and he wanted revenge for what Russek did.

No one said a word. After several minutes, Rema took Savenek's hand and they turned, exiting the room.

Once they were back in the Royal Chambers, Rema's shoulders dropped and Darmik finally blinked, showing slightly more emotion than before.

"Do you know how she died?" Savenek asked before thinking the question through.

Darmik's fingers curled into fists, his knuckles turning white. "Russek kidnapped her. They sent a ransom note telling Rema to abdicate the throne. When she refused, they sent us Allyssa's fingernails and a detailed note on how each one was removed. King Drenton made sure to tell us about the pain she suffered." He took a deep breath. "Then they sent another note stating it was the last time they'd ask. We could either hand over Emperion or Allyssa would die."

"Did you think about handing the throne over?"

"No," Rema responded. She sat on the sofa, folding her hands on her lap. "Russek would have destroyed the citizens of

Emperion. I couldn't do that to my people." She focused on Darmik, her chin wobbling, her eyes red.

"They would have killed her no matter what we did," Darmik said. "Jana wanted revenge. Killing our child and making us suffer is the best form of punishment she could have inflicted upon us." He turned away from Savenek and Rema, going over to the window and staring outside.

Savenek ran his hands through his hair. Being a ruler was filled with tough choices. His life was no longer about what he wanted but what was best for his kingdom. "What's the plan?" He recalled Darmik saying he was leaving today.

"Neco and I are heading for the frontlines. When we get there, we'll attack Russek."

Savenek wanted to ask details such as how many men were at the frontlines, where would the attack take place, and how did Darmik intend to reach King Drenton? However, with Rema sitting on the sofa, tears streaming down her cheeks, Savenek didn't think it was the proper time to discuss battle strategies. Instead, he asked, "When are you leaving?"

"Now."

"Right this minute?" Savenek asked.

"Yes." Darmik squatted in front of Rema, taking her hands and holding them between his own. "I promise I'll be back. And I will extract revenge on King Drenton and Prince Kerdan. I swear to you I won't return until they're dead."

Rema threw her arms around Darmik's neck. "I can't lose you, too."

"You won't. And Savenek will be here in my place."

Rema and Darmik turned to Savenek. He still couldn't think of them as his parents. He couldn't even imagine ruling this kingdom. It was all too much. "I'll help in any way I can."

"Good." Darmik stood. "While I'm gone, you will do what we discussed earlier. You will appear to be a carefree prince. Rich, entitled, nonthreatening. Understood?"

"Yes."

"Your father's right," Rema added. "The other kingdoms all have spies here. We want those spies to see you out and about. You will be happy and laid-back. No one can suspect you were trained with the Brotherhood. No one can find out there is more to you than what they see."

"While I'm gone fighting Russek, you and Rema will be in charge of the Brotherhood."

Savenek couldn't believe what he was hearing. In charge of the Brotherhood? That was an honor he hadn't expected, and it was a challenge he would gladly take.

"Make sure Apethaga doesn't sell poison to the other kingdoms. If you can, see that production ceases."

Savenek nodded. He could do that, especially since he'd been to Apethaga and knew firsthand how potent the poison was, as well as where one of the mines was located.

"You will also be in charge of monitoring our borders. And watching the sea. No ships from other kingdoms are permitted to dock in our port until this war is over."

"Yes, sir." Nathenek had sheltered Savenek for so long he found it hard to believe he was not only involved in the kingdom's politics and the upcoming war, but that he was also being given such huge responsibilities. He wouldn't disappoint Darmik. And maybe in the process, he'd impress Neco.

Darmik smiled. "And remember, you are the crown prince of Emperion. You don't answer to anyone. They answer to you."

CHAPTER 3

Savenek

After Darmik said goodbye to Rema, he came over to Savenek. "Come with me. There's something I want to show you before I leave."

The pair exited the Royal Chambers, making their way to the first floor of the palace. "While I'm gone, this belongs to you." Darmik reached in his pocket, then pulled out a thin skeleton key. "It unlocks my office."

Savenek took the key, closing his fingers around it. He couldn't believe Darmik was entrusting him with something so valuable and important. As a trainee of the Brotherhood, Savenek had never been privy to a high-ranking official's office. If he'd wanted to gain access, he'd had to break in.

"Here we are." Darmik stopped before a nondescript door. "Unlock it."

It couldn't be that simple.

Darmik smiled, as if sensing Savenek's thoughts.

Savenek unlocked the door, then pushed it open it. There was a short hallway with another door at the end.

"This one requires some finesse." Darmik demonstrated how to push the stone four over and three up from the floor before inserting the key and unlocking the second door. "The previous emperor was a little paranoid."

For good reason, Savenek thought, seeing as how Darmik and Rema had killed Emperor Hamen.

Savenek stepped inside the large office. In the middle of the room stood a round table, papers strewn all over it.

"On that wall," Darmik said, pointing to his right, "are maps of Emperion, where our soldiers are stationed, and places of importance. The maps on the wall behind you are of our neighboring kingdoms. Study the maps. Know them well. On the table, you will find several letters and correspondence with other kingdoms, reports from spies, and treaties we've signed. I tried to put anything you need to know or might find useful here."

Savenek went over, scanning the table. He saw a letter signed by King Drenton, a hastily written letter with only a *B* for the signature, indicating it was from a member of the Brotherhood, and a list of weapons and supplies at a camp in the Romek mountains.

"With regards to the Brotherhood," Darmik said, "Rema has been in charge of that organization since it began almost twenty years ago. She will explain the inner workings and what you will be doing in my place."

Savenek couldn't believe Darmik was giving him access to all of this. That he trusted Savenek enough to give him this responsibility.

"Rema feels guilty for Allyssa's death. She sent two members of the Brotherhood after the princess. We don't know what happened to them. It is rare for the Brotherhood to fail on a mission." Darmik went over to the map of Russek and studied it. "Russek must be stopped. Rema is too distraught to effectively manage the Brotherhood alone. You will act in my place and aid her. And if I don't make it back, it's up to you to stop Drenton, Jana, and Kerdan."

Savenek would gladly take up the reins and stop Russek and their machinations. The thought of killing the king, queen, and prince and seeking revenge on behalf of Emperion gave him direction and purpose.

"They killed your sister." Darmik's voice was tinged with disbelief.

Savenek came over and stood next to Darmik, staring at the map of Russek. "We'll get our revenge." One way or another, Savenek would make sure of it.

"If you need anything, ask your mother for help. She is the only one you can trust implicitly. Out there," Darmik pointed out of the room, "you're a carefree prince, calm, collected, and in control—no matter what you are thinking or feeling. In here," he pointed at the floor, "you're the one keeping this kingdom running. You will be lethal, unwavering, and steadfast in your commitment to Emperion and its success."

"Understood." It was just like being on a mission. Savenek was given a role to play, a job to do, and he would do it.

"Any questions before I leave?"

"Just one. Will I be able to see Nathenek?" He needed to talk to him about everything so he could understand why Nathenek hadn't told him his identity.

"Eventually. For now, he is being utilized elsewhere."

Before Savenek could ask what mission Nathenek had been sent on, Neco entered the room. "Everyone is saddled and ready to go."

"Take care of your mother while I'm gone," Darmik said. He patted Savenek on the back and started to leave. "Are you coming?" he asked Neco.

"I'll be along in a second. I need to speak to Savenek alone."

Savenek vaguely noted how informally Neco spoke and acted around Darmik. Almost as if they were brothers. And he didn't fail to notice Neco was extending that same familiarity toward him—calling him by his first name and not using his title. Savenek wasn't sure what that meant; however, he didn't think it was a good thing like it was between Darmik and Neco.

After Darmik left, Neco closed the door. "I have something to discuss with you."

Savenek moved to the other side of the table so there was a buffer between them. Neco's eyes narrowed, the corners of his lips rising as he fought a smile. *Blasted.* Neco knew he intimidated Savenek. He wanted to kick himself for giving Neco the upper hand.

"I came here to ask you for a favor," Neco said.

That surprised Savenek. "Of course." Anything to help Ari's father.

"If something happens to me, I want you to honor my wishes and leave my daughter alone."

Savenek wasn't sure what Neco meant. Professionally? Or personally? He decided to press Neco a bit. "I was just on my way to speak to Rema about bringing Mayra here to assist me. I want to surround myself with people who are intelligent and who I can trust. I could use someone with Mayra's linguist abilities at my side."

Neco remained standing still, watching Savenek.

Savenek tried not to smile as he forged on. "Now that Allyssa is dead, Mayra is no longer her lady-in-waiting. I'm assuming she needs a new job?"

Neco nodded. "She will be reassigned. But that isn't what I'm referring to. I do not want you pursuing my daughter for the purpose of marriage."

"Why is that?" Savenek folded his arms, challenging Neco to answer. Was Savenek not good enough for Mayra? How could that be now that he was the prince of Emperion? Did Neco have someone else in mind for his daughter? That thought nettled Savenek. He raised his eyebrows, waiting for Neco's response.

"I want to make sure you marry for the benefit of Emperion. I don't want my daughter getting in the way of that."

It wasn't the answer Savenek expected. It almost sounded as if Neco wasn't sure Mayra was good enough for Savenek—which was insane. She was perfect. "What if Mayra is what's best for the kingdom?"

"Right now, we're on the brink of war. We need to keep our options open in case an alliance or truce is needed."

"Understood." This wasn't about Savenek or Mayra. It was about Emperion. Like Rema, who'd given up her son for her kingdom, Neco was willing to sacrifice Mayra's happiness for Emperion. "I will do what is best for my kingdom." Because right now, that was all that mattered.

"Good."

"And if that means utilizing your daughter as part of my intelligence team, so be it."

Neco's jaw twitched. He must not have expected such a response from Savenek. After an uncomfortable minute in which neither of them spoke, Neco gave a curt nod and left the room.

Savenek sat on one of the chairs before his legs gave out. He couldn't believe he'd just spoken to Neco—one of the greatest military leaders of all time—like that. It was a bold move, and he hoped it paid off.

SAVENEK SPENT THE FOLLOWING DAY GOING OVER THE documents and letters Darmik had left for him. Most of the information he was aware of—like the fact Landania, Kricok, and Fia had willingly joined the empire in order to gain the protection of the Emperion army in case Russek invaded them. Some he hadn't known—like Jana's son, Soma, was skilled in the art of poison, and King Drenton's previous wife Queen Elenk had died suddenly after Soma came to court. Once Queen Elenk died, King Drenton married Jana, Darmik's half-sister, who was determined to overthrow Rema and Darmik so she could claim the Emperion throne. Savenek rubbed his forehead, realizing Jana had to be crazy, and he was related to her.

"Your Highness," a sentry yelled from the other side of the door. "The empress wants you. Immediately."

The urgency in the sentry's voice spurred Savenek into action. He jumped up from his chair and exited the office, going directly to the Royal Chambers.

Rema was pacing in the sitting room. When she saw Savenek, she rushed over to him and grabbed his upper arms. "Russek attacked." Her eyes were wide with shock. "There's no way Darmik and Neco have reached the frontlines yet. That means our men are fighting without their commander."

Russek attacked? "Darmik has competent men in charge," Savenek answered. At least, he assumed Darmik would only have the most proficient men leading the army.

"He does," Rema agreed. "But he should be there."

"You're not relieved he's missing the war?"

"If you were in Darmik's position, would you be happy if you weren't there to fight?"

"No."

"Darmik is going to be furious. I know how important this is to him, and our chances for success are higher with him there."

Sometimes, Rema surprised him. She wasn't like a lot of the other women he'd met over the years. Even though she looked regal and elegant with her fancy dress and her hair all done up, there was a fierce determination to her that he understood.

"Come with me," Rema said. "We must get to work. We can't win this war sitting around. There is much to be done."

MEANDERING DOWN THE HALLWAY, SAVENEK FORCED his steps to be slow and casual. He smiled at those he passed by, acting as if he didn't have a care in the world. At the fifth door on the right side, two sentries stood guard. Savenek nodded to them, and one opened the door. Stepping inside, Savenek straightened and hurried to his desk. After he sat, he started going through the correspondence that had been left for him.

For the past few days, most of his time had been spent in here. Originally, this room had been used for dancing and parties. Now, it had been dubbed the War Room, and the entire space was filled with long tables serving as desks. Rema and Savenek managed everything from here. It also allowed messengers and spies reporting in to easily find them. Rema and Savenek worked side by side, dispatching spies, monitoring the progress the army made, taking note of the casualties, and sending additional supplies as needed. At any one time, day or night, there were at least fifty people working in there.

Savenek read the most recent report. It stated the Emperion troops were steadily holding the line, and Russek hadn't managed to advance any farther. Darmik and Neco had also arrived at the frontlines and were rallying the men.

Rema had written a letter to Fren requesting their immediate aid. So far, no Fren troops had responded to the request for help. Most of the fighting was taking place in Landania and Fia. Emperion casualties were high, the Russek soldiers unmercifully brutal.

Savenek leaned back in his chair, tossing the report on the table.

Rema joined him. Picking up the report, she began to read through it. "Excellent," she murmured. "Having Darmik there should help."

Savenek felt queasy knowing the emperor was there fighting. Russek would stop at nothing to capture or kill him. As strong as Rema appeared, he didn't think she could handle another loss right now.

"Your Majesty," a soldier yelled as he entered the War Room. He bent over, panting. "I have a message."

"What is it?" Rema demanded, her face paling.

"The Russek army is retreating. I rode straight here to deliver the news." Someone handed the soldier a cup of water, and he quickly gulped it down.

"Russek has ceased fighting?" Rema clarified.

"Yes, Your Majesty."

Rema abruptly sat on the chair next to Savenek. "What do you make of this?"

"I'm leery. Are they retreating for a reason?" Savenek said. He considered various reasons Russek would withdraw. "What if they're planning to attack with poison? They could be simply moving their soldiers out of harm's way."

Rema stood and began pacing. "What are our options?"

Several officers had gathered.

"We could go after the Russek army," one suggested.

"We should stay where we are and monitor the situation," another said.

"And what if Prince Savenek is right? What if Russek plans to attack tomorrow with poison?"

No one said a word.

Savenek leaned his elbows on the table, trying to decide the most effective way to administer large doses of the poison. What would he do in Russek's situation? "The poison will be administered through the air."

"How so?" Rema asked.

A feasible idea came to him. "They could have hidden containers with the poison in the ground. Maybe the Russek army retreated in order to get our army to follow. When our men step on the hidden containers, the poison will be released into the air, killing anyone who breathes it in."

The room fell silent as everyone stopped to stare at him, imagining the horrific implications of such a catastrophe.

"We need to prevent that from happening," Savenek added.

"You." Rema pointed at the soldier who'd delivered the message. "Make haste back to the frontlines. Tell the commander not to go after the Russek army. Tell him of the potential for a lethal attack like the prince suggested.”

“Yes, Your Majesty.” He turned and ran from the room. Savenek hoped the soldier at least took a fresh mount.

“Everyone else, dispatch messages throughout the army. Let them know of this new danger.” Rema turned to Savenek. “What sort of quantities are we looking at?”

“A small amount will do a lot of damage.”

“That’s what I was afraid of.” She sat down again. “What can we do?”

“I’ve sent spies into Apethaga. I know of one location where the kepper flowers are taken and turned into poison. The Brotherhood is searching for more mines.”

“I hope you told them to destroy these locations.”

He’d wanted to. “We can’t. We need to know where the poison is going. If we destroy the mines, Apethaga will know we’re aware of what they’re doing and hide all traces of sales and what they’ve done. If we leave the mines alone, we can follow the poison and see who is getting it and what they’re doing with it.”

Rema clasped her hands together, staring at Savenek with her bright blue eyes. “Once we have that information, I want each and every mine destroyed.”

“With pleasure.”

A few hours later, a letter arrived via another messenger.

Rema—

King Drenton is dead. Murdered by his own son who wants the throne for himself. Jana is refusing to relinquish it to him. She has declared herself the queen of Russek and Kerdan a traitor. Russek is now in a brutal civil war as the two battle for the throne.

I'm tempted to return home. However, I must consider that this could be a ruse. I will remain here with my men another week. At that time, I'll reassess the situation.

Yours,

Darmik

"What do you think?" Rema asked after she read the letter.

"I'd like to believe that's why the army retreated." Savenek wondered whose orders the army was following—Jana's or Kerdan's? "But…"

"What is your intuition telling you?"

"That it couldn't be that simple. It seems too easy, too convenient."

"I agree."

A WEEK LATER, THE REPORTS ALL SAID THE SAME THING: Russek was indeed in the middle of a nasty civil war. Jana had the backing of several rich, powerful nobles, while Kerdan had the support of a substantial portion of the army and the poorer citizens of the kingdom.

Darmik wrote to tell them he'd decided to keep a unit of the Emperion army along the Russek border to monitor the situation. He sent the rest of the army home.

Savenek plopped on the sofa in the Royal Chambers. He was glad to be out of the War Room. He'd spent the better part of last week disassembling it and moving his stuff back to Darmik's office. There, he'd finally received word from a member of the Brotherhood stating there was only the one active mine in Apethaga producing the kepper poison. The Brotherhood was tracking shipments that had recently left the facility.

Rema entered, gliding across the room to peer out the window. "I've received word your father and Neco have returned."

At first, Savenek thought Rema was referring to Nathenek, but then he realized she'd meant Darmik. Savenek still didn't consider Darmik his father. He didn't know if he ever would.

A few moments later, the door swung open and Darmik

entered. He still wore his commander uniform, his face was unshaven, and he had mud covering his boots. He stormed across the room, grabbed Rema, and slammed his lips against hers. Savenek had to turn away.

"I missed you," Rema murmured.

"You two done?" Savenek asked.

Darmik chuckled. "Sorry, I couldn't help myself." He stepped away from Rema. "I'm going to bathe. When I'm done, we'll talk."

"Before you leave," Rema said, "did Fren truly not come to our aid?"

Darmik's eyes darkened. "No. And I sent multiple messengers."

Now that Allyssa and Odar were both dead, any hope of aligning the two kingdoms must be over. Savenek thought it a bold move on Fren's part not to send help because if Russek attacked Fren, Emperion would not step in.

Darmik moved toward the hallway.

"Are you certain Odar is dead?" Rema asked.

Savenek reconsidered what he'd learned about the kidnapping. Allyssa's guard, Marek, reported he'd seen the assassin shoot and kill Odar. "Why are you questioning it?" Did Rema know something he didn't?

Darmik rubbed his jaw. "When Odar came to Lakeside to court Allyssa, he switched places with his squire Jarvik. Marek did not know of the deception. I think Jarvik was killed, not Odar. Somehow, the assassin knew who the prince really was. Which means the assassin took Odar and Allyssa to Russek."

"And you didn't bother to tell Fren their prince was still alive?" Savenek guessed. The more he was around Darmik, the more he liked him. If the king and queen of Fren believed their son was dead, Russek couldn't use Odar as a bargaining piece like they'd done with Allyssa.

"I did not," Darmik answered. "However, from Fren's actions, or lack thereof, I think it's safe to say they're back to being an isolated kingdom only concerned with their own welfare."

"What has become of Odar?" Rema asked. "Where is he? Is he still in Russek? Is he dead?"

"If he's in Russek, our spies haven't seen or heard anything about him," Savenek replied. He'd sent a few members of the Brotherhood to Clovek to try to find out exactly what had happened to Allyssa and to determine if her body could be recovered.

"Since Fren refused to help us, Odar is no longer my concern," Darmik said.

"And what of revenge?" Savenek still wanted Russek to pay for what they'd done, not only killing Allyssa, but also for killing Emperion's soldiers.

"Jana has to be assassinated for her crimes."

"Now would be the perfect time for us to accomplish such a feat," Rema said. "Especially with the civil war going on."

"I agree. But first, I need to bathe." Darmik headed down the hallway, away from them.

THE DAYS QUICKLY PASSED. IT HAD BEEN FOUR WEEKS since Allyssa had died and Savenek had taken her place. Four weeks of living with Rema and Darmik in the palace. Four weeks of running the Brotherhood, sending spies into Apethaga to follow the trail of poison, and working alongside Darmik to learn the intricacies of the army and the kingdom.

Sprawled on the sofa, Savenek stared at the ceiling, tossing a small ball with his right hand and catching it with his left. He was finally alone. Well, as alone as he could get now that he was the prince. Two sentries stood near the doors of the sitting room.

At least there weren't any distractions here. And he could think. Tossing the ball, he caught it. Something was...off. He could feel it. Fren, Telmena, Apethaga, and Dromien were too quiet. Had Jana truly been the instigator of everything? And now that she was busy fighting for the Russek throne, the other kingdoms had just backed off? Were they waiting to see what happened with Russek? Savenek didn't think the other kingdoms would invest so much time into an alliance just to let it fall apart. He was missing something—he was sure of it.

Rema and Darmik entered the sitting room holding hands. "I was hoping we'd find you here," Rema said, taking a seat on the sofa across from Savenek.

Darmik sat next to her, crossing his legs and stretching his arms along the back of the sofa.

"What's going on?" Savenek asked absently, tossing the ball, thinking about the other kingdoms.

"The former royal families of Kricok, Landania, and Fia are all coming to Lakeside. We are to meet there to discuss how these three kingdoms now fit into the Emperion empire. They must also pledge their fealty to you, now that you've been crowned as the prince of Emperion."

"Russek still maintains a large presence in Melenia," Darmik mumbled. "We need to decide how to handle that as well."

"Have you—"

Someone banged on the door. The sentry answered it, and a soldier entered. "Your Majesties, there is a messenger here from Fren. He seeks a word with the two of you in private. He is downstairs in the Receiving Room."

Darmik stood, pulling Rema up alongside him.

"Do you want me to come?" Savenek asked, still tossing the ball.

"No," Rema answered. "Stay here. If you're needed, I'll have someone fetch you."

They exited the Royal Chambers.

Savenek remained on the sofa, tossing the ball, his mind still churning.

Twenty minutes later, Rema and Darmik returned. Rema's eyes were red as if she'd been crying. However, there was an excitement on her face that Savenek hadn't seen before.

"Is everything okay?" he asked, setting the ball aside and sitting up.

"We don't know yet," Darmik said. His voice had an odd hitch to it, and he wouldn't look at Savenek.

Savenek was about to ask what was going on when Neco came into the sitting room. "I was told you sent for me?"

"I did," Darmik replied. "I have an assignment for you of the utmost importance. Pack your bag. You leave in five minutes. I'll meet you out front with your horse." The two men left.

"What is it?" Savenek asked.

Rema smiled, her eyes filling with tears. "I don't want to say anything until I confirm our information. It could just be a ploy. Once I know for sure, I'll tell you." Covering her face with her hands, she began crying.

"Are you okay?" He wasn't sure what to do with her. Comfort her? Leave her alone? Try talking to her?

Rema came over and grabbed Savenek's hands. "Everything is perfect," she said with a smile, tears streaming down her cheeks.

A couple of weeks later, Neco returned. He went straight to Darmik's office with Rema in tow. While Savenek paced the halls and contemplated what was going on, a letter from Russek arrived via a messenger. Since the empress and emperor were both engaged, Savenek took the letter and examined it. He considered opening it; however, he didn't want to break the seal until Darmik had a look at it. He decided to take the missive directly to the emperor in case it contained vital information. After knocking on the door, he entered Darmik's office and handed the letter over. "This just arrived from Russek."

"Interesting timing," Darmik mumbled as he examined it.

"We have something to tell you," Rema said, capturing Savenek's attention. She was sitting at the conference table, Neco to her left.

Savenek sat on the chair to her right, curious to hear what she had to say.

"A couple of weeks ago, a messenger from Fren arrived." She took a deep breath and smiled, the simple act lighting up her face. "Allyssa is alive. Neco confirmed it."

Savenek was sure he'd heard her wrong. "Excuse me?"

"King Drenton lied when he said he'd killed your sister. Allyssa managed to escape from Russek with Prince Odar. Neco went to Fren and brought her home."

"She's here?" Savenek jumped to his feet, eager to meet the sister he never thought he'd have a chance to know.

"She is not at the palace." Rema folded her hands on her lap, focusing on them instead of anyone else in the room. "Neco took her to Nathenek's place."

Why were they all sitting there? Why weren't they with Allyssa? Dread filled Savenek. "Is she okay?" He sat back on the chair, suddenly afraid for his sister. He remembered Darmik saying she'd been tortured, her fingernails removed. What sort of state was she in?

"Allyssa has endured a great deal," Neco said, speaking for the first time. "Your mother thought it best that the princess spends some time away from the palace so she can fully heal."

"I want to make sure she's capable of returning to her life, facing her responsibilities, and that she's not only able to rule, but also that she wants to," Rema said.

"I'm not following you." Was his sister okay or not?

"Your mother gave her a choice," Darmik explained. "She can live a normal life as a commoner with Nathenek. Or she can resume her role as the princess of Emperion."

"Where does that leave me?" Did everything depend on

Allyssa and what she decided? If she stayed away, he'd have to continue as the crown prince? But if she returned, was he no longer needed?

"No matter what Allyssa chooses, you are going to remain here with us. That isn't going to change," Rema said with firm conviction.

Savenek rubbed his face. "I want to meet her."

"She needs time," Neco said. "A lot has happened." He tugged his right earlobe. "On our way to Nathenek's, we encountered Prince Kerdan of Russek. He proposed to Allyssa."

No one said a word.

Savenek blinked. Prince Kerdan of Russek, Emperion's enemy, had proposed to Allyssa? Not only that, but he'd also been on Emperion soil? "I hope you ran him through with your sword."

"I think his proposal is sincere and worth considering," Neco replied.

"I must have heard you wrong," Savenek said. Kerdan had kidnapped Allyssa. Why would he want to marry her?

"Allyssa spent some time with him in Russek," Neco explained.

"Yes, as his prisoner."

"It wasn't like that. He saved her life and aided in her escape."

"You can't be serious," Savenek said.

"Did he kill his father to take the throne?" Rema asked.

"That's what Jana is claiming," Darmik replied. "However, I'm not sure I believe it. Kerdan is the prince and next in line to inherit the throne. The only one who truly benefits from this is Jana. I think Jana killed the king and is blaming it on Kerdan to get him out of the way. Then she can have the throne."

"Why propose to Allyssa?" Rema asked.

"I only spoke to Kerdan briefly," Neco said. "Kerdan explained he needs Emperion's support. A union between Russek and Emperion will enable him to overthrow Jana and bring peace to his kingdom."

"A lofty notion," Rema mused.

"I told him I would let the two of you know about the proposal. However, an answer could not be quickly given."

"Do you believe him to be sincere?" Rema asked.

"I didn't spend enough time with him to get a sense of his personality. However, Allyssa speaks highly of him and insists his intentions are honorable."

Savenek snorted. The bloke had kidnapped his sister. How could he be honorable in any sense of the word?

"I'd like to discuss the matter with Allyssa first before I consider this in more detail," Darmik said.

Savenek couldn't believe they were even entertaining the idea. "If Prince Odar and Allyssa are alive, doesn't that mean they're still engaged?"

Neco shifted uncomfortably on the chair. "Fren severed the contract. They are no longer engaged."

Rema raised her eyebrows. "They did?"

"Yes. And Allyssa is extremely upset over the matter. She said it was handled poorly."

"If that is any indication of Odar's moral character, I'm glad he ended the engagement." Darmik finally opened the letter from Russek.

"What does it say?" Savenek asked.

"It's a letter from Prince Kerdan."

"Is it about his proposal to Allyssa?" Rema asked.

"No. And something feels off about the way it's written."

"Off how?" Savenek leaned over Darmik's shoulder, reading the letter.

"Given what Neco has just told us, this letter doesn't make any sense. I don't believe Kerdan wrote it." Darmik handed the letter to Neco.

"I concur. This isn't from Kerdan."

"Jana?" Darmik said.

"Most likely."

"Why would Jana send a letter posing as Kerdan?" Savenek asked. "Is she trying to lure us into a trap?"

"That is precisely what I think," Darmik replied.

"What do you want to do?" Neco asked, a wicked gleam to his eyes.

"Make it look like we're falling for the trap, while we set a trap of our own. It's time to end Jana once and for all."

"We'll need Allyssa for this to work," Neco mused.

"Give me the letter." Rema held her hand out. "I'll see that Allyssa receives this and Nathenek sets things in motion." She stood. "If you'll excuse me, it's time for me to see my daughter."

CHAPTER 4

"I'm not going in the carriage," Savenek said, folding his arms and imitating Darmik. "If you're riding, I'm riding." Not wanting to give Darmik a chance to argue, Savenek turned and mounted one of the horses. It felt good to be back in the saddle. It had been far too long.

The person on the horse next to him chuckled. "It seems no one in our family cares for confined spaces," a familiar female voice said.

Savenek scrutinized the woman dressed in a basic army uniform with a cap concealing her hair. "Rema?" he asked, still not able to call her Mother. Thankfully, she hadn't pressed the issue.

She nodded.

"If you're out here, who's in there?" He pointed at the carriage.

"A decoy."

"And you wanted me in there with a stranger?"

She shrugged. "I figured you'd ride."

"You two can't make anything easy," Darmik muttered as he mounted his horse.

"Oh, please," Rema chided him. "Like you'd ever ride in a closed carriage."

Instead of responding, he gave the signal. The unit of soldiers escorting the royal family moved out, exiting the palace compound.

As they left Emperor's City, Savenek glanced over his shoulder, not sure when he'd be back. This had been his home, where he grew up, where he lived with Nathenek, where he had his first love, first kill, and first sword fight. Where he had trained as a member of the Brotherhood.

"Are you okay?" Rema asked.

Savenek faced forward. "Yes." He knew he didn't fool her. She was far too observant sometimes. Not wanting to talk about it, he kept his attention on the soldier in front of him, trying to envision what life in Lakeside would be like.

His hands became sweaty, and he gripped the reins of his horse tighter. Mayra would be there. In Lakeside. Living in the castle. How would she act around him? Would she be the woman he had gotten to know and fell in love with during their mission in Apethaga? Would she treat him like she always had? Or would things be awkward between them now that he was the prince? It wasn't as if he was a different man. However, instead of not being worthy of Mayra, he now felt he had something to offer her. The two of them would make a good match. That was, if Neco allowed it. Now that Savenek was thinking on the matter, he wasn't sure if Rema and Darmik would allow it, either.

"I'm going to the front to speak with my captain," Darmik said. "The two of you remain here." He nudged his horse, riding ahead of them.

"Is something the matter?" Rema asked. "You seem worried or nervous."

"I'm just thinking about Lakeside."

"And a certain someone who will be there?"

Bullocks. How did she know about Mayra?

"Oh, please," Rema said. "Neco and his wife Ellie are our closest friends."

Savenek pulled the collar of his shirt away from his neck, not knowing what to say to that.

"I understand you and Mayra worked well together in Apethaga?"

A question that wasn't a question. He cleared his throat. "We did." Sweat beaded on his forehead.

"And I understand Neco has raised some concerns regarding a possible match between you and his daughter?"

Savenek glanced over his shoulder to make sure Neco wasn't riding right behind them. Not seeing him nearby, he replied, "Yes, he has."

"I can understand his point of view."

Savenek forced himself not to respond to that comment. Of course Rema would understand—she put her kingdom above all else. She viewed marriage with one purpose in mind: How could it benefit Emperion?

After a few moments of awkward silence, Rema said, "However, I saw what an arranged marriage did to my daughter. The toll it took. I am not keen to see you go through what she did."

Savenek didn't know how he would handle an arranged marriage. Could he eventually learn to love someone who was chosen for him simply for political reasons? He didn't think so. He wondered if Allyssa had experienced the same issues with Odar. Allyssa. He shook his head, unable to believe she was alive and they hadn't told anyone. Not only that, but he also couldn't believe he hadn't met her yet. What sort of person was she? Had Russek changed her? Broken her? "You don't plan to consider Kerdan's proposal, do you?"

"Consider it? Yes. Allow it? Probably not. Russeks are known for being brutal. I wouldn't wish that upon my enemy, let alone my daughter."

"Then why even think about it?"

"Because I'm the empress. I must give it some consideration.

Why was the proposal made in the first place? Does Russek need Emperion's support? What does that show? Does Kerdan seek a true alliance with us? I know if Jana succeeds, she will send Russek's army against Emperion."

"Kerdan would destroy Allyssa. Then he'd destroy Emperion."

"How can you be so certain of that?" Rema asked. "What do we know about him? What has he done in the past to show who he truly is?"

Kerdan was one of Russek's commanders. He was a typical Russek—brutal, crazy, and a lying pack of horse crap. Savenek didn't trust him.

"Which brings me back to you," she said.

Why did Savenek have a feeling Rema was setting him up?

"You have done everything we've asked of you." A wisp of her hair came loose, and she quickly tucked it back under her cap. "If you continue to play the part of the prince, help our kingdom be successful in all endeavors, I will see that you have the opportunity to court Mayra."

He eyed her sidelong. She was trying to bribe him. Guarantee his cooperation by dangling something he wanted in front of him. *Blasted woman*. She knew he wouldn't be able to resist.

"You must understand that Mayra is one of the highest ranking and most important women in Emperion. Marrying her off to another kingdom would be highly beneficial."

The thought of Mayra marrying another man strictly for political reasons made Savenek want to vomit. And punch something. He readjusted his hands on the reins, trying to calm himself. Up until this point, he'd only thought about *himself* marrying for political reasons. He'd never considered the possibility Mayra would have to. And knowing Mayra, she wouldn't hesitate to do what was best for Emperion. Rema knew this. Now she was making sure Savenek knew it as well.

"Don't look at me like that," she said.

Instead of answering or agreeing to Rema's terms, he asked, "If

Allyssa returns to court, do you still plan on ransoming her off for Emperion?"

"I don't have to. She will do what is best for this kingdom, regardless of what she wants or needs. That is one of her faults and virtues. She loves Emperion more than she does anyone or anything else."

"She takes after her mother in that regard," Savenek said. "After all, isn't that how you gave me up so easily? You care more for your kingdom than for me?" He hadn't meant to say that out loud, even if he'd been thinking it.

"Sometimes being a mother and an empress forces me to make difficult choices. Yes, I put my kingdom first. One day, you'll understand what that's like. There is tremendous pressure and responsibility being the ruler of Emperion."

Darmik joined them. "Everything all right?" He looked from Rema to Savenek, his brow pinched with worry.

"Fine," Rema and Savenek snapped in unison.

THE TOWN OF LAKESIDE CAME INTO VIEW. THE LAST time Savenek was there, he'd been poisoned and fighting for his life. Since he'd been holed up in the infirmary, he hadn't had a chance to see the castle or visit the town. He'd wanted to return so he could properly enjoy the place. However, he'd never imagined it would be as the prince.

The unit of soldiers escorting them broke into two groups. One went with the carriage containing the decoys to the front of the castle, while the second went around the side, entering through the military entrance. After traveling for a week, Savenek was glad to finally be there.

He dismounted and stretched.

A woman came running out of the castle, heading straight to Neco. He wrapped his arms around her. The woman had brown hair and wore a gown befitting of a lady. She turned her head, resting her cheek against Neco's chest. She had the same nose and cheekbones as Mayra. This had to be her mother, Ellie.

Savenek glanced at the side entrance of the castle, wondering if Mayra would come running out to see her father. He tugged the tunic away from his neck, suddenly hot and uncomfortable. A stable boy came over and took Savenek's horse. Darmik moved off to the side, speaking quietly with Rema.

"Your Highness," Neco said, suddenly at his side. "May I have a moment of your time?"

Savenek had never heard Neco refer to him as *Your Highness*, and the formality unnerved him. "Yes."

Neco's wife went over to Rema and Darmik. Rema hugged Ellie, and Darmik left the women alone. He joined Neco and Savenek, motioning them farther away from the soldiers so no one could overhear their conversation.

"Neco and I are leaving," Darmik said.

"Right now?" They'd only just arrived.

"Yes. Kerdan has agreed to meet us at Duke Womek's estate in Russek. From there, we will formulate a solid plan to assassinate Jana."

"What about assassinating Kerdan while you're at it?" There was no sense in leaving one of the crazy royal Russeks alive.

"Right now, the threat is from Jana, not Kerdan," Darmik replied.

"Kerdan wants an alliance with us," Neco reminded him.

"Who wouldn't want an alliance with Emperion?" Given that Russek had just tried to conquer Emperion and Kerdan was one of the commanders of the army, Savenek didn't trust him. Kerdan probably only wanted to marry Allyssa in order to gain control of Emperion without having to go through the trouble of war.

"I understand," Darmik said, adjusting his riding gloves. "However, right now, Kerdan is willing to work with us. I will go to Russek and meet with him. After assessing the situation, I will decide whether I trust him or not."

"And if you don't trust him?"

Darmik put a hand on Savenek's shoulder. "Then I'll kill him myself."

Good. That was what he wanted to know. "What do you need me to do while you're gone?"

Darmik removed his hand from Savenek's shoulder. "Have your mother show you where your office is. Since you're intimately connected with the Brotherhood, we want you to continue running the organization. You should also familiarize yourself with the castle, the people working in it, the town, and the soldiers stationed here."

"Yes, sir." Those were all things he would enjoy doing. And none of which required him to attend a ball, a fancy supper, or a formal event.

Rema and Ellie headed into the castle, at least six soldiers following them.

A soldier approached. "Commander, fresh mounts have been prepared."

"Thank you. We'll be there in two minutes." Darmik turned to Neco. "Ready?"

Neco held up a finger, addressing Savenek. "My son, Marek, is the head of Allyssa's personal guard. You may utilize him until she returns."

"An excellent suggestion," Darmik said. "So long as you two don't get into any trouble."

"What about Mayra?" Savenek asked.

"What about her?" Neco said.

Savenek made sure to carefully word his request. "I could use someone with her skillset. She would be a valuable asset to the Brotherhood."

Darmik chuckled. "You're not fooling anyone."

Savenek forced his face to remain blank as if he had no idea what Darmik meant.

Neco's eyes darkened, making him appear menacing. "I will consider the request while I'm gone. When I return, I will give my answer regarding your *professional* relationship with my daughter." He glanced at Darmik. "I can't be worried about my baby girl when I'm off in a foreign kingdom trying to assassinate its ruler."

Mayra was neither a baby nor a girl. She was a grown woman capable of making her own decisions. However, Savenek kept that tidbit to himself.

"We need to be on our way," Darmik said. "I promised Rema I'd return in time to celebrate your seventeenth birthday. If anything happens and I'm not back in time, take care of your mother."

"I will. And I'll do everything you've requested." Not because Darmik was his father and asking him to, but because Darmik was his emperor and commander. Savenek wanted to do his part to ensure Emperion's success. As far as Mayra was concerned, there would be plenty of time for them to work together—professionally, of course.

SAVENEK ENTERED THE CASTLE TO FIND REMA WAITING for him, Ellie nowhere in sight.

"I'll show you to the Royal Chambers." She took hold of Savenek's arm and led him along the corridors, pointing out various rooms and saying the names of the people they passed but not doing any formal introductions.

Savenek only listened with half an ear to what she said because he was too busy keeping an eye out for Mayra. A smile spread across his face just thinking about her. She was somewhere in this castle, and it was only a matter of time before he saw her.

"Here we are," Rema said.

They entered a quaint sitting room. The walls were gray stone, the windows framed with burgundy drapes, and the few pictures were informal paintings of the royal family. Two sofas and a couple of chairs were situated in the middle of the room on a thick, worn rug. A fire roared in the hearth. Where the palace had seemed opulent, the castle was welcoming and lived in. Savenek immediately felt at home.

He went over to one of the windows and peered outside. Most of the structures in the town were only a few stories tall, each a different shade of white, tan, or brown. Trees stood in the distance, hinting at a forest not far away. Smoke rose from many buildings. In Emperor's City, all the structures were the same color. The landscape was barren, the place sandy, and the weather hot.

"I can see why you live here." Even though the castle was significantly smaller than the palace.

"Your room is this way." Rema led him down a hallway with three doors. "The first door is for my room, the second is for Allyssa's room, and the last belongs to you."

Savenek went to his door, standing before it.

"I've always kept a room for you." She came up behind him. "Just in case." Reaching around him, she pushed the door open.

He stepped inside. The room was massive—easily ten times the size of the room he'd had at Nathenek's house. There was an empty fireplace, several armoires, a four-poster bed, and a row of windows along one wall. The sun shone through, lighting the space in a soft glow. Near the fireplace was a sofa and two chairs along with a low table.

He exited his room, not wanting to think about what life would have been like if he'd grown up at Lakeside. Instead, he decided to focus on the sister he would soon meet. "Can I see my sister's room?" While he didn't feel comfortable calling Rema his mother and Darmik his father, he had no qualms whatsoever about calling Allyssa his sister.

"Of course." Rema opened Allyssa's door.

Savenek stepped inside her room. Like his, it was huge and the furniture was similarly situated. The only differences were the two archways on one of the walls. One appeared to lead to a bathing room and the other a dressing closet.

"Huh." He turned in a slow circle.

Rema stood just inside the door, watching him.

"Her room seems sort of sterile." He didn't get a feel for his sister by being in here.

"How so?"

"What distinguishes this as Allyssa's room and not some other woman's?"

Rema smiled ruefully as she came farther into the room, pointing toward the dressing closet. "Go peek in there."

Savenek went over to the archway, sticking his head inside. It was a bloody mess. Clothes were strewn all over the place. Several pairs of shoes had been carelessly tossed on the floor. Going over to one of the dressers, he pulled opened the top drawer. Fabric popped out. He lifted it, revealing a brown cloak with dirt caked on the bottom hem.

He raised his eyebrows. "I assumed a princess would have someone cleaning up after her." He thrust the cloak back in the drawer, then tried to shove it closed.

"She does."

"The closet would indicate otherwise."

"You should have seen this place before the servants cleaned it."

Allyssa would never have survived growing up with Nathenek. He chuckled, imagining them together. Nathenek wouldn't put up with her lazy, unorganized, chaotic messes.

STANDING ON THE DAIS NEXT TO REMA, SAVENEK GAZED

out at the crowd before him. There had to be over one hundred people crammed in the Throne Room, all vying for a chance to see him. The women were bedazzled in lavish dresses and extravagant jewelry, while the men wore tunics sporting their family's crest. The way several of the younger women were watching Savenek made him feel like a piece of meat dangling before a pack of hungry wolves.

"Thank you for coming," Rema said, addressing the people. "In case you haven't heard, my son Savenek is alive. He has been officially crowned prince. I asked you here today to declare your loyalty to him." She gracefully turned and sat on the middle Throne Chair, gesturing for Savenek to sit in the chair on her left.

Knowing he had a part to play, Savenek smiled at the crowd as he took his seat. He wanted them to love him. He scanned the room, making eye contact with as many people as he could, trying to keep a pleasant—yet seductive—grin on his lips. Most people smiled back, a hint of curiosity on their faces.

Savenek wondered if he resembled Allyssa. While he hoped there was a familiarity between them—they were twins after all— he didn't want to actually look like her since she was a woman. He'd never considered his features delicate. Shaking his head, he tried to banish those unwanted thoughts.

A few women batted their eyelashes, smiling coyly at him. In Emperor's City, the palace had mostly consisted of military personnel and servants. Here, in Lakeside, this was another beast entirely. How had Allyssa managed this on a daily basis? He didn't have the time or the energy to deal with courtesans pursuing him because of his position.

Movement caught Savenek's attention, and he scanned the area to his left. Mayra entered the Throne Room from a side entrance, a young man dressed as a soldier accompanying her. Savenek hoped the man was her brother. They sat in the front row next to Ellie. Now that they were next to one another, the resemblance between them was unmistakable.

Savenek's focus drifted to Mayra. She was just as beautiful as he remembered with her brown hair and eyes. The navy-blue dress she wore covered her from the neck down—a far cry from the brightly clad, skin-showing outfits she'd worn in Apethaga. He longed to talk to her, to find out what she'd been doing since the last time he saw her. Mayra's attention was on Rema, listening to every word the empress said.

Savenek realized he should probably pay attention, too.

"Since there are so many people here today, I ask that you simply state your name, swear your fealty to Prince Savenek, and exit through the side door. If you wish to speak to the prince, you will need to do so at another time. A ball will be held in Prince Savenek's honor, celebrating his seventeenth birthday as well as his coronation." Rema motioned to the first row.

One by one, the people came forward, kneeling before Savenek and pledging their allegiance. He made sure to keep an agreeable smile, nodding his head at the appropriate times. It was hard not to assess each person who came before him. Hard not to focus on each person's body language, eyes, how he or she spoke, and what words were emphasized. Years of training couldn't be turned off. He filed the information away, making sure his facial expression revealed nothing but a pleasant prince sitting on a throne as the most powerful and wealthy families in Emperion came before him to vow their allegiance. It was difficult to grasp the reality of his situation. It still felt like he was playing a role and none of this was real.

Mayra came forward, kneeling on the dais. She spoke in a clear, articulate voice. "I, Mayra, pledge my loyalty to Prince Savenek, heir to the Emperion throne." She stood and moved to the side, barely looking at him. Her brother made a similar declaration. When Ellie finished, they headed to the adjacent room. Mayra didn't glance back at him. Not once. She acted as if she'd never met Savenek before. As if she didn't care for him at all. Maybe she no longer did. The mere thought deflated his mood.

Once the last person had spoken, Rema took Savenek's arm and led him from the Throne Room. After sitting on that chair for so long, his legs were stiff and his back sore. He ached to do something physical.

Strolling along the corridors, he tried to memorize each turn, room, and courtyard. It would take him another day or two until he knew the place inside and out. They passed a group of courtiers who'd been present in the Throne Room. Three women and two men. They'd been sitting in the fifth row, left side, toward the middle. They bowed as the empress passed by. Well, he supposed they bowed for him, too. He wasn't sure he'd ever get used to that.

"Do all these people live here?" he asked.

"No. They have homes they maintain on their land. However, each family who owns land over a certain size is required to attend court for a couple of weeks each year. It allows me to discuss with them how their land is doing, make sure they're paying taxes, and ensure the family is loyal."

"How do you know everyone comes? What if someone stays behind?"

"I have people who oversee that." Her eyes gleamed.

It was moments like this that solidified why she was such a formidable empress. It both pleased and scared him to know she was his mother.

They stopped before a closed door, one sentry standing guard. "This room is only for the royal family's use," Rema said. She opened the door, revealing a training room. "If you're anything like your sister, I'm sure you're eager to do something after being stationary for so long."

"I am." Savenek went into the room. The wall directly ahead had several windows revealing open land on the other side and a forest in the distance. Another wall held various weapons such as wooden practice swords, spears, and knives. There were also a couple of straw dummies set up for punching. After everything he'd experienced lately, this room was the first familiar setting he'd encountered in weeks. "The soldiers stationed at the castle don't train here?"

"They have their own quarters and facilities on the castle grounds, but not inside the castle."

"How often do you come here?"

Rema remained standing near the door. "Only once or twice a week when your father drags me here." She smiled before turning to someone behind her. "Ah, Marek is here." She stepped aside to let a soldier enter.

It was the man who'd been standing beside Mayra during the fealty ceremony, the one who Savenek had assumed was her brother.

"Your Majesty, Your Highness." The man bowed.

"This is Marek, the head of Allyssa's personal guard. I asked him to come here to meet you."

Relief flooded Savenek. Marek *was* Mayra's brother. Savenek stuck his hand out to shake the other man's. Marek glanced at Rema.

"Royalty never shakes hands," she informed him.

Savenek should have known that. Dropping his hand, he said, "Your father told me to put you to work."

Before Marek could respond, Rema said, "I understand there is a lot to do. However, I hope you will be friends, not simply work acquaintances."

Savenek scratched his head. Friends? He didn't have many of those. Marek eyed him briefly, and Savenek noticed the same confusion mirrored on his face.

To Marek, Rema said, "I expect a full guard assembled by supper. I am placing the prince in your care."

"Understood." Marek bowed, and Rema left the room.

Savenek wasn't sure how they were supposed to be friends when Marek was responsible for *his care*. He tried not to let it irk him, he really did. But honestly, he could take care of himself. He did not need a friend or a babysitter.

"So you're Allyssa's brother, the infamous Savenek."

He nodded, trying to discern what sort of fellow Marek was.

"I understand you were raised by a member of the Brotherhood?"

Savenek tried not to laugh as Marek questioned him. He reminded him so much of Neco right now. There was no doubt they were father and son. "Yes." He wondered if Mayra had told Marek anything about him. "Nathenek raised me."

"Nathenek?" Marek strolled over to the wall, picking out two wooden practice swords. "That's impressive. I guess I don't have to worry about you being able to defend yourself."

"No, you don't."

"Regardless, your mother wants a royal guard. That means I have to pick twelve men who will be responsible for your safety."

"Twelve?" That seemed a bit excessive.

"You'll have six with you at all times. They rotate since they have to eat and sleep."

"Is there any way we can cut that in half?" And make it more tolerable? Less suffocating?

"I'm afraid that's not possible. Not only does a royal guard consist of twelve soldiers, but the court also expects you to have an entourage at all times."

While Savenek wanted to tell himself this was only a part, that it wouldn't last forever, he knew otherwise. This was his new life now.

Marek chuckled. "You're a lot like your sister. She also hated having a guard around her all the time." He tossed one of the swords at Savenek, who deftly caught it.

"Is it necessary to be guarded while I'm inside the castle?" He could understand the need for a royal guard in public, but inside? Weren't there already sentries everywhere?

Marek swung, and Savenek easily deflected the blow. "I can

choose men who will keep a respectable distance and give you space." He swung again.

Did that mean he could also choose men who would hover around Savenek and drive him crazy? He thought carefully before answering. "Only men?" Savenek smiled ruefully, imagining Mayra guarding him. That would be fun. Then he wouldn't mind it so much.

Marek swung low, knocking Savenek's legs out from under him. *Bullocks*. He'd been too distracted thinking about Mayra that he'd missed the attack.

"Keep your mind off my sister," Marek said, his voice low and laced with fury. He stood over Savenek, trying to intimidate him.

Savenek couldn't help but smile. Mayra had obviously told her brother about him. "How's she doing?" Before Marek could answer, Savenek swung his legs, knocking Marek over. Then Savenek pinned him to the floor. "I don't think the help is supposed to threaten royalty."

"She's my baby sister," Marek snarled.

"And?"

"I don't want you using her and leaving her brokenhearted. She's not a distraction or a plaything." His face was red with fury.

Ah. Marek was worried about Savenek's intentions. That he could work with. He'd been afraid it had something to do with his upbringing and that he'd been raised as an assassin. "I care for Mayra. As a friend and possibly more. I would never use her or lead her on."

"You're the prince. You can have anyone you want."

Savenek released him and stood. "That may be the case, but that's not who I am." He picked up the practice swords, then replaced them on the wall. "I was not raised a prince. I only know one thing—and that is protecting Emperion. I am here for my kingdom, not my own personal pleasure."

Marek sat up, but he didn't respond. He probably didn't know what to think. Whether he should believe Savenek or not.

If Savenek wanted a chance of courting Mayra, he had to win over her brother. "Right now, my priority is adjusting to my position. I need someone I can trust who can show me around the castle and the town, who can also help me get up to speed with the inner workings of the army. Can you do that?"

Marek stood and rubbed his arm across his forehead. "Yes, I can. Just leave Mayra alone."

It was hard to reconcile the independent and resilient woman Savenek traveled through Apethaga with to the one seemingly sheltered and protected by her father and brother. "Okay. But I think it's a shame she isn't being utilized by the Brotherhood. She's intelligent and could be valuable as a spy."

"She can't be a part of the Brotherhood. She's a woman, not a man. And just because you went on one mission with her doesn't mean you really know her."

"Fair enough. However, would you consider allowing her to work with my spies to help decipher correspondence from other kingdoms?"

Marek sighed. "I'll think about it."

That was good enough for Savenek. At least, good enough for now.

CHAPTER 5

Savenek

Sitting at the desk in his office, Savenek read over the reports his spies had sent from Telmena and Apethaga. Telmena hadn't acquired any more poison from Apethaga. They did, however, buy a large shipment of swords. In addition, Telmena was actively recruiting men for their army. There were numerous reports that the army was gathering in Lumar, the capital of Telmena. Drills were being conducted, but most of the soldiers were clumsy and untrained. Regardless, that didn't bode well with Savenek.

Apethaga, on the other hand, was still mining the kepper flowers and producing the poison. None of the reports indicated any of the poison had left the kingdom. Savenek drummed his fingers on the table. This was problematic as well. It was time to intervene. The mine needed to be destroyed. But how to do so without risking the lives of those who worked there? The kepper flowers should be demolished as well. He wondered if he could burn the fields in which they grew.

"I figured I'd find you in here," Rema said as she came into the office. She smiled at Marek—the only soldier Savenek had let inside—and he bowed. "You're making the rest of your royal guard wait outside?"

"Technically, Marek isn't a member of my royal guard. But yes, I made them stay in the hallway so I could think." What a boring job it must be to follow him around all day and stand there doing nothing. Even though he'd been in Lakeside a few weeks now, he still hadn't gotten used to being watched all the time.

Rema held out a piece of paper. "This is from your father. He sent it last week, but it only just arrived."

Savenek took the letter and read it. "It says Jana is dead."

"Yes."

It also said Allyssa had killed Jana, that Kerdan aided in the planning and assassination, and that Neco and Nathenek were fine. Rema paced back and forth in front of the desk.

"What's the matter?" Savenek asked. He slid the reports into the bin to be burned.

"Did you read what Darmik wrote?"

Savenek nodded.

"Allyssa killed Jana."

"That's why you're upset?" She was distraught over the fact that her daughter had been involved in the assassination?

Rema balled her hands into fists. "Allyssa has been through hell. While I knew she'd read the letter and rush off to Russek, I assumed your father would have kept her at the Womek estate where it was safe." She raised her arms in the air. "Not take her traipsing through Russek during a civil war trying to lure a deranged woman out of hiding so my daughter could murder her!" She sat abruptly on one of the chairs.

"I don't know Allyssa," Savenek said. "However, if I were in her position and had a chance to be involved, I would have taken it."

"I know. I would have, too."

"And it's done now. We can't change anything."

"I know."

"Then what's the problem?" Savenek must be missing something.

Rema stood. "Your birthday celebration is tonight. I hope your father and sister make it home in time." With that, she swept out of the room, closing the door behind her.

He glanced at Marek.

"Don't ask me," Marek said. "She's your mother."

Savenek rubbed his face, wanting to talk to someone about the spy reports. Usually, he did this sort of thing with Nathenek. But Nathenek wasn't here. Pointing at the chair on the other side of his desk, he said, "Sit."

Marek did so without question.

Savenek quickly wrote a letter. First, he told the Brotherhood to come up with a feasible way to destroy the Apethaga mine without killing everyone in it. Second, he instructed them to keep watching Telmena's army and to track all its movements. After he folded the letter, he slid it into the box nailed to the top of his desk. A member of the Brotherhood came daily to deliver and pick up correspondence. Savenek had never seen who came.

"Did you want to ask me something?" Marek said.

"No. I want to talk through what I'm thinking."

Marek waved his hand, gesturing for Savenek to continue.

Pushing his chair back, he propped his feet on his desk and clasped his hands behind his head. "When I was in Apethaga with Mayra, we found a letter. Mayra was able to decipher it. That's how we knew Apethaga was going to send poison to Russek."

"The shipments that you and my sister destroyed?"

"Yes." So Mayra had told her brother about her trip with Savenek. He tried not to smile like an idiot. "The letter also mentioned uniting the four kingdoms of Russek, Fren, Telmena, and Apethaga."

"Uniting how?"

"Through marriage. Prince Kerdan is to marry Princess Conditto, Princess Lareissa is to marry Prince Jem, and Princess Shelene was supposed to marry Prince Odar."

"Allyssa told me Fren severed the contract between Shelene and Odar." Marek steepled his hands in front of his face.

"Interesting that Prince Odar then came to Emperion seeking Allyssa's hand in marriage."

Savenek considered the implications. "Do you think Fren wants out of their arrangement with the other kingdoms?"

"I don't know. Let's assume the other marriages take place. That will unite Russek with Apethaga, Telmena with Apethaga, and Fren and Telmena already have a treaty through the marriage of Prince Kren and Princess Jestina."

"Maybe now that Jana and Drenton are dead, the kingdoms will no longer want to unite," Savenek suggested. He really hoped with Russek in its current state, that would thwart the other kingdoms' plans.

"I don't know."

Most of the spy reports showed each kingdom was staying within its own borders. The issue with so many kingdoms uniting would be who ruled over them once they came together and went after Emperion. Although, maybe they would no longer try to overthrow Emperion. Maybe the four kingdoms would start fighting one another. That was an intriguing idea, and one he'd have to explore in more detail later. "Did you know Kerdan proposed to Allyssa?" As much as that bothered him, it did indicate Russek no longer wanted to align with those other kingdoms. Russek had always wanted Emperion. Savenek didn't intend to let that happen.

"I heard."

"Kerdan has just taken the throne. He has a lot to contend with." Controlling the nobles, ending the civil war. "I think the real threat is going to come from Fren, Telmena, and Apethaga. Russek has too many problems right now to join with them. However, I do believe we will need to deal with Russek in the future."

"I agree." Marek crossed his legs. He was about to say something when someone banged on the door.

"Enter!" Savenek called out.

A sentry burst into the room, breathing heavily as if he'd just ran a mile as fast as he could. "Commander Darmik has arrived. And...Princess Allyssa is with him." The sentry looked as if he'd seen a ghost. "Did you hear me? The princess is alive!"

Savenek presumed most people would react this way when they learned that the princess was back from the dead.

"Thank you. You may go." When the door closed, Savenek took a deep breath. "Now that my sister is back, I presume you have other duties besides babysitting me?"

Marek grinned. "Mind if I leave?"

"Go right ahead."

Savenek stood, wondering if he should go find this notorious sister of his. His body grew hot, sweat beading on his forehead. Why was he nervous? It wasn't like he had anything to prove. She was just a woman. And his twin sister. He gripped the edge of the desk.

"Prince Savenek?" Madelin said, sticking her head into the room.

He straightened. "Yes?"

"I have someone who wants an audience with you." She opened the door wider, and Nathenek strode in.

Savenek hadn't expected to see him. He ran his hands through his hair, unsure if he was happy or upset with this man who had lied to him his entire life. Regardless, Nathenek had loved him as a son. Taken care of him as a son.

"I'll leave the two of you alone," Madelin said, closing the door.

"I'm sorry I didn't tell you," Nathenek said.

"I can't believe you kept something that important from me." Savenek wanted to say more. He wanted to yell and punch Nathenek for lying to him. However, he'd grown up respecting Nathenek and his authority. To question him now, to behave so childishly, would not only be impertinent, but it also wouldn't accomplish anything. What was done was done.

"I was under strict orders."

"I figured," Savenek said. Nathenek would never have gone against a direct order from the empress. His loyalty to Emperion was one of the things Savenek loved most about him. "How are you doing?" It appeared as though Nathenek hadn't bathed in days.

"I'm fine."

"I assume you were involved with Jana's assassination." Otherwise, he wouldn't have shown up at the same time as Darmik and Allyssa.

"I was. Although your sister is the one who killed her."

Of course she was. It seemed she could do no wrong. Everyone claimed she was the perfect princess who loved her kingdom. She had even been kidnapped and tortured, yet she'd managed to escape and receive a proposal out of it. "What's the situation? Is Kerdan a threat? Is Russek going to attack us again?"

Nathenek took a seat. "Do you have anything to drink?"

Savenek went over to the side table, hurriedly pouring Nathenek a cup of water. "Here."

"The situation with Russek is under control." He took several gulps. "But we'll have plenty of time to talk about that later. For now, tell me how you're doing."

Savenek plopped onto the chair next to Nathenek. "I'm fine. Darmik has given me a lot of responsibility." Unlike Nathenek. "I'm running the Brotherhood and getting familiar with the castle, army, and town."

Nathenek nodded as if he already knew that. Perhaps he did. "How is your relationship with your parents?"

"Fine." Savenek wasn't prepared to have this conversation right now since he hadn't figured out how he really felt about everything.

"You can talk to me."

"Can I?" Savenek snapped. "Clearly your allegiance is to the empress, not me." Otherwise, Nathenek would have told him the truth.

The older man took a sip of water, not bothering to respond.

"Sorry," Savenek mumbled.

"I suppose I deserve some of that hostility. I did what I thought was best. Right or wrong."

Nathenek hadn't said anything about Allyssa other than the fact she'd killed Jana. Was he waiting for Savenek to ask about her? Because he didn't want to have to ask. He wanted Nathenek to volunteer information. He couldn't help but wonder what Nathenek thought of her. Some childish part of him wanted Nathenek not to like her. As irrational as that was, it was how he felt.

"What do you want to know?" Nathenek asked, setting the cup on the desk.

"About what?"

He chuckled. "Allyssa. I can tell you're curious about her."

Savenek shrugged. He didn't know where to begin. She was the one his parents had chosen to raise, love, and be the heir to Emperion. Now that Allyssa was back, how did Savenek fit into this family? Was he even part of it?

Instead of asking about his sister, he said, "How long are you going to be in Lakeside?"

"I can stay as long as you'd like me to."

For some reason, an overwhelming sense of relief filled him. "Do you want to stay? Or are you eager to return home?"

"I'd like to remain here. Even though I'm not your biological father, I raised you. I think of you as my son."

Savenek hadn't realized how much he'd missed Nathenek until now. "I could use an advisor I can trust." He smiled, knowing it would be difficult for Nathenek to remember Savenek outranked him now.

"We can talk later about how I can be of use to the crown. For now, we should get ready. I hear there's a celebration tonight."

Right. Savenek's—and Allyssa's—birthday party. She would be there, and he'd finally meet his twin.

Standing outside the Great Hall alongside Rema and Darmik, Savenek waited to be announced. It seemed silly that they couldn't enter the party until some herald told everyone who they were. However, Rema insisted it was tradition.

"Relax," Rema said, patting his arm.

"I am relaxed." He tilted his head from side to side, stretching his neck. His black tunic and pants were a little snug, making him sweat. The royal family's crest had been embroidered on the front of his tunic, signifying his position.

"Allyssa will be along shortly," Darmik said. "We'll go in without her."

The sentry opened the doors, and the herald announced, "Prince Savenek, Emperor Darmik, and Empress Rema."

"Let's go," Darmik said.

Rema stood between Darmik and Savenek, each holding one of her arms. They entered the Great Hall together. People parted, making an aisle to the center of the room for the royal family. As they passed by, everyone bowed. Savenek saw people tracking his movements. He was suddenly keenly aware of holding Rema's arm and made sure he played the part of the doting, carefree prince. He knew people were curious as to how he would affect the dynamics at court. He had to tread carefully.

They stopped in the center of the room. "Thank you for coming to celebrate with us tonight," Rema said. She gave a single nod, and everyone resumed talking.

Darmik took Rema's hand, then pulled her in for a hug. The music began, and Savenek watched his parents dancing together. Several other people started dancing. Savenek scanned the room, searching for Mayra. She was nowhere to be seen.

When the song ended, Rema joined Savenek. "I'll introduce you to anyone who comes over looking for an introduction. It is important you meet the dukes and members of the Legion. However, I don't want to seek anyone out."

Because she wanted to keep power and control. She didn't want to look weak. Savenek knew there were five regions in Emperion, a duke in charge of each. When treaties were signed and important decisions made, each duke had one vote, along with each Legion member. The theory was that by having input from people who lived and worked around the kingdom, everyone's voice was heard. Savenek wondered what would happen if Rema didn't agree with how they voted.

The doors swung open, and Allyssa was announced. Turning, Savenek saw her standing there as everyone in the room dropped to a knee.

Even if no one had told him, he would have known she was his sister. She had the same hair and skin color as Darmik, but she had Rema's mouth and piercing blue eyes.

"I'm afraid of the mischief the two of you are going to make around here," Rema said.

Darmik chuckled. "They are going to be a lethal combination. I pity the fool who gets in their way."

Mayra joined Allyssa, and the two women approached. When they were about halfway there, Mayra threw her hands up in the air and stormed off. Allyssa's brows drew together as she watched her friend walk away. Allyssa turned back toward Savenek, twirling her fingers together as if nervous. She started moving toward him again. Her face was so familiar even though Savenek had never seen her before.

Allyssa stopped a couple of feet away. "Happy birthday, brother," she said, a smile hovering on her lips. Her eyes twinkled, hinting at a cheeky personality.

"Happy birthday, sister."

"I told myself I wouldn't cry," Rema said. "But I can't help it.

I'm so happy right now. It has been seventeen years since I've had both of my children with me."

Allyssa wiped the tears off her mother's face. The simple, intimate gesture startled Savenek.

"I'd like to dance with my daughter." Darmik took Allyssa's hand, leading her to the dancing area.

Savenek blinked. He'd known Allyssa grew up with Rema and Darmik, but to actually see the love between the three of them felt like a punch to his stomach. He would never have that.

"Well," Rema said, recapturing his attention. "Care to dance?"

Remembering he had a part to play, he forced a smile on his face and replied, "I would love to." Savenek took Rema's arm, and they made their way to where everyone was dancing. It was a slower song, allowing them to easily converse. "Allyssa looks well." Considering she'd been kidnapped, tortured, injured, and involved in an assassination.

"You of all people should know that appearances can be deceiving." Rema glanced over Savenek's shoulder to where Allyssa and Darmik were dancing. "This life has never been easy for her. She values her privacy, and she doesn't have the natural ability to charm a crowd like you do."

Savenek snorted. "You think I'm charming?"

Rema smiled at him. "When you want to be. I've seen you sulking one minute and grinning the next when you notice someone watching you. Allyssa cannot control her emotions so easily. I've also noticed that when you walk into a room, you command everyone's attention. Allyssa would rather remain in the shadows."

"Ironic considering how each of us was raised."

The song ended, and Rema turned toward Darmik. He took her hand, leaving Savenek alone with Allyssa.

"Care to dance?" he asked.

She shook her head. "I'm quite tired. It has been a long week." She wove her way through the crowd, and Savenek followed her.

When she reached the balcony, she addressed the guards on duty. "I'd like a moment alone with my brother."

One of the guards asked everyone to leave the balcony. Once it was cleared, Allyssa stepped outside. She casually leaned against the railing, resting her arms on top of it. Savenek imitated her stance. A gentle breeze blew.

They stood in silence for several minutes. Savenek breathed in the heady pine scent, so vastly different from the dry, sandy conditions he grew up in.

"Have you spoken to Nathenek?" Allyssa asked.

"Yes. He came to see me shortly after he arrived."

"He was eager to see you. I haven't known him that long, but I like him."

Savenek scratched the side of his head, trying to figure out how to respond to that. *Thanks? I like him, too? He was a great fake dad?*

She abruptly turned toward him. "Do you hate me?"

"No. Why do you ask?" He knew why. She must feel guilty Rema and Darmik chose to raise her as their child instead of him.

"I had no idea you were alive. I'm still mad at Mother and Father for hiding that from me. I'm sorry." Her hands gripped the railing so hard her knuckles turned white.

"There's nothing to be sorry for. Like you said, you didn't know." He leaned his arms on the railing, trying to see the trees in the distance. The moon was hidden behind thick clouds.

She sighed. "Mother gave me a choice. She said instead of coming back here, I could live a regular life, free from the confines of being the heir to the throne."

"Why did you choose to come back?" Did she seek power? He didn't think so. Maybe she missed her parents. She seemed close with both of them.

"As enticing as it was to imagine living a regular life, I couldn't do it. Not only do I want to help Emperion, but I also wanted the chance to meet you. After living seventeen years without my twin brother, I didn't want to live the next seventeen years wondering what you were like, if you enjoyed the life you lived, if you were like me." She shrugged. "So here I am."

"Being here feels right." The truth of his statement shocked him.

Allyssa smiled. She had Rema's smile. "I agree."

They stood next to one another in silence, staring out at the forest in the distance.

"What's going on with you and Mayra?" Allyssa asked.

"Why do you think there's something going on between us?" Did Mayra say something to Allyssa?

"When I mentioned your name, she seemed rattled. I've never seen her react that way before."

His sister was rather astute. "I was sent on a mission last season to Apethaga. Mayra went with me."

"What?" Allyssa said a little louder than necessary. "I was wondering where Neco had sent her. What was this mission? Tell me everything."

He was surprised she didn't already know about it. Perhaps she wasn't involved with the Brotherhood. Savenek spent the next hour talking to Allyssa about his and Mayra's escapades in Apethaga. She laughed, asked questions, and seemed genuinely interested in everything he had to say. She was easy to talk to, and all awkwardness between them melted away.

Savenek was careful not to ask her too many questions about what happened to her in Russek. He knew she would talk when she was ready. And tonight wasn't about trudging up painful memories, it was about getting to know one another and celebrating their birthday together. The first of many more to come.

THE NEXT MORNING, SAVENEK ROUNDED THE CORNER,

about to enter the sitting room, when he noticed Allyssa standing by the sofa, a blank expression on her face. He watched her for a moment. Her eyes were unfocused, and her stillness unnerved him. He entered the room. "Are you okay?"

She blinked, her face instantly changing as life flooded back into her. "I'm fine."

"What were you thinking about?" he asked casually, hoping she'd open up and talk to him.

"My friend, Grevik." She moved around one of the chairs, trailing her fingers over the back of it. "He died protecting my identity."

"Friend?" Or lover? Did he live here in the castle? Was he a courtier or a soldier? Savenek suddenly had a hundred questions he wanted to ask her.

"He was one of my best friends." Punching the back of the chair, she let out a frustrated sound. Hands now on her hips, she cocked her head to the side and said, "There's something I want to show you." She strode to the door. "Are you coming?"

He hurried after her and they left the Royal Chambers, their guards trailing them.

Allyssa raised her chin and rounded her shoulders back, standing up straighter, which gave her a regal appearance. She walked slowly down the hallway, giving off an air of confidence and fortitude. "How are you adjusting to life here at the castle?"

"I'm getting used to it." While at her side, he made sure to keep a lackadaisical posture. "Where are we headed?"

"To one of my favorite places." On the first floor, she led him into the library. "I like coming here because the room is often empty. If you ever need to find me, chances are I'm here."

Allyssa headed toward the back of the library where several alcoves were. Each had a table and two bench seats. She entered the alcove on the end and sat down, sighing. Savenek slid onto the seat across from her. Their guards remained at the entrance to the library, giving them the allusion of privacy.

"Tell me what's going on," Allyssa demanded as she slouched against the wall.

"With regards to what?" Her question could be interpreted multiple ways.

"Now that Russek is no longer threatening us, is Emperion safe? Or are there other issues I need to be aware of? Father mentioned something about Telmena not being happy with us."

"I didn't think you'd be concerned with the political machinations of the kingdom." He was only half serious.

She reached across the table and whacked his arm. "Honestly. I didn't expect my own brother to be so pigheaded."

"I'm only teasing you."

"Well, don't. I'm eager to get to work."

There was that look in her eyes again—a strange, haunted light. He'd seen it a couple of times last night. It usually only lasted a second. If he hadn't been paying attention, he would have missed it. He glanced out the window to his left. A light fog covered the land. It was early in the morning, and most of the people living in the castle were still asleep. Focusing back on Allyssa, he noticed a restlessness to her. After everything she'd been through, she probably needed to be kept busy so the memories wouldn't overwhelm her. A pang of sympathy and regret filled Savenek, making him want to know what had happened to her so he could help her recover.

"Does knowing Drenton is dead and being the one who killed Jana help?" The times he'd been forced to kill, he hadn't known the person, nor did he have a vendetta against his target.

Allyssa stared at the table, and Savenek wasn't sure if she was going to answer. When he'd asked the question, she hadn't flinched at either of the names like he thought she would.

"I saw her die. Same with Soma." She rubbed her face.

Savenek moved his hands to his thighs, curling his fingers into fists. She hadn't thought twice about Drenton. Instead, she'd brought up Soma—Jana's son, the one skilled in the art of poison.

It took every ounce of control Savenek had to keep his face blank, not revealing how livid he was at the thought the man had hurt Allyssa. It was a good thing Soma was dead; otherwise, Savenek would have killed him.

"He still haunts me," she whispered. "I have trouble sleeping."

He, not *she.* Closing his eyes, Savenek took a deep breath. He had to know. Steeling himself, he looked at his sister. "Tell me what he—"

Soft murmuring came from the library's entrance. Savenek glanced over his shoulder. It was Mayra talking with one of the guards.

Allyssa straightened, the horror that had been on her face only a moment before vanished, replaced by a pleasant smile. "Oh, good. Mayra's here." She waved her friend over.

As Mayra approached, she kept her focus on Allyssa, not once even peeking Savenek's way. Not that he minded. It gave him the opportunity to watch her. Today, she wore a dark green dress, the sleeves trailing to the floor. Her hair had been braided around her head, showing off her slender, elegant neck. He wished he could kiss that neck right now.

Allyssa kicked him under the table.

"Do you need something?" Mayra asked, standing before them.

"Yes." Allyssa patted the seat next to her. Mayra hesitated and then sat. "What's going on between you and my brother?"

Mayra's eyes widened, and her face turned a bright shade of red, making her even more stunning. "Nothing, I swear."

Allyssa rolled her eyes. "Oh, please. I'm not blind. I see the way you look at each other. Plus, my brother told me all about Apethaga."

Savenek noticed Mayra had a necklace on, the chain visible. If the key he'd made her was strung on there, it was tucked under her dress so he couldn't see it. However, just knowing she wore it, that it was snug against her skin, was more than enough for him. It meant she still cared about him.

When she didn't respond, Allyssa stood. "If you won't talk to me, at least talk to Savenek. If you'll excuse me, I have a meeting with my mother." She sashayed out of the room, her head held high.

Savenek chuckled. His sister was rather blunt. Once she exited the library, he turned his attention to Mayra. "How are you?" He wanted to reach across the table and hold her hand, but he knew not to.

"I'm well. And you?" She finally met his eyes.

He couldn't believe she was being so stiff and formal around him. This would not do. Leaning forward, he wiggled his eyebrows. "Now that you're here, I'm peachy." He winked.

Her face turned an even brighter shade of red. He'd missed seeing her blush.

"I should go."

"Wait." Unable to help himself, he reached across the table. As he'd feared, Mayra didn't take his hand. Instead, she kept hers firmly clasped together. "I spoke with Rema."

Her brows bent together. "About what?" she said softly.

"About courting you."

She covered her face with her hands.

He reached forward, peeling her fingers away so he could see her beautiful face. "Ari."

She made a funny noise.

"Talk to me."

"You're the prince."

"So?"

"You need to marry for political reasons." Her eyes filled with tears. "When we were in Apethaga, I had no idea who you were."

"I know. I didn't either." He firmly held her hands in his. "And Rema said I can choose who I marry."

"She did?"

He nodded. "So what do you say?"

"Have you spoken to my father?"

Neco had already voiced his concerns. However, Rema said she would take care of everything. "I haven't formally asked him yet. I wanted to make sure you still, you know, liked me first."

She smiled, a dimple forming on her right cheek. "I still like you."

"Good." His eyes focused on her red lips. He wanted to kiss her. "I did ask you father about you working with the Brotherhood."

"What did he say?"

"He's considering it." Now that Neco was back, he should have an answer. "Has he said anything to you about it?"

"My father hasn't mentioned anything to me."

"I haven't mentioned what?" Neco asked, his voice loud in the quiet library.

Savenek wanted to crawl under the table and hide. He couldn't believe Neco had walked in on him holding Mayra's hands while speaking to her privately.

"I was here talking with Princess Allyssa," Mayra said. "She just left. I was telling Savenek that you hadn't mentioned the possibility of me working with the Brotherhood."

Folding his arms, Neco stared pointedly at Savenek.

"Hello, sir." Savenek swallowed. Was that how he should address Neco? Under normal circumstances, that was what he'd say. However, now that Savenek was the prince, he wasn't sure if it was proper. There was still so much he needed to learn.

Neco turned his attention to his daughter. "Your mother is in the solarium waiting for you. Prince Savenek, the emperor is in the War Room. He expects you. Immediately." The formality of his tone wasn't lost on Savenek.

"Yes, sir." He stood and left the room.

CHAPTER 6

Allyssa

Allyssa headed to the training room, quite pleased with herself for managing to throw Savenek and Mayra together. She opened the door, breathing in the familiar smell of wood and sweat. As she'd hoped, Marek stood in the middle of the room waiting for her.

"It has been a long time," she said by way of greeting.

"Shall we spar with or without swords?"

"Without."

"Why are you smiling?" He eyed her suspiciously. "Is there something I should know about?"

"It appears my brother and your sister care for one another." No one had ever caught Mayra's fancy before, and Allyssa rather liked the idea of her best friend in love with her brother.

Marek put his hands on his hips. "My father doesn't approve."

"Why not?" Was it because Savenek had been raised in the Brotherhood?

"He doesn't want Savenek rushing into something without thinking the consequences through."

She stretched her arms in front of her, loosening up. So this wasn't about what Mayra and Savenek wanted; rather, it was about what was best for Emperion. If anyone was going to raise that concern, she thought it would have been her mother, not Neco. "Is there another kingdom seeking an alliance with us?"

"Not at the moment. But who knows what the future may hold."

He had a point. Marrying Savenek off could be beneficial. Before Allyssa would entertain that idea, she needed to talk to Savenek to determine how much he cared for Mayra. Because if he truly loved her, then Allyssa would make sure Savenek wasn't forced to marry for political reasons.

"Speaking of which," Marek said, "what about you?" He started to walk around her.

"What about me?" She prepared for him to attack. He liked to strike when she least expected it.

"I hear you received a proposal from Prince Kerdan." His voice sounded as if he didn't quite believe it.

"You mean King Kerdan." She rather liked the way that sounded—the way it rolled off her tongue. Speaking of tongues, she remembered the last time they were together and the way he'd kissed her.

"I guess that answers all my questions."

As much as she tried not to, she blushed.

"Kerdan? Seriously?" He wrinkled his nose as if he'd tasted something sour.

"What's that supposed to mean?" If one of her dearest friends didn't take well to her marrying Kerdan, no one else would.

"He's from Russek," Marek said, like that was supposed to explain everything. He stopped in front of her. "Russek kidnapped you." His eyes flashed with something she couldn't quite discern. Fury?

Allyssa reached out to touch Marek's shoulder. She owed him an explanation, especially since she intended to keep him on as the head of her personal guard after she married. "Jana arranged my kidnapping. Not Kerdan. He's the one who saved me." She explained how she was tortured on Jana's orders, how Drenton had ordered her execution, and how Kerdan had stepped in and saved her. She explained how Kerdan and her became unlikely allies and then friends.

"You really care for the guy?" Marek asked.

"I do." She let her arm fall to her side. He was going to attack her at any second.

"I had assumed this was a political match." He started circling her again.

"I can assure you I love him." She twisted the ring Kerdan had given her, realizing she probably shouldn't wear it when she sparred since it would leave a nasty mark.

"Even though he's a Russek?"

Now he was simply goading her. "He can appear a little rough," she admitted. And unrefined, but she kept that to herself. "But once you get to know him, you'll see he's dedicated to his kingdom, he cares about the well-being of his people, and he is a good person." She withheld the fact he was an excellent fighter and could best Marek.

"Will you please stop smiling?" Marek shook his head in disbelief. "I can tell you're thinking about him just by the expression on your face." He pinched the bridge of his nose. "Does your father approve of the match?"

"He does." The hiccup lay with the provision Darmik put on the engagement. "However, he insists that Mother and Savenek approve of the marriage before we sign the contract."

Marek started laughing. "Good luck with that."

"Are we going to spar? I didn't come here to gab about my love life."

"Maybe not. But I did come here to gab about yours," he teased.

She swung, and he ducked. It was time to put some of the Russek fighting moves Kerdan had shown her into action.

ALLYSSA ENTERED THE PRIVATE DINING ROOM IN THE Royal Chambers. Rema had insisted they eat as a family tonight without the distraction of members from court. Which was just fine with her. Allyssa had been avoiding as many people as possible since she'd been back. She didn't want to have to answer questions about where she'd been and what had happened to her. Or listen to people say how grateful they were she'd returned. The fact of the matter was that everyone—*everyone*—knew she'd been kidnapped. It was logical to assume she'd been tortured. The pity in people's eyes was too much to handle. And if anyone discovered she'd been holed up in Kerdan's private bedchamber, her virtue would be ruined.

The dark wood walls and lack of windows gave the room a cozy feel. A fire roared in the hearth, warming the space. Rema, Darmik, and Savenek were already seated at the small square table. Her brother raised a single eyebrow. She rolled her eyes. She wasn't late, but she wasn't early either. When she took her seat, a servant set several platters of food on the table and then left.

"We're alone?" Allyssa asked, glancing at the closed doors. The guards had been posted on the other side.

"We need to talk," Darmik said. "And I don't want anyone overhearing our conversation."

Savenek reached forward, taking a scoop of potatoes and plopping them on his plate. "Don't you normally eat as a family?" He grabbed a hunk of the duck, but bypassed the carrots altogether.

"Yes," Allyssa said. "But we usually eat in the Dining Hall with about fifty members of our court." She watched her brother shove a piece of duck in his mouth. "It's great fun. We're always on display." She leaned forward, helping herself to the food. "What do you want to discuss?" She waited for Darmik to lead the conversation.

Rema kept glancing at Savenek. It was more than a mother watching over a son. It was almost...concern. Why would her mother be worried about Savenek? He seemed perfectly fine to Allyssa.

"We need to talk about Telmena," Darmik said. "They sent me a strongly worded letter objecting to any sort of a union between Emperion and Russek."

"Do they know Kerdan proposed to Allyssa?" Savenek asked.

"Yes." Darmik took a drink from his goblet. "Does anyone have any thoughts on the matter?"

"I can see why aligning Russek and Emperion makes sense," Savenek said. "But I don't like the idea of my sister marrying the enemy."

Allyssa blinked. *What?* Savenek hadn't been prince that long. Why did he think he had any authority on the matter?

"I understand why you say that," Darmik said.

"He killed his father," Savenek added.

"No, he didn't," Allyssa interjected. "Jana killed Drenton." Although Kerdan *had* intended to kill his father. But she didn't feel like getting into that right now. "Kerdan is a good man."

"He kidnapped you," Savenek said.

"No. Soma kidnapped me on Jana's orders. Kerdan saved me."

"Then you must be blinded by some misguided notion that you owe him."

Darmik cleared his throat, garnering everyone's attention. "I had the same concerns and beliefs as you," he said to Savenek. "However, after spending time with Kerdan, I found him to be a good man."

"You also thought Prince Odar would make an excellent match for our daughter," Rema said. "And look how that turned out."

"Why can't either of you believe what I say?" Allyssa asked. "I want to marry Kerdan."

Rema reached out, taking Allyssa's hand. "I love you dearly, but you have been through a trying ordeal. I think you need some time and space to make sure this is what you really want."

Oh, hell. Did everyone think she was some injured creature that needed to be coddled? "Why don't we ask what Neco and Nathenek think about Kerdan?"

"I've already spoken to them both, and they have some reservations," Rema said.

Allyssa squeezed her hand out from under her mother's.

"I have agreed to the union on one condition," Darmik said. "I told Kerdan that once he is crowned king and establishes control in Russek, he needs to come here for the formal negotiations. After he receives both Rema and Savenek's approval, the marriage can take place."

"Excellent," Savenek said. He shoved another spoonful of potatoes in his mouth.

Did he think that settled it? When Allyssa agreed to this, she hadn't known her brother would be so pigheaded about the situation. And to think she'd tried helping him with Mayra. Well then. If he was going to be difficult, she would be difficult, too.

"Allyssa," Darmik said, a warning in his voice.

"What?" she asked innocently.

He raised his eyebrows. "Stop plotting. It isn't very becoming."

She huffed but didn't argue.

"It will take Kerdan some time before he gets everything under control and makes his way here," Rema said. "Until he arrives, I want you to make sure this is what you desire. Distance might make you see things differently. Please keep an open mind."

Allyssa rolled her eyes.

Savenek chuckled. "You must have driven Nathenek mad," he said around a mouthful of food.

Where was a dinner roll when she needed one? Not seeing a piece of food suitable for chucking at her brother, she cocked her head to the side and said, "Actually, we got along quite well."

His smile widened. "Sure you did."

She flung her leg out, trying to kick him under the table, but missed.

"You have quite the temper," he commented.

"Stop irritating your sister," Darmik said.

"He's doing it on purpose?" Allyssa asked. Why would he do that?

"I can tell you were raised as a princess," Savenek said, sitting back in his chair and watching her. "You're very prim and proper, you expect everyone to do what you want, and you're…what's the right word…prissy." His eyes gleamed with mischief.

She jumped up from her chair and reached across the table, intending to strangle him.

"I told you not to provoke her," Darmik said, shaking his head.

"I thought we'd have a nice family dinner," Rema added.

Unable to reach him across the table, and not wanting to climb on said table, Allyssa was about to run around the side of it.

Savenek started laughing. "Trying to prove me wrong by acting like a Russek?"

She froze. What was she doing? Besides trying to murder her brother—though she really only intended to cause him moderate harm—she wanted to prove she had the upper hand. However, her brother had been trained by the Brotherhood. By Nathenek. She probably couldn't best him physically. Another approach was needed then.

Holding her head high, she straightened her dress and took a seat. "I apologize for my outburst." She gracefully picked up her fork and resumed eating her meal. If he thought she was prissy, she'd give him prissy.

"Are the two of you done?" Darmik asked.

Savenek lifted the corner of his mouth in a half smile. "For now."

"Back to Kerdan. If we move forward with the marriage, Telmena will oppose it."

"I think they'll find something to oppose, regardless of what Allyssa does or does not do," Savenek said. "They're determined to invade Emperion and have been involved in this from the get-go."

"Why?" Allyssa asked. "We've never bothered them."

"I sent Nathenek to Telmena to verify a few things for me," Rema said. "I knew Hamen, the previous emperor, had married into the royal family here in Emperion. When he discovered Empress Eliza was not the true heir, that the line had shifted because of Nero all those years ago, he was furious. It is why he sought me out and tried to have me killed."

"Where was Hamen from?" Allyssa asked.

"I'm assuming it's Telmena," Savenek said.

"Correct," Rema replied. "And that is why Telmena has been aiding Jana in any way they can. However, now that she's dead—now that we have killed her entire family—I expect some sort of retribution from Telmena."

"Instead of sitting here waiting for them to make the next move, I suggest we attack," Savenek said. "We do what they least expect."

"Until they physically make a move against us, I can't sanction our army marching into Telmena," Rema said.

Allyssa agreed with her mother. "What would you hope to accomplish by attacking them?" she asked Savenek.

"I'd remove the entire royal family."

"And then what? Take over the kingdom? Expand Emperion yet again?"

"Or put someone we want in power there. Someone who won't threaten us."

"We can't just go around murdering people because we don't agree with them."

"Each of you have valid points," Rema said. "And everything will be taken into consideration. I want both of you to think on the matter some more. We will discuss it in greater detail tomorrow with the Legion members and the dukes."

"Aligning ourselves with Russek will only strengthen us," Allyssa added.

"Or be seen as an act of war," Savenek mumbled.

"Correct," Darmik said, leaning forward on his elbows. "And know this, no matter what we do, which path we choose, we are going to war."

～

ALLYSSA STROLLED NEXT TO MAYRA, THEIR ARMS linked as they made their way to the archery range.

"I know you fancy my brother," Allyssa said.

Mayra tried pulling free, but Allyssa held onto her friend.

"I just want to know if it's a fling or something more?"

The archery range came into view. Allyssa's arms tingled with anticipation. It had been far too long since she'd shot a bow.

Instead of answering, Mayra nodded up ahead to where Madelin stood waiting for them. "Did you hear Marek and Madelin are no longer courting?"

The news shocked Allyssa. "What happened?" She glanced over her shoulder at Marek, who trailed about ten feet behind her with the rest of her guard.

"I don't know all the details," Mayra said, lowering her voice. "But I think Madelin ended their relationship when she realized Marek would always put you first."

"What are you talking about?" Marek didn't have feelings for Allyssa.

"When my brother returned after you'd been kidnapped, he was frantic to rescue you. He thought of nothing else. You must realize that Marek's first love always has been and always will be Emperion."

For some reason, this saddened Allyssa. "I want him to be happy." Not shackled to his job.

"He is. Especially now that you're back."

Allyssa had thought the royal family was the only one making extreme sacrifices for Emperion. She didn't realize—hadn't known —others were doing the same thing.

They stopped before Madelin, who was impatiently tapping her right foot on the ground. "What took you so long to get here?" Without waiting for an answer, she continued, "I don't know why you're so eager to be at the archery range. You know how I feel about this sort of thing."

Allyssa knew Madelin didn't have the patience or the skill to shoot. Her lady-in-waiting would much rather be dancing at a ball than standing about an archery range. Especially knowing Marek was here. "You don't have to stay."

"There is something I need to discuss with you," Madelin said.

Allyssa went over to the table where several different-sized bows and a handful of arrows had been placed. She found her favorite bow and picked it up, feeling the weight in her hands. "What is it?"

"I received a letter from my parents requesting that I visit. The empress has given me permission to go. However, I want to make sure you don't need me here before I leave."

Allyssa knew that Madelin's parents, Audek and Vesha, lived in a cottage a couple of days' journey from here. They preferred the quiet countryside to life in town. "I will miss you terribly, but you may go. Enjoy the time with your family."

"Thank you." Madelin hugged Allyssa and left, practically skipping back toward the castle.

Grabbing an arrow, Allyssa moved over to the shooting line. She nocked her arrow and raised the bow. Five targets stood at various distances. Closing her eyes, she reveled in the feel of the bow and the soft wind against her face. It was good to be home. Aiming at the closest target, she released the drawstring. The arrow sailed through the air, landing on the target but missing the center by an inch. *A bloody inch!*

"I don't think I've ever seen you miss," Mayra said.

Allyssa didn't miss. Ever. Nocking another arrow, she aimed. This time, she narrowed her focus to the center of the target, ignoring everything else going on around her. Slowly breathing out, she released the bowstring. The arrow flew faster this time, hitting the inner target. Not dead center, but at least she'd struck it.

Nocking her third arrow, Allyssa aimed at the next target. She was just about to release the bowstring when another arrow went whizzing by her, striking the second target dead center.

"Now that's how it's done," Savenek said from behind her.

Lowering her bow, Allyssa turned to glare at her brother.

"The princess hasn't shot in weeks," Mayra reminded him. "As I've said before, your sister is better than you." She folded her arms over her chest, daring Savenek to argue.

"Not possible."

He was far too cocky and arrogant for Allyssa's liking. "Instead of standing back there," she drawled, "come up here so we can have a proper contest."

"If you insist." He strode up next to her. "You want to just stand here and hit a stationary target? That doesn't sound very difficult. I think I could hit that when I was five." He smirked.

How in the world had Savenek caught Mayra's attention? She glared at her friend, as if it was Mayra's fault Savenek was here making Allyssa's life difficult. She could have sworn she heard Marek chuckle from behind her. The traitor.

Rolling her shoulders back, she tried to maintain some sense of dignity. "To make the contest more challenging, I'll meet you at the stables in thirty minutes." Without waiting for a response, she turned and glided away.

"Bold move," Mayra said, trying to keep up with her quick pace.

"Are you certain I'm a better shot?" She didn't want to be embarrassed today.

"Savenek is good, especially from a long distance. He's been trained to make those intricate, detailed shots. However, you're precise, quick, and you never miss. Other than that one time today, I mean."

"Have two horses saddled and ready to go. Make sure each has one bow and a quiver with a dozen arrows." She would put her brother in his place. Wipe that smug expression off his face.

"Will do. Do you need help changing out of that dress?"

"No. I can take care of myself." She'd been forced to figure out how to lace up her own dresses over the course of the past few weeks since she didn't have anyone helping her at Nathenek's or on the road.

Mayra nodded and left.

Marek came alongside Allyssa. "I hope you know what you're doing."

"Don't I always?" She glanced over her shoulder to make sure her brother wasn't following her. "What's your impression of Savenek?"

"From what I've seen, there are two sides to your brother. Before the members of court, he is cocky, arrogant, conceited, and he flirts with everyone. In private, he's intelligent, quiet, and levelheaded."

"Why do you think that is?"

"That's the role your father told him to play."

"Then he has my father's shrewd intelligence."

"Or your mother's."

"I wonder why he's showing me his court face."

"Maybe he's just trying to get to know you better."

"Perhaps. Or he could be trying to prove he's a better shot than me."

"If that's the case, I don't want to be anywhere near this castle if you lose."

"If?"

"Sorry, my money's on the assassin."

Allyssa cursed.

DRESSED IN HER RIDING PANTS AND A FORM-FITTING tunic, Allyssa entered the stables.

"It's about time you showed up," Savenek said, leaning against one of the stalls. "Thirty minutes must mean something different to you than it does to me." Pushing off the stall, he pointed at the stable boy who held the reins for two horses. "I presume those are for us."

"They are."

"Is our entire guard going to ride with us?"

"Yes. I've instructed them to keep a safe distance." Allyssa noticed his cheek twitch. She tried not to smile at this small revelation. And she tried not to take comfort that being watched all the time bothered him as much as it did her.

Going over to the closest horse, Allyssa mounted.

"What exactly are we doing in this contest of ours?" Savenek said, mounting the other horse.

"There is a field behind the castle. Past the field is a forest. Ride straight to the forest and you will find a narrow dirt path that cuts through the trees. Each side of the path has five targets hung somewhere on the trees. Your arrows have a blue mark, mine have a red. Whoever hits the most targets, closest to the center, wins."

"It's not fair if you know where the targets are. It puts me at a disadvantage."

"Don't be such a baby," she chided him. "I had a soldier place the targets at random. I don't know where they are."

He studied her. "Do we both go at the same time?"

"Yes. On the way out, you can only hit targets on your right; on the way back, only shoot to your right again. I'll do the left." She nudged her horse, exiting the stables.

"I'm surprised you're allowed to wear pants," Savenek said. He rode his horse alongside hers.

Instead of responding to him, she addressed Marek. "Are we good to go?"

"Everything is ready."

"Count us off."

"Three, two, one, go!"

Allyssa nudged her horse, bringing it to a full gallop. The wind tossed her hair as she leaned forward on the saddle, reveling in the feel of the animal's speed. When she neared the forest, she grabbed her bow and an arrow. Slowing her horse to a steady canter, she scanned the trees, searching for the first target. Savenek was slightly behind her. She felt, rather than saw, him raise his bow and aim. Not bothering to look back at him, she kept her focus on the left side of the path since that was where her targets were.

The first target came into view. Squeezing her legs against the horse, she made sure her balance was secure before aiming. If she fell off the horse, she'd never be able to look her brother in the face again. She pulled back the bowstring, checked her aim, and released the arrow. Not wanting to slow to verify she made the shot, she continued on the path, searching for the next target. There it was, a little higher this time. She aimed and shot. Two down.

The horse flew around the bend in the path, kicking up dirt as it ran. Two targets came into view. As quickly as possible, Allyssa released an arrow, grabbed another, aimed, and released the second. She was positive the first one hit its mark. The second one might be off-center.

The last target came into view dead ahead. She needed to make the shot, turn the horse around, and prepare to hit the targets on the other side of the path this time. After shooting an arrow, she watched it sail straight for the center. As her arrow embedded in the middle of the target, another arrow split hers in half. *Bloody hell!*

She turned her horse around. Somehow, Savenek had already managed to turn his horse and was heading back along the path, now ahead of Allyssa. Grudgingly, she acknowledged he was an excellent rider. Of course he was. Nathenek had raised him.

However, she simply refused to lose to him. Adjusting her grip on the bow, she prepared to shoot an arrow at the next target. She found it quite some distance away, deeper into the forest than the other targets had been. She nocked an arrow, aimed, and released. Hopefully her arrow didn't strike a tree before it hit the target.

Her horse slowed as it went around the bend. When the path straightened, Allyssa urged it to run faster. The next target came into view. She shot another arrow, reveling in the *thunk* she heard as she rode past it. Pushing her horse faster, she came alongside Savenek.

"There isn't room for us to ride side by side," he yelled.

She knew that, but she ignored him and focused on searching for her remaining targets. If he was concerned about his horse colliding with hers, then he would have to slow down or maybe watch her more closely. Perhaps he'd even miss a target. It was a dirty trick, but she didn't care.

A target came into view. She released an arrow. Her arms started to tire. As she grabbed another arrow, it slipped between her fingers and fell to the ground. Trying not to let it rattle her, she plucked another one, aimed, and shot.

She almost missed the next one. Fumbling for another arrow, she nocked it, swerved back toward the target, and shot. When she twisted around, the last target came into view. The soldier must have put these two closer together to make it more challenging. If Savenek could accurately shoot two arrows at once, which he probably could because it was something Nathenek would have insisted he know how to do, then she was sure to lose.

Slowing her horse to a trot, she patted its neck and said soothing words, congratulating it on how fast and steady it rode.

"You're crazy," Savenek said. He flew by her and slowed his horse, waiting for her to catch up. "Were you trying to get yourself killed?"

"I was trying to win." She pulled her horse to a stop.

"I'll go and measure the targets," Marek said as he darted off into the forest.

"I understand you wanted to win, but that doesn't mean you should take unnecessary risks." His eyes were filled with fury.

"I didn't take any unnecessary risks," she said with more confidence than she felt.

He ran his hands through his hair. "Then what do you call that stunt where you practically ran me off the road?" His voice was borderline hysterical.

"I didn't run you off the road. Stop being so dramatic."

"You're the princess, and you shouldn't endanger your life." He patted his horse's neck.

"Are you worried about my well-being?" Was he concerned about her? Like a brother?

"Of course I am. I don't want to be the emperor. I'm fine with helping Darmik out and running the Brotherhood. But all this..." He pointed at the royal guard not far away. "I don't want to deal with this my entire life. Keep yourself in good health and don't break your neck."

She had a tough time reading him. Was he serious? Joking? Some of each? "Why do you call Father by his name?"

He gripped his horse's reins. "He's your father, not mine." Angling his horse away from hers, he started heading back toward the stables.

She stared at his back. "What do you call Nathenek?"

He stopped. "Nathenek is my father. He raised me."

"I understand. However, here at court, you must realize how it can be misinterpreted if you call Nathenek Father." They couldn't afford for anyone to question the legitimacy of the crown.

He glanced over his shoulder at her. "It's always about the kingdom, isn't it?"

Always. "If we don't put Emperion first, who will? We have a duty and responsibility to our people."

"I know that." He turned his horse around so he was facing

Allyssa. "When I trained with the Brotherhood, I'd assumed the royal family was ordering everyone about. I didn't realize how much you each sacrifice personally."

"Are you not up for the challenge?" she asked, half teasing, half serious.

"No. I can do it. It's just different than I thought it would be."

Marek came sprinting out of the forest. "I have a winner," he said as he joined them.

"Who is it?" Allyssa asked, suddenly nervous.

"It was close," Marek said. "Both of you struck each target. However, only one of you hit the center on all ten."

Her heart pounded waiting for Marek to declare the victor.

"Princess Allyssa won."

Joy and smug satisfaction washed through her. Throwing her arms up in the air, she yelled, "Yes!"

Savenek cursed. "Are you sure?"

"Positive. She was more accurate than you."

Savenek bristled.

Allyssa laughed. "I can't wait to share this news with Nathenek."

"He'll have my hide for losing. He always says my aim is better with a dagger than an arrow."

"I'm excellent with a dagger too," she bragged.

"Is there somewhere we can throw?"

"Haven't the two of you had enough?" Marek asked.

They both turned to Marek. "No," they said in unison.

CHAPTER 7

Savenek couldn't believe he'd lost. To his sister. *A woman.* How was that even possible? He was a trained assassin. His shot should be far more accurate than a pampered princess's. Mayra had been right—Allyssa was an excellent marksman. And that grated on his nerves.

He made his way to Darmik's office knowing he'd never hear the end of it. Allyssa would constantly goad him about her victory. The only way he could redeem himself would be by winning their dagger competition later today.

Turning the corner, he almost bumped into Mayra.

"Excuse me, Your Highness." She tried stepping around him.

He reached out, taking hold of her upper arms to steady her. "Your Highness? Really?" He didn't want her to call him that. It was too formal. His fingers trailed down her arms, but then he took a step away from her.

"Would you rather I call you Prince Savenek?"

The thought of calling her Princess Mayra crossed his mind, but he didn't say anything. If he did, she'd probably whack him. Instead, he smiled his devilish grin at her. "Maybe."

"I need to be on my way. I'm expected elsewhere."

"I miss you," he whispered, taking a slow, measured step toward her.

"How about you meet me in the solarium after supper?"

That sounded intriguing. "Alone?"

She glanced at his guards. "That would be nice."

"I'll see what I can do."

"Until then." She bowed and hurried away.

Savenek entered Darmik's office. Darmik was standing in the middle of the room, leaning on a table surrounded by men wearing high-ranking military uniforms. Neco and Nathenek were hunched over another map.

"Your Highness," one of the soldiers said.

It took Savenek a minute to realize the soldier meant him. Which would explain why everyone was bowing. Was he supposed to say something?

"At ease," Darmik said. Everyone righted themselves. "I'm glad you're here." He waved Savenek over to the table. "Take a look at this."

Savenek quickly read the letter.

King Viscor,

You should not have severed your son's marriage contract with Emperion. Since you have done so, Emperion is now considering an alliance with Russek. Jana's death has changed everything. We needed Russek on our side. We can't lose them to Emperion. Do whatever you have to in order to secure a marriage between your son and Princess Allyssa. Once they're married, Prince Odar can work from within and destroy Emperion.

King Metek of Telmena

"Is this authentic?" Savenek asked, not seeing an official seal on the letter.

"One of the spies you sent to Telmena intercepted it. This is a copy. He allowed the original to continue to its destination." Darmik folded his arms. "We've been discussing the best course of action."

"At least Telmena isn't outright attacking us," Savenek mused.

"Agreed."

"What are our options?" Savenek wanted to know what the men in the room had suggested before he'd arrived.

"The empress believes we should go along with it," Darmik said.

"I recommend we attack," one of the soldiers said.

"I think it's odd Prince Jem of Telmena hasn't sought a marriage with Princess Allyssa," Neco said.

"Isn't Jem in his thirties?" Savenek asked.

"Yes. Which may be why Telmena didn't go that route," Darmik said. "Besides, the princess has a history with Prince Odar. I think it makes sense."

Savenek couldn't believe he was being included in a meeting of this magnitude and that his opinion was sought after and valued. "What are the pros and cons of allowing Princess Allyssa to marry Prince Odar?" He honestly didn't see the point, but there was no harm in considering it. "And what do we want to accomplish?" He was of the opinion the entire Telmena royal family should be eliminated. Why live always having to worry about them? Especially knowing Telmena had bought poison from Apethaga. He needed his spies to find where the poison was being stored so it could be destroyed.

"Our goal is to protect Emperion from outside threats," Darmik said. "If we allow Prince Odar and Princess Allyssa to marry, we are taking a gamble. Would Odar attempt to destroy us? Or could we persuade him to help us? It could go either way. However, we do avoid a war. At least for the time being."

"I think if all we care about is keeping the peace," Savenek said, "then we should have Allyssa marry Jem." He couldn't believe they were talking about his sister's life so casually.

"Is that what Allyssa wants?" Nathenek asked.

No one had said anything about what Allyssa did or did not want. All Darmik was focused on was avoiding a war. Savenek wasn't sure how he felt about that. His gut reaction was to tell Darmik he was wrong. That sometimes war was necessary. And could Darmik really sacrifice his daughter's happiness like that? The thought made Savenek sick.

"What if the princess marries King Kerdan?" Neco asked. "Would that be enough to scare Telmena into behaving?"

"I don't know," Darmik said. "If this had happened a few seasons ago, I would have taken the stance that peace was the right course of action. However, after dealing with Jana, after seeing the consequences of our past leniency, I am apt to say going to war with Telmena might be the right thing to do." He rubbed his face. "Regardless, we must present two options to the Legion members and the dukes so they can vote. Let's review our options and then decide what is going to work. We also need to come up with one solid plan and one outlandish plan to ensure they approve the one we want."

Sometimes Darmik shocked Savenek. And right now was one of those times. He'd not only said that war might be the way to go, even though Rema had said otherwise, but he'd also indicated he could manipulate the situation to make sure he got the outcome he wanted. It was impressive.

"I'll outline a plan for what happens if Princess Allyssa and King Kerdan marry," Neco said.

"And I'll come up with a plan for if Princess Allyssa and Prince Odar marry," Nathenek said.

"I'll outline what a full-scale invasion into Telmena will look like," Savenek said. "Including what happens after we successfully remove the royal family." He would love for the chance to ride into war with Darmik.

"We reconvene in two days," Darmik said. "Dismissed."

Savenek left the room, thankful no one had suggested marrying him off for the betterment of Emperion.

After instructing his guards to remain in the

corridor, Savenek entered the solarium. The large room had a glass ceiling, fragrant flowers growing throughout, and a water fountain was situated toward the center. Straight ahead was a wall of windows overlooking a garden outside. He strolled through until he found Mayra standing near one of the windows. The sun had just set, casting the room in an orange glow.

After all the weeks he'd spent fantasizing about Mayra, he was finally here with her. Alone. There was so much he wanted to say to her that he didn't even know where to begin. "I never got to thank you for saving my life," he said by way of greeting.

She smiled. "It was nothing."

He stood next to her, looking outside without really seeing anything. "If you hadn't put that paste on my wounds and stopped the poison from spreading, I'd be dead. I'm grateful for your quick thinking."

"All I remember is being so scared you'd die on me. I kept thinking I'd finally found someone I cared for, and I couldn't lose you."

Her words thrilled him. Instead of jumping up and down or grabbing her for a kiss, he asked, "How'd you figure out who I am?" He needed to remain calm and collected.

"The tattoo on your leg. Allyssa has the same one on her shoulder." Taking a deep breath, she faced him. "There's something I must say to you. I need to apologize for how horribly I treated you in Apethaga."

He almost laughed. She'd definitely given him a hard time, putting him in his place. "You don't need to apologize."

"I was rude and condescending."

True. But he'd loved her sassy attitude. It was part of her charm. "You also kissed me," he reminded her.

"I thought you were a member of the Brotherhood. If I had known you were a prince, I would never have been so casual around you."

He chuckled. "I rather like your casualness."

Blushing, she moved away from the window. It was turning dark outside. "You must have been shocked when you found out."

"I was." To put it mildly.

"You seem to be adjusting to life here in Lakeside."

He took hold of her hands, rubbing his thumbs over the back of her hands. "I am. There's only been one thing missing."

"What's that?"

"You. I want you by my side every day."

"You're supposed to be running a kingdom, not thinking about me."

He chuckled. She was always so practical. "Ari," he whispered. "I have been focused on Emperion. But I've also been thinking about having you at my side helping me."

She stilled. "Are you certain that's what you want?"

"Positive." He leaned down and kissed the side of her mouth, breathing in the distinct scent of her lavender perfume. "I plan to speak to your father on the matter." Although he didn't look forward to that conversation.

"Please do it soon."

Savenek kissed her again, this time taking his hands and sliding them down her back, pulling her closer to him. He could feel the heat from her body.

She put a palm on his chest and gently, but firmly, pushed him away. "We shouldn't do this until you have permission from my parents."

Was she serious? He raised his eyebrows.

"If my father sees us kissing before you speak to him, I'm fairly certain he'll never let you anywhere near me ever again—even if you are the prince of Emperion." Her eyes sparkled, and it took every ounce of his self-control to step away from her.

Taking her right hand, he slowly lifted it to his lips and kissed her fingers. "I understand."

"And I understand Allyssa beat you in the archery contest earlier today."

Nice way to ruin his happiness. "We also had a dagger-throwing contest. Did she tell you about that one?" He strolled over to the rosebush on his left and plucked a white rose.

"I did not hear about that."

He meandered back toward Mayra. "I won that contest." Although it had been closer than he cared to admit. He placed the rose behind her right ear.

"Speaking of your sister, can I ask a favor?"

"Sure."

"I'm afraid Allyssa is going to leave the castle tonight. Can you assign someone to watch the laundry room? I meant to ask Marek earlier but forgot."

He remembered Darmik saying something about Allyssa using her laundry chute to sneak out. "I'll take care of it." It seemed odd that Allyssa would leave the castle unprotected knowing how important her safety was to the kingdom. The more he learned about her, the more he realized she took unnecessary risks.

AFTER SAVENEK LEFT THE SOLARIUM, HE ASSIGNED TWO sentries to monitor the laundry room during the night. Although he couldn't imagine Allyssa sneaking out since she'd already been kidnapped once. She couldn't possibly do something that stupid.

Heading to the Royal Chambers, he thought about how he was going to ask Neco and Ellie for permission to court Mayra. Where would be the best place to talk to them? Should Rema and Darmik be present? He had no idea how these things worked. Maybe he needed to ask Nathenek for his advice first.

When Savenek passed the library, a faint light from inside caught his attention, and he wondered if Allyssa was in there. At the next hallway, he rounded the corner and instructed his guards to wait there, out of sight. Then he double-backed and peered inside the library. Allyssa was in her alcove, hunched over several books. Her guards were spread throughout the library, some standing around the perimeter, others sitting at desks, most looking bored. Savenek considered going in to talk to her, but intuition held him back. Glancing down the hallway, he saw his own guards poking their heads around the corner in order to keep him in sight. Instead of spying on Allyssa to see what she was up to, Savenek decided to head to his room and retire for the night. Or at least pretend that was what he was doing so he could ditch his guards.

Entering the Royal Chambers, he didn't see Rema or Darmik anywhere. He went to his room. Protocol dictated that two men from his guard remain on duty for the night. Luckily, they both stood outside in the hallway. After locking his door, he quickly changed into plain black pants and a shirt. He blew the candles out before hurrying over to the windows. One readily opened, and he climbed outside. The castle had been built with large stone blocks, allowing him to easily climb the side of it.

Once on the ground, he headed toward the main gate that led to the town. If Allyssa planned to sneak out, she'd have to pass through there. Since Savenek wasn't familiar enough with the workers to pass off as one, he decided climbing over the wall would be easier. He headed north about fifty feet. Leaning against the wall, he waited for the sentry on duty to pass by. Once he did, Savenek quickly scaled the wall. When he reached the top, he rolled onto his stomach, trying to remain flat so no one would see him. Then he slid over to the other side and climbed down as quickly as he could. At the bottom, he sprinted across the street to the closest building. Once hidden in the shadows, he headed back toward the gate.

Savenek found an excellent alcove that allowed him to remain hidden, yet see everyone who came or went. He stayed there waiting for Allyssa to exit.

After an hour, he started to wonder if he'd been wrong. Maybe Allyssa didn't plan to sneak out. Or maybe she'd tried to, but the guards stationed in the laundry room had caught her. Savenek let his head rest against the stone wall behind him. He could be in bed sleeping by now instead of standing there like an idiot waiting for his sister who may or may not show up.

He was just about to leave the alcove and return to the castle when he saw someone exit the castle's gate. The person wore pants and a cape, making it difficult to tell if it was Allyssa. Sliding out of the alcove, he decided to follow the person to see who it was. He or she headed along the street, toward the main section of town. Savenek followed from a safe distance. At a rather bland building, eleven blocks south, three blocks east, the person went over to a ladder attached to the side, climbed up to the window on the second level, and went inside.

If it was Allyssa, he had no idea what she was doing. Standing across the street, he watched the window. After a few minutes, the person exited through the window and climbed down the ladder. Stepping out from the shadows, Savenek approached the person. As the person's hands clung to the rungs of the ladder, he caught a glimpse of a ring he recognized.

"What are you doing?" he demanded.

Allyssa jumped and spun around. "You scared me."

He folded his arms, waiting for her to answer.

She scanned the street. "Follow me."

Curious to see what she was up to and why, he followed her. They walked two blocks south and then Allyssa climbed another ladder, waving Savenek up after her. At the top of the building, he stepped onto the flat rooftop. Allyssa went to the center and laid on her back, staring up at the night sky. Savenek stretched out next to her. Instead of asking her one of the hundreds of questions he wanted to, he kept his mouth shut, hoping she would talk on her own. She would probably be more apt to share if he didn't push her.

After several minutes, she finally spoke. "I went to Grevik's house." She then told him about her best friend who Soma had brutally murdered. She explained how the two of them used to sneak out at night to track down criminals and put them in prison. "The only reason I went there tonight was to check on his mother. I wanted to make sure she's okay. And I wanted to leave her some money."

While he understood her compulsion to help, it wasn't safe for her to be traveling through the town all alone. "You should have asked me to come with you—not because you're not capable of taking care of yourself, but because our neighboring kingdoms want you dead. You owe it to our people to keep yourself safe."

"I know. And I promised Neco I wouldn't sneak out anymore."

"Then why did you?"

"Since I've been back, I've felt suffocated," she admitted. "I just needed one night to myself. I'm sorry."

"I guess you can't be perfect all the time," he replied dryly.

She whacked him. "I'm not perfect."

"You appear to be."

"Of course I do. That's what Emperion wants and needs. I'm simply giving them that."

Interesting. "What about you?" he asked. "What is it that you want?" He saw the corners of her lips rise in a tiny smile.

"Peace. Love. Family."

"Do you think peace is possible?"

"Eventually."

"Have you heard about Telmena's letter?" If not, she had a right to know. It was about her after all.

"No." She turned her head to face him. "Mother and Father said they need to speak with me on an important matter tomorrow."

"Telmena wants Odar to marry you."

She started laughing. And not a normal laugh, but a laugh with a slightly hysterical quality to it.

CHAPTER 8

Allyssa

Allyssa couldn't control her laughter. Telmena wanted Odar to marry her. That was just her luck. Telmena had originally opposed the union, fearing it would make Emperion too strong. Now that Telmena's plans were falling apart with Russek, they wanted Odar to marry Allyssa in order to worm their way into Emperion. It allowed them to take control without the expense of a nasty war. Too bad she no longer wanted to marry Odar.

"Why are you laughing?" Savenek asked. He looked at her as if she was deranged. Maybe she was. This entire situation was ridiculous.

"Your mother wants you to go through with it," he added. "She mistakenly thinks it'll prevent a war."

Allyssa wiped the tears from her face. She hadn't laughed that hard in a long time. "Did you talk to my mother about it?" Why would Rema have discussed it with Savenek before Allyssa?

"Your dad."

"Father already said I could marry Kerdan." Which meant her parents were planning something. She was fairly certain that even if her marrying Odar was the only way to prevent a bloody war, Darmik wouldn't let her. Not after the way Odar had treated her.

"You might want to be prepared for your parents changing their minds."

She reached over and patted his arm. "Oh dear, sweet Savenek," she sang, teasing him.

"What?"

"I'm positive my parents don't intend for me to marry Odar."

"Then why did Darmik suggest it? Why did Rema say that's what she wanted?"

"It has to be a ruse." If she pretended she was going to marry to Odar, it would give them time to come up with a permanent solution to Telmena. The problem was, she didn't care to pretend anything with Odar. "I wonder if he would even go along with it." Because if he didn't, then there was no point entertaining the idea. And whose side was he on? And how would they know if they could trust him or not?

"Wouldn't Odar do whatever his parents tell him? I mean, they are the king and queen. He doesn't have much choice."

She wondered if that was how Savenek felt sometimes—that he didn't have a choice. She'd have to think about that in more detail later. For now, she needed to consider the situation with Odar. He'd refused to marry Princess Jestina of Telmena. Instead, he'd had his younger brother marry her. Allyssa had a feeling his parents could influence him, but not force him to do anything he didn't want to do. Which was why it stung knowing he'd severed the marriage contract with her. No matter, it was for the best.

"What do you think we should do about Telmena?" she asked. If Telmena was so determined to destroy Emperion, they wouldn't stop until they accomplished it. Even if Telmena didn't wage war against Emperion, they could hire an assassin to kill off Rema, Darmik, Allyssa, and Savenek. There were so many options.

"I think we should kill the Telmena royal family," Savenek said. "Then we should take control of the kingdom." He sounded so confident in his assessment.

"I'm not sure we could govern the people. If they rebel, our army would have to step in to neutralize them. I don't know if we can be spread so thin." She didn't know if she could send

Emperions to their deaths. Because Emperions would die. Making these tough decisions weighed her down.

"Good point. Is there someone we can place in power that the people would want?"

"I don't know offhand." It was late, and she was too tired to think straight.

"I'll look into it to see if I can come up with some possibilities. In the meantime, what do you want to do about Odar?"

"If pretending to marry him buys us time, I'll go along with it."

"What if your parents want you to actually marry him?"

"They won't." Her voice cracked, although she'd been trying to hide her feelings from Savenek. Feelings she didn't care to discuss. Especially with a brother who she couldn't decide how she felt about.

She gazed up at the stars, shoving Odar out of her mind. She'd said goodbye to him in Russek. While she'd known there would be a possibility she'd have to deal with him in the future, she hadn't thought it would be so soon.

"You were engaged to him," Savenek said.

"Yes."

"But Fren severed the contract?" His voice revealed nothing but interest.

She sighed. "Yes."

"You don't talk much."

She chuckled. "And you talk far too much." She thought about probing him about Mayra just to prove how annoying it was to have to talk about that sort of thing. Instead, she decided to be honest. "He broke my heart."

"Odar?"

"Yes." She didn't know how much Savenek knew about the situation, and she didn't feel like going into details. How could she explain the prince had switched places with his squire? That she'd fallen in love with the squire who was really the prince? That once she realized he was the prince and he'd been deceitful on more than one occasion, she no longer loved him? That her heart now belonged to another man?

"Then pretending to be engaged to him is going to be rough."

His words caught her by surprise. "Yes." How did he understand so easily? If it had been Madelin, she would have questioned Allyssa relentlessly about what had happened and why she felt that way.

"If you don't want to go through with the farce, we can come up with something else."

"I know." She hated when he acted like he knew more than she did. She knew they could do something else, but this was the most logical thing to do. It was what was best for Emperion. In her mind, there was no question about it.

"Are you sure?"

She nodded, realizing belatedly he couldn't see her since they were on their backs.

"You probably won't have to see him or anything," Savenek said. "Just a few letters of correspondence should be all."

She nodded, this time trying to convince herself that everything would be fine.

"So," Savenek said, a hint of mischievousness to his voice. "Are we going to sit around here doing nothing? Or are we going to find a criminal to imprison?"

"You'd do that with me?" She'd known better than to ask Marek to accompany her. But her brother, well, he trained with the Brotherhood. He'd make an excellent companion.

Chuckling, Savenek jumped to his feet. "As long as you can keep up." He started climbing down the ladder without waiting for her to respond.

He could be so cocky sometimes. She got to her feet, eager to join him.

On the street, Allyssa took the lead and headed toward one of her favorite taverns, The Crow's Cave.

"You armed?" Savenek mumbled.

"Always." She had two knives strapped to her thighs and two daggers on her forearms. She suspected her brother had even more weapons on his body. Occupational hazard.

When they came to the black door with a crow carved on it, Allyssa went inside.

"You sure know how to pick them," Savenek said under his breath.

Stifling a laugh, Allyssa made her way to the bar. The place was packed, and she could barely maneuver between the people. The walls were black, the ceiling black, the tables black. Barrels of ale hung on the wall behind the bar. At the other end of the room, there was a stage where people would sing, act out a play, or even dance. It was one of the reasons she enjoyed coming here—and one of the reasons Grevik had hated it.

At the bar, Savenek ordered two drinks, tossing a coin at the bartender. Allyssa brought her cup to her mouth, turning to watch the room. A man teetered up the steps to the stage where he began to bellow a song completely out of tune. People threw food at him until he got off the stage.

She scanned the room, searching for anything unusual or out of place. There were two men who were dressed like everyone else, but something felt off. She watched them, trying to figure out what it was about them that bothered her.

"Those guys over there, third table from the left, two back, are from Telmena," Savenek said as he turned his head toward her and scratched the side of his neck.

Allyssa didn't know what someone from Telmena was supposed to look like, so she'd have to take his word for it. She counted the tables until she came to the one he'd pointed out. It was the same one she'd been watching.

Another person climbed onto the stage. This time, the man stomped his foot while chanting a song. It was rather catchy, and the crowd allowed him to finish. As everyone was applauding the man, the two people from Telmena stood and moved toward the exit.

Allyssa set her cup down, then started heading to the door. She didn't bother to make sure Savenek was following her; she knew he'd be close behind. When they exited the building, she spotted the men moving toward an inn a block away.

"We can't arrest them if they haven't done anything wrong," she whispered.

Shrugging, Savenek picked up the pace. He went between the men, wrapping his arms around each one's neck and leading them down the closest alley as if they were the best of friends.

After making sure no one was following them, Allyssa darted between the buildings. Savenek had each man pinned to the wall. "What are you doing here?" he demanded.

"We were just getting a drink at the pub," the one on the right answered. His speech was clear and articulate. He sounded like an Emperion to Allyssa.

"Why are you in Emperion?"

"We live here."

"You're lying." Savenek raised an eyebrow at Allyssa. "Do you want me to handle this, or are you in the mood to rough one of these buggers up a bit?"

"I want one." Preferably the smaller of the two.

Savenek released the man he'd been holding with his left hand. "Take that one."

The man swung toward Allyssa, pulling a knife out of his boot. He rushed at her. When he was close enough, she spun and kicked, hitting his right hand. The knife dropped to the ground.

Savenek slammed his forehead against the other man's. The brutality of it stunned her.

The man Allyssa had kicked said something in a language she didn't know. When he swung, she ducked, the punch narrowly missing her. She rammed her knee into his side, but he barely moved. His right hand shot out, clutching onto her arm. Using the momentum, she spun in toward him so her back was against his chest. Then she leaned forward, flipping him over her shoulder. When he hit the ground, she slammed her fist into his stomach. Not having any rope to tie him up with, she withdrew her dagger and smashed the hilt against his forehead, knocking him out.

She righted herself. Savenek stood leaning against the wall, watching her. "Are you done?" he asked. The man he'd struck was lying at his feet. She hoped he was still alive.

"How did you know they were from Telmena?" She wiped her brow. "And how did you know they were up to no good?"

He pushed off the wall and came over to the man she'd fought with, kicking him in the side to ensure he was indeed knocked out. She tried not to be offended that he felt the need to check.

"See his ear." He pointed to the man's right lobe. "It has a mark. That is a hole for an earring. People in Telmena often wear them."

She'd never heard of such a thing. "And you managed to see that from where we were standing at the bar?"

"Well, no." He smiled. "I noticed when we walked past him."

They needed to take these men to the City Guard. She'd let them handle the investigation.

Savenek rolled each man over before checking pockets, boots, and sleeves. He found one small tube filled with red liquid.

"What is it?"

"Kepper poison," he said, pocketing the container. "The castle is fourteen blocks from here. That's roughly a mile." He scrutinized the men. "I'm not sure I can carry both that far."

"The prison is two blocks from here." She pointed to the left. "Can you drag them there?"

"I guess that will do. But I want them turned over to the Brotherhood for questioning."

"Because they're from Telmena?"

"No," he said, reaching down and grabbing the arms of the larger man. "Because of the kepper poison."

Allyssa flicked her eyes at her brother's poison-filled pocket. "What are you going to do with it?"

"Destroy it."

That was good enough for her. "I'll help you."

SOMEONE BANGED ON ALLYSSA'S DOOR, STARTLING HER awake. Darmik poked his head inside her room. "Get up. It's time for our run. You have fifteen minutes."

Groaning, she pulled one of her pillows over her head. It was still dark outside, and she'd only just crawled into bed. It seemed as if Darmik always wanted to run the mornings when she'd been up late gallivanting the night before. It was almost as if he knew. She flew upright. Somehow, he knew. She was sure of it. Allyssa threw her pillow at the door even though Darmik was no longer there. If Savenek had told Darmik she'd snuck out, she'd kill him. He was just as guilty as she was.

Allyssa slid out of bed, then headed to her dressing closet. Half asleep, she pulled on her army pants and tunic, the standard uniform the soldiers wore. Pulling her hair back, she quickly braided it and wrapped the braid around her head. As ready as she'd ever be at this forsaken hour, she headed to the sitting room where she found Darmik and Savenek waiting for her. Savenek was similarly dressed. He yawned and rubbed his eyes. Apparently, Darmik was going to punish them both. Maybe this run wouldn't be so bad after all.

They headed out of the castle, joining a dozen soldiers.

Darmik led the way, keeping a steady pace toward the forest. Allyssa and Savenek followed him, the soldiers running in two lines behind them. The sky had started to lighten, but it was still fairly dark out.

They made their way to the dirt path that cut through the trees.

"I don't know why I'm jogging alone," Darmik said.

Allyssa rolled her eyes and caught up to him, running on his left side. Savenek did the same, coming up to Darmik's right.

"How far are we running today?" Savenek asked.

"Five miles," she answered.

"Actually…" Darmik said. "I was going to head around the lake today."

"Bloody hell! That's ten miles." There was no way she could run that far right now. She was barely managing to remain upright.

"Watch your language," her father chided her.

"Are you too out of shape to run that far?" Savenek teased.

"She can run that far," Darmik said.

"Too tired?" Savenek asked. "Need your beauty sleep?"

Reaching behind Darmik, she hit her brother. "How are you not tired?"

"Neither of you should be tired," Darmik said pleasantly. "You both should be well rested and ready for this run."

"I could run all day," Savenek said. He pulled ahead of them. "In fact, I think I'll run at a faster pace."

Blimey. She would not let him outrun her. Pushing her legs faster, she caught up to him.

"Let's make a bet," he said. "Loser has to stand up at supper before the entire court and sing a song."

Allyssa sounded like a dying dog when she sang.

He chuckled. "That's what I thought. You can't sing worth cows, can you?"

"How'd you know?"

"I was watching you closely last night. I might have even heard you trying to hum along."

She had no idea if he could sing or not, but she was certain he wouldn't be embarrassed standing in front of all those people. "If I win, you have to let me help you run the Brotherhood."

He stumbled but caught himself. "You're not involved with the Brotherhood?"

"No. My mother has been solely in charge of it. I'm quite surprised she's letting you have as much control as you do." Nope, Allyssa definitely didn't sound bitter when she said that. She had enough other duties to tend to. However, there was something alluring about the secret organization.

"Fine. Because you're never going to win."

"I didn't bring you out here to bicker," Darmik said from behind them. "I thought the three of us would have a nice jog around the lake."

"I say we shorten it to five," she mumbled to Savenek.

"Okay, but you need to tell me where we're going ahead of time."

That was only fair. "Take this path for about two miles. When we reach the lake, turn right. The path will loop back to the castle. First one to step foot in the stables wins."

"Deal."

She wasn't about to let him win. Using her elbow, she nudged him in the side. Hard. He grunted. She stuck her foot out, trying to trip him. He jumped right over her foot, not missing a step.

"You're going to have to do better than that," he said with a wink. And then he took off, kicking up dust from running so quickly.

Dread filled her. The prospect of losing to her brother was bad enough. But to have to sing before her entire court? Unthinkable. Sucking it up, she sprinted as fast as her legs would go. Time seemed to stop, and all she could see was the back of Savenek's head. She focused on that, running hard, trying to breathe in and out. She had no idea if her father and the soldiers were following. All that she cared about was keeping her brother in sight. Then when they neared the finish, she'd sprint around him.

It didn't help that she was starving, tired, and not in the mood to run. She would not let her cocky, arrogant, think-he-knew-everything brother win.

A cramp formed in her side, but she ignored it. Or at least she tried to. It was getting harder and harder to breathe. They came to the lake. Savenek veered to the right. This was the halfway point. The first part was always the worst. She'd made it this far. She could finish.

Savenek smiled over his shoulder at her. She didn't know what she looked like, but there most definitely was not a smile on her face. He didn't even look winded! She should have known better than to make a bet with him. Of course Nathenek would have trained Savenek to survive on very little sleep and be able to run long distances. She was out of her league.

One foot in front of the other. Was Savenek getting farther away from her? She had to run faster. Her legs started going numb. Allyssa never ran this fast for this long. She couldn't breathe. The stables came into view. Someone was standing near the entrance, waiting for them.

Savenek started running backward. "And here I thought this race was going to be close," he teased.

Using every last ounce of energy she had, she sprinted toward the finish line. She just prayed her feet didn't get tangled up and cause her to fall. Savenek's eyes widened and he spun around, facing forward as he ran the rest of the way to the stables.

Savenek reached the door first and he slowed to a jog, crossing the entrance. Neco stood there with his arms folded, watching them. Allyssa started swaying on her feet, veering to the left and then the right. She motioned for Neco to move out of the way. He stepped to the side, and she ran past him into the stables. Savenek stood there with his hands on his hips, a light sheen of sweat on his forehead.

Allyssa ran right past him and out the other end. She slowed to a walk and went to the first bush she saw, bending over and vomiting.

Her brother came up behind her. "Are you okay?"

"I hate you." She wiped her mouth with the back of her sleeve. Everything hurt. She had sweat dripping off her face, running down her back, and covering the front of her shirt. Her legs wobbled, barely holding her upright. She wasn't sure she could make it to her bedchamber—where she planned to collapse and sleep for a very long time.

"I thought Darmik said he was going on a nice jog with his children," Neco said as he joined them. "I'm not sure what this is, but I'm certain it's not what Darmik had in mind."

Allyssa and Savenek stared at one another.

Her brother grinned. "No, but he might enjoy the entertainment at supper tonight." With that, he turned and strolled away, whistling as he went.

Allyssa entered the Dining Hall holding her head high. She would not let Savenek see how much she didn't want to do this. Earlier in the day, he'd told her which song he wanted her to sing. It was one she'd never heard of. He'd gladly volunteered to write the lyrics down for her so she could memorize them before supper.

She strode to the head table, taking her seat alongside Savenek.

"You're here before Rema and Darmik," he said. "I'm shocked. I thought you were always late."

"When do you want me to sing? Shall I do it before we eat? Or wait until people have food in their mouths so they can spit it out from laughing?"

He snorted. "You're entertaining."

"Glad I can be of amusement." She took a sip of her wine.

"How about you sing in the middle of supper? That way you

can spend the first half dreading it and the second half facing everyone you've serenaded."

"You're evil."

Rema and Darmik entered, taking their seats next to Allyssa. The food was brought out and served.

She scanned the room, estimating there were about forty people present tonight.

As she ate, she went over the lyrics in her mind. They were crude and would humiliate her. No doubt it was why Savenek had chosen this particular song—if one could even call it that. The only way to pull this off was to stand up and be absolutely ridiculous. She hadn't told anyone what she was going to do tonight, not even Mayra. Her face heated up just thinking about it.

Savenek nudged her. "It's time."

Pushing away from the table, she stood and went to the center of the room. Everyone stopped talking to stare at her.

She cleared her throat. "Thank you for joining us for supper. My esteemed brother Prince Savenek has suggested I provide you with some entertainment this evening." She could have sworn she heard Darmik groan. How would she convince them she wasn't looney from her time in Russek? "I'm going to sing a favorite of the prince's. In fact, he specifically requested it. If I had chosen a song on my own, it would have been a very, very different song." She glared pointedly at her brother.

Instead of seeming embarrassed, a smirk spread across his face. She wanted to throttle him.

Taking a deep breath, she tried to calm her nerves. There was nothing to do but get it over with.

So she sang.

A song appropriate for a pub—*not* a royal court.

And she made sure she bellowed it out:

"Pour a cup, yo ho
Down your belly it goes, oh no

Drink another cup
Before you barf it up
Tallie ho
Yo ho
Drink another cup before you go."

She was going to die of embarrassment.

The entire room was silent, every single person's eyes wide with shock or horror, she couldn't be sure. She curtseyed and returned to her seat, holding her head high. Savenek started slowly clapping.

"Well done, Your Highness," Mayra said as she began to clap enthusiastically.

Soon, everyone in the room was applauding.

Allyssa glanced over at Darmik, who sat there shaking his head. Rema blinked several times, but said nothing. Yup, this was going to earn Allyssa a stern lecture tonight. She sighed. At least it was over.

And the night couldn't possibly get any worse.

The door flew open, and a sentry entered. "Your Majesties." He bowed and hurried forward, stopping before the head table. "A messenger just arrived with this letter." He held out the sealed parchment.

Darmik reached forward and took it, dismissing the sentry. Since everyone was still focused on the head table, he told them to resume eating their meals. Once attention was diverted, he examined the seal and opened the letter, reading its contents. He folded the letter back up, then tucked it into his tunic.

He didn't rush from the room, which meant the news couldn't be that dire. Allyssa lowered her gaze to her plate.

"That certainly was entertaining," Savenek mused. "I think I enjoy life here at court."

"I need you two to hurry and finish eating," Darmik whispered to Allyssa and Savenek. "Then leave and go straight to the Royal Chambers."

Maybe the news wasn't so good after all.

Darmik stood, Rema joining him. They headed out of the room. As Darmik passed Neco, he pulled on his ear.

Blimey. That was the sign Darmik gave Neco whenever he needed him.

Not bothering to finish her meal, Allyssa stood and hurried after her parents.

"Wait for me," Savenek said, catching up with her. "Do you have any idea what's going on?"

Shaking her head, she glanced back. Sure enough, Neco was following them. A thought suddenly occurred to her. Could Kerdan be here? She wanted to shove past her parents and run to the Royal Chambers. Instead, she forced herself to stroll slowly behind them. Reaching up, she made sure her hair was in place. She hadn't heard from him since they parted ways in Russek. She'd sent many letters, but he hadn't responded. Darmik said Kerdan probably didn't write back because he was too busy being crowned king, gaining control over the army, putting an end to Russek's civil war, and not being assassinated. Which meant if Kerdan was here, things were going well and he was safe.

"Are you okay?" Savenek asked.

Unable to form words to respond, she simply nodded. She hadn't realized how much she missed Kerdan until now.

They entered the Royal Chambers. It was empty. Maybe he was being escorted here at this very moment. She eagerly waited for Kerdan to join them. What would her mother and brother think of the man she'd chosen to spend her life with? Would they approve of him?

A sentry opened the door, revealing a visitor. Only, it wasn't Kerdan who stood there dressed in his finest. Instead, Prince Odar of Fren strode forward, his eyes focused on Allyssa. He looked like a prince should. A crown atop his head, the royal crest embroidered on his blue tunic, a fine sword strapped to his waist.

Allyssa couldn't breathe. What was he doing here? And where was Kerdan?

"Prince Odar," Darmik said dryly. "Welcome." Folding his arms across his chest, he waited for Odar to speak.

He seemed healthier than the last time she'd seen him. He'd gained some weight and his coloring was better. She went over to the sofa and sat, not having much energy left to stand about after the long day she'd had.

"Thank you for admitting me so readily. I need to speak with Princess Allyssa." He purposefully scanned the guards around the room.

"Everyone out," Darmik commanded. All the guards filed out of the room, leaving only the royal family, Odar, and Neco.

"My parents have officially sent me here to reestablish my relationship with Allyssa. They expect us to marry as soon as possible." Odar rubbed his face. "However, that's not why I'm really here." He went over to one of the chairs and sat.

"I'm not following you," Darmik said, sitting across from him on the sofa.

"As you know, Fren has a treaty with Telmena since my brother and Crown Princess Jestina married. When I refused to marry Princess Jestina, certain…elements…were put into the treaty. Me being here is now one of those requirements if you will."

Allyssa wasn't sure she was following him. However, she kept her mouth shut and let her father handle this one.

"I know Allyssa doesn't intend to marry me. I don't want to be married to someone who doesn't care for me." He rested his elbows on his knees, leaning forward on the chair. "I'm here because I have to be. I'm hoping you have a way out of this mess."

Darmik sat back on the sofa, studying Odar. "What does Telmena have to do with this?"

Allyssa had forgotten there was a lot of information they

weren't supposed to know. By asking Odar this, they'd learn how much they could trust him.

"Telmena has always feared Emperion. They financed Jana. Helped her rise to power in Russek, hoping she'd take control of Emperion one day. When that didn't work, they came to me. They want me to marry Allyssa and then help assassinate the empress and emperor, so I'd have control."

"And through you, Telmena would have control," Darmik said.

"Correct. You know the previous emperor, Hamen, was from Telmena?"

Darmik nodded.

"And Jana was related to the Telmena royal family?"

Darmik nodded again. Allyssa also knew her father was related to Jana since they both had the same father. Which meant Darmik was also related to the Telmena royal family.

"They hold you responsible for killing Jana and her children."

"Why are you telling us this?" Rema asked, speaking for the first time.

"I'm tired of these political games. I'd like to end them."

"Even if that means going against your king and queen? Your own parents?" Rema inquired.

Odar nodded.

"Tell me," Darmik said, "do you have any idea how to accomplish this?"

"No," Odar admitted. "I just figured coming here would buy me some time. And if anyone could figure out what to do, it would be you."

"I have a few ideas," Darmik said, not offering any of them up right now. "Anything else we need to be aware of?"

"Yes." Odar glanced at Allyssa briefly before answering. "My father said that a marriage contract has been signed between King Kerdan and Princess Conditto of Apethaga."

Allyssa felt as if a horse had kicked her in the stomach. Was that why she hadn't heard anything from Kerdan? Had he found someone else to marry?

"That contract was signed over a season ago, and it might not be valid," Savenek said, taking a seat next to Allyssa. "I think Jana may have signed it, not King Drenton."

How did Savenek know this? Regardless, Allyssa held onto that hope.

"For your sake," Odar said, eyeing Allyssa again, "I pray it isn't. However, I know Telmena is counting on Fren and Apethaga to join forces and overthrow Emperion. Whether that is peacefully through a marriage or by war, one way or another, Telmena plans to destroy you."

"As of this moment," Rema said, "Odar and Allyssa are engaged."

"Mother," Allyssa said. Rema was jumping to conclusions and making rash decisions.

"It's just for show. Pretend you're engaged. While the attention is on the two of you, Darmik and I will come up with a solution to the situation with Telmena. Permanently."

Odar nodded and stood. "That sounds like an excellent plan. Thank you for your time. Good night." He turned and left.

"Do we trust him?" Savenek asked the second the door closed.

"I trusted him enough to help assassinate Jana," Darmik said.

"What about his relationship with Allyssa?"

"I think he still has feelings for her. And when feelings are involved, that's when things tend to go wrong."

"Excellent," Savenek said. "That was my impression as well."

Allyssa still couldn't believe that Odar was here. That he'd just shown up.

"Neco, see that Odar gets settled in. Make sure there's nothing we're missing."

"My pleasure." Neco headed out of the room.

"I don't know if I can do this," Allyssa said. "I can't pretend to be in love with him."

"No one said anything about love," Rema replied.

Savenek placed his hand on Allyssa's shoulder. "You need to stop worrying. You're strong and resilient. Don't let some guy unravel you."

"You're right." It wasn't like she cared for Odar. So why was she getting all worked up over a simple engagement that wasn't even real in the first place? She smiled briefly at her brother. It was nice to have someone on her side. "I'm glad you're here," she said to him. Because he didn't have to be. Her parents had sent him away for the sake of the kingdom. He owed them nothing.

"You're welcome." He abruptly stood and left the room.

CHAPTER 9

Savenek

Savenek was becoming rather fond of Rema and Darmik. Leaning back on his chair at the head table in the Dining Hall, he watched as Rema introduced Odar to her court, asking him to please explain who he was since they were under the impression he was Jarvik, Odar's squire.

Savenek knew Rema could have easily cleared the issue up. However, she wanted to watch Odar squirm before her court, to humiliate him as revenge for breaking Allyssa's heart. While Allyssa didn't need protecting, her parents were slightly overprotective of her. Savenek felt the same way, which he thought was strange. It had to be that she was his twin. Not because he cared about her like a sister. Because that didn't make any sense. He barely knew her. And she could be annoying.

Odar was not an eloquent speaker. Granted, he was clear, direct, and to the point. But he didn't have the finesse Rema did. He didn't hold the court rapt with attention. Part of it was he didn't try to woo them. Savenek couldn't figure out Odar's angle. What was he playing at? He'd have to talk to Nathenek afterward to discuss the matter. For now, as far as he was concerned, Odar was a threat that needed to be monitored. And he eagerly anticipated the opportunity. After all, this was the man who'd hurt Allyssa.

Odar wasn't tall, he wasn't particularly handsome, and he

didn't appear to be witty. So why had Allyssa fallen for him? He remembered Marek saying something about Odar helping her with the assassin. Allyssa hadn't known Odar was the prince then. So perhaps she was attracted to regular guys who showed a propensity to help others?

Odar took his seat next to Allyssa.

"I'm glad that's over," Allyssa mumbled, twisting her hands together.

Savenek had noticed whenever she was nervous or unsure, she either played with her fingers or her hair.

"Talk to me," she said. "I need a distraction."

He glanced over to where Mayra was sitting next to her parents and her brother. "It's strange to see Marek wearing a fancy tunic." Savenek was so used to seeing Marek in his soldier's uniform that it was odd to see him dressed as one of the members at court.

"I hear you're speaking to Neco and Ellie tomorrow."

Savenek nodded, not really wanting to talk about it. If he thought about it too much, he'd get nervous. And a nervous Savenek was never good.

"I suggest you try to be humble when speaking to them."

He snorted. "Not my style."

She rolled her eyes. "Fine. Don't listen to me. I've only known them for seventeen years."

He knew she was right and that he should listen to her. But humble?

"What are the two of you talking about?" Darmik asked.

"Savenek is going to speak to Neco and Ellie tomorrow," Allyssa said with a hint of glee from disclosing this tidbit of information.

"I know you like Mayra," Darmik said. "But are you certain you're ready to court someone?"

Mayra wasn't just *someone*. Savenek had never met anyone like her before. She was loyal, strong, intelligent, and beautiful. "I thought you'd be happy if I married since you're all about securing the royal line." That may have come out harsher than he'd intended.

"That's what we have Allyssa for."

Savenek blinked.

"He's joking," Allyssa said, shaking her head. "What Father is trying unsuccessfully to say is that he feels bad for neglecting you for seventeen years so he's going to let you choose who you want to marry and there is no rush."

Darmik shot her a stern expression. "I'm letting you choose who you want to marry."

"Well, now you are. But before you weren't."

A thought occurred to Savenek. "What about Kerdan? Are you marrying him because that's what you want or because that's what's best for Emperion?" Did she ever do anything selfish?

"They are one in the same," she answered.

His eyes narrowed. Was it so ingrained in her to do what her kingdom needed that she put herself second?

"It's what I want," she admitted. "I love him."

Hearing his sister say she was in love with a Russek was a bit hard to stomach. Savenek would try and reserve his judgment of Kerdan until he met him. Once he saw Kerdan and Allyssa together, he'd be able to decide how he felt about the union.

"Perhaps this is a conversation for another time when not so many people are around?" Darmik suggested.

Savenek had been careful to keep his voice down; however, he understood what Darmik was saying. He glanced over at Odar sitting on the other side of Allyssa. Odar's focus was on his plate as he ate his food. He'd probably heard every word of their conversation. But Savenek didn't care. It was probably good for the guy to hear that Allyssa had moved on.

"Just so you know," Darmik said to Savenek, "Rema and I are of the same opinion. Mayra would make an excellent partner, and we support your decision. You may court her if Neco and Ellie agree."

A huge sense of relief overcame Savenek. Not that it really mattered—he would have pursued Mayra regardless of what Rema and Darmik had to say about it. But having their approval definitely made it easier.

After dinner, Savenek decided to escort Odar to his bedchamber so he could assess the guy better. As they made their way through the hallways, he tried to figure out how to ask him about Allyssa. In the end, he decided to just come out and say it. When they reached the door to Odar's rooms, Savenek said, "I want to know if you still care for my sister." He made sure to keep his voice low, so it wouldn't carry.

Odar folded his arms, uneasily staring at the guards standing about fifteen feet away. "Yes."

"Why are you really here?" Was it because Odar's parents wanted him to be? Or because he hoped to win Allyssa back?

"Allyssa made it clear the last time we spoke that she wants nothing to do with me."

"Yet, you still came here."

Odar nodded. "If I didn't, Telmena would have attacked Emperion. Regardless of what you may think about me, I don't want any harm to come to Allyssa."

Savenek got the feeling Odar would double cross his own parents in order to win Allyssa back. Which said an awful lot about Odar's character. Savenek decided it was a good thing Odar severed his marriage contract with Allyssa.

SAVENEK BID GOODNIGHT TO HIS GUARDS AND CLOSED his door, thankful to finally be alone. He quickly changed into his plain black tunic and pants. After strapping several knives to his arms and legs, he slid two daggers in his boots. Satisfied, he went over to the window and peered outside. Last time, he'd snuck out this way to the castle grounds easily enough. This time, he needed to go up and over the roof so he could get to the correct wing of the castle.

He climbed outside, pushing the window closed so no one would notice it. He easily scaled the side of the castle. When he reached the roof, he traversed his way across it.

"Savenek?"

Bullocks. He almost lost his footing and fell. Glancing up and to the right, he saw Allyssa standing at the railing. Reluctantly, he made his way over to her. "What are you doing?"

"Sometimes I come out here to think. The real question is, what are you doing?" She peeked over her shoulder, presumably at her guards.

"You don't want to know," he mumbled.

Thankfully, she didn't push the matter. She gazed out at the town, sighing.

"Are you okay?" he asked. After announcing her upcoming marriage to Odar, he wasn't sure how she was holding up. Even if the marriage wasn't real.

"I'm worried about Kerdan."

He hadn't considered that. "He still hasn't responded to any of your letters?"

"No. And I really wish I could discuss the Telmena situation with him."

Even though Savenek was standing precariously on the rooftop, he said, "You can discuss it with me."

She eyed him, as if she wasn't sure she could really trust him. The expression on her face stung.

"Whatever you tell me stays between the two of us," he said, hoping she'd talk to him.

That seemed to be the right answer. "You are of the opinion that we should assassinate the Telmena royal family?"

Now she was speaking his language. "Yes. However, I've been doing some investigating and have concluded that if we take out the royal family, there will be riots if we attempt to establish control. Which is why I've been trying to come up with other viable options besides us taking over."

"Have you come up with anything?" Gripping the railing, she kept her focus toward the town. Probably so her guards wouldn't know she was talking to someone. He appreciated her discretion.

"Not yet. However, I've come up with a way to assassinate the royal family." As to whether anyone would go along with his plan was another matter entirely.

"What's your plan?"

"You agree to a wedding date. We invite everyone of importance from the other kingdoms. Once the king and queen from Telmena are here, we kill them."

"And start a major war."

"What if they die while traveling here? It can be a nasty accident. Killing them on the road would be infinitely easier than in a fortified castle." He could even plan all the details. The Brotherhood would have no problem executing it.

Allyssa shivered, and he wondered what he'd said that had made her eyes go so blank. Was talking about murder too much for her?

"And what of Princess Jestina and her husband?" she asked.

"The princess is married to Odar's brother?"

"Yes."

"I assume we'd kill them, too." No sense in leaving any of them alive.

She pursed her lips. "Do you think Odar's brother, Kren, might be willing to work with us?"

"I have no idea." Savenek had never learned anything about either Kren or Jestina. "I guess that's something we should discuss with Odar." Not that Savenek trusted Odar. However, since Odar still cared for Allyssa, he'd probably be willing to help them in some capacity.

She straightened, pulling her cape tightly around her body.

"My parents won't condone the plan. Especially after we were involved with Jana's murder. The move is far too aggressive."

"I agree." Which was why he was discussing this matter with her instead of Darmik.

She eyed him suspiciously. "Are you suggesting we do this without their knowledge?"

He didn't think they could pull off something of this magnitude without telling them. "I'm suggesting we start making plans without their input. We can discuss the matter with them once we have all the details figured out."

She stood there staring at him for quite some time. "I'll speak with Odar. Get a feel for what he thinks of his brother and Jestina."

"Are you okay doing that?" Savenek had no qualms about talking to Odar. Granted, he didn't have the history with him that she did.

The wind tossed her hair, and she tucked it behind her ears. "I will do what is best for Emperion." She craned her neck to see her guards. "I can't have the threat of Telmena hanging over our heads. I won't risk the safety of my kingdom and my family. I'll do what needs to be done." Her eyes were vacant, and it sent a chill through Savenek. The way she spoke seemed so final. As if she'd sacrifice herself for her kingdom—which she probably would. But there was no need for her to do that. Savenek would help her. Together, they would destroy Telmena. He just needed to make sure his sister didn't destroy herself in the process.

"Once you've spoken to Odar, let me know."

"I will." She left without another word.

Savenek continued over the rooftop, staying in the shadows so he wouldn't be seen. Once he reached the right place, he lowered himself over the side until his feet found purchase. He began his descent, counting the windows until he came to the correct one.

After double counting to make sure it was Marek's window, he knocked gently. It would have been easier if Marek had been on duty guarding Allyssa tonight.

The curtains pulled aside. A moment later, the window opened. "What the bloody hell are you doing out there?" Marek demanded. "No, don't answer that. I don't want to know. Actually, just tell me if this has something to do with my sister?"

Savenek chuckled. The thought of sneaking into Mayra's room hadn't crossed his mind. If he did something like that, Neco would kill him and ask questions later. "No, I'm here for you."

Marek rubbed his eyes, then shook his head. "Fine." He opened the window wider. "Come in before you fall and break your royal neck."

Savenek climbed inside the bedchamber. "I need your help."

"What is it with you and your sister?" Marek asked. "Do neither of you sleep?"

Actually, Savenek was rather tired and wouldn't mind turning in for the night. However, there was too much that needed to be done. "Get dressed. Wear nondescript clothing."

Marek groaned. "Aren't you running the Brotherhood?"

"Yes." That was how he knew two men from Telmena were here and staying at the Alleyway Inn.

"Can't you send someone to do whatever it is you want done?" Marek asked.

Well, yes, Savenek could. But he didn't want to. Not only was he itching to go on a mission, but his men were also all occupied elsewhere. He would have had to pull two men off another assignment, and he didn't want to do that. "Stop being a pansy," Savenek said. "You have five minutes."

"I'm only going because if I don't, you'll go alone." Marek headed into his dressing closet to change.

Savenek couldn't help but smile. That was exactly what he would have done if Marek had refused to go.

Once Marek was dressed, they climbed out the window and down the side of the castle.

"Follow me," Marek whispered. He led the way over to the military garrison. "We can exit through the military gate."

That was certainly easier than climbing over the wall while trying to evade the sentries on duty.

Once in the town, they headed south. "What exactly are we doing?" Marek asked.

"Going to the Alleyway Inn."

"And then what? I take it we're not going there for a drink."

"There are two men from Telmena staying there. I want to talk to them." Actually, Savenek wanted to knock them out and search the room they were staying in. He hoped to find some correspondence stating why they were there and what they were planning to do. Given that he'd found those other two men from Telmena with poison not that long ago, these men warranted a thorough investigation.

Thankfully, Marek didn't argue. He nodded his head to the right, and they headed that way.

Since it was late, not many people were out and about. They easily traversed the streets until they came to a narrow alley.

"It's down here," Marek mumbled, leading the way. About thirty feet into the alley, there was a door with a sign above it reading *Alleyway Inn*. Marek opened the door and stepped inside.

Savenek entered after him. There was a small taproom to the left with only a handful of tables, most of them empty. He patted Marek on the shoulder and stepped around him, entering the taproom. Savenek went straight to the bar, leaning on it with his elbows.

"Can I get you something?" the bartender asked. He was a middle-aged man with a thick beard.

"Cup of ale," Savenek mumbled.

The man poured ale into a cup, then handed it to Savenek. Taking a sip, Savenek casually moved to where he could survey the room. Marek was nowhere in sight. Excellent.

"I have two friends staying here," Savenek said to the

bartender. "Both not from around here. One usually wears a ring in his ear." He took another sip of his ale.

"Yeah," the bartender replied. "Second floor, third door on the left."

Savenek nodded his appreciation. After tossing a coin on the bar to pay for the drink, he left the taproom and headed for the narrow stairwell. Halfway up, Marek joined him. Without saying a word, the two men crept along the hallway until they came to the third door on the left.

Savenek withdrew a dagger from his boot. Marek did the same before nodding he was ready. Savenek put his hand on the doorknob, counted to three, and burst into the room. One man was sitting on the bed tying his boots while another was staring out a small window. Savenek ran over to the man on the bed, smashing his elbow into the stranger's face. The man crashed back onto the mattress. Savenek rolled the man over, hitting him on the back of his head and knocking him out.

Marek had managed to incapacitate the other man as well.

Rushing over to the door, Savenek closed and locked it.

"Now what?" Marek asked.

"Check the room." Savenek grabbed one of the satchels, starting to rummage through it. He only found clothes and one knife. He searched under the bed, in the chest of drawers, and in the closet, but found nothing. "Any luck?"

"No," Marek said.

"Let's check the clothes they have on." Savenek rolled the guy on the bed over, searching his pockets. Not finding anything, he opened the man's jacket and felt around for a hidden pocket. Nothing. The guy had a hole on his right ear, which meant he wore an earring, so Savenek was certain the guy was from Telmena.

"There's this," Marek said, unfolding a piece of paper he'd found. "It says: *Midnight under the bridge*. Nothing else."

There was only one bridge in Lakeside. Savenek guessed it was about an hour away from midnight. "Let's drop these two off at the City Guard and then head to the bridge. We'll pretend to be these guys."

Marek rubbed his face. "You're assuming they don't actually know whoever they're meeting."

"It's a gamble," Savenek admitted. "But I think it's worth it."

"I can't believe this, but I agree with you."

Savenek removed the top sheet from the bed and handed it to Marek. "Roll your guy up in here." Savenek then took the other blanket and wrapped it around the guy on the bed, tying each end together. Once done, he hefted the body up on his shoulder. "Blasted bugger weighs a ton."

Marek hoisted his guy up on his shoulder. "Let's go."

"I'll follow you. Get us to the closest City Guard station as quickly as possible."

Marek nodded and exited the room, heading down the narrow stairwell, the guy's head smacking against the wall as he went. Savenek followed closely behind, hoping they didn't have to travel very far. Out in the alley, Marek headed south. Savenek had to readjust the body he was holding a couple of times, making sure he didn't drop it.

After four blocks, they arrived at a City Guard station. Inside, only two men were on duty.

"I'm Marek, head of Princess Allyssa's personal guard. This is Prince Savenek." He dropped the body he was carrying to the floor.

Savenek did the same. He massaged his shoulder, glad to be rid of the weight. "I need you to lock these men up in separate cells. I will send a soldier from the castle to transfer these prisoners to another facility tomorrow. Understood?"

Agreeing, the guards hurried around the desk to reach the prisoners. Keeping both men wrapped in the blankets, they dragged each one into a cell.

Not having any time to waste, Savenek and Marek left. "Which way to the bridge?" Savenek asked. He thought it was east of here.

"To the left."

He was right. They headed in that direction. Savenek hoped they reached the bridge before whoever it was they were supposed to meet arrived. He wanted time to make sure the area was secure.

They traveled about ten blocks until they reached the lake. Jogging through the park, they made their way to the bridge.

Savenek sent Marek north to do a sweep while he checked the south end. Not seeing anyone or anything of concern, he headed under the bridge where the water lapped against land. There was approximately eight feet from the water to the bridge, just big enough to hold a clandestine meeting.

A few minutes later, Marek joined him.

"All good?" Savenek asked.

Marek nodded.

Remaining under the bridge, Savenek watched southward while Marek kept an eye on the north. Crickets chirped in the distance.

Savenek hoped there weren't more than two people who came. Ideally, he'd like for it to only be one person. He shoved his hands in his pockets, trying to stay warm. The minutes ticked by.

"Someone's coming," Marek whispered. "Only one individual."

"Protect my back," Savenek said. He turned to face the oncoming person while Marek took up watch from the other direction, making sure they weren't taken by surprise.

A single man approached. "Good evening," he said with a deep voice.

Savenek didn't hear an accent. "You're late."

The man smiled. "But I'm here."

"Hurry this up," Savenek said.

The man stopped three feet away from Savenek. He wore nondescript clothing. "My partner and I arrived this morning. We are in position."

Savenek wondered what they were in position for. He needed to give a generic answer. "Good. Do you need anything?" He blew his breath into his cupped hands, trying to warm himself.

"Na," the man said. "I already gave the third group their vial." He reached in his pocket, then pulled out a small canister. "Here's yours. Don't break it—it'll kill you."

"I know." Savenek took the canister, trying to keep his hand steady even though it was shaking. He slid it in his pocket. The lid had better be on nice and tight. "Same plan? No changes?"

The man nodded. "Once the king and queen arrive, if the signal is given, put yours in the lake and drinking wells. The other group is going to get it into the castle. I've got the inns."

"Will do." Since Savenek knew this was a Telmena phrase, he said, "Luck in days."

"And in nights," the man replied. With a final nod, the man left.

Savenek turned to go. Marek was nowhere in sight. He hoped Marek was following the man. They needed to know where he and his partner were staying so they could be apprehended. Savenek also had to figure out where the third pair was since they already had the kepper poison in hand.

Why could nothing be simple or easy? Rubbing his forehead, Savenek decided there was no point in freezing his arse off under the bridge. He headed back to the castle, knowing Marek would return there after he'd tracked the man to where he was staying.

Once inside, Savenek went straight to his office. After he lit a candle, he sat at his desk. He wrote a letter to the Brotherhood detailing the events of the evening. Savenek informed them he wanted the men in the City Guard prison taken to a secure location and questioned. He wanted someone to speak with Marek to learn the location of the second pair. Then he wanted them arrested and taken to the same secure location. Lastly, he wanted that third pair found. He folded the letter, then placed it in the locked box of correspondence with the Brotherhood. Once that was done, he headed back to his room.

Fully dressed, he crawled onto his bed and fell asleep, shoes and all.

~

SAVENEK KNOCKED ON THE DOOR TO NECO AND ELLIE'S wing. Neco opened the door. "You look as if you haven't slept," Neco said.

Savenek didn't know if he truly looked that bad, or if Neco somehow knew he'd been out all night. Not acknowledging the remark, Savenek turned to his guards and instructed them to remain in the hallway. The last thing he needed was for the men who guarded him to witness this spectacle.

Neco led Savenek down a narrow corridor to a spacious sitting room. Several windows were along one wall, bathing the room in early morning sunlight. Ellie stood in the center of the room, waiting. Neither Mayra nor Marek were anywhere to be seen. When Savenek had inquired after Marek, one of his guards told him Marek had returned to the castle early this morning.

Savenek swallowed. He needed to pretend Neco was just another man—not one of the greatest military leaders of all time. Not his hero. Not one of the most powerful men in Emperion.

"Good morning, Your Highness," Ellie said, curtseying. "To what do we owe this honor?"

Bullocks. Neco and Ellie were going to make this as difficult as possible. "I have come to speak to you about your daughter, Mayra." Neco hadn't invited him to sit so he stood there, trying not to appear nervous. Allyssa had suggested Savenek wear his tunic with the royal family crest embroidered on the front. He'd listened to her, wanting to impress Mayra's parents, but now he was sweating from the thick clothing.

Neco stood next to his wife, folding his arms across his chest, waiting for Savenek to continue.

"I had the pleasure of working with your daughter in Apethaga. While there, we became friends. She is intelligent and kind. I wish to get to know her better." When he'd practiced this speech, it had come across more eloquent and refined. Right now, his tongue felt two sizes too big for his mouth. *Blasted*. He was never this nervous. Even his hands were sweating.

Ellie smiled. "May we dispense with pleasantries?"

"Please." He just wanted to know if he could court Mayra.

"Have a seat." She motioned toward the chair.

Savenek did as instructed. Neco and Ellie sat on the sofa across from him. Savenek recalled staying in Mayra's family estate a few miles from Lakeside when he'd been recovering. This room had a similar feel as that house—lighter walls, well-worn dark rugs, paintings of horses. It wasn't ostentatious but warm and homey. He rather liked it here.

"Our daughter speaks highly of you." Ellie had the same kind smile as Mayra.

"I care for her a great deal. With your permission, I wish to court her with the intention of marrying her." There, he'd said it. Was it getting even hotter in here? He tugged the collar away from his neck.

"I've spoken to Mayra on the issue," Ellie said. "She cares for you, too."

"But we have some concerns," Neco added.

"I understand." Not really, but it seemed the right thing to say. Sweat beaded on his forehead. He didn't want to wipe it off. It might draw attention to the fact he was nervous.

"We hadn't intended for her to marry a prince," Ellie said. "Being married to you will present some complications."

Savenek wiped his hands on his thighs, waiting for them to explain.

"We haven't groomed her for such a position," Neco stated.

A valid concern that Savenek needed to address. At least Neco and Ellie were considering it instead of outright saying no. He held onto that. "I believe Mayra is more than capable of being a princess. She has grown up at Allyssa's side and understands what the position entails." Mayra was elegant and refined. She would make the perfect partner. In fact, she would probably help him be a better prince.

"And she will be a target," Ellie said. "So will your children."

"Since she will be a princess, she will have her own security detail. I would like for you to choose the men most capable of protecting her." Before Neco could respond, Savenek added, "And let's not forget, I was trained by the Brotherhood. I grew up in Nathenek's home. I am able to keep her safe."

Ellie stood and went to the side table, pouring herself a cup of water. A tactical move so Savenek couldn't see her face. Had he convinced her or not?

"I always knew this day would come," Neco said, leaning back against the sofa and propping his right foot on his left thigh. "And I still find myself ill-equipped to handle it. Mayra is my baby girl."

Ellie joined him on the sofa, patting his leg.

"I had no idea you were alive," Neco said. "Rema didn't tell me what she'd done. I hope you can understand that you being here is a surprise to us all. I'd never considered Mayra marrying a prince because we didn't know you existed. I feel like if you'd grown up here, I would have had time to decide whether you're worthy of my daughter and to come to terms with the possibility."

"However," Ellie interjected, "if you'd grown up here, Mayra would probably consider you as a brother, and a relationship between you may never have blossomed."

Savenek realized he was going to have to court Mayra's parents as well. He would have to spend time with them so they could get to know him.

"I see both Rema and Darmik in you," Neco said. "While I

don't know you that well, Mayra has told me enough that I have a sense of the person you are."

"I think the two of you are meant to be together," Ellie said softly. "I think fate threw you together in Apethaga."

Neco raised his eyebrows at Ellie, mirroring Savenek's shock.

"If Mayra wishes to be with Savenek," Ellie said, "I think we must honor her wishes. I have no objections to them courting."

Savenek breathed in a huge sigh of relief. One approval. Now for the second one.

"I still have some reservations," Neco said. "If you were anyone other than Rema and Darmik's son, I wouldn't even consider it. However, Rema and Darmik are like family. Which makes you one of us."

"What are you saying?" Savenek asked.

"I will allow you to court my daughter," Neco said. "However, I insist you court for a year. Then, if you wish to marry, we will discuss it at that time."

"That seems fair." Because really, what else could he say? That he didn't want to wait that long? That he was too impatient? Neco would smack Savenek over his head, and for good reason.

Neco stood. Savenek did the same, placing his right fist over his heart. "I promise to honor your daughter."

"You better. Because if you hurt her in any way, I don't care who your father is…I'll kill you."

CHAPTER 10

Allyssa

*A*llyssa needed to speak with Odar. However, she didn't particularly care to be alone with him. Somehow, it made her feel guilty. As if she was being dishonest with Kerdan whom she missed dearly.

At court, appearances were everything, so Allyssa instructed Mayra to take a letter to Odar inviting him to meet Allyssa at one of the inner courtyards where everyone would see them together. If they were to pull off this engagement, people needed to believe it. She also wanted to move quickly so they could end the threat from Telmena as soon as possible. Allyssa was eager to get on with her life.

Strolling into the courtyard, she headed toward the fountain. It would help block out their conversation. When she neared, she saw Odar was already there waiting for her. She motioned for her guards to stay back so she could speak freely with him.

"I thought Kerdan may be here in Emperion with you," Odar said.

"No, he's busy being crowned the king of Russek and making sure there is peace among his people." She wished Kerdan was there with her. She missed his quick assessment of a situation, his intelligence, his piercing eyes, and the way he treated her as an equal instead of a weak woman. *Blimey.* She missed everything about him.

"Well," Odar said. "Him not being here certainly makes this easier."

Easier for Odar, but not for Allyssa. "We need to talk about Telmena." Not her love life. She had no intention of discussing anything with him other than what was absolutely necessary.

He scanned the courtyard before lowering his voice and answering. "My parents don't want to be involved in this mess. My father ordered me to come here and clean it up—by whatever means necessary."

"Explain."

"Father said if I have to marry you, so be it. But he'd rather I found a solution that didn't involve tying our kingdoms together."

She tried to not let the comment sting. "And his feelings on Telmena?"

"Same. He doesn't want Telmena telling us what to do. My father is content with his little corner of the world. He wishes to be left alone."

Perfect. Then her and Savenek's plan might be possible. "What do you think about assassinating the king, queen, and prince of Telmena?"

Odar went very still. "I must have heard you wrong." His eyes darkened.

"What if we leave your brother and Jestina in charge?"

He shook his head. "You're unbelievable." Turning, he stomped away several paces before turning back to face her. "Has Kerdan changed you that much?"

She forced her temper under control. "What's that supposed to mean?" This had nothing to do with Kerdan.

He came closer, much too close, invading her personal space. She tried not to flinch. "The Allyssa I first met would never have considered assassinating someone."

That was back when she had been naive and didn't know any better. "Kerdan hasn't changed me," she said, balling her hands into fists. "Being kidnapped by Soma, thrown in the dungeon, being tortured, and facing Jana has changed me."

Odar flinched. Allyssa forced her fingers to unfurl. People were watching them, and she couldn't appear angry. *Calm and in control,* she told herself.

"Telmena is a threat to all of us," she said. "They've been buying poison from Apethaga for quite some time. Who knows what they plan to do with it. And what's to stop them from taking over every kingdom on the mainland?"

"They only want Emperion since you've murdered half their family members. Maybe if you hadn't killed so many people, you wouldn't be in this mess." He pinched the bridge of his nose. "This is why my father wants to remain out of politics."

How could Odar be so close-minded? How had she ever loved him? "I used to think as your father did. I mistakenly assumed that if I didn't act, the problem would go away. I learned that doesn't happen, so I plan to eliminate those who wish to harm me and my family."

He stood there, less than a foot away, his eyes searching her face. She couldn't decipher his thoughts or feelings. He was always good at concealing them from her. He'd never let her in.

"Fine," he whispered. "What do you need from me?"

"Are you certain you want to be involved? That you wouldn't rather run home to your kingdom where it's safe?" If he wasn't fully committed, she didn't want him here.

Odar took a step back, running his hands through his hair. "I've been instructed to end this debacle. Father gave me control of the situation. And...I agree with you. You won't be safe until the threat from Telmena is eliminated. My brother has told me stories. I always thought he was exaggerating. Now I'm not so sure."

She noticed he'd said, *you won't be safe* and not *your kingdom* or *we.* Didn't he want his people to be free from the clutches of Telmena? Didn't he want peace? Taking his arm, she started strolling through the courtyard with him. "Can we leave Jestina and Kren in charge of Telmena?" She hadn't met either one, which meant she didn't know what sort of people they were.

"Yes. They will be competent rulers. If Jestina becomes a problem, I'll deal with her myself. I shouldn't have forced my brother to marry her in the first place. That was my fault."

Allyssa wasn't sure how he would deal with it himself, nor did she want to know. All that mattered was eliminating the threat from Telmena while leaving someone in place to rule who would be just and fair. "Is Jestina amenable?" Or would she put up a fight? If Jestina learned what happened to her parents, would she seek retribution? Or would Kren be enough to keep her in line? And did Odar even know her well enough to make these sorts of determinations?

"She'll follow my brother if that's what you're asking. My brother and I are close. I'll make sure that aspect is taken care of. What else?"

Now for the tricky part. "My brother wants to take care of this ourselves. He doesn't want to involve anyone other than the three of us. At least for now." She prayed telling Odar this was the right thing to do and he wouldn't double-cross them.

"I agree." Odar stopped, abruptly swinging his body toward Allyssa. "Are you sure about this?"

She nodded. They didn't have a lot of options.

"It's a risky, bold move."

"I know."

"If we're not successful, it has the potential to backfire and cause a war."

"We face a war if we don't do anything. At least this way, we have the potential to stop one."

OVER THE COURSE OF THE NEXT FEW WEEKS, ALLYSSA

watched her mother send out wedding invitations to all the kingdoms on the mainland. Rema asked every king and queen to come, saying that not only would there be a royal wedding to celebrate, but also that it would give them all a chance to sit down and talk about politics, trade, and treaties.

Late at night, Allyssa would meet with Savenek and Odar to hash out a plan for stopping Telmena. So far, they'd agreed that when Telmena's king, queen, and prince were on their way to the Emperion castle for the wedding, a tragedy would befall them, leaving them dead. However, Kren and Jestina would be unscathed, allowing them to continue on to the castle. Once they were there, Odar would speak with his brother to ensure Kren and Jestina would work together with Emperion.

Savenek and Odar still debated which tragedy should befall the Telmenas and how to execute said accident. Allyssa wanted the entire thing to be over with. She just had to keep up the charade with Odar for a few more weeks.

Too bad nothing ever went as planned.

Allyssa made her way to the rooftop, as she tended to do almost every night. When she stepped onto the roof, she saw Odar and Savenek were already there, standing near the edge at the railing. They were far enough away so the guards couldn't hear what they said.

"What's the matter?" Savenek asked as she joined them.

Gripping the railing, she let the cool metal soothe her hands as she gazed out at her beautiful town. The sky was dark, clouds concealing the stars and moon. She sighed. "Mother just informed me that Kren and Jestina aren't coming." The way the letter was worded caused Rema to believe that Jestina might be with child.

He patted her back. "We can still proceed without them."

"It's too risky. We need to know where Kren stands before we attempt the assassinations." Thunder boomed in the distance. The thick air smelled of rain.

"I agree," Odar said, leaning against the railing next to her.

"I'm not comfortable moving forward until I've spoken to Kren. If he won't go along with the plan, then we'll need to come up with something else."

Allyssa released the railing and paced back and forth, considering their options. Everything hinged on Kren working with them. If he refused to, then they'd have to get rid of him and Jestina as well. She didn't think Odar would agree to that.

"We can't send any correspondence to Kren. Too much of a risk that someone will intercept it," Odar said.

Silently, they gazed between each other, an unspoken knowledge apparent. They'd planned to keep this between the three of them. However, none of them could go to Telmena to speak with Kren. Allyssa resumed pacing. Who else could they involve? "What about someone from the Brotherhood?"

"Each member is loyal to the empress," Savenek said. "If I send someone with information about an assassination plot, Rema is going to hear about it."

"What about Nathenek?" Odar suggested.

"He's loyal to Rema," Savenek answered without hesitation.

Allyssa stopped pacing, facing Savenek and Odar. "We have to send either Marek or Mayra."

"Don't you think Neco will question where one of his children has gone off to?" Savenek asked.

"Those are the only two people who I not only trust, but who are also capable of handling the mission."

"Mayra can't go," Savenek said, leaving no room for argument in his voice. Folding his arms, he leaned his back against the railing.

"Fine." Allyssa went over to one of her guards still standing near the door. She asked him to fetch Marek immediately. When she came back to Savenek and Odar, she started pacing again. "Marek will have to travel fast." The wedding was only a couple of weeks away. Most people would start their journey to Emperion shortly.

"What if he doesn't agree with us?" Odar asked. "He could run straight to his father or Rema and tell them everything."

True. "I've known Marek my entire life. He won't like what we're doing. He probably won't agree with it. However, he is loyal to me."

Savenek smirked. "Maybe his loyalty stems from a secret love for you."

Allyssa whacked her brother on the arm. "Be serious. We are friends. Nothing more."

"Speaking of which," Savenek said, rubbing his arm, "you should probably tell Mayra what we're doing so she can help cover for Marek."

Allyssa groaned—so yet another person was going to be privy to this secret mission. The more people who knew about it, the higher the chance it would be foiled.

The wind blew over the rooftop, making Allyssa's eyes water. She yawned, ready to crawl in bed for the night. The guard finally returned with Marek, who was dressed in his nightclothes.

"I don't even want to know," Marek said. "I'm certain whatever you three are planning can't be good."

"I need you to hear me out," Allyssa said.

"Do I have a choice?" Marek crossed his arms, his face suspicious.

"I have done everything my parents and kingdom have asked of me—whether I agreed with it or not. And now, as we stand on the brink of war with Telmena, I do not believe we should try to resolve this peacefully. Sometimes peace is the best policy. But not now. Not when Telmena plans to destroy us no matter how long it takes. We can't live knowing any moment could be our last." She regarded her dear friend, willing him to understand the gravity of what she said. "I need your help. I want you to go on a secret mission. We plan to destroy Telmena."

~

Allyssa entered Neco's office. Mayra was sitting at the desk, no one else in sight. "What are you doing?"

"My father asked me to decipher this letter." She didn't even bother to raise her head from her work.

Allyssa closed the door, thankful she'd found her friend alone. "I need to talk to you."

Mayra held up her finger. She finished reading the letter, biting her bottom lip. "I think I have it," she mumbled. "Although…it doesn't make any sense."

"What does it say?" Allyssa asked as she took a seat across from her.

"It says: *I'm sending another to replace the first. Don't lose this one.*"

"Where did this letter come from?" Allyssa glanced over her friend's arm to see the writing on the paper. She couldn't tell what language it was in.

"Prince Savenek found it on someone." She folded the letter up, scribbled a few words on the outside of it, and then faced Allyssa. "What do you want to talk about?"

Allyssa hoped Mayra wouldn't be too upset at what she had to disclose. "I sent your brother on a mission last night." While Marek hadn't liked the plan, he had agreed to go along with it. He'd said he understood, especially the part about some people being too dangerous to be left alive.

"Why are you telling me this?"

Now for the part Allyssa had wanted to avoid. Lowering her voice to a whisper, she explained how she'd formed a plan with Odar and Savenek to assassinate the Telmena royal family, leaving only Jestina and Kren alive to rule. She explained how she'd sent Marek to speak to Kren on their behalf to make sure he'd be amiable to work with.

"You did what?" Mayra said, her words laced with fury.

"Marek will be back in a fortnight." Allyssa hoped.

"And no one, not even my father, knows about this?"

"No." Allyssa took comfort in the fact that Savenek was

running the Brotherhood. If something went wrong, at least they had those men at their disposal. But nothing would go wrong. She had to believe everything would go according to plan. At least from here on out.

"Marek went alone? What if he gets into trouble? How could you do that?" Her voice was getting louder and louder as she spoke.

Allyssa reached out and took her friend's hands, squeezing them reassuringly. "I love him, too. He'll be fine. Your brother is going to speak with Kren and that's it. As a precaution, I sent him with a letter from the empress in case he gets into trouble." Granted, the letter was forged, but it should buy Marek enough time to escape or for them to send a member from the Brotherhood to extricate him.

"You sent my brother into a hostile kingdom with only a letter?" Mayra asked, her words clipped.

Allyssa needed to calm Mayra down before she ran to her father and told him everything. "Yes, a letter. It asks if any special accommodations need to be made for the esteemed king and queen while they are visiting in Emperion for the wedding, such as any dietary restrictions or things of that nature."

Mayra took a deep breath, slowly letting it out. "I wish you had told me ahead of time," she said. "I would have gone with him." She squeezed her hands out from Allyssa's, tiredly rubbing her face.

Savenek had told Allyssa not to say anything to Mayra until today for that exact reason.

Mayra's hands fell to the table. "You are the princess of Emperion. I am loyal to you." She shoved away from the desk and stood. "I take it I'm not to say anything to anyone?"

"Correct."

Mayra picked up the letter without sparing Allyssa even a glance, then left the office.

Well, that hadn't gone as smoothly as Allyssa had hoped.

Mayra was furious, although she'd never admit it since Allyssa outranked her. A pang of regret filled her. However, she shoved it aside, knowing she needed to be strong in order for this plan to work.

WHILE ROAMING THE CORRIDOR, ALLYSSA SPOTTED HER father and Odar. She was just about to turn the corner to avoid them when Darmik called her over.

Sighing, she pasted on a fake smile and joined them.

"Care to tell me where the head of your guard is?" Darmik asked, clasping his hands behind his back.

Well, no, Allyssa didn't particularly care to tell him where Marek was. She tried to keep her expression neutral. "I sent him on an errand. He won't be gone long." She went to move past him but he put his hand on her shoulder, holding her in place.

"When he gets back, have him come see me."

"I'll let him know you're looking for him." The only way for their plan to work was for no one to know Marek had left Emperion. Savenek estimated it would take about a fortnight for Marek to make it there and back. She sincerely doubted they could last that long without Darmik or Neco suspecting something. Savenek, Odar, Mayra, and Allyssa had decided they would try their hardest to stall. Pretend they'd just seen Marek or that he was otherwise engaged. And with all the activity and preparation for the upcoming wedding, Allyssa hoped they could elude Darmik and Neco.

"I want you and Odar to take a stroll through the castle so people can see the two of you together."

"Of course." Allyssa took Odar's arm.

She could feel her father watching her as she walked away. He had to suspect something. At first, she felt guilty for deceiving him. However, this was for his benefit. A little deceit and deception was needed for the betterment of Emperion.

Strolling along the corridors draped on Odar's arm made her uncomfortable. Allyssa had no desire to be there with him. She didn't want people believing they were going to marry. However, she played her part and nodded to the courtiers as they passed. Pretending to be happy. Pretending to be in love. Always pretending.

"I'm sorry we're in this predicament," Odar murmured. "But I want you to consider something."

They turned the corner and entered the solarium. The rain had started to fall, pinging against the glass. It reminded her of the last time they were in this place together, back when Odar had been Jarvik. So much had changed since then.

Their guards remained near the entrance.

"What is it?" she asked, not really caring.

"Have you considered that fate keeps throwing us together for a reason?"

"No." And she didn't believe in fate. She headed over to the hydrangeas, her fingers trailing over the leaves.

"Allyssa."

"Stop." She held up her hand. "We are not fated to be together. Please don't push me on the matter. I've already said everything I had to say to you back in Russek." She couldn't rehash old memories with him right now.

Sliding his hands in his pockets, he moved closer to the window, staring outside. "You were always so obstinate."

Allyssa bristled. "Like you're one to talk." Why was she alone with him? The only point of spending time together was to put on a show for court. Now that they weren't in front of anyone, there was no point in continuing the charade.

He smiled wryly. "Truce."

"Fine."

"Your brother seems…like you."

"I suppose." Savenek reminded her more of Darmik.

"How do you feel about having a brother after all these years?"

Odar wanted to talk to her about Savenek? Was he trying to be friends with her? She meandered closer to him, looking outside at the puddles forming on the ground. "Sometimes it's awkward. Other times, it feels like he's always been a part of our family. He fits in so well."

"I can't imagine having a sibling sprung on me like that." He rubbed the back of his neck.

Odar never talked about his own brother. "Kren is younger than you?"

"Yes, by a couple of years."

"Did the two of you fight?" She'd seen Mayra and Marek bicker over the years.

"All the time. That's normal."

"Savenek seems to think he can boss me around." She didn't like being told what to do.

Odar chuckled. "That's just the way siblings are. You'll get used to it."

"I hope so." The rain started coming down harder. "Father said Savenek has to approve of Kerdan before we can marry." She feared Savenek wouldn't care for the Russek warrior.

Odar's smile faded away. "Do you still want to marry Kerdan?"

"Yes. And I don't care to discuss him with you."

"Then why bring it up?" Odar's face flushed red, lips tightening.

His sudden loss of composure made Allyssa's words catch in her throat. She opened her mouth, but nothing came out.

"What are you two doing?" It was Savenek.

Whirling toward him, Allyssa breathed an internal sigh of relief. She had never been more grateful to have a brother than she was at this moment. "We just took a walk around the castle. Father wanted people to see us together."

"Are you done?" Savenek asked.

"We are," Odar answered.

"Good. I have a favor to ask." He came over to Odar's side, surprising Allyssa. "Now that Marek is gone, I need someone to spar with. I don't want any of my guards or members at court to see me."

"Ah," Odar replied. "I understand. You need to keep up the appearance of the aloof prince."

"Exactly."

"Well, you certainly came to the right person."

Savenek put his arm around Odar, guiding him out of the solarium and away from Allyssa. Her brother could be far more astute than she gave him credit for.

CHAPTER 11

Savenek

anting to keep Odar as far away from Allyssa as possible, Savenek led him straight to the private training room he'd been using with Marek. Shoving Odar inside, he shut the door. His guards already knew to remain out in the hallway.

"When you said you wanted to train with me, I didn't think you meant right now," Odar said sullenly. "I'm not even dressed for practicing."

"Don't be a pansy." The guy had pants and a tunic on. If he was attacked, what did he think he'd be wearing?

Glancing out the windows, Savenek saw the rain had stopped. He went over to the wall and grabbed two swords, tossing one to Odar, who deftly caught it. Odar held his sword with such ease that Savenek had no doubt he was a good swordsman. Anticipation coursed through Savenek. He always enjoyed sparring with someone new.

"I hadn't noticed you were left-handed," Odar said. He swung.

Savenek parried the blow. "I'm not."

"I wish you wouldn't insult me like that."

Smiling, Savenek moved the sword to his right hand. "Just trying to give you a fair advantage."

"I don't need it." Odar lunged, swinging his sword low in an attempt to catch Savenek off-guard.

Laughing, Savenek twisted, avoiding the blow. He jabbed his elbow back, hitting Odar's side. Odar attacked with a series of strikes. Savenek met each one. He got the feeling Odar was testing him to see how proficient he was with a sword. Savenek made sure to keep his skill reined in. He met Odar strike for strike. Odar was actually a very good swordsman, especially considering he was from Fren.

Time to turn the tables. Savenek went to swing high. When Odar blocked the hit, Savenek punched him in the stomach—not hard enough to do any damage. He stepped back as Odar caught his breath. "Do you intend to try to win my sister back?"

Odar didn't answer. He remained bent over, breathing heavily. After a minute, he straightened and readjusted his grip on his sword. Odar struck low. Savenek parried the blow, then countered with one of his own.

"Your sister and I said our goodbyes in Russek." Odar sped up his strikes.

Savenek deflected each one. "That's not an answer."

Odar lowered his sword, panting. "Are you asking if I'd still like to marry Allyssa?"

"I am." Although Savenek already knew the answer. Odar clearly still cared for her. Savenek often found Odar staring at Allyssa or trying to start up a conversation with her.

Odar nodded. "I still love her."

"Even though she is engaged to another man?"

"That engagement isn't official," Odar replied. "But it doesn't matter. She's made it clear she wants nothing to do with me romantically."

Whenever Odar was around Allyssa, Savenek watched his sister tense up. "I want you to leave her alone. She's been through enough."

"I am better acquainted with her than you are," Odar said. "You don't know what's best for her." He readjusted his grip on the sword.

"And you do?" Savenek demanded.

"It sure as hell isn't Kerdan."

"Even if that's what she wants?" Savenek was trying to get a better read on Odar. The man was usually quiet and kept to himself. It was nice he was finally talking. And Savenek had never thought he and his sister's ex-fiancé would agree on anything where Allyssa was concerned.

"She's just confused." Odar wiped his brow.

"I'm not crazy about her marrying some guy from Russek," Savenek admitted.

Odar eyed him, his facial expression not giving any sign of what he was thinking or feeling. "Allyssa loved me once. With time, she may learn to care for me again." He hesitated a moment before continuing. "Besides, the wedding is already planned. The empress could change her mind and let the ceremony take place. Maybe that really is what's best for Emperion in the long run."

"Even if Allyssa doesn't love you?" Savenek tried to keep the loathing out of his voice.

"Marriage has little to do with love. People of our station marry for political reasons far more than they ever do for love."

Savenek readjusted his grip on the sword. While he'd never cared for Odar, he decided he truly didn't like the guy. Odar wanted to marry Allyssa because that was what *he* wanted. He gave little thought to what Allyssa wanted or why. Savenek hoped he never behaved so selfishly.

He turned to strike Odar. A shadow outside one of the windows caught his attention. When Savenek peered at the window, Odar swung his wooden practice sword, striking Savenek's legs and knocking him on his back.

The shadow shifted. It was a man.

Odar loomed over Savenek.

"There's someone outside," Savenek grunted, his back stinging from the fall.

"Distraction doesn't work with me."

The window burst open as someone jumped through it, landing on his feet. Odar cursed.

Savenek sprang up, wishing he had a real sword. The man dove for Odar, tackling him to the floor. The two men grappled, rolling on top of one another.

Savenek wondered if he should help Odar. Probably not. Savenek didn't much care for him anyway. He noticed belatedly that his guards hadn't come into the room at the sound of shattering glass. Savenek decided to see how this played out before he intervened.

The man punched Odar in the side, saying something Savenek couldn't understand because his accent was so thick. And that was when Savenek realized where the attacker was from. He'd been so wrapped up in the fact Odar was having his butt kicked that Savenek hadn't bothered to see who was doing the butt kicking. The man had pasty white skin, tangled dark hair, and his shoulders were twice as wide as Odar's.

Savenek pointed his wooden practice sword at the Russek man. "Stop," he said. "Back away from Prince Odar."

The man stilled. He'd managed to pin a wildly bucking Odar to the floor. When the man turned his head to Savenek, pure hatred shone on his face, causing Savenek to tighten his hold on the sword.

"I'd put that down if I were you," the man said, speaking slowly so Savenek could understand him.

"You leave me no choice," Savenek said as he slid his dagger from his sleeve, preparing to throw it at the man's neck.

"Savenek, stop," Odar said. "This is Kerdan."

While Savenek had known this man was from Russek, he hadn't considered the possibility the man was Kerdan. Savenek slid the dagger back up his sleeve.

"That's Allyssa's brother, Savenek," Odar said to Kerdan.

"And to what do we owe the honor of your visit, may I ask?" Savenek inquired.

"I want to see Darmik and Allyssa," Kerdan said. "Take me to them." He released Odar and stood. "Now." Kerdan towered over Savenek.

Savenek couldn't believe this was the man his sister wanted to marry. He was huge. And lacking in manners. Although, Savenek had to admit, he didn't mind watching someone else knock Odar around. However, he kept that to himself.

It was probably best not to say anything since he didn't know what Kerdan wanted, why he was at the castle, or why he'd decided to join them by crashing through a window instead of through proper channels. "Follow me." Savenek headed toward the door, hating to turn his back on Kerdan.

Kerdan followed. For such a large man, he was quiet on his feet.

Odar stood, straightened his tunic, and glared at the new guest.

"Are you coming?" Savenek asked Odar when he opened the door.

Odar shook his head. "But I do have one thing I'd like to say to Kerdan before he leaves."

Kerdan raised a sardonic brow at Odar, motioning for him to get on with it.

"Thank you for sending men to replant the fields your soldiers destroyed during your civil war."

Kerdan narrowed his eyes, lips curling into a smile that was anything but pleasant. "You're welcome, Prince." He said the word *prince* with such disdain that Savenek was glad he wasn't on the receiving end of this man's hatred. Kerdan gave Odar his back, dismissing Allyssa's ex-suitor as if he were a peasant, then brusquely addressed Savenek. "Let's go." It was more of an order than a request.

Savenek bristled. It was one thing for the man to treat Odar in that manner, but quite another for him to think he could speak to Savenek like that. It had been a while since someone had dared to.

Shaking the insult off, he decided to let it pass. It wasn't as if it bothered him. Since he'd been raised as a commoner, it felt more awkward to be treated like royalty than to be ordered about.

In the hallway, Savenek found his guards standing in a group. Their weapons had been confiscated and three Russek warriors surrounded them with their swords drawn. Had the castle been taken over? Was Russek declaring war on Emperion? Savenek was fairly sure he could escape if he needed to. However, Kerdan hadn't threatened him directly so far. Kerdan had only insisted on speaking to Darmik and Allyssa.

"Hurit and Larek, stay here with these—what do you call them? Guards?" Kerdan's haughty question was directed at Savenek, his judgement clear.

Savenek nodded once, knowing his guards shouldn't have been so easily overpowered by three men.

"Brookfel, you're with me," Kerdan said.

Still going along with Kerdan—for now, anyway—Savenek led Kerdan and Brookfel down the hallway. Both men were so large they practically filled the entire space. Not wanting members of the court to see these Russek men and panic, Savenek led them to the servants' passageways. He'd only been in this area a couple of times, and he hoped he didn't get lost in the maze. He headed toward where he thought the Royal Chambers were located.

"What are you doing here?" Savenek asked. He considered leading these men to an empty storage room and locking them in there.

"I'm here to speak with the emperor and princess."

While Kerdan's words were still heavily accented, Savenek could understand what he'd said. "I'm the prince. Why not talk with me?"

"Because I have no dealings with you."

Fair enough. They traversed the stairwell and exited the servants' passageways not far from the royal family's chambers.

Savenek stopped at the doors where four sentries stood guard. "Is my father inside?" he asked.

One of the sentries ran an assessing gaze over Kerdan before answering. "He is, Your Highness."

Savenek was about to tell Kerdan and Brookfel to wait there while he went in to let Darmik know he had a visitor. However, Kerdan shoved past Savenek and burst into the sitting room. All four sentries withdrew their weapons and charged after him.

Savenek and Brookfel exchanged a quick glance before running after the sentries. Inside, Darmik was standing next to the sofa where Rema and Allyssa sat, a knife clutched in his hand.

Kerdan stopped a few feet away from Darmik. The four sentries surrounded Kerdan, their swords pointed at his chest.

"What is the meaning of this?" Rema demanded.

"It's about time you showed up," Darmik said, sliding the knife into his back pocket.

"Kerdan?" Allyssa stood, her tone sounding confused. "What are you doing here?"

"I think I should be the one asking questions," Kerdan said. "Call off your dogs."

"Stand down," Darmik ordered the sentries.

Savenek came farther into the room, standing next to Darmik. Folding his arms, he waited for Kerdan to explain his unexpected appearance.

Kerdan kept his focus on Darmik, not looking Allyssa's way. "I am here to find out why the woman I love is to marry another man. Explain."

Savenek chuckled. The next thing he knew, he was flat on his back, his face stinging from the punch Kerdan had thrown at him. *Bullocks.* He hadn't even seen it coming. He couldn't remember the last time he'd been caught off-guard like that. He'd be mad if he wasn't so impressed.

"I hardly think punching my son was necessary," Darmik said. He offered Savenek his hand.

Savenek didn't bother to take it as he stood, trying to decide what to do with Kerdan. Should he punch him back? Tackle him? He rubbed his jaw, his head ringing from the blow.

Rema stood, moving to put her arm around Allyssa's shoulders. Allyssa's brows were pinched. Darmik glanced around the room. "Everyone out," he said. Two servants curtseyed and exited the room. The remaining sentries and Brookfel also left. Once the five of them were alone, Darmik pointed at the chair. "Sit."

Kerdan didn't move.

"Kerdan," Allyssa said, a bite to her voice. She put her hands on her hips, knocking her mother's arm off her. "How dare you come in here treating my family like this?"

He slowly turned to look at her, expression inscrutable.

"And how dare you ignore me?" she said. Savenek half-expected her to stomp her foot—she seemed that close to a full-on hissy fit. "I haven't seen you in weeks. *Weeks.* Do you have any idea how much I've missed you? How many letters I've sent you? And now you just show up and act like, well, a typical Russek!"

"You missed me?" he asked.

"Of course!" She threw her hands up in the air, exasperated.

A slow smile spread across Kerdan's face. He took two large strides over to Allyssa, grabbed her, and lowered his head to hers. He murmured something, then kissed her.

CHAPTER 12

Allyssa

Allyssa lost all sense of time and propriety as she stood with Kerdan's mouth on hers. His warm hands seared her back, holding her close. The feel of his body against hers, his lips devouring her, and his arms keeping her upright made her never want this moment to end.

Rema cleared her throat, interrupting Allyssa's hazy thoughts. "I take it this is Kerdan?" Rema asked.

Allyssa broke away from Kerdan. They stared at one another, breathing heavily. "Yes, Mother. This is Kerdan." She couldn't take her eyes off him. He was here. In Emperion.

"I heard you were going to marry Odar," Kerdan said. "So I came here to kill him."

She wasn't sure if he was joking or not. But she didn't care. "I'm not really marrying him."

Closing his eyes, he inhaled deeply before slowly letting it out. "I was afraid you'd changed your mind." He took her hand and examined it.

"I still wear the ring you gave me." His mother's ring.

A slow smile spread across his face. "I don't have to kill Odar?"

"No," she whispered, wishing they were alone. She wanted to run her hands through his hair and kiss him some more.

"If the two of you are done," Rema said, her voice clipped and irritated.

Allyssa forced herself to step away from him. "Mother, I'd like to introduce you to Kerdan."

"It is a pleasure to meet you, *King* Kerdan," Rema said.

"I always forget how formal you Emperions are with your manners." He turned toward Savenek. "Sorry about the face." He positioned himself so he stood next to Allyssa instead of in front of her.

Savenek kept his arms crossed, his stance mirroring Darmik's. As Allyssa watched the two of them, she tried not to laugh. Rema glided over to Darmik, whispered something in his ear, and then stood on his other side. Allyssa suddenly became nervous. What did her mother think of Kerdan?

"Are you here on official business?" Darmik asked.

"No. I snuck away with some of my men. You've met them before: Brookfel, Hurit, and Larek."

Allyssa liked all three of Kerdan's men. They were part of his elite force, which he called Hunters. They'd worked together in Russek to help assassinate Jana.

"Just to be clear," Darmik continued, "you snuck into this castle and managed to make your way here?"

"I brought him here," Savenek said.

"Into the castle?" Darmik asked.

"Well, no. He did get into the castle, and he even managed to capture my guards." Savenek shrugged. "But I willingly brought him to the Royal Chambers when he asked."

"I'm pleased to know our security is so lacking," Darmik muttered. "Savenek, make sure we address the issue with Neco after this."

"Yes, sir."

It still irritated Allyssa that Savenek didn't call their parents Mother and Father. That he refused to form that intimacy with them.

"I want to know why everyone on the mainland has received an invitation to Allyssa and Odar's wedding," Kerdan demanded.

"We're using the wedding as an excuse to lure everyone here, so we can talk about a truce between all our kingdoms," Darmik said.

"Explain. I did not like hearing from my men that my woman is being married off."

Allyssa noticed both Savenek and Darmik bristle when Kerdan called her his woman. She, on the other hand, had to stop herself from preening.

"Why don't we all sit down so we can discuss this?" Rema said.

Kerdan sat, pulling Allyssa down on the sofa beside him.

Darmik quickly told Kerdan about the letter he'd intercepted, Odar showing up, and the need for the farce in order to buy time so Telmena didn't attack them.

"Let me see if I understand this correctly," Kerdan said. "When the royal families show up for the wedding, you plan to force them into a room to broker peace?"

"That's my mother's plan," Allyssa said.

"We won't force them into a room," Rema said. "I will ask everyone to join me for a meeting, so we can discuss the future of the mainland."

"And you think talking to the king and queen of Telmena, in front of everyone, will be enough to make them stand down?" Kerdan asked.

"Yes," Rema answered. "Right now, they think everyone supports them and it is emboldening them. If they come here and see no one stands with them, they'll have no choice but to abide by the rules we all set forth."

"And this is to take place next week?"

"It is."

"Then I am staying here. If something goes wrong, I will see to Allyssa's safety."

Savenek snorted, but he didn't say anything.

"Very well," Darmik said. "I will have a room prepared for you."

"I would like some time alone with Kerdan," Allyssa said.

"That's not possible," Rema replied. "We must keep up appearances that you are engaged to Odar."

While Allyssa understood that, she didn't see the harm in being alone with Kerdan in the Royal Chambers where no one could see them. She was about to argue with her mother when Rema said, "I'd like to remind you that both Prince Savenek and I must approve of a union between the two of you." Her voice was smooth like water.

Allyssa swallowed, realizing her mother was not happy right now.

"I'll announce that you've arrived for the wedding," Darmik said. "I'll have you placed in the wing with the other families that will be arriving shortly."

"Where is Odar staying?" Kerdan asked.

"In the guest wing."

"Then I will stay in the guest wing with him."

Rema smiled politely, folding her hands on her lap. Allyssa could tell her mother wasn't sure what to make of Kerdan and his brash personality. She remembered when she'd first met him, thinking the same thing and assuming he was a Russek brute because he didn't have the manners similar to other royals. But she'd quickly learned that those manners often times hid sinister thoughts, devious traits, and heinous personalities. With Kerdan, he didn't put on airs. He didn't need to. However, she knew he also wore masks. His were just different.

"While you are here, you will be the king of Russek," Rema said.

"I am the king of Russek."

"Yes, I understand that. However, what I am trying to say is that you are here as the king of Russek and only the king of Russek."

Savenek smirked. "In other words, you are not interested in my sister in any capacity. That way, she can continue pretending to be engaged to Odar."

Oh, he was enjoying this far too much. Sometimes having a brother could be annoying. If Allyssa was sitting closer to him, she'd smack him upside his head.

"At what point do you plan to announce my engagement to Allyssa?" Kerdan asked. "I've already told my entire court we're engaged."

"If I agree to the marriage," Rema said, enunciating her words clearly, "we will announce it after the engagement between Allyssa and Odar is dissolved."

"You mean the *pretend* engagement."

"Yes."

Darmik leaned forward, resting his arms on his legs. "I want you to understand, Kerdan, that I don't like the idea of Allyssa being around Odar any more than you do."

"I highly doubt that," Kerdan said dryly. "I find his presence here too much of a coincidence."

"I've considered many angles," Darmik said. "However, I believe he is here because it is in his best interest to be here. I know he still cares for Allyssa, and he will keep her safe in whatever capacity he can."

"Even though it is not his place?" Kerdan asked.

"He doesn't want war."

"Fine." Kerdan stood. "I want my men with me."

"It's just the four of you?" Rema asked.

"Yes. Easier to travel. Faster."

She nodded. "Do you have clothes for court?"

He was dressed for traveling. Allyssa doubted he'd brought anything with him.

"No. I will take care of it tomorrow."

"We'll expect you to join us for supper this evening in the Dining Hall. Make sure you're dressed appropriately."

"I would like a minute alone with Allyssa," he said.

"That's not possible." Rema stood, smoothing out the front of her dress. "She cannot be alone with you. It is highly improper."

Allyssa rolled her eyes. It was a good thing her mother didn't know she'd stayed in Kerdan's room while in Russek.

"We'll probably have some time to talk later this evening," Allyssa assured him.

He reached out, placing his rough hand on her cheek. She leaned into his hand, smiling.

"It is still strange to see you wearing a fancy dress."

She blushed, imagining *not* wearing a dress.

"I'll escort you to the guest wing," Savenek said, a little louder than necessary. He placed a hand on Kerdan's shoulder, shoving him away from Allyssa.

"I'm glad to see you taking your role as her brother seriously," Kerdan said. "We need to talk. Alone." Savenek and Kerdan exited the Royal Chambers.

"So that was Kerdan," Rema said, taking a seat. "You were right," she said to Darmik. "He is a little unrefined. I'm not sure how our court will receive him."

"It doesn't matter how they receive him," Darmik said. "Right now, we need to worry about Telmena. I must speak with Neco and Nathenek about our lax security."

Rema nodded. After pressing a kiss to her forehead, he left. Allyssa tried exiting the room before her mother could say anything.

"Don't think you're getting out of here that easily," Rema said. "Get back over here and sit. We need to talk."

When Allyssa had been in Russek, she'd wanted nothing more than to sit and talk with her mother to ascertain her opinion on Kerdan. However, that had been before Allyssa had fallen in love with him. Now she feared her mother's opinion. What if Rema didn't like him?

Rema patted the sofa next to her. "Sit."

Taking a deep breath, Allyssa held her head high and sat next to her mother. "What is it you'd like to discuss?"

"I want to talk about your relationship with Kerdan."

Allyssa forced a smile as she waited for her mother to continue. What would she say? That Kerdan was too unrefined? More soldier than king? Not the man she pictured her daughter marrying? That he wouldn't make a good emperor for Emperion?

"Tell me what you like most about him," Rema said.

Allyssa hadn't expected that. "He doesn't treat me like a fragile princess." She recalled all the times he'd treated her as an equal.

"What else?"

"He understands me."

"How so?" Rema asked, tilting her head to the side and observing Allyssa.

How could Allyssa explain that he wore masks like she did? "He knows that sometimes I have to show my people one side of me, my parents another, and the people at court yet another."

"I see." Rema folded her hands on her lap, looking down. "Anything else?"

Allyssa leaned back on the sofa, thinking about Kerdan. She thought about how he went to the local towns in Clovek, handing out food to those in need, and about how he'd helped her escape Russek by providing his beloved horse along with maps. "He is dedicated to Russek. He wants to improve his kingdom and help his people." He had the same devotion to his kingdom that she had to hers.

"That is important. Someone in your position must consider such things." Rema reached out, gently touching Allyssa's arm. "If it's not too bold of me to say so, the two of you seem to be attracted to one another."

Bloody hell. Had her mother seriously just said that out loud?

"Yes," Allyssa agreed, suddenly very interested in the ring on her finger. The ring Kerdan had given her. "I find him quite handsome." It was far easier to talk to her ring than to look her mother in the eyes and admit she found Kerdan attractive. Her face felt like it was on fire.

"That is good considering you will need to produce an heir."

Why did her mother insist on having this conversation right now? It was utterly embarrassing to talk about. She wanted to crawl under the sofa and hide.

"I just want to make sure you and Kerdan truly know one another. I also want to ensure he is the right choice for not only you, but also for Emperion as well."

Allyssa wanted to tell her mother he would make a wonderful emperor, that Emperion would be lucky to have him, that she already knew him, and that she wanted to marry him. However, now was not the time to make such declarations. "I understand."

"Good." Rema leaned forward and hugged Allyssa. "If there's anything you ever want to talk about, I'm here for you."

"Thanks, Mother."

Rema released Allyssa and stood. "Please keep in mind that you are a princess. I expect you to behave like one. I don't want to see you and Kerdan displaying any sort of public affection until after you're married. Are we clear?"

"Yes, Mother." Allyssa would make sure all displays of affection were done in private, without the audience of her family.

ALLYSSA STOOD IN FRONT OF THE MIRROR, OBSERVING herself. "I'm not sure this is the right dress," she mumbled.

"The blue complements your eyes," Mayra said. "I think you look lovely."

But blue was the color of Fren. "I want to look exceptional tonight."

"I know." Mayra smiled. "Savenek told me someone special arrived." She went over to the side table, then picked up the tray of dusting powder. "Wear the blue. It suits you. I'll do your face so Kerdan won't be able to keep his eyes off you."

Allyssa sat while Mayra applied dusting powder to her eyes.

"I'm surprised you're allowing me to do this," Mayra said. "I usually have to fight with you."

It was because Allyssa had never wanted to impress a man before. She started fiddling with her ring.

"I can't believe you're going to marry the king from Russek." Mayra took a step back, examining Allyssa's face.

"Meaning?"

Mayra shook her head. "I never pictured you with someone like him."

Allyssa's heart sank. Why did everyone assume he was such a brute? "Have you met him?"

"No, not yet."

Allyssa knew her family and closest friends would like Kerdan once they got to know him. It was just the getting to know him part that would be a little rough. However, she could help in that regard.

"Your face is done," Mayra said. "Would you like me to make any adjustments to your hair?"

Allyssa glanced at the mirror again. Half her hair was braided on top of her head while the rest hung down her back in soft waves. After placing the crown atop her head, she hugged her friend. "No adjustments are needed. Thank you for your help."

Mayra smiled before slipping out of the room.

Allyssa headed to the sitting room to wait for her parents. She found Savenek on the sofa reading a book.

"Mayra said she is joining us for dinner," she said as she sat across from him.

He smiled ruefully and closed the book, setting it on the side table. "Since we are officially courting, she will be sitting next to me so we can get to know one another better."

His jaw had bruised over, and a twinge of guilt washed through Allyssa. She still couldn't believe Kerdan had punched him. "What did you and Kerdan talk about?"

"You."

When he didn't extrapolate, she asked, "What about me?"

"If we wanted you to know, we would have included you."

She rolled her eyes.

He leaned back on the sofa, stretching his arms over the back of it. "We're going hunting tomorrow."

"Just the two of you?" Kerdan had promised to take her.

"All of us," Savenek said. "Kerdan, Odar, Mayra, you, and me."

"What's the purpose of the trip?" Had Kerdan suggested it?

"There are two reasons. One, I need to get to know Kerdan better so I can decide if I trust him or not."

That was probably a good idea. She was certain once her brother became better acquainted with Kerdan, he would wholeheartedly approve. "And the second reason?"

"We need to discuss the assassination plot."

"In front of Kerdan?"

"Do you want him involved?"

"Yes." He would be vital. Plus, she didn't want to have to lie to him about what she was doing and why. If anything, he would ensure the plan went, well, according to plan. "I'm just surprised you'd allow him to be included."

Savenek leaned forward, lacing his fingers together and resting his elbows on his thighs. In that moment, he looked so similar to Darmik. "It's what you want, isn't it?"

"Yes."

He spread his hands apart, showing that was why he'd done it.

"Thank you," she replied. He'd taken her feelings into consideration. The action touched her.

"And Odar vouched for his skills. Said he'd be a huge help."

Her eyes narrowed. "Odar?"

Savenek nodded.

"When did you talk to him?"

"While you were getting ready. Do you have any idea how long it took you to put that dress on?"

Rema and Darmik entered the sitting room, both exquisitely dressed for dinner.

"Let's go," Darmik said.

Allyssa and Savenek stood, exiting the Royal Chambers. She wasn't used to walking with anyone besides her parents. However, now that she had a brother, she and her twin led the way as they strolled through the castle. People bowed as the royal family passed. What surprised Allyssa was that Savenek addressed each person by his or her name.

"How do you know so many people?" she asked. "You haven't been here that long."

"I made it a priority. After all, we live here together. It seems only right I should know everyone living at the castle."

She suspected it was more of an occupational hazard than a sincere desire to get to know the people.

Stopping at the entrance to the Dining Hall, they waited to be announced. Allyssa wondered if Kerdan was already in there. And if so, where would he be sitting? She knew she'd be next to Odar. However, she hoped Kerdan wasn't far away. She wanted the opportunity to talk to him.

"His Highness Prince Savenek, Her Highness Crown Princess Allyssa, His Majesty Emperor Darmik, and Her Majesty Empress Rema."

The royal family entered. The head table was a little more expansive than usual today. Rema and Darmik took their places at the center. Savenek sat at Rema's side, Mayra next to him, and Mayra's parents next to her. A pang of fear stabbed Allyssa as she thought about Marek all alone on his journey to Telmena. Allyssa took her seat next to Darmik. On her other side sat Odar, and next to him were two additional empty chairs. She hoped Kerdan would be sitting in one. Although, she couldn't imagine Kerdan and Odar behaving civilly to one another over the course of an entire meal.

The tables next to the head table consisted mostly of the dukes and their wives. The table across from the head table seated the Legion members. Courtiers filled the remaining tables farther away from the royal family.

Rema gracefully stood, and the people in the room went silent. "I have an announcement to make," she said, commanding everyone's attention. "As most of you are aware, my daughter will be getting married soon. Many of the kings and queens from the mainland are coming to join us as we celebrate this joyous occasion. The first of our guests has arrived."

The door swung open to reveal Kerdan.

"Ladies and gentlemen, may I present King Kerdan of Russek."

Everyone stood, bowing in deference as Kerdan stalked into the room. He wore thick black pants and an emerald green tunic that hit him at mid-thigh, befitting of the harsh Russek weather. He'd draped a fur over his shoulders. A crown sat atop his head. He was probably rather hot in that getup.

Kerdan focused directly on Allyssa, and her breath caught at the intensity of his gaze.

Nathenek entered the room after Kerdan, following him as he made his way to the head table. Kerdan and Nathenek sat in the two remaining chairs. Servants immediately started bringing out platters of decadent food.

Allyssa covertly peeked around the room, trying to gauge everyone's reaction to Kerdan. That was when she noticed that most of the women were batting their eyes and staring at Savenek. Frowning, Allyssa glanced at her brother. There was no way someone as astute as him was oblivious to the attention of the women in the room. However, he kept his focus wholly on Mayra, talking and smiling at her and ignoring everyone else.

One of the dukes approached Kerdan. "Your Majesty," the duke said, bowing. "I'd like to offer my condolences on the death of your father. I'd also like to congratulate you on ascending to the throne. I believe you'll make an excellent king." After a final bow, the man returned to his seat.

"This is going to take some getting used to," Kerdan muttered.

"Being king?" Allyssa asked.

"No." He looked over at her. "Your Emperion formality."

She tried not to smile.

"By the way," he said, "you look beautiful tonight."

"I'm sitting right here," Odar said with a groan. "Must you talk over me?"

"Yes, since you are sitting between us," Allyssa said.

He opened his mouth to say something when Kerdan placed his heavy hand on Odar's shoulder. "I'm sorry for attacking you earlier today," Kerdan said. "I thought you'd wormed your way back into Allyssa's life, and I wanted to kill you." Releasing Odar, he surveyed the plate before him. "It was silly of me to be jealous. Clearly, I have nothing to be jealous of." He took a bite of his food.

Odar stiffened. "Sometimes I wonder why I do this to myself. I could have told my parents no and refused to come here. Or I could have left once the engagement was in place. But no, I stay here and this is what I get."

"I know," Kerdan said around a mouthful of meat. "And I appreciate you being here. Even though I don't like you, you are a good man and will make a good leader for Fren."

Trying to hide a smirk, Allyssa took a drink from her goblet. That was Kerdan's way of saying Odar belonged in Fren...away from Allyssa.

CHAPTER 13

Savenek laughed, pretending not to have a care in the world. But the sight of Kerdan at the other end of the table grated on his nerves. Kerdan. The ruler of Russek. The enemy.

Many of the people seated around the tables were sneaking peeks at Kerdan. Some were whispering to one another behind hands or napkins. Savenek didn't feel any hostility coming off the crowd. It was more curiosity than anything else. The reason for Nathenek being there suddenly made sense—it was in case someone decided to attempt to harm Kerdan. Savenek almost laughed. He doubted Kerdan needed protecting. And where were Kerdan's men? Did Rema think it too risky to have so many Russeks in one room?

Savenek scanned the back wall. Rema and Darmik's usual guards were stationed there. He peered down the table at Nathenek, who sat eating and not paying attention to anyone in the room. Earlier in the day, Nathenek had spent over an hour trying to convince Savenek that Kerdan could be trusted. Nathenek claimed that even though Kerdan was a Russek, he did care for Allyssa and the alliance between them would be highly advantageous. Savenek didn't care about any of that. What mattered to him was that his sister must have been deceived to have fallen for Kerdan.

In a room full of Emperions, Kerdan stood out. He was so tall and muscular that he barely fit on his chair. What did Russek people eat? And his skin was unusually white, as if he'd never seen the sun before. And what was the guy thinking wearing a fur over his shoulders like that? No one in Emperion wore fur. But maybe that was the point. Kerdan didn't want to fit in.

"What's the matter?" Mayra asked.

"Nothing." Savenek took a drink from his goblet to have something to do.

"Have you talked with Kerdan yet?" Mayra whispered.

"Yes." He remembered Kerdan's hands all over Allyssa. Right in front of Rema and Darmik. As if he were too high and mighty to have to adhere to Emperion customs. It had been too much to witness, so Savenek had escorted Kerdan out of there as fast as he could.

Only, he hadn't expected Kerdan to take control of the situation and start grilling him. Kerdan had wanted to know all about Savenek's life. Who'd trained him, what missions he'd been on, if he really cared for his new royal family. Savenek could tell from the questions that Kerdan didn't trust Savenek any more than Savenek trusted Kerdan. However, it was clear Kerdan cared for Allyssa. Even now, he kept gazing at her as if she were the only one in the room.

"We're not going to be able to pull off Allyssa and Odar's fake engagement with Kerdan here," Savenek quietly told Mayra.

"He hasn't seen her in a while. I'm sure it'll be fine." Mayra didn't sound convinced.

"She's my sister."

"What are you implying?"

He didn't know. Running his hands through his hair, he tried not to be irritated by Kerdan. "He's not good enough for her."

"How do you know?"

He didn't. Savenek just didn't like the idea of Allyssa marrying the king of Russek. Their enemy. Kerdan didn't even look or act like a king. His clothes, his mannerisms, and his speech all showed what he was—a warrior.

"Are you done eating?" Savenek asked.

"Yes."

"Meet me in the solarium in fifteen minutes." He stood, then shoved his chair back. "Your Majesties," he said to Rema and Darmik, bowing.

"Leaving so soon?" Rema asked.

"I have business to tend to." Without waiting for a response, he hurried from the Dining Hall.

Out in the corridor, his guards surrounded him. "Any news?" Savenek asked.

"None, Your Highness."

He hoped Marek was doing okay and that he'd had a chance to speak with Odar's brother. If anything happened to Marek, Mayra would never forgive Savenek for sending him on the mission alone. And neither would Neco. He entered the solarium, instructing his guards to remain at the entrance. No candles had been lit so the room was cast in darkness. He went over to the window, staring outside into the night.

It was much more peaceful here than it had been in the Dining Hall. Savenek hadn't realized how being around so many people all the time could be so exhausting. He didn't know how long he stood there. After a while, he finally felt calm and in control again.

"What are you doing here?" Odar asked from somewhere behind him.

"Waiting for Mayra."

"Ah," he said as if that explained everything. "Can we talk?"

"You have five minutes," Savenek answered.

"What do you think of Kerdan?"

"Why?"

Odar shrugged. "I don't like him."

"Of course you don't." Because Allyssa preferred Kerdan over

Odar. And for good reason. Odar had broken her heart. He didn't deserve Allyssa.

"But," Odar said, coming to stand alongside Savenek, "as I said before, the guy is skilled not only with a sword, but also in a fight."

"That's why we're going to include him in our plans." Savenek slid his hands in his pockets, wondering where Marek was and what he was doing. It was different sending someone he knew well on a mission.

"I'm glad to hear it." They stood in silence for several minutes, each lost in his own thoughts. "I get why she likes him," Odar said. "I've screwed everything up so badly between the two of us. I know there's no chance she'll ever forgive me. I get it. But I do still care for her, and I want to make sure she's safe."

Savenek kept his focus outside so Odar wouldn't see how perturbed he was. Whenever Savenek spoke to Allyssa, it was always her trying to decide what was best for Emperion or how her decisions would affect her people. She always put others before herself. She was like her mother in that regard. Odar, on the other hand, had mixed priorities. While he did seem to care about Fren, he seemed to care for himself more than his kingdom. And when Allyssa was factored into the equation, things became even more muddled.

"You don't like Kerdan, but you trust him?" Savenek mused.

"As much as it pains me to say it, yes."

"We'll discuss the matter with him tomorrow when we go hunting."

"Hunting?" Odar asked.

"Yes." Savenek didn't know if Kerdan suggested it because he enjoyed the sport, or if it was simply to get them out of the castle so they could speak without the chance of anyone overhearing them.

"Someone is here to see you," Odar said. "I better go."

As Odar left the room, Mayra entered. "Do I even want to

know what that was about?" she asked as she came to stand next to Savenek.

He shook his head. "Did I miss anything?" He hoped Rema and Darmik hadn't been upset he'd left the Dining Hall early. But he'd felt his temper rising. In order to keep his reputation as the dashing prince, he'd hightailed it out of there.

"No." She placed the palm of her hand against the glass. "Well," she smiled ruefully at Savenek over her shoulder, "when Odar helped Allyssa stand and he escorted her from the room, Kerdan bent a spoon."

"Kerdan and Odar don't like each other."

"I gathered that."

Savenek came up behind her, placing his hand over hers. Lacing his fingers with Mayra's, he leaned down to whisper in her ear, "We're finally alone."

"Your guards are back there near the entrance to the solarium."

"It's dark in here so they can't see us." He missed Apethaga when it was just the two of them.

"So," she said, leaning against him. "What should we do?"

He ran his hands up her arms. "I much preferred you in Apethaga."

"How come?"

"Less clothes, more skin." He wrapped his arms around her, resting his chin on her shoulder. In Apethaga, the clothes reflected the hot, humid climate. Here, the Emperion outfits mirrored the colder weather. Even in the dark, he could see her blush. "I've missed that." He kissed her cheek.

"I suddenly find myself with a lot of enemies at court," Mayra said, changing the subject.

That surprised him. "Why?"

"Because every woman is enamored with you."

"I hadn't noticed."

"Liar." She smiled. "But that's the right answer."

"I know."

She twisted in his arms, so they now faced one another. He bent and kissed her. Mayra's mouth molded around his. He slid one of his hands up her back, twining his fingers in her soft hair.

Someone cleared his throat from the entryway. Mayra jumped. Savenek chuckled, taking a step away from her and turning to see who'd interrupted them. When he saw Neco standing in the doorway with his arms crossed and the light behind him keeping his face in shadow, Savenek cursed.

"When I said that you could court my daughter," Neco said, stepping farther into the room, "I didn't mean like this."

"We were just talking," Mayra said.

"You are alone, in a dark room, and it looked to me as if you two were doing more than talking." Neco took another step closer to them.

Savenek noticed the dagger sticking out of the waistband of her father's pants. "I'm sorry, sir," Savenek said. "I meant no disrespect. It's just that when I'm around your daughter, she takes my breath away."

"Probably because your lips are locked together." Neco said each word clearly, distinctly, sending a chill through Savenek.

"I'll make sure that when we're together, we are supervised at all times," Savenek assured Neco—one of the greatest military commanders of all time. *Bullocks.* "I love and respect your daughter. I promise nothing untoward will happen."

"Mayra, wait for me outside."

Mayra nodded and hurried from the room, leaving Savenek alone with Neco.

Neco stopped right in front of Savenek. "Just because you're the prince of Emperion, and my best friend's son, doesn't mean I'm going to allow you to marry my daughter."

The words were sharp, like a knife jabbing into Savenek.

"That's right," Neco said, leaning forward into Savenek's personal space. "You have to earn the right to marry her. You will respect my daughter. You will treat her like you want your own sister treated. I will not find the two of you kissing in a dark room again. Are we clear?"

"Yes, sir." Sweat beaded on Savenek's forehead.

"Meet me tomorrow morning before breakfast."

Savenek wanted to ask what for but knew better. Nathenek had trained him well. "Yes, sir."

"We need to spend some time together," Neco explained. "It will give me an opportunity to value your worth."

Savenek swallowed.

Neco turned to leave. When he reached the door, he paused. "Make sure you wear training clothes."

Oh, hell. Savenek didn't want to have to spar against Neco. "Yes, sir. I look forward to it."

Neco chuckled, the sound deep. "That's because you don't know what you're in for."

SAVENEK HEADED TOWARD NECO'S WING. HE WIPED HIS hands on his pants. Again. He couldn't remember the last time he was so nervous.

Neco stepped out of the shadows, blocking the corridor. "Glad to see you're on time."

Savenek knew not to say anything. He simply nodded, waiting for Neco to take the lead.

"You're all dismissed," Neco said to Savenek's guards. Once the men left, Neco started striding down the corridor away from his rooms, waving at Savenek to follow him.

Savenek didn't know if he was supposed to walk alongside Neco or behind him. He settled for behind him. He also decided to refrain from making idle conversation.

They entered the royal family's training room on the first floor. The sun had not yet risen, and the sky outside was only just starting to turn gray.

Neco moved around the edge of the room, lighting the torches so they could see. "I know Nathenek trained you and that you were raised in the Brotherhood."

"Yes, sir." That seemed to be all Savenek was capable of saying to Neco.

"Even though your sister is the crown heir and will become empress, your father wants to leave the army in your hands instead of Kerdan's." Neco stood across from Savenek, his feet shoulder-width apart. "What do you think of that?"

Was this a test? "I'm trained to spy and kill. If Darmik wants me to lead his army, I'll need further training on battle strategy." In theory, Savenek knew what methods worked and were effective. However, he'd never been in charge of men, much less leading them into battle.

"I don't want my only daughter to be a widow."

That was a gloomy thought. "I understand." Sort of. Was Neco implying Savenek would die if he led the army since he lacked experience? Or was Neco declaring his plan to kill Savenek? Really, it could go either way.

Neco swung, punching Savenek in the stomach. Savenek doubled over, shocked from the strength of the hit. Knowing another one was likely coming, he allowed his body to fall to the floor. He immediately rolled to the side in case Neco decided to try to kick him. Once Savenek caught his breath, he reached out, grabbing Neco's ankle and yanking it. Neco flipped in the air, landing upright on his feet.

Savenek used the time to stand back up. Now that he was watching Neco for an attack, he noticed the slight shift of his feet. Savenek raised his arm, blocking the punch before it hit him. He countered with a jab from his right fist, hitting Neco's side.

Neco grabbed Savenek, tossing him to the floor. Savenek rolled, realizing he needed to do something unexpected if he wanted to survive. He flung his legs up, catching Neco and slamming him to the floor. Neco swung his legs around, pinning Savenek down. In retaliation—and a hope to get free so he didn't embarrass himself—Savenek reached out, clutching Neco's wrist and pinching a pressure point. Neco didn't release him; however, he did loosen his grip ever so slightly, which allowed Savenek to shift his body, breaking the hold.

Both men got to their feet, circling one another.

"Care to tell me where my son is?" Neco asked.

Bullocks. "No."

Neco ran at him, tackling him to the ground. "What if I tell you I have an idea of where he is, what he's doing, and why?"

Grappling on the floor, Savenek managed to flip Neco over, sitting on top of him. The second he had the upper hand, he knew it had been a setup. Neco hit the back of Savenek's head, knocking him over. Everything went black.

WHEN SAVENEK WOKE UP, HE FOUND HIMSELF LYING ON the sofa in the Royal Chambers. His clothes were sweaty, and the back of his head ached. He sat up and rubbed his face. His session with Neco had not gone as he'd intended. Based upon the light filtering in through the windows, it had to be almost time to go hunting. He stood and dragged himself to his bedchamber to change. Opening the door, he saw Nathenek stretched out on his bed. "What are you doing here?"

"I just had a nice talk with Neco," Nathenek answered.

Great. This day kept getting better and better. Sitting on the chaise lounge, Savenek removed his boots.

"Do you know why Neco bested you?" Nathenek asked.

"Yes." Neco had known exactly what to say to throw Savenek off. It was a rookie mistake, and Savenek should have known better. But that was what happened when emotions—like love— got in the way. Neco had been trying to prove a point, and he did.

Not only that, but Neco had also hinted he knew about the assassination plot. Savenek didn't know if Neco knew something specific, or if he was guessing in order to rattle Savenek.

"Then I won't waste my time lecturing you." Nathenek stood. "Are you going somewhere?"

"Kerdan is taking us hunting." Savenek pulled on his black tunic.

"Hunting?"

"Yes. Allyssa, Odar, and Mayra are also going."

"Hunting?"

"Yes, hunting." What part of this did Nathenek not understand?

"Animals?"

"Yes," Savenek said, exasperated. "As opposed to what?"

"People."

"I can't tell if you're joking," Savenek said, pulling on his sturdy boots.

Nathenek went to the door. "That's a nice bruise on your face."

"Kerdan gave it to me."

"I heard."

"Then why did you bother mentioning it?"

"Because you're going hunting. With Kerdan."

"It was a total misunderstanding." He rubbed his jaw, which was still rather sore from the hit.

"I know Kerdan," Nathenek said. "I believe your sister loves him."

"I know." Savenek stood. "We've been over this before." He folded his arms across his chest.

"During the hunting trip, try to smooth things over with Kerdan. Get to know him better. You may find you like him."

"I doubt it." Kerdan was from Russek. That was reason enough to hate him.

After Nathenek left, Savenek finished dressing.

Once he was ready, he headed to the stables where they were

supposed to meet up. He found Odar, Kerdan, and Mayra already there with horses saddled and ready to go.

"We're waiting for my sister?" Savenek asked. Shocking. Allyssa always arrived last. It was surprisingly annoying.

"I'm here," Allyssa said from behind him as she glided into the barn. She went over to her horse and mounted, not bothering to specifically address any of them.

Relieved he wouldn't have to see his sister kiss Kerdan hello, Savenek led his horse out of the stables before mounting. Three of Kerdan's men were already outside on horses. A dozen Emperion soldiers were off to the side. Two riderless horses were loaded with weapons—one had bows and arrows, the other spears and swords.

Allyssa exited, followed by the rest of their party. "Are you finally going to let me teach you how to shoot a bow and arrow?" she said to Kerdan.

"Only after I teach you to throw a spear." He nudged his horse onward, leading the way toward the forest.

Mayra steered her horse alongside Savenek. "I heard you were with my father at the crack of dawn."

He wondered if Neco had told her about their encounter. He really hoped not. "We trained together," was all he said, trying to be evasive.

The fog had disappeared leaving the morning air crisp and cool.

"My mother had a talk with me over breakfast. She wants to make sure I behave properly."

"I'm sorry about last night." Savenek had been alone with women before. He'd even spent time with Mayra in Apethaga. For him, it was difficult to remember that the rules had changed because of his position. Perhaps he should apologize to Mayra's mother for kissing her daughter alone in a dark room.

"It was worth it," she said.

"I agree." Savenek lowered his voice and asked, "Do your parents suspect anything?"

"With regards to what?"

"The assassination plot."

It took her a moment to answer. "I'm not sure. My father has been questioning where Marek is. I've continued to tell him what we decided upon, that he's training at the barracks, meeting with the City Guard, or that you sent him on a personal errand. My father is starting to question why he hasn't seen Marek at all."

Savenek had known it would be difficult to mislead Neco. But Marek was the only person capable of carrying out the mission. "I should probably tell your father I sent him to do something for the Brotherhood."

They entered the forest, traveling along a narrow path. Under the cover of the pine trees, the air was colder. Savenek could see his breath coming out in tiny white puffs.

"I don't know," Mayra said. "My father is pretty tense with everyone due to arrive for the wedding. We may be able to get away with it."

Savenek wasn't sure how much longer they could last. And Marek should be back by now. However, Savenek couldn't stress over the fact Marek was a day late because it would only upset Mayra. Marek probably got held up because of the weather or something along those lines.

Kerdan and Allyssa were riding side by side leading the group, followed by Odar, then Savenek and Mayra, with the soldiers trailing behind them. "Let's go and keep Odar company."

"I thought you didn't like Odar."

"I don't."

"Then why do you want to ride with him?" She eyed him suspiciously.

"I like Russek less than I like Odar."

"Ah," she replied, as if that explained everything. Mayra nudged her horse, joining Odar.

Savenek came up on Odar's other side. "So, Kerdan's a big hunter?"

Odar nodded.

Savenek glanced back at the soldiers accompanying them. They weren't Allyssa's guards, nor were they his. He looked closer. They were members of the Brotherhood.

"Whose idea was it for these guards to go with us?" Savenek asked.

"When I arrived at the stables, Nathenek was ordering this squad of men to go with us." Odar peered over his shoulder at the guards. "Why? Is something the matter?"

The trees parted. They came to a small clearing—six people standing in the center of it.

Rema, Darmik, Neco, Ellie, Nathenek, and Marek.

Savenek was about to ask if they were going to join them on their hunting expedition when everything suddenly fell into place. They knew. As to whether Rema was about to yell at them for their treasonous actions or not, Savenek couldn't be certain.

The Brotherhood surrounded them, spreading out in a circle facing outward. Savenek dismounted and joined Odar, Mayra, Allyssa, and Kerdan as they stood before the empress.

Rema had on brown pants and a tunic, her hair braided and wrapped around her head. Her eyes scanned the five of them, and Savenek had no idea what she was thinking or feeling. However, seeing her dressed like that—standing in the middle of the forest, a sword at her waist—he understood one thing. There was a reason Rema had kept control over Emperion for the past two decades, despite being a woman who'd grown up on Greenwood Island.

Kerdan was the first to speak. "Your Majesties, I'm going to take my men and do another sweep of the area. We'll return shortly."

Rema gave a curt nod.

Savenek groaned. Kerdan didn't seem the least bit fazed by

seeing them here. Plus, he'd arranged for this outing. Which could only mean one thing—the Russek king had snitched on them. Savenek curled his fingers, making two fists. He would pummel Kerdan.

Kerdan withdrew his sword, gliding past the Brotherhood into the dense trees, his three men following silently after him.

CHAPTER 14

Allyssa

Allyssa ran forward, wrapping her arms around Marek. "You've returned." She'd been so afraid something had happened to him.

"I have." He hugged her back.

While she was curious to know about his trip and what Prince Kren, Odar's brother, had said, she knew not to say anything until her mother had spoken. Had Marek discovered something? Had he been the one to tell her parents about the assassination plot? Not that it really mattered. She was just thrilled her friend was home and he appeared to be unharmed.

Rema cleared her throat. Allyssa released Marek and moved back to stand alongside Savenek, Odar, and Mayra. Kerdan still hadn't returned.

"Killing another person is never to be taken lightly," Rema said. "I was forced to kill Emperor Hamen in order to take back my throne. Allyssa and Odar, you had to kill Jana and her children to protect Emperion and Fren. Savenek and Mayra, you've had to kill for the betterment of Emperion as well. We all understand that taking a life is never easy." Pausing, she nodded at Darmik, apparently wanting him to chime in.

"I agree," Darmik said. "Which is why Rema and I have been hard at work with our most trusted advisors," he pointed to Neco and Nathenek, "trying to decide what to do should our peace talks fail."

Allyssa bit her bottom lip to ensure she didn't say something she'd regret.

"You four are playing a very dangerous game," Rema said, taking a slow, measured step forward. "I am first and foremost your empress. You must obey me, or I will have you charged with treason."

Bloody hell. Her mother and father not only knew about the assassination plot, but they were also pulling rank—speaking as the empress and emperor of Emperion instead of as her mother and father.

"I suspected something when Marek went missing," Neco said.

"And like I mentioned before, Rema and I are working on several contingency plans," Darmik said. "It didn't take Neco and I long to figure out what you are up to."

"Thankfully, Kerdan confirmed our suspicions," Neco said.

Kerdan?

"Yes," Darmik said. "Kerdan suspected Savenek and Odar were up to something. He immediately came to me fearing that if there was an assassination, there would be far-reaching consequences, especially if the empress and emperor did not know ahead of time."

Well, when her father said it like that, it did make their plan seem a bit naive. But they didn't intend for anyone to know it was an assassination. It was supposed to appear as an accident. So, in theory, there shouldn't be any consequences. Allyssa shifted her weight from foot to foot. "Sorry?"

Rema's piercing gaze fell on Allyssa. "I expect better from you."

Her mother's words felt like a punch to the stomach.

"If there's going to be an assassination," Rema said, "it needs to be a flawless plan."

"What are you saying?" Savenek asked.

"That assassinating the Telmena royal family has always been a possibility," Darmik replied.

"We just need to try for peace first," Rema added. "Then if peace fails, we will be justified in killing."

"Why are we all here?" Allyssa asked. Out in the middle of the forest, alone.

"To plan," Neco answered. "We can't risk anyone overhearing."

Which included servants and soldiers. Thus, the reason for the Brotherhood.

Kerdan returned with his three men. "All clear." He stood next to Allyssa, clasping his hands behind his back.

"Then let's get to work," Rema said.

"The first order of business," Darmik pointed at Marek, "is a report on your mission."

Now that Allyssa was paying closer attention to Marek, she could see the lines under his eyes and the stubble on his cheeks. His appearance seemed to suggest he'd barely slept the entire time he'd been away.

"I was able to secretly meet with Prince Kren. He says the king and queen are building up the army and plan to take over Emperion if Odar doesn't produce results shortly. The people of Telmena aren't happy about being forced into the army, and there is a lot of unrest. Kren is worried because his wife, the princess, is pregnant. He's afraid the people will rebel, which will throw Telmena into the midst of a bloody civil war. When I asked Kren if he would be opposed to us killing the king and queen and he and Jestina taking over the kingdom, he seemed relieved. He made it clear he didn't want to know the details, but would work with us after it was done."

"Anything else?" Darmik asked.

"Yes. Kren insists Telmena remain its own independent kingdom, free from Fren and Emperion rule. He said that while he and Jestina will work with us, they don't want to be controlled by us."

"Odar," Darmik said, "what do you think?"

"I know my brother well. Kren is insisting on this to make sure my overbearing father doesn't control Telmena—or him. Kren left for a reason. I made him a promise, and I intend to honor that promise."

Interesting. Odar rarely spoke about his brother. But listening to him here, it almost seemed like Kren married Jestina not because Odar didn't want to, but to get away from his father and live his own life. Perhaps Odar wasn't as selfish as Allyssa had thought.

"Good to know," Darmik responded. "Marek, is there anything else?"

"Yes." Marek pulled out a small satchel, handing it to Nathenek. "It was right where you said it would be, still buried and undisturbed."

Nathenek undid the tie, then pulled out several papers. "Here is all the evidence we need to show Telmena is conspiring against us."

"Evidence?" Allyssa asked, trying to get a better look at the papers.

"Documents showing Hamen is from Telmena. Also, these show that Telmena considered Hamen to be the true ruler of Emperion. It is their belief the line should have shifted to them upon Hamen's death, therefore making the king and queen of Telmena the rulers of Emperion."

"Do you think they intend to challenge our rule?" Rema asked.

"Yes," Nathenek responded. "When they come here for the wedding, I expect they'll make a bid for the throne. They know you'll deny it. However, the seed of doubt will be planted in the other kingdoms. Once Odar marries Allyssa, it will only be a matter of time until they ask Odar to kill the empress and emperor. Upon Rema and Darmik's deaths, they will expect Odar and Allyssa to graciously hand over Emperion to them. They will have what they want with minimal loss to themselves."

"Is this why you were in Telmena?" Savenek asked. "To discover their plan?"

"Yes," Nathenek answered. "They are also building up their army as Marek mentioned. When Russek lined their army along the Russek border, we responded to the threat at once. Telmena feels that if they do the same, you will take them seriously."

Allyssa's heart pounded. She'd had no idea Telmena had been planning to overthrow Emperion for so long.

"The Brotherhood has also discovered that there are small groups of Telmena people in Emperion with kepper poison," Savenek said. "Two of the three groups have been apprehended."

"How has this happened?" Allyssa asked, furious their enemy could so easily enter their kingdom.

"It is easy for a man or two to slip past our defenses," Darmik said.

"What is the point of these Telmenas? Why are they here? What do they hope to accomplish?" Allyssa started pacing in the small clearing. She glared at her brother. Why hadn't he told her any of this information sooner?

"I think they plan to assassinate the Emperion royal family if things don't go their way," Nathenek said.

So basically the Telmenas planned to do exactly what Allyssa and her family intended to do. The irony wasn't lost on her. She stopped pacing and faced everyone.

"I agree," Kerdan said. "That's what I would do in their situation."

Allyssa shivered. Everyone was due to arrive shortly. This was one deadly game they couldn't afford to lose.

"Do we still intend to broker peace when everyone is here for the wedding?" Allyssa asked. It seemed too dangerous to continue with the plan, especially knowing Telmena wouldn't agree to it.

"We have to," Rema said. "Otherwise, there will be war on the mainland. I can handle discord with one kingdom, but not with all the kingdoms."

"After they refuse to broker peace and leave, we'll assassinate them," Darmik said. "Before we start planning the details, I have one last question for Odar. How will your parents react to you not marrying Allyssa?"

Odar rubbed his face. "I'm not certain." He hesitated, scratching the back of his neck.

"What is it?" Darmik demanded.

"My parents would handle the situation with Telmena much better if I were to marry Allyssa and sit on the Emperion throne."

Allyssa heard the noise of fist hitting flesh. Odar's breath *whooshed* from him in an audible sound. He stumbled, losing his footing. Allyssa glared at Kerdan, but he shook his head. When she whirled around, she realized her brother had been the one to punch Odar. "What did you do that for?" she asked.

"This devious little snake is trying to use the situation to marry you," Savenek spat.

"I was just being honest," Odar said, righting himself. "I didn't say I wanted to marry her."

"You didn't have to," Kerdan said, voice menacing. "It was implied."

"I'm sorry, Odar," Allyssa started to say.

"No," he replied. "I know you don't want to marry me. The last thing I want is to be wed to someone who doesn't like me and would rather be with someone else." He massaged his side.

"What is your solution to ensure your parents don't retaliate?" Kerdan asked.

"When all of this is done, I will return to Fren with my parents. We will remain there. They won't be able to do anything if I insist I didn't want to marry Allyssa and am relieved to be home."

"We won't ever make a move against Fren," Darmik said. "Not as long as there is peace between us. I give you my word."

"That is all I want," Odar replied.

"Now that we have that out of the way," Rema said. "Let's get to work."

ALLYSSA PACED IN HER ROOM EVEN THOUGH SHE WAS exhausted from plotting with her parents all day. They'd come up with a handful of plans, some more dangerous than others, all of them risky. The entire ordeal was starting to make her stomach twist in worry. To top it off, the first royal party traveling to Lakeside had been spotted about twenty miles away. It was due to arrive late tomorrow.

She plopped on the chair in front of the fireplace, staring into the flames. Kerdan had been here for two days, and she still hadn't had a moment alone with him. It was driving her mad. She couldn't believe he'd rode all the way here from Russek just to make sure she wasn't marrying Odar. It was romantic in a wild sort of way.

She sighed.

A light tapping came from the wall. Getting up, she went closer to the wall and listened. The sound was coming from her laundry chute. Pulling it open, she yelped in surprise. Savenek was wedged in the chute.

"Don't laugh," he said. "I'm barely hanging on."

"What are you doing?" If he was trying to get into his room, he'd missed a turn.

"I'm here to see if you want to sneak out."

Surprise washed through her. "Give me five minutes." She ran to her dressing closet, then quickly changed into pants and a tunic. Grabbing a cap, she headed back to the laundry chute. Savenek was nowhere to be seen. After climbing inside, she slid to the bottom, finding Savenek standing there waiting for her.

He motioned for her to go ahead. Without uttering a word, she led him out of the laundry room, through the castle, and off the grounds. Once they were in the town, the twins walked side by side along the street.

"Feeling restless?" Allyssa asked.

Savenek shrugged. "I figured that once everyone arrived for the wedding, we wouldn't be able to leave the castle. And I really needed to be away from my guard. I never have a moment alone."

While Allyssa loved being back in Emperion, she was having a tough time getting used to her guard following her around, too. At first, when she had been in Russek or with Nathenek, she'd felt isolated and alone. However, she'd gotten used to the privacy, the independence, and the freedom. Even though she was thrilled to finally be home with her family, it was hard to have someone watching her all the time.

"Where to?" she asked. "Are you in the mood to fight? Drink? Or walk?"

"Drink."

That surprised her. She didn't think Savenek was the drinking sort of man. Not questioning him, she led the way to one of the more crowded taverns, thinking he'd like the atmosphere there. It had been one of Grevik's favorite places to meet. When Allyssa stepped inside, she breathed in the smell of ale and stew. The familiar sight of men playing cards at the tables, people dancing off to the side, and the sound of people laughing, made her tear up.

"What's wrong?" Savenek asked.

"Nothing. Go order us drinks. I'll find a table." She made her way through the crowd until she found an empty table. After wiping off the bread crumbs with her sleeve, she sat and scanned the crowd. There weren't any familiar faces from the City Guard or the army. Relaxing, she leaned back on the chair, slouching and taking it all in. The musicians were playing some lively music and about two dozen people were dancing.

"Here." Savenek set two mugs on the table, then took a seat across from her. "This is almost as good as a tavern back in Emperor's City."

She eyed him. "Almost?"

He took a sip of his ale. "It's missing the distinct stench that fishermen have. Doesn't feel like a tavern without the awful smell of fish." He smiled wryly.

Allyssa couldn't help but laugh. "You hate the smell of fish, too?"

"Loathe it."

"Same here. The smell makes me nauseous." She took a drink of her ale, taking note of yet another similarity between them. "How are things going with Mayra?" Since Savenek and Mayra started officially courting, Mayra hadn't been very forthcoming with details. And Allyssa wanted details.

He groaned. "I think Neco hates me."

Neco didn't hate Savenek. If he did, he never would have allowed Savenek and Mayra to court. "Neco can be intimidating." Luckily, she'd grown up with him and knew his antics well. "He just wants to make sure your intentions are honorable."

"I understand he wants what's best for his daughter. But you'd think," he lowered his voice to a whisper, "he'd be thrilled to have his daughter marry a prince."

Allyssa wrapped her hands around her mug, considering what Savenek had said. "Perhaps after watching what I went through, he's more concerned about his daughter being happy than her station in life."

Savenek ran his hands through his hair, messing it up. "Don't hit me for saying this, but I'm thankful you've been through what you have. Otherwise, I'm not sure Rema and Darmik would approve of me marrying Mayra. They would probably have insisted on a political match."

Allyssa hated to admit it, but he was right. Not wanting to talk about her past, she changed the subject. "Why don't you call them Mother and Father?"

He shrugged before taking a long drink from his mug. When he set the mug down, he focused on the people dancing. "They didn't raise me so it's hard to think of them as my parents."

"You seem comfortable around them." He fit right in as if he'd always been a part of their family.

"I am." He finally looked at Allyssa. "But Nathenek raised me. He's my father."

She couldn't imagine what her life would have been like if someone other than her parents had raised her. She was fairly sure she wouldn't be as accepting of it as Savenek appeared to be. "For what it's worth, I'm sorry."

"It's not your fault."

"Still, I feel bad." And thankful she wasn't the one her parents had sent away. Which only made her feel even more guilty.

Instead of answering, he said, "It's getting loud in here."

"More people just came in." There was barely any room to dance and every single table was occupied.

"At least the ale is good," Savenek said sardonically.

The ale tasted like stinky socks. She scrunched up her nose.

Someone near the door caught her attention. Someone taller and wider than everyone else in the room. She blinked. "You've got to be kidding me." Kerdan was here.

"I was wondering how long it would take him to come in," Savenek murmured.

"You knew he was out there?"

"I felt him following us. Probably because he's not familiar with the town, he stayed a little closer to us than he normally would have."

"Why didn't you say anything?" She would have asked Kerdan to join them.

"I wasn't sure if he was following to protect you, spy on you, or to see you."

Kerdan spotted Allyssa and headed her way. When he reached their table, he sat on one of the empty chairs. "What are you doing out of the castle?" he demanded.

"I needed a break," she said.

"Me too," he admitted.

"Are you alone?" Or had he brought one of his men?

"I came here by myself. I figured one Russek was hard enough to blend in. Any more would be too difficult."

"Smart man," Savenek muttered, taking another sip of his ale. "I'm not leaving my sister alone with you."

"I didn't ask you to."

"I came here to enjoy myself," Allyssa said. "Can you two please not argue for one night?"

Kerdan drummed his fingers on the table. "It is nice to see you dressed like normal," he said to her.

"This isn't normal. The fancy dresses are."

"I prefer this."

"You prefer me drab?"

"No, not drab." He raised a single eyebrow, sending a jolt of pleasure through Allyssa. "Like a fighter."

Savenek groaned. "I can't believe I have to sit here and listen to this."

"Apologies," Kerdan said. "Allyssa, want to dance? That way your brother won't have to listen to us."

"It would be my pleasure." She stood and followed him to the dancing area. The last time she danced with him had been at a tavern in Russek.

He grabbed hold of her waist, playfully tugging her to him so their chests touched. She met his eyes, and her breath caught. He reached out, brushing her cheek with the back of his hand. While she was aware of everyone dancing around them as she and Kerdan just stood there, she didn't care. Kerdan's eyes revealed so much. Sadness—probably for the lives lost during the war; happiness—from being with her; anger—at what Jana had done to his kingdom and his father for allowing it to happen; and longing —for peace, contentment, and a bright future.

Going up on her tiptoes, she kissed his cheek and then reluctantly stepped away from Kerdan so she could dance.

"You're right," he said. "Your taverns are very different from mine."

The music sped up, and people clapped every two beats, stomping on the third and fourth.

"Ours are tame compared to yours. No organized fighting." She still remembered when he'd fought the man in the ring. That had been a thing of beauty to see. She'd thoroughly appreciated Kerdan's brute strength and watching his muscles ripple as he moved.

"Why do you have that devilish expression on your face?" he asked.

"Me?" He couldn't possibly know what she'd been thinking.

"Yes, you."

Her face warmed.

"Now you have to tell me."

It was difficult to carry on a conversation over the music, people talking, clapping, stomping, and mugs clinking. But at least no one could hear her when she replied, "I was just remembering when you fought shirtless."

He leaned in until his lips touched her left ear. She stopped dancing, unable to move with him so close. "I wouldn't mind watching you in that situation." He chuckled, the sound deep and sultry.

Her legs went weak, and she almost fell over right there on the dance floor. Kerdan gripped her elbows, holding her upright. Was it getting hot in there or was it just her?

The song ended and another one began. This was a quick tune usually played at celebrations. Allyssa clapped three times while stomping on either foot. She spun to the right, then to the left, and stomped again. Kerdan caught on quickly, imitating her movements. The music sped up, and the dancing became quicker. Allyssa couldn't help but smile as she watched Kerdan match her move for move. When the song ended, everyone in the pub pounded on the tables or the bar while those who had been dancing applauded the musicians.

"I need a drink," Kerdan said, breathing heavily.

Allyssa made her way back to the table where Savenek sat while Kerdan went to the bar to get a drink.

"How can you marry a Russek?" Savenek asked, his lip curled in disgust.

She rolled her eyes. "I almost married a man from Fren. What's the difference?"

"Russek is our enemy."

"Was."

He ran his hands through his hair. "I find it hard to trust him."

"I know you do." And she understood his reluctance to trust him. However, Darmik, Neco, and Nathenek had all vouched for Kerdan. Wasn't the opinion of the three most highly regarded men in Emperion good enough for Savenek?

"I can't decide who I like more. Kerdan or Odar," Savenek muttered.

"It doesn't matter who you like more because I'm only in love with one of them."

Savenek raised his eyebrows, giving her a half smile. "Fair enough."

Kerdan joined them. "Where do you go if you want to fight?" He took a swig from his mug.

"Into the army," Savenek replied.

"That's not what he meant," Allyssa said. "In Russek, they fight at taverns. They place bets on who will win."

"Maybe I like Russek a little more," Savenek drawled.

Kerdan finished off his drink. "Are you two ready to leave?"

It was getting late, and Allyssa was tired. They exited the tavern. The air had turned cold. Allyssa folded her arms, trying to stay warm.

"I need to meet up with my men," Kerdan said. "We're going to spy on the royal party that is arriving tomorrow."

"Mind if I come?" Savenek asked.

"I thought you didn't like Kerdan," Allyssa said.

Savenek elbowed her in the side.

Kerdan slapped his arm around Savenek's shoulders. "I think we should spend some more time together. I'm not sure I like you, either."

"At some point, I hope you and I will have a moment alone?" Allyssa stared pointedly at Kerdan.

"If Emperion didn't have their backward ways, I'd be staying in your room." He kissed her forehead.

"I hope that's a joke," Savenek said.

Allyssa didn't respond.

"Come." Kerdan nodded his head to the north.

"Aren't we going to walk Allyssa back to the castle first?" Savenek asked.

Kerdan scrunched his eyebrows together. "Why would we do that?"

"To make sure she gets there safely," Savenek replied, as if talking to a two-year-old.

"Your sister can take care of herself." Kerdan started to walk away.

"I guess," Savenek said, not sounding convinced at all.

Kerdan turned and winked at Allyssa. "I know."

Allyssa watched Savenek and Kerdan walk away. Once they were out of sight, she made her way back to the castle.

～

Allyssa had to be dreaming. It felt like Kerdan's arms were pulling her closer to him. Her eyes opened. "Kerdan?" she whispered.

"Shh," he said.

The darkness of night had started to fade to a pale, gray light.

"What are you doing here?" she whispered.

He was stretched out on the bed alongside her. "I just got back and wanted to see you."

"Is everything okay?" she asked.

"Yes." He gently stroked her hair, his hand practically covering her entire head as he did so.

She started to drift off to sleep, breathing in the smell of him.

"It is strange to be here," he mumbled. "Your cities are so different from mine. Both of your parents are still alive. You have a sibling. There is a feeling of peace and contentment here."

"Do you think you could live here?"

"I could live anywhere as long as you are with me. But it is a little hot here for my liking."

She smiled, feeling the warmth of his fully clothed body next to hers.

"Your father has been an immense help to me," Kerdan said. "He has given me a lot of advice on how to handle the army and those vying for power. Not that I've done everything he's said, but most of his advice has been worthwhile." He continued to stroke her hair, lulling her back to sleep.

"I'm not ready for the responsibility of being king," he admitted. "But I have no choice. Russek must have a king, and I am him."

"Why aren't you ready?" she asked drowsily. He'd make a great king.

"I was raised for the army, not politics."

"That's why we're perfect together. I have politics covered, and you'll take care of the army."

"Your father is putting Savenek in charge of the Emperion army."

Well, there would still be the Russek army to run. But she didn't want Kerdan in Russek; she wanted him here in Emperion with her. There was so much that needed to be sorted through and figured out.

He leaned forward and kissed her cheek. She didn't want a kiss on her cheek. She wanted to feel his lips. Rolling over so she faced him, she wound an arm around him and lifted her chin. His lips touched hers.

The door to her bedchamber opened. Kerdan cursed. Allyssa peeked over her shoulder to see a very stunned Mayra standing there.

Mayra came in and closed the door. "Sorry," she whispered. "But Her Majesty bid me to come wake you."

"The royal family from Dromien must have arrived," Kerdan said as he got off the bed.

"How'd you get in here?" Mayra asked. "There are guards right outside the door. They have strict orders not to let anyone other than the royal family or me in here."

"That is my secret," Kerdan whispered.

There was no way he fit in the laundry chute.

"I suggest you get out of here before someone finds you." Mayra eyed Allyssa. "You know how your parents would react if they found him in here."

"I know," Allyssa said.

Mayra headed to Allyssa's dressing closet.

Kerdan leaned down and kissed Allyssa's forehead.

"How did you get in here?" she asked.

"Your brother let me in. He said I could have five minutes."

"My brother?" She found that hard to believe.

"I won a bet."

Now that she did believe.

"The bookshelf in the corner of your room swings open and

leads into your brother's room. Didn't you know that?" He straightened.

She did not know that.

Kerdan headed toward the bookshelf. When he was about five feet away, the bookshelf swung open and Savenek stood there.

"Time's up," Savenek said.

Kerdan exited through the secret passage Allyssa hadn't known existed.

"Did you know he can kill and skin a rabbit in less than two minutes?" Savenek asked.

Well no, she hadn't. "Why are you asking?"

"He's a king."

"And?"

"I didn't think royalty knew how to do that sort of thing." He placed his hands on his hips.

"Can you kill and skin a rabbit?" she asked.

"Of course."

"Aren't you royalty?"

"Yes, but that's different. I wasn't raised as a prince."

And Kerdan didn't have a typical childhood either. However, Allyssa didn't feel it was her place to reveal Kerdan's secrets. "I'm quite surprised you let him in my room."

"Only for five minutes. And he promised me he wouldn't do anything untoward."

"And you believed him?"

"Yes."

"Are you coming?" Kerdan called from Savenek's room. "We still have work to do."

"Yeah," Savenek answered him. "I need to go. I swear I don't know where that man gets his energy." He turned and left, closing the bookshelf behind him.

Allyssa smiled. They must have gotten to know one another a little better last night.

Mayra exited the dressing closet holding a lovely lavender dress. "Will this do?" she asked.

Allyssa stood and stretched. "That one is fine." She needed to hurry so she'd be ready to receive the Dromien royal family. The last time she'd met the prince, he'd made fun of her, saying she was a skinny, ugly runt. She'd punched and yelled at him. But that had been years ago. Still, she'd already made up her mind she wasn't going to like the Dromien royal family.

STANDING IN THE THRONE ROOM, ALLYSSA GREETED the king and queen from Dromien as they explained that their son had not come along with them for the wedding.

Odar was at Allyssa's side, playing the part of the doting fiancé perfectly. He was very good at playing parts. The squire, the prince, the victim, the warrior. She shoved those thoughts aside as Rema and Darmik expressed their pleasure at seeing their friends. Allyssa tried not to roll her eyes.

Savenek was slightly behind her, smiling and charming to those who'd bothered to come today. Now that Allyssa was paying attention, most in attendance were young, unmarried females. She twisted to glare at Savenek. He simply shrugged.

Rema announced that supper, followed by dancing, would be held that evening to welcome the king and queen from Dromien.

Allyssa glided down the aisle and exited the Throne Room. She was immediately joined by Marek.

"I'm glad you're back," she said by way of greeting. She much preferred having him guard her.

"We need to talk."

"About what?" she asked.

"Mayra told me what she saw this morning."

Son of a harlot! Allyssa wanted to strangle her friend. "It was nothing."

"It is definitely something," he said. "We need to speak somewhere private."

Savenek joined them. "I just heard," he said.

Maybe they weren't talking about the same thing.

CHAPTER 15

Savenek entered his office, running his hands through his hair.

"Will someone please explain to me what's going on?" Allyssa asked, looking from Savenek to Marek and back again.

Savenek hadn't wanted to tell her before and worry her unnecessarily. However, she deserved to know the truth. "Mayra went to the barracks early this morning."

"What was she doing there?" she asked.

"Translating for Nathenek," Marek said. "He was having a prisoner questioned."

The thought sickened Savenek. Mayra shouldn't have to see someone being questioned like that. However, if he wanted to her do work for the Brotherhood, this was what it entailed. And it wasn't like it was being forced on her—Mayra had not only volunteered to translate, but also seemed eager to do the job.

Savenek sat on the edge of his desk, facing his sister. "When Mayra was finished, she left the barracks and proceeded to cross the castle grounds. She saw something near the wall so Mayra being Mayra, she hid alongside a tree and watched. It ended up being a person carrying a box of what seemed to be bread. Mayra didn't recognize him, so she followed him inside the castle. The guy delivered the box to the kitchen." Savenek stood and went around the desk, sitting on the chair and propping his feet on the desk.

"Mayra hid and watched the man. He shoved the bread aside and pulled out a small container. After which, he then proceeded to uncork the container, pouring its contents into various jugs throughout the kitchen. When he finished, he corked the container, slid it in his pocket, and left."

Allyssa's face paled. She sat on one of the chairs across from Savenek. "Is Mayra okay?"

"She is," Marek answered.

"After the man left, Mayra ordered a guard to stand at the entrance to the kitchen. She told him not to let anyone enter. Then she ran straight to Darmik and told him everything." Savenek was still shaken up over the incident. If the guy had caught Mayra, he could have hurt or killed her.

"What did my father do?"

"He got me," Savenek said, lowering his feet off the table. "I went to the kitchen with him where I examined the substance the intruder had left behind. I was able to confirm it's the kepper poison from Apethaga." He rubbed his face. He'd just received word from the Brotherhood on a workable plan for destroying the mines with minimal loss of life. After perusing the plan and running it by Rema, he'd given it the go ahead. Four members of the Brotherhood were going into Apethaga. Two would create a fire in the forest not far from the mountain where the mines were located, prompting an evacuation. Once everyone was out of the mines, the other two members of the Brotherhood would set a handful of explosions, destroying the mines. They'd planned to do it when it looked like rain was coming so the fires wouldn't rage out of control.

Savenek rubbed his face. Even when the mines were destroyed, the poison that had already been produced and shipped to other kingdoms would still exist. And so would those blasted kepper flowers.

"I don't think it was an assassination attempt," Marek said, sitting on the chair next to Allyssa. "I think it was supposed to poison most of the people in the castle, thus creating widespread panic."

"I agree," Savenek said. This guy was probably part of the third pair of men they'd been searching for. The other two pairs were locked up in the dungeon below the barracks. This third pair must have been sent to target the castle. What Savenek found even more concerning was the man he'd previously spoken to had said to wait for the signal from the king and queen from Telmena before they were to do anything. Had the signal been given? Or did this man have different instructions? There were too many questions and not enough answers.

"What measures have been taken for security?" Allyssa asked. She was always the practical one. Thinking ahead.

"Guards and patrols have been doubled," Marek answered.

It would be difficult to monitor everyone with so many people coming for the wedding. No doubt part of their enemy's plan.

"What does the poison look like?" Allyssa asked.

Savenek recalled seeing the flower back in Apethaga. A very small plant that produced deadly results. "It's a red substance." He didn't know what it entailed to make the poison, but he knew the flower was red and so was the poison.

The door opened, and Kerdan and Darmik entered the room.

"I assume everyone has been apprised of the situation?" Darmik asked.

"They have," Savenek answered. Kerdan moved to the corner of the room and leaned against the wall, watching everything.

"Good. The kitchen has been cleaned and is poison free," Darmik said. "The suspect managed to escape without further notice. All sentries are on alert and have been given his description."

"Excellent," Allyssa said. When she stood to leave, Darmik put his hand on her shoulder, pushing her back onto her chair.

"There is more we must discuss. The Apethaga royal family is due to arrive in two days. Savenek, share what you and Mayra discovered while you were there."

Savenek sat up a little straighter. "We found correspondence between Princess Conditto of Apethaga and Jana. Before Jana died, the two of them managed to negotiate marriage contracts between Prince Jem of Telmena and Princess Lareissa of Apethaga."

"Does Princess Conditto have authority to authorize such contracts?" Allyssa asked, sounding very much like Rema.

"I do not know," Darmik answered. "Apethaga is very different from Emperion."

"There is one more contract." Savenek looked at his sister as he said, "Kerdan and Princess Conditto."

"Of which I was unaware until Savenek told me last night," Kerdan stated.

"Is the contract valid?" Allyssa asked.

"No," Kerdan answered. "Jana had no authority to negotiate such a contract."

"Then what's the issue?" Allyssa asked.

"Jana could have forged my father's name and seal," Kerdan said. "I don't know since I haven't seen the contract."

"If she forged the contract, it's not enforceable, is it?" Allyssa asked.

"No," Kerdan said, leaving no room for argument.

Darmik turned to Savenek and asked, "What's your take on the Apethaga royal family? What do they have to gain from this union?"

Savenek had spent enough time in Apethaga to have an opinion of the royal family. Everything they did made sense. They sold weapons and poison to other kingdoms for money. Conditto had brokered the contracts in order to tie the various kingdoms together. They valued wealth and power. "I believe that since Jana is dead, they aren't as eager to move forward with the plan to overthrow Emperion as they had been before. I'm sure they'll be looking for an out."

"What should we do about the contracts?" Allyssa asked. She pulled a section of her hair over her shoulder and started braiding it.

"Has Prince Jem acknowledged his contract with Princess Lareissa?" Savenek asked.

"Not that I know of," Darmik said. He pinched the bridge of his nose. "I think we wait and see on the contracts. Agreed?"

Kerdan nodded.

"Also, I need for Allyssa and Savenek to give the weekly address to the people today," Darmik said.

"Why can't Mother do it?" Allyssa asked.

"Your mother is with the Brotherhood right now. She is putting contingency plans in place."

Savenek hadn't been involved with any of the weekly speeches here at Lakeside. Hopefully Allyssa would do the talking and all he'd have to do was stand there and smile, wooing the crowd.

"Make sure you tell the people about your engagement so everyone is talking about it," Darmik said. "However, keep it vague."

"Got it," Allyssa responded.

"Anything else?" Darmik asked Savenek.

"Not that I'm aware of." He didn't think they could handle anything else at the moment.

"I need to meet with Neco and Nathenek." Darmik left the room.

"I need to go and write my speech," Allyssa said. She smiled at Kerdan before exiting the room, Marek following her.

"Come," Kerdan commanded.

Savenek raised his eyebrows. "Where to?"

"The training room." He turned and left, not waiting for Savenek to join him.

Was everyone in Russek so rude? Or was that trait unique to

Kerdan? Savenek reluctantly followed him to the training room. He found Kerdan standing in the middle of the floor, his hands on his hips.

Savenek remembered seeing Kerdan burst through the window and tackle Odar. That had been fun to watch. While the broken glass had been removed from the window, the window hadn't been repaired yet.

"Thanks for letting me come with you last night," Savenek said. Spending time with the three Russeks had given him a good idea of who Kerdan was as a man, soldier, and friend. It also allowed Savenek to understand the Russeks a little better. Granted, he still thought of them as bloodthirsty, vicious soldiers. However, when they were on the right side, they could be valuable allies. Savenek had been relieved the men listened to orders and worked so well together. They also proved to be apt in stealth, which he appreciated. And, begrudgingly, they were funny, and he'd enjoyed his time with them.

"I must say, you've surprised me," Kerdan said.

"How so?"

"You seem to have taken to your new position. You seem to care for your sister. You seem to put Emperion first."

Savenek noticed the use of the word *seem* over and over. As if it only seemed that way but it wasn't so. He kept his mouth shut and let Kerdan speak.

"The court thinks you're a princely man. You wear the right clothes, look the part, smile at the ladies." He tilted his head to the side, cracking his neck. "But that is only the perception. Raised in the Brotherhood, by Nathenek specifically, makes you something other than what you seem."

Well, Darmik had told Savenek to act the part so no one would suspect him of anything.

"At first, I didn't know what to think of you. After last night, I get what you are doing, and you make sense to me."

"Same here. I can see why my sister cares for you." Kerdan and

Allyssa were both passionate about their kingdoms, dedicated, and they both had an inner side they kept hidden from others but shared with those close to them.

"Your sister is a remarkable woman."

Savenek had never heard Kerdan speak so much. "I care for my sister and want her to be happy. Yet, I haven't known her that long. It is not for me to decide what's best for her. She seems to know her own mind and can decide for herself."

"Now I officially like you," Kerdan said. "I have seen far too many people treat Allyssa like a child incapable of taking care of herself. It bothers me. She is smart, strong, and she doesn't need someone watching over her. As much as I want to protect her, treating her as a submissive woman who is not my equal would be grievous to her."

Savenek hadn't expected him to say that. "Do you think Darmik treats her poorly?"

"No. He is her father, so his overprotectiveness is understandable and warranted."

"And if you were Allyssa's husband, you would not assume that role?"

"In Russek, men and women are equal. We do not have Emperion's backward ways. Women can fight, work in a trade, or farm the land."

Women could do those things in Emperion as well. However, there was a difference between what was expected of women verses what was expected of men. Savenek ran his hands through his hair. "What is the point of this conversation?" Hadn't they spent enough time together last night?

"I understand you do not like Russeks. We are different from Emperions. We have also treated Emperion badly in the past. I am not my father. I plan to rule justly. I want you to know that."

"I am glad to hear it."

Kerdan took a step closer to Savenek, and the air shifted. "However," Kerdan said, his voice low, "if anyone threatens

Allyssa or myself, I will retaliate. In Russek, we act first, talk later. I won't let my enemies see me being weak."

"Good to know." Savenek wasn't sure what to make of Kerdan's threat.

"Now that we have that out of the way," Kerdan said, taking a step away from him, "we fight." He threw a punch, and Savenek ducked, narrowly missing it. Savenek countered with a blow of his own, hitting Kerdan's side.

~

"Are you certain that doesn't hurt?" Allyssa asked for the tenth time as she headed toward the balcony with Savenek. They were about to give the weekly address to the town.

"No," he said. "I'm fine." Sore, but fine. Kerdan and him had spent over an hour sparring against one another. It had been a while since Savenek had been challenged like that. Even though Kerdan had gotten a few jabs in, Savenek didn't mind. The aches and pains reminded him that he could always improve. Plus, he knew Kerdan would be sporting a few bruises himself.

"When we're on the balcony, make sure you don't go all the way to the railing. Keep a two-foot buffer. There are marksmen on the rooftops and a few behind windows."

Allyssa didn't need to tell him where the marksmen would be; he'd be able to tell the second he stepped on the balcony. He was trained to know where the best places to hide were.

"Neco and Nathenek will also be scanning the crowd for threats. There are soldiers dressed as civilians among the crowd. The City Guard is also spread throughout."

"Is this normal?" If it was so dangerous, why did they bother speaking to the people? Or, as he suspected, was Allyssa simply nervous and jabbering uncontrollably?

"Normally, security is tight. Today, it's a little heavier than usual because of the recent threat with the poison."

They entered a small room where four heavily armored guards stood. Mayra came up behind Allyssa, draping a cape over her shoulders. Once it was fastened, Mayra grabbed another cape and attached it to Savenek. The weight of it surprised him. Then Mayra handed each of them a crown. Reluctantly taking it, he set it atop his head.

Savenek was about to thank Mayra when Allyssa grabbed his arm and said, "Let's go." They stood before a set of double doors. "Remember to smile, wave, and look regal."

"In other words, act normal," he said, teasing her and trying to lighten the mood.

She whacked his arm. "Sometimes you're impossible."

"Sometimes?" He laughed.

She finally smiled. "You're right. All the time."

When the doors swung open, he and his twin stepped onto the balcony. The crowd roared from the courtyard below. Savenek did as instructed, keeping a smile on his face and waving at everyone. He scanned the people, not seeing anyone who stood out. Of course, an assassin would be doing his best to blend in. Regardless, he didn't notice anything of concern.

Cool air blew. The afternoon sun was behind them. Savenek glanced at his sister, hoping she would be the one to speak.

"People of Emperion," Allyssa said, her voice booming throughout the courtyard. The crowd went silent, everyone straining to hear what the princess had to say. "Thank you for coming. As you know, the war with Russek is over. King Kerdan has withdrawn the Russek troops out of Emperion. He has sent his apologies for those killed in the tragic war. He also apologizes for his father, the late King Drenton's actions. He promises there will be peace with Emperion."

The crowd cheered and clapped, showing their approval. Savenek side-eyed Allyssa. Darmik hadn't said anything about her mentioning Kerdan during this speech. However, Savenek was glad she did. She was setting up her future union with Kerdan in a way the people would welcome and accept.

"As many of you may have heard, there will be a wedding here at the castle. Royal families from all over the mainland are traveling to Lakeside to witness the event. While the leaders of other kingdoms are here, our great empress will be discussing a path to peace with them. She plans to ensure there is peace and open trade on the mainland. We all live here and should be able to coexist for the betterment of one another."

Again, the crowd cheered their approval. Allyssa held up her hands. "Before I leave to attend to my duties, I want you all to welcome my dear brother, Prince Savenek." She turned to face him. "He will be studying under our father, Emperor Darmik, commander of our great army. One day, I hope Prince Savenek will lead our army as our father does."

People stomped and clapped, expressing their approval of the news. Allyssa bowed her head and then glided off the balcony. Savenek waved one last time, scanned the crowd, and exited.

Back inside the small room, Savenek removed his heavy cape, instantly feeling lighter. "You're very good," he said to his sister. "I can tell you've been groomed to be the next empress." He had to admit, he was thankful the task no longer fell to him since he was nowhere near as qualified as Allyssa.

"Do you want to go for a ride?" He wouldn't mind taking one of the stallions on a short jaunt to the lake.

"I need to get ready for the ball tonight."

"Ball?" He thought it was just supper followed by dancing.

"Yes. I'm sure Mother is going all out."

They started walking along the hallway, their guards trailing behind them. "I thought she'd be more concerned with security and keeping you safe than hosting a party for a small kingdom nobody cares about."

"Security isn't the issue," Allyssa said. "The poison is concerning. It will be problematic no matter what we do."

A few female courtiers stood up ahead talking. When they noticed the royal siblings, they immediately moved off to the side, bowing. Savenek smiled at them under hooded eyes. Most didn't even give Allyssa the time of day. When they were far enough away, he asked, "Are you friends with many of the women at court?"

"No."

She'd answered too quickly. "Why is that?" he asked.

"A conversation for another time."

He shrugged. Well, at least Allyssa had Mayra. "Back to why your mother is going to throw an extravagant ball when not all the guests are here and the wedding hasn't taken place yet?"

"Mother wants word to reach Telmena of our wealth. In addition, she wants Dromien to feel important and valued. Lastly, Mother is going to make sure Telmena knows our army is strong. If they think us weak—which they may since we sought Fren's help with the Russek issue—they'll be more likely to attack or do something stupid. If they think us rich, with many friends, as well as strong, they may think twice about pushing us into a corner."

Growing up, Nathenek had always taught Savenek to have a plan, then a contingency plan, and then a backup plan if everything failed. Rema seemed to have so many plans he couldn't keep track of them all. At least he knew when it was all said and done, Rema was okay with assassinating the Telmena royal family. Granted, she preferred it as a last resort, but at least she was willing to make the tough choices. Choices he could respect.

"And she's not just *my* mother. She is *our* mother," Allyssa said.

Nathenek stepped out from an alcove up ahead.

"I need to talk to Nathenek." He'd almost said *my father*.

"I'll see you this evening." Allyssa nodded a hello to Nathenek before continuing on her way, her guard trailing her.

"Is there a problem?" Savenek asked.

"Follow me." Which meant there was an issue. They exited the castle and went to the army barracks. Nathenek instructed

Savenek's guards to wait outside the building. He and his adopted father stepped inside an expansive room with several doors. "This way." Nathenek waved him over to the first door on the left. He opened it, then descended a steep staircase, Savenek following close behind.

At the bottom, Nathenek grabbed a torch from the wall and continued along a narrow stone hallway, cells lining either side. This was the first time Savenek had stepped foot in this dungeon.

At the end of the hallway, they came to a closed door. Nathenek knocked three times and entered. Inside, a man sat on a chair, his arms and legs chained together. Neco leaned against the back wall, his arms crossed and his gaze intent on the prisoner.

"We apprehended him in the courtyard while you were on the balcony with Allyssa," Nathenek said.

Savenek observed the prisoner, trying to discover what Neco and Nathenek had seen that warranted this man's arrest. He wore plain brown pants, a brown shirt, and boots. His hair was cut close to his head. The man's belly was large, his arms beefy. If Savenek had to guess, he'd say the man worked in a tavern. No facial hair. And that was when he saw it—the tips of the man's fingers were red.

"Good catch," he said to Nathenek.

Neco smiled, probably because Savenek had figured it out without having to be told.

"Do you think he's the one who brought the poison to the castle?"

"Mayra confirmed it," Nathenek said.

"Have you discovered where he's staying?" Savenek asked. They still needed to find the second man.

"No," Neco replied. "We were just about to have...a conversation with him to determine where that is and who his partner is."

"Why am I here?" Savenek asked.

"A member of the royal family must give consent for a prisoner from another kingdom to be questioned or tortured," Neco said.

Savenek knew Darmik had been tortured when he was younger. He suspected Darmik had put this rule in place as a result of what he'd endured. "I give you my permission to use whatever means necessary to extract the information we need."

"I'll take care of it," Nathenek said.

Savenek and Neco left the dungeon.

"My daughter told me what she did for you to help slow the poison from spreading through your body," Neco said.

Savenek shivered. He hated remembering what he went through, not being able to feel parts of his body. "I'm grateful for Mayra's quick thinking." Otherwise, he'd be dead.

"Rema wants to know if there's an antidote."

"If there is, I don't know about it." He would have to send a member of the Brotherhood to Apethaga to investigate.

"Rema wants us to come up with one of our own," Neco clarified.

Savenek didn't have enough knowledge on poisons and herbs to be able to take this job on. There had to be people better suited. "What about the healer who tended to me? What did she use?"

"I'll speak with her. I'll also have Mayra write down exactly what she did for you. Between the two of them, they should be able to find something that works. If a person is accidentally exposed to the poison, we need to have an antidote readily available."

"I'm sure the healer will be able to come up with something," Savenek said.

Neco patted him on the shoulder. "I hope so. In the meantime, stay safe." He veered to the right, going into the castle from the servants' entrance.

Stunned by the gesture, Savenek wondered if he'd finally made some headway with Neco.

CHAPTER 16

Allyssa

*A*llyssa entered the Great Hall draped on Odar's arm. She hated being presented with him. Not only because it was a lie, but also because it wasn't fair to Kerdan. He shouldn't have to stand there and watch her touch another man.

Odar led Allyssa to where Savenek and Mayra were standing at the front of the room, Kerdan and his men on one side of them, the royal family from Dromien on the other. Rema and Darmik were announced, and they glided into the room regally, like the empress and emperor that they were.

"My parents are coming," Odar mumbled.

"For the wedding?" Allyssa asked.

He nodded.

"They'll probably be relieved when they learn the truth," she said. When she'd met them, they clearly didn't care for her. Not only had they treated her poorly, barely speaking to her, but they'd also made it known they didn't want their son to marry her.

"As long as they get what they want at the end of the day, they won't much care what does and does not happen to me."

"I'm sorry."

He shrugged. "Let's get our dance over with so you can be with Kerdan."

The music started. Those with the rank of prince, princess, or higher were invited to dance for the first song. Odar swung

Allyssa into his arms. So much had changed from the first time they'd danced together. Back then, he'd been hostile toward her, angry even. Now he seemed almost deflated. As if none of this mattered anymore.

"If your parents just want to be left alone and for Fren to remain isolated, why did they allow your brother to marry Jestina of Telmena? Why link your two kingdoms together?" After all, that was what had dragged them into this mess in the first place.

Odar sighed. "Telmena threatened to overthrow us unless I married Jestina. I refused, knowing it would be detrimental to Fren since I'm the crown prince. My brother offered to marry her to avoid war. I think he may have been a little besotted with her."

Allyssa wondered if Telmena had the physical strength to pull off an invasion like that.

"At the time, we didn't have a standing army," Odar explained. "We do now. That has been my mission since this all began." He spun her around and pulled her back to him.

"What will you do when you're done here?" Would he go home? Continue to train his army? Marry someone else?

"I'll do what I've been doing. Although I suspect I'll need to keep a close eye on my brother."

"We've been through so much. I hope we can be friends." She didn't have many friends.

"I think it's in both our best interest to maintain a good working relationship with one another. But know that Fren will stay to itself. Even once my father steps down from the throne and I take his place. It is what our people want and expect." He kept his focus on her forehead—not on her eyes.

"You've done so much for my kingdom," Allyssa said. "I hope to be able to repay you. If you ever need my help, just ask and it will be freely given."

He finally looked into her eyes. "I haven't been helping you out of the goodness of my heart," he admitted. "I've been doing this for purely selfish reasons."

"I don't understand." She stopped dancing and stood there, waiting for him to explain.

His eyes remained penetrating and intense. "I've been trying to make amends for all the wrongs I've done, for the injury I've caused you. I'm doing all of this for you."

Not knowing how to respond, Allyssa glanced over Odar's shoulder and spotted Kerdan watching her. Looking to her left, she noticed Savenek and Mayra dancing close by, Savenek also staring at her. The song ended. When she turned to go, she noticed her parents observing her, too.

Her skin crawled. Why did everyone feel they had to watch her every move? It was infuriating.

Savenek came over and requested the next dance. Kerdan remained standing near the front of the room. No one had dared to approach him.

The music started up, and Allyssa and Savenek began dancing.

"Why are you in such a foul mood?" he asked.

"I can take care of myself."

"I know."

"Then why is everyone watching me?"

He chuckled. "I can't answer for everyone else, but I was looking out for Odar, not you. I was afraid you'd punch him and start a major incident between our kingdoms."

Her eyes narrowed. Was he telling her the truth or trying to appease her?

"You two have a history," Savenek said. "I don't know how to explain it, but I feel protective of you even though you don't need protecting. I don't want him saying things that cause you pain or hurt you."

Allyssa could understand that. "Thank you."

"For what?"

"Being my brother. I've never had one before, and I sort of like it."

The song ended. Savenek hugged her, then turned to find

another partner. Allyssa moved toward Kerdan. Only, Mayra got to him first. If he was surprised, he didn't show it. That was nice of Mayra to dance with him since no one else was.

"My turn," Darmik said, taking Allyssa's hand. "How's my daughter doing?"

"Fine." She placed her free hand on her father's back. He led her in a dance.

"This may cheer you up," he said. "Kerdan spoke to your mother and me earlier today." Amusement flickered in his eyes.

She groaned. What taboo had he inflicted upon Rema?

"He said that while he understood us not wanting him to be alone with you, he wanted to respectfully request us to reconsider."

She raised her eyebrows. Her father knew that when she was in Russek, she'd stayed in Kerdan's room. Alone. Granted, nothing had happened. Back then, they hadn't cared for one another that way. "And?" Had her mother lectured Kerdan? Was he having second thoughts about marrying her now that he'd met Rema?

"He stated his case as to why we should allow you to spend some time with him."

"How did Mother take it?" Kerdan was not the most eloquent speaker.

"Kerdan spoke from his heart. Your mother listened to his request, and she granted it."

Was her father serious? Allyssa was going to spend some time with Kerdan? "Thank you."

"But," Darmik said.

There was always a *but*.

"I ask that you not dance with him tonight."

"Why not?" As the princess, she was expected to dance with each visiting royal. It wouldn't make sense to skip Kerdan. People might view it as a slight.

"Several reasons," he said. "The main one being that whenever you and Kerdan are together, it is clear to anyone watching that you're in love with him, and he with you."

The real reason for Mayra asking Kerdan to dance suddenly became clear. It wasn't out of the goodness of her heart—it was because Darmik had told her to. Allyssa sighed.

"When?" she asked her father.

"Later tonight. You may ask Marek to escort you back to the Royal Chambers in an hour or so. Kerdan will intercept you along the way. I expect you to return to your bedchamber by midnight. Understood?"

She was going to spend time with Kerdan. Alone.

"Wipe the smile off your face," Darmik said.

"I'm not allowed to smile?"

"Not like that you're not."

She studied her father's stern face, trying to determine if he was teasing her.

"I'm glad you and Kerdan are happy together," he said, a warm smile spreading across his face. "I never saw that with you and Odar."

She couldn't stop grinning. Even though her kingdom was on the brink of war and Telmena was trying to dethrone her family, she was happy. Somehow, she knew that no matter what obstacles she faced in her life, she could survive them with Kerdan at her side.

Allyssa walked with Marek toward the Royal Chambers, eagerly anticipating her time alone with Kerdan.

Brookfel stepped out of the shadows, blocking the way. "Princess," he said, bowing. "The king wants me to escort you to the rooftop."

Allyssa loved hearing Kerdan referred to as king. She went to take Brookfel's arm when he abruptly turned and stalked down the corridor. Allyssa and Marek hurried after him.

"Russeks have very different manners from us," Marek said under his breath.

She didn't respond because there was nothing to say to that. They climbed the stairwell leading to the rooftop. When they reached the top, Marek asked her to remain there while he did a quick sweep of the area.

"The rooftop is secure," Marek said when he returned. "I'll wait in the stairwell with Brookfel so you can have some privacy. If you need anything, a simple shout will suffice."

"Thank you." Allyssa squeezed Marek's hand before stepping onto the rooftop. She often came out here because no one from court even knew about this hidden gem. This section of the castle had been designed for star gazing. It was flat, surrounded by a half wall, and allowed unobstructed views of the sky and town.

Kerdan stood in the middle of the rooftop waiting for her. "You look beautiful."

"And you are very handsome in that tunic." It had the royal crest of Russek embroidered on the front. "It's very kingly."

"I know." His shoulders slumped. "And all I want to do is to put my army uniform on and join my men. But that is no longer my destiny."

Allyssa took Kerdan's hand, pulling him to the edge of the rooftop where the half wall was. She leaned against it, observing the flickering lights from the town in the distance. "My brother is also having a tough time coming to terms with his newfound position." She didn't know if Kerdan and Savenek had talked about that when they'd gone off spying together. "I think it's hard when you expect your life to travel down one path, but you end up taking another."

Kerdan stood behind her, wrapping his arms around her waist and resting his head on her shoulder. "I knew I'd be king one day.

I had mistakenly assumed it would be when I was older. Much older. I thought I'd control the army, roam the land, be free."

Allyssa was fortunate to have grown up knowing what was expected of her. As she came closer to becoming the empress, she felt ready for the position. Kerdan, on the other hand, would never be happy sitting in a castle all day. "We will need to discuss how we're going to manage two kingdoms, especially since both are large."

"We are going to be busy." Kerdan kissed her cheek, then released her. He moved to stand beside her, gazing out at the town.

She sensed there was something else bothering him. "What is it?"

"I know you only think of my father as an evil man, but I miss him."

King Drenton was an evil person. He'd murdered, butchered, and harmed thousands of people. She was glad he was dead. "Regardless of how I feel about him, he was your father. I can understand you'd miss him. It's only natural."

Kerdan moved toward her, leaning his forehead against hers. "A part of me hates him. I don't know the extent to which he was involved in my mother's death, but he was involved in it. He was cruel, vicious, and mean. He brought Jana into our lives. Allowed her to run Russek into poverty."

"But he was still your father."

"Yes." His eyes bore into hers. "And this is one of the reasons I love you. Not only can I speak openly with you, but you also understand. I have greatly missed our conversations."

"I thought I drove you nuts with my incessant talking."

Kerdan grinned. "At first you did. But I grew to like it." He reached forward and took a strand of Allyssa's hair, twirling it between his fingers. "I grew to like a great many things about you. Including these lips." He leaned forward and kissed her.

Allyssa trailed her hands up his arms to the back of his neck.

He deepened the kiss, his tongue sliding into her mouth. Her arms tightened around him, pulling him into her. She twined her fingers into his thick hair.

He pulled away, breathing heavily. "We should stop."

"We should. But I don't want to."

He chuckled, the sound deep and throaty. "Neither do I. But I fear your father. And I'm confident that if he were to walk out here and see us like this, he'd throw me off the rooftop."

Allyssa knew her father would do more than toss Kerdan off the roof. "Fine." Since they couldn't kiss, they might as well talk. She figured she had about an hour until she had to be back in her bedchamber. Her father would probably be waiting to make sure she returned on time. "Tell me what happened after I left the duke's house in Russek."

He leaned on the half wall. "I returned to Clovek with a good number of soldiers. I feared I'd have to fight my own army when I got there. However, once everyone learned Jana was dead, they put down their weapons. I was crowned king shortly thereafter."

"What about the rest of Russek?" She'd spent weeks hearing rumors of fighting going on and worrying about him.

"There have been several small uprisings. Mostly citizens who didn't know or understand what's been going on. Once I, uh, educated them, they stood down and the problem was resolved."

"And by educate you mean?"

"A short fight in which someone may or may not have been injured, but no one died."

She could envision Kerdan dealing with the Russek citizens. He must be a sight to behold. "Are any of the dukes giving you a hard time?"

"I sent five hundred soldiers to each duke's residence to ensure their loyalty." He dropped his eyes to his folded hands resting on the wall. "Your father has been offering his advice on how to handle these situations."

"I'm glad he has been able to help you."

Kerdan nodded. "My kingdom will be in turmoil for quite some time. I need to reestablish trade, get production of food up, and help those in need."

"Then it's a good thing you'll have me by your side to help." This time, she was the one who leaned in, kissing him on his lips.

ALLYSSA STOOD IN THE THRONE ROOM AS THE ROYAL families from Kricok, Landania, and Fia arrived for the wedding. When these three territories joined the Emperion empire, Rema and Darmik granted the rulers of each territory retention of his or her status. Among those present was Prince Zek of Fia. Allyssa remembered when he'd come here seeking her hand in marriage for the benefit of his kingdom. While they'd had nothing in common and she found him rather droll, she did respect his loyalty and dedication.

Rema requested the kings and queens from these three territories join her for a private meeting. Allyssa and Savenek invited everyone else to the back lawn for a picnic.

Odar dutifully escorted Allyssa out of the castle and to the back lawn where long tables and benches had been placed throughout the grassy area. One of the tables held food for everyone. She'd already eaten and had been needlessly instructed not to touch anything. Three sentries stood near the table, keeping watch over everything.

To the side, several targets had been set up for archery. Off to the other side, several baskets had been placed in one area while a handful of balls were in another. The goal of the game was for a person to see how many balls he or she could toss into the baskets.

"Care to play a game?" Odar asked.

"Not right now. I've been instructed to make sure people enjoy themselves."

Besides the members of the royal families, several courtiers from the castle had come out to join in the festivities. Allyssa strolled around, talking to several people. It was all rather boring, but she did her duty, making sure everyone was greeted and had food. Savenek also meandered around, talking with everyone and playing the part of the carefree prince. He seemed to take to his role with more enthusiasm than Allyssa did.

Kerdan sat at one of the tables with his men. They looked out of place with their fur wraps, hulking statures, and severe facial expressions.

Prince Zek of Fia approached Allyssa and bowed. "Your Highness." He was the same as she remembered—tall and lanky. "I would like to personally thank you for stopping the war with Russek."

"I'm sorry there was any fighting at all." And she felt horrible so many good men had died.

"If the Emperion army hadn't come to our aid, we would have been slaughtered."

Fia's army was small and no match for Russek's soldiers. "I'm glad our kingdoms have joined together for the mutual benefit of all our people." That sounded politically correct to her. And she liked reminding him that he fell under her jurisdiction now.

"I'm surprised to see anyone from Russek here." He nodded at the table where Kerdan was sitting with his men.

"That is King Kerdan," Allyssa informed him. "He is the person responsible for stopping the war. Once his father died, King Kerdan immediately withdrew all Russek troops from Emperion."

"I did not know that."

Which was why she'd told him. She forced herself not to roll her eyes or say some snide remark.

Odar joined her. "Would you like to begin the games?"

"I would love to." After excusing herself from Prince Zek, she went with Odar over to the archery area.

Savenek already stood there holding a bow. A handful of women surrounded him. Several other courtiers came over to join in the archery competition while a dozen or so stood back to watch.

"I'll go first," Allyssa announced. She nocked an arrow, aimed for the first target, and released the bowstring. The arrow sailed through the air, landing in the center of the target. Everyone clapped.

With a smirk on his face, Savenek raised his bow and released an arrow. It wobbled through the air and landed on the outer part of the target. He smiled, pretending to be pleased with the shot. Allyssa knew it was hard for him to appear as anything less than extraordinary—especially at something he was so good at. Luckily, he played his part well.

While the next person prepared to shoot, Allyssa glanced over at Kerdan. He was still sitting at the table; however, he'd angled his body so he could watch her. Russek people didn't use bows and arrows. She'd offered to teach him to shoot. Too bad she couldn't do it today. Allyssa wouldn't mind the feel of her arms wrapped around him as she tried to show him the proper angle and hand placement.

Savenek nudged her. "Your turn," he said, winking.

Everyone taking part in the archery competition had already taken their first shot. And she'd missed them all while standing there thinking about Kerdan. She needed to focus. It appeared that everyone had managed to get an arrow on the target. So far, hers was the closest while Savenek's was the farthest from the center. Everyone else was somewhere in between.

She nocked another arrow and shot, once again striking the middle of the target. Only this time, she could feel Kerdan watching her, and it pleased her immensely.

CHAPTER 17

Savenek

ord came that the royal family from Apethaga had been spotted not far from the castle. When Savenek had escaped from Apethaga, he never thought he'd see the royal family again. And now here he was, getting ready to greet them as the prince of Emperion. They would be shocked to learn his identity.

He vaguely wondered if they'd be dressed in typical Apethaga clothing. If so, they were sure to cause a stir since they liked to show a lot of skin, especially around the shoulders, arms, and neck. Granted, it was so hot and humid in Apethaga that the clothing made sense. But in Emperion, people were always fully covered.

"Let's go," Darmik said from the doorway to Savenek's bedchamber.

Savenek gave himself one last look in the mirror. His black pants fit snugly, accentuating his long legs. The dark red tunic complemented his skin tone, making his hair seem more blond than brown.

"You look fine." Darmik pinched Savenek's upper sleeve, pulling him from his room.

When Savenek entered the sitting room, he saw Mayra standing there. She was beautiful in her navy-blue dress.

"You have five minutes," Darmik said. "I'm going to get Rema and Allyssa." He left the room.

Savenek went over and kissed Mayra on the cheek.

"Bold move considering your parents aren't far away," she said.

"It's just a friendly hello." It felt good to see her.

"As long as you're not giving anyone else those friendly hellos," she teased.

While he may harmlessly flirt with women at court in order to keep his appearance as the aloof prince, he would never consider kissing another woman. He reached out and took hold of her hand. "I assume you know who's just about here." He didn't know how King Theon and Queen Elesseni would react once they realized they'd imprisoned and tried to kill Savenek and Mayra—not Ven and Ari.

"I do." Mayra pulled her hand free and sat on the sofa. "Which is why I'm here."

Running his hands through his hair, he sat on the sofa next to her, knowing she was about to be overly practical. "I thought you were here because you missed this dashing face." He grinned.

"Be serious."

Sometimes he didn't want to be serious or practical. It was too much work. And thinking about King Theon and Prince Patteon being under the same roof as Mayra made Savenek anxious. He'd spoken to Neco about assigning a handful of guards to watch Mayra. Neco had decided against it, stating he needed his daughter to be able to move through the castle undetected. "I want you to avoid the Apethaga royal family as much as possible. I also want you to be extra cautious."

"I understand your concern," she said, patting his thigh. "But they're the ones who should be careful. Once they realize what they've done to Emperion's prince, I expect them to be on their best behavior, scared your father will retaliate."

Darmik entered the room with Rema and Allyssa. Savenek

stood, pulling Mayra up with him. Dipping his head toward her, he whispered, "Meet me in the library at midnight."

"Mayra," Darmik said, "your father and I want you in your rooms while the Apethaga family is getting situated. I don't want them accidentally running into you."

"I understand." She bowed and left.

"Are we heading to the Throne Room?" Savenek asked.

"No. We're going to greet them outside in front of the castle," Darmik said. "I want their bags, clothing, and anything else they bring with them searched for poison before they step foot in the castle."

"Our family must put on a strong, united front," Rema said. "From this point forward, watch your back."

They exited the Royal Chambers. Twice the number of usual guards surrounded them. Savenek had a feeling this would last until all the guests—and enemies—left. They made their way through the castle. Many of the servants were cleaning, others were bringing in fragrant flowers, and another handful carried in freshly baked bread from town.

In front of the castle, Rema and Darmik stood next to one another, holding hands. Savenek and Allyssa were on either side of them. The Emperion army lined the pathway that led to the main entrance in the outer wall.

The gates swung open, and twenty-four mounted Apethaga soldiers rode onto the castle grounds, followed by four carriages. When the Apethaga soldiers arrived at the front of the castle, they dismounted and stood off to the side, allowing the carriages to pull up to the front.

The first carriage door opened, and servants exited. They began unloading trunks from the second carriage. They did know they were only welcome here for a week or so? Just long enough for the wedding, and then they were going home. The last two carriages remained shut with their curtains drawn.

Neco came around the side of the castle, going straight to the

Apethaga soldiers. He started barking out orders, making it clear he was in charge and they needed to obey. He ordered the soldiers to take their horses to the stables. Once the animals were taken care of, the soldiers were to report to the barracks where they would be given rooms for the duration of their stay.

After Neco was done ordering them about, he turned to the servants. He instructed them to follow one of his men around the side of the castle to the servants' entrance. Savenek was certain that once the servants were out of sight, Neco would be thoroughly searching them and the trunks for poison.

Savenek looked expectantly at the two remaining carriages. One of the doors finally opened, and Lareissa stepped out wearing a purple dress that hung off her shoulders, revealing her bare arms and neck. She was just as stunning as Savenek remembered. She stood to the side while Zare exited. Conditto stepped out next, her eyes scanning the Emperion royal family before taking her place next to her siblings. She wore a soft orange dress that clung to her shapely body. There was a slit up the front revealing long legs. The color of the dress complemented her dark skin. Patteon exited, standing next to his siblings. The door to the last carriage opened, and Theon and Elesseni stepped out. They approached Rema and Darmik.

"Welcome," Darmik said. "This is my beautiful wife, Empress Rema; my daughter, Crown Princess Allyssa; and my son, whom you already had the pleasure of meeting, Prince Savenek."

The king narrowed his eyes at Savenek. "I do remember you," Theon said. "I believe you called yourself Ven."

Savenek didn't let the intended jab bother him. "Ven is my nickname. It's short for Savenek." He smiled, indicating it should have been obvious.

"You didn't introduce yourself as the prince," Theon accused him.

"At the time, I wasn't."

Theon looked at Darmik for an explanation.

"I'm sure you've heard that Allyssa and Savenek are twins," Darmik said. "Allyssa grew up here in the castle, while Savenek grew up with a close, trusted friend."

"Yes," Rema added. "We are so pleased both our children are finally living with us."

Theon waited for them to say more. When neither Darmik nor Rema offered further explanation, the king waved his children forward and introduced them.

"We are so very pleased you all could make it," Rema said, her voice so sweet it made Savenek want to gag. "Please come inside for some refreshments."

"We prefer to be seen to our rooms first," King Theon said. "We've had a long journey and wish to freshen up."

"Very well," Darmik replied. "My most trusted advisor will show you to your rooms. Supper and dancing will be held this evening. We look forward to seeing you then." Without waiting for a response, Darmik turned and strolled inside the castle.

Rema, Allyssa, and Savenek hurried and joined him.

Once they were inside, away from the Apethaga royal family, Savenek ran his hands through his hair. "Well, that was awkward."

"If you think that was awkward," Rema said, "just wait. The king and queen of Fren, Odar's parents, are due to arrive within the hour."

Allyssa paled.

Darmik wrapped his arm around her. "It'll be okay," he said. "It won't be much longer until this is over."

"I know," she replied. "It's just that the last time I saw King Viscor and Queen Lutia, they were rather rude toward me, flaunting they didn't need the marriage contract any longer."

Savenek curled his fingers into fists. His poor sister had been kidnapped, drugged, tortured, and when she'd finally escaped, thinking she was getting her happily ever after with Odar, Odar's parents had severed the marriage contract. And to hear her say they did it so callously made him want to punch something—preferably King Viscor.

"Let me know when they arrive," Savenek said. "I have a few things to tend to."

He left before he lost his temper in front of Allyssa. She didn't need to see that. Instead of going to the training room to work out his aggression like he wanted to, he headed toward the infirmary. He needed to check on the healer to see how she was progressing with the antidote. Now that Apethaga was here and Telmena was due to arrive within the next day or two, the antidote was a priority.

Savenek found the elderly healer coming out of a patient's room.

"Prince Savenek," she said, her voice gravely from old age. "Come to my office."

She led him down the hallway to a small room. There was a table in the center and shelves lined the walls. On the shelves were various plants, ferns, and flowers. Built into the ceiling of the office was an oversized window, which allowed the sunlight to filter in.

Savenek instructed his guards to wait out in the hallway. He closed the door and faced the healer. "How's the antidote coming?" An odd smell permeated the room. He couldn't pinpoint where it was coming from.

Picking up a pot of water, the healer started pouring a small amount into the plants on the west wall. "It's coming. I only had the one glass container to work with."

"And Mayra's notes."

"Yes." She set the water pot down and stood before the table in the center of the room. There were several mixing bowls and containers spread over it. "Mayra's paste significantly slowed the poison from spreading throughout your body. However, it didn't stop or neutralize the poison." She pulled one of the bowls forward, picked up a spoon, and started grinding the leaves in it against the side of the bowl. "I had to use a couple of different medicines on you before one of them worked. The trick is to discover if the last one I administered did the trick, or if it was a combination of them that healed you."

On one of the shelves directly behind the healer, a vial with red liquid stood inside of a glass container. "Is that it?"

"Yes. I don't have much left. I've been mixing it with various substances trying to determine what works and what doesn't." She set the bowl aside, then grabbed another one. "Once I mix the leaves from that bowl with the ingredients from this bowl, I can neutralize the poison."

"Meaning?"

"It is no longer harmful to touch or smell."

That was a start. "What about if the poison is ingested?" he asked, coming to stand beside her so he could examine the contents of the bowls in greater detail. "Or, like me, someone is cut with a knife laced with the poison? Does that concoction neutralize the poison once someone is infected with it?"

She raised her head, pinning him with a steady gaze. "I won't know until we test it on someone."

That was what he'd been afraid of. "Let's use one of the Telmena prisoners who brought the poison here." Not that he liked the idea of using a person to test the poison on. However, at least these men had planned to use it on Emperions. It seemed only fitting for the healer to test the antidote on one of them.

She nodded. "You get the poison, and I'll carry the antidote."

Savenek went over and opened the glass container, removing the vial of poison. He carefully set it on the table, trying to think of the best way to do this. "Do you have a cup?"

She pointed at a shelf near the door where odds and ends were. Savenek went over and grabbed a wooden cup. He withdrew his dagger, engraving an "X" on its surface. Then he filled the cup halfway with water. Uncorking the poison, he poured two droplets into it. After re-corking the vial, he set it back in the glass container on the shelf.

The healer mixed the contents of the two bowls together. When she finished, she scraped the antidote into another bowl. "It's ready."

Savenek exited the room, the healer right behind him. After she locked the door, they made their way out of the castle and to the barracks. Inside, Savenek found Neco talking with several soldiers.

"I need your assistance," Savenek said to him.

Neco immediately came over. "Are you going to the dungeon?"

"Yes."

Neco unlocked the door on the left, then led them down the stairwell to the dungeon. "I assume you want one of the Telmena prisoners?"

"I do," Savenek answered.

Neco stopped before one of the cells and unlocked it.

"Back for more," the guy inside taunted. "Think I'll tell you something now?"

Savenek recognized him as the man from under the bridge the night he and Marek had gone out. The man would never willingly drink from the cup knowing it could contain poison. After sizing him up—six feet, one hundred eighty-five pounds—Savenek handed the healer the cup of poison and entered the cell. Reaching for the man's throat, Savenek grabbed him, slamming him onto the floor.

Neco rushed in, pinching the man's nose. Savenek used his weight to pin the man's legs down. The healer entered, carefully holding the cup. She knelt and began pouring it into the man's mouth. He tried spitting it out, but Savenek pushed on the man's stomach. When he did, the prisoner inhaled, ingesting the substance.

Neco released the man's nose, now forcing his mouth closed.

After about a minute, Savenek nodded. They let go of the man, exiting the cell.

"Fools," the prisoner said, his voice hoarse.

"Did either of you get any poison on your skin?" the healer asked.

Savenek examined his hands. "I don't think so."

"I did," Neco said.

"Do you have any cuts?" The healer pulled out a handkerchief.

"No."

"Good." She handed the handkerchief to Neco, and he wiped his hands off. "If it went in through a cut, it would spread much more quickly." She gave him the antidote. "See the spots on your palm?" He nodded. "Put the antidote there."

Neco scooped up some of the paste the healer had made and then spread it on his palm, covering the dark spots. "It already feels better."

Savenek noticed Neco's hands were shaking. They stood there for about a minute, no one talking.

"Do you feel anything burning?" the healer asked.

"No," Neco replied. "I am fine."

She nodded. "I'm glad you're doing well, because he certainly isn't."

They turned to look at the prisoner. His legs were stiff, and white foam ran out of his mouth.

"That happened much quicker than I thought it would," Savenek said. It scared him that only two drops of the poison could be so severe. "How do we administer the antidote?"

"Orally," the healer said. "I need it in his system to see if it works."

Neco opened the cell door. "I hope he's not already dead."

"If it kills that quickly," the healer said, "then no one stands a chance." Hurrying over to the prisoner, she moved to crouch beside him. Using a spoon, she shoved the pasty antidote into his mouth.

The man's eyes rolled back, and he stopped breathing. The healer picked up the cup and bowl, exiting the cell. "He's dead."

"Let's try it again," Neco said. "This time, let's give the antidote first, the poison second. See if that works."

The healer handed the cup to Savenek. There was just enough left inside to try it on one more Telmena prisoner.

Neco led the way farther down the corridor, stopping before another cell.

The man Savenek had knocked out at the inn was inside. He was roughly two hundred pounds, his lumbering frame propped in the corner of the cell. Loud snores emanated from him.

Neco unlocked the door. The healer waved both men back, so the prisoner wouldn't see either of them. Once the healer entered the cell, Savenek couldn't see what she was doing. He heard her talking softly. He wondered what she was saying in order to get him to take the antidote. A minute later, the healer exited and joined them.

"Let's wait five minutes," she whispered. "Then we'll give him the poison."

When the allotted time had passed, Savenek strolled forward until he was standing in front of the prisoner's cell. "Finally," Savenek said, "someone's awake." He squatted. "What are you in here for?" He hoped the man didn't recognize him.

"Why do you care?" the man asked.

"They said I can give a cup of ale to anyone who's in here for stealing but not for murder." He slid the cup between the bars.

The man smiled, revealing a missing tooth. "I'm not in for murder." He heaved himself forward and snatched the cup, gulping it down. "Hey! This ain't ale!"

Savenek jumped to his feet, standing a safe distance away with Neco and the healer. The three of them watched the prisoner. Nothing happened.

"Why's the lot of you standing there?" the man asked.

They didn't answer.

The man's breathing sped up, sweat started to bead on his forehead. After another minute, the man gasped for air. His legs starting to shake, foam bubbled out of his mouth and down his chin. His eyes rolled back.

Neco cursed.

"I'll get back to work," the healer said. "There has to be something that will neutralize the poison once a person ingests it or it enters the bloodstream."

"Why did it work on my hands?" Neco asked.

"Because it hadn't penetrated the surface of your palm yet. If you'd had a cut and the poison got in it, you'd be in the infirmary by now. The poison is slower when it's administered through a wound." She pointed at the dead prisoner. "But if it's swallowed, you're dead within seconds."

Savenek remembered when he'd been cut by the contaminated sword. Within minutes, he'd lost feeling of his arm and leg and had blacked out.

"I have a few more ideas," the healer said. "Give me another day or two and we'll try again."

Savenek hoped they had another day or two to spare.

When Savenek exited the barracks, a soldier ran up to him. "Your Highness," the man said. "You're needed in the Throne Room."

Savenek jogged across the lawn, then entered the castle from one of the side doors. His guards' swords clanked as they ran after him.

Odar's parents must have arrived. *Blasted.* Savenek had wanted to be there with Allyssa. He entered the Throne Room from the front, slowly easing his way across the dais until he stood a few feet from his sister.

The room was only half-full of courtiers. Odar stood with a

couple in their fifties, all facing the dais. Allyssa remained on the first step, Rema and Darmik on either side of her.

"I presume this is your missing son," King Viscor said, his eyebrows raised as he took in Savenek.

Savenek immediately hated the arrogant guy.

"Yes, Father," Odar said. "This is Prince Savenek, the princess's twin brother."

The king slowly inclined his head. Savenek guessed that was as much of a hello as he would get from the prick.

"I must say," the king said to no one in particular, "we're surprised you're still here. We thought that once Princess Allyssa returned, you'd leave again."

Savenek wondered who the *we* he was referring to. Him and his wife? Or Fren and Telmena? Both perhaps.

Rema smiled, and Savenek eagerly anticipated what she had to say to put the king in his place. "I must confess," Rema purred, "when you severed the marriage contract with my daughter, I did not expect for Prince Odar to come groveling back seeking to reestablish the union. Since the original contract was destroyed, we signed another one. This new contract is very beneficial for Emperion, and I'm quite pleased with it."

The king's face contorted with rage.

"It's a good thing you gave your son permission to negotiate terms and sign contracts on your behalf," Darmik added.

"Come, Mother, Father," Odar said. "I'll show you to your rooms." He ushered them from the Throne Room.

Savenek started to ask Allyssa how she was doing, but she glided from the dais and exited the room through a side door. He noticed Neco standing in the shadows of the corridor, watching everything. Neco nodded his chin to the left, and Savenek hurried to join him.

"What is it?" Savenek asked as they headed farther away from the Throne Room.

"Another complication," Neco mumbled. "In here." He entered

a small storage room piled high with boxes. "The mines have successfully been destroyed. We need to figure out how to make sure the Apethaga royal family doesn't hear the news until after they've left the castle."

"I'll see what I can do." Savenek knew a couple of tricks on how to prevent messages from getting through to them. "What else?" Because it seemed like Neco had more to say.

"There have been small riots sprouting up throughout the kingdom of Telmena."

This was both good and bad news. Good because it meant people wouldn't be upset once the king and queen of Telmena were dead. Bad because Kren and Jestina would have to get the citizens under control. "There are things we can do to help." Savenek had a few ideas on how to calm the people *after* the king and queen were dead.

"I'll escort you back to the Royal Chambers."

Savenek was shocked Neco had come to him with this information instead of going straight to Darmik. When they neared the Royal Chambers, he heard several angry voices arguing from within. He raised an eyebrow at Neco, who shook his head.

Savenek opened the door. Allyssa stood with her hands on her hips, her face red. Kerdan was near the hearth, his back to everyone in the room. Darmik paced behind the sofa where Rema was perched, her back ramrod straight.

"Is everything okay?" Savenek asked. Had Kerdan done something to upset Allyssa? If he had, Savenek would pummel him right there in the middle of the sitting room. He stretched his neck, loosening up. The last time he'd fought Kerdan, the guy had gotten in some good punches. This time, Savenek was sure Kerdan wouldn't be so lucky.

"Princess Conditto," Allyssa said, her voice clipped, "informed everyone of her impending marriage to Kerdan. She even had the nerve to suggest she and Kerdan wed while they are both here." Allyssa's face was getting redder as she spoke. "Conditto asked the empress if she and Kerdan could hold their ceremony after Odar and I wed."

Savenek wondered why Allyssa was so upset. He glanced over at Darmik, who shook his head ever so slightly. Savenek kept his mouth shut.

Neco excused himself and exited the room. Savenek wished he could do the same.

"Allyssa," Rema said, her voice calm and placating. "Telmena is due to arrive any day. I need you to get your temper under control. Everyone thinks you're engaged to Odar, so you cannot be upset over anything related to Kerdan."

"I don't want to watch that evil woman put her hands on my man, Mother."

Savenek raised his hand to point out Kerdan had to see her with Odar, but Darmik shook his head again. Savenek closed his mouth, forcing himself to keep quiet.

Kerdan pivoted to face Rema. "What's our plan?"

"How would you normally respond to an allegation such as this?" Rema asked him.

"I would demand to see the contract."

Rema smiled. "And that is what you will do. You will speak with King Theon and ask to see the signed contract. Inform him you know nothing of the engagement and are quite surprised."

"I agree with Rema," Savenek said. "If Kerdan goes along with the marriage contract, they might think he's working with Emperion." Savenek was the one who'd discovered the information and told Rema and Darmik about it in the first place. "However," and now for the part his sister was going to hate, "Kerdan should state he is willing to discuss a potential alliance through marriage as the Russek king."

Tears welled in Allyssa's eyes.

"That is a wise move," Rema said. "Demand to see the contract, state it isn't valid, and then propose negotiations. That not only makes sure the contract is null and void, but it also buys us additional time."

"Conditto isn't a flirt," Savenek said, trying to appease his sister. If it was Lareissa, Savenek would say Allyssa had reason to be concerned. But Conditto was cold.

"I should go to my bedchamber and prepare for tonight," Kerdan said. He left the room before Allyssa could say a word.

"Allyssa," Rema said.

"I don't want to hear it." Allyssa held up her hand, whirled around, then stormed out of the room.

"I'll talk to her," Savenek said, even though he didn't have the slightest idea what to say. He went to Allyssa's bedchamber where he found her standing at the window, staring outside.

"I don't need you to tell me I'm overreacting, being unreasonable, or that I need to calm down. I already know."

Savenek chuckled. "If you already know, then why are you acting this way?" If the situation was reversed, he'd feel the same way. The difference was he'd hide it while Allyssa wore her emotions plain on her face for everyone to see.

"I can't help it." She spun in his direction. "When I was in Russek, I saw Kerdan wear so many different masks. I finally uncovered the real Kerdan. And now, we're asking him to wear another mask. I hate it."

Understanding this was more than mere jealousy, Savenek came farther into the room and sat on the sofa, propping his feet on the low table in front of it. "Isn't that what you do every day, though? Play different roles?"

Allyssa came over and sat next to him, leaning her head against his shoulder. The act of seeking comfort and familiarity stunned him.

"I suppose," she muttered. "I know I act one way in front of members of our court, one way in front of my family, and yet another when I'm out in the town."

"Each job I perform requires a different personality." The

beggar, the shopkeeper, the prince, the diplomat…the list went on and on. "Sometimes it can be fun. Most of the time, however, it is difficult not to lose who I am underneath the façade."

She lifted her head, staring directly into his eyes. "That's exactly it."

"I'm sure Kerdan knows and understands this. I wouldn't worry."

"I know you're right. And I know we'll both continue to wear masks throughout our lives."

Savenek couldn't believe he was going to say this. "Kerdan's a good man. You don't need to worry about him being unfaithful or untrustworthy."

"It's not like I'm jealous." Folding her arms, she pouted. "Well, maybe I am just a little bit."

"You have nothing to worry about." Savenek had been going over it in his head. Originally, Jana was the one insisting on the marriages to tie the kingdoms together. Now that Jana was dead, what reason could Apethaga have to want the marriage to go through? The only reason Savenek could think of was to thwart Telmena. Without the marriage, Apethaga would always be under Telmena's thumb. But with such an advantageous marriage, Apethaga would be strong enough to stand against Telmena. Which meant Emperion might have a chance at getting Apethaga over to their side.

Savenek sighed. Things were getting rather complicated, and Telmena wasn't even here yet.

CHAPTER 18

Allyssa

"Your Highness," Nathenek said to Allyssa. "Can I please have a moment of your time?"

"Of course." She pushed her chair back and stood, thankful to be leaving the Dining Hall. She didn't think she could sit there and finish her breakfast while pretending not to look at Kerdan, who was sitting next to Conditto. Allyssa wanted to tear the woman's eyes out.

She followed Nathenek out of the room. In the corridor, her guard fell in step behind her. They entered the library and Allyssa breathed in the smell of books, immediately feeling more relaxed. Her guard remained near the entrance. She went over to her alcove. The drapes were open. She didn't remember leaving them that way when she left here yesterday. Maybe one of the servants had cleaned the area for her. She sat on the bench, motioning for Nathenek to sit across from her. The stack of books she'd been reading was in the middle of the table, so she shoved them closer to the window. She thought she'd organized them into two stacks—ones she had to read and ones she wanted to read.

"Two things," Nathenek said, pulling something out of his pocket. He set a tiny glass jar on the table. "I want you to swallow the contents of this."

"What is it?"

"It could be an antidote for the poison Apethaga has been producing."

"Could be?"

"The healer is still working on it. However, since Telmena is due to arrive today, I want you to take it. It's better than nothing."

She reached forward and took the glass jar, uncorking it. It smelled like rotten fish.

"Pinch your nose. It'll help."

"Did you give some to Savenek already?"

"No, you're first. I'll administer it to your parents and brother next."

She pinched her nose and tossed the contents of the jar in her mouth, swallowing the thick gooey substance as quickly as possible. It got stuck in her throat, making her gag. Nathenek withdrew a flask and handed it to her. She chugged it, washing the gooey stuff down. Her throat burned, and she slammed the flask on the table.

"That was ale," he said. "I only meant for you to have a sip." He took the flask and the jar, closing both and putting them away. "Now for the second item of business."

Allyssa leaned back on the bench, her chest feeling warm and her head pounding. Her foot hit something. Glancing under the table, she saw something had fallen on the floor. When she reached down, she picked up a book and a scrap of material—one of Mayra's handkerchiefs. The book was about a woman who fought for the king in his army of men. She set it on the table, sure she'd loaned it to Mayra seasons ago. Mayra had returned it —she was certain of it. So how had her book and Mayra's handkerchief gotten on the floor?

"Everyone is watching you," Nathenek said, recapturing her attention.

"I know."

"You're not doing a good enough job."

"What?" She sat up straighter.

"If we're going to pull this off, you need to act the part. You're marrying Odar. You're smitten with Odar. You're too stupid to suspect he's using you."

She folded her arms. "I'm not going to act like an idiot."

"I'm not asking you to. I'm telling you to pretend you're in love with Odar and stop publicly mooning at Kerdan. He has his own part to play."

"Can't we just kill them all and get it over with?" She put her elbows on the table and massaged her temple. Playing these dangerous games was taking its toll on her.

"I wish we could." He chuckled. "To be the leader we need to be, there is an order to how things must be done. Talks first, assassinations second."

"Fine. I'll pretend to be a naive woman in love with Odar."

"And you'll stop watching Kerdan. Even when you think no one is paying attention, someone is."

"Very well."

"Remember, act as nonthreatening as possible. Talk about clothes, hairstyles, and things along those lines. Give them what they expect, and that's what they'll see."

"Anything else?" she asked.

He leaned back on the bench, assessing her. "How are things going between you and Savenek?"

"They're going well." Especially now that they weren't trying to outdo each other. "Why do you ask?"

"I'm worried about him. He's had to deal with a lot over the last few weeks. He's not as tough as you think."

She found that hard to believe. Savenek was not only raised by Nathenek, but he was also in the Brotherhood. He was as tough as they came.

Nathenek's face was serious. "Keep an eye out for him."

"I will."

"He won't ask for help, even if he needs it."

As much as she hated to admit it, she understood not wanting to ask for help.

A soldier ran into the library. "Your Highness! Telmena has just arrived. Your parents want you outside."

As Allyssa made her way to the front of the castle, she spotted Kerdan striding along one of the corridors, his men close behind him. They were quite a remarkable sight. All four wore drab pants and tunics with furs draped over their shoulders. Kerdan also wore a simple crown to show his status, but other than that, no one would ever know he was the king of Russek.

Allyssa tried not to smile as she watched people practically falling over themselves to get out of the Russek men's way. Then she remembered her recent conversation with Nathenek and forced herself to look away.

"Sister," Savenek said as he came up alongside her, his hands clasped behind his back.

"Brother," she replied, playing along with him.

"Shall we go meet our most esteemed guests together?" His eyes sparkled with mischief.

"We shall." She tried not to laugh.

He held out his arm, and she took it. They made their way to the front of the castle where Rema and Darmik stood waiting.

Several carriages were parked in the courtyard; however, no one had exited yet. A few more carriages rolled in, parking alongside the ones already there.

"This is a bit extreme," Rema mumbled.

"It's just a show of wealth," Darmik replied.

"Or they could be transporting a lot of soldiers or a copious amount of poison in those carriages," Savenek pointed out.

Everyone looked at him.

"What?" he asked innocently. "I'm just stating the possibilities."

Her brother analyzed things differently than she did. Sometimes Allyssa wondered what was going on inside that head of his.

Odar came running out of the castle. "Sorry I'm late." He stood next to Allyssa, kissing her cheek.

She released Savenek, forced a smile on her face, and said, "I'm just glad you're here." Reaching out, she took hold of his arm, hugging it. She wished he hadn't kissed her—even though it was only on the cheek. It made her uncomfortable, and it wasn't necessary.

"My parents wish to have tea with you this afternoon."

"That will be lovely," she said, trying not to cringe at the thought. She didn't want to spend any time with them.

"Your parents are invited as well."

"We'll see," Rema said. "Now that everyone has arrived, I'm going to call a meeting this afternoon. I don't want these people here any longer than necessary."

"I agree," Savenek said. "The longer they're here, the higher the likelihood something could go wrong."

Savenek was always so pragmatic. Darmik was right to hand the army over to him.

Odar put his mouth close to Allyssa's ear and whispered, "Relax. We want this fixed the right way since we will be dealing with these kingdoms for decades. It is better we come to an understanding now rather than have years of conflict."

She took a deep breath. Odar was right. But it didn't mean she had to like the role she played. Allyssa was eager for this entire ordeal to be over. "How long are we going to stand here?"

"Good question." Darmik waved one of his soldiers over. "Find out where the royal family is. Either they exit the carriage within the next five minutes, or we're going inside—even if it's considered rude on our part. I will not have my wife standing here unnecessarily."

"Yes, Your Majesty." Hurrying over to one of the drivers, the soldier gestured he wanted a word.

"My parents confirmed my brother and his wife stayed in Telmena," Odar said.

Excellent. At least they had that going for them. Now if only the king, queen, and prince would exit, they could get on with it. Thick clouds rolled in, concealing the sun. The chilly air held the promise of rain.

A third row of carriages rolled in. There had to be fifteen in all.

"You have got to be kidding me. This is worse than that production you put on," Allyssa said, jabbing Odar in the side.

He chuckled. "That seems like a lifetime ago."

Because it was.

A dozen soldiers exited from the first row. They surrounded one of the carriages in the third row. That had to be the one the royal family was traveling in. When the door swung open, a man descended. Allyssa didn't know what she expected, but this was not it. The man was in his late sixties with gray hair. He wore what appeared to be tights on the bottom half of his legs with short, puffy pants on the top. His tunic was rather frilly, making the entire outfit seem feminine. Not at all imposing or intimidating.

Next, a woman exited. Her dress contained layers and layers of fabric. Allyssa wondered how the woman moved without falling over or getting stuck in a doorway. The top part of the dress was tight, her breasts bulging up and down as the she breathed. Her graying hair was artfully arranged on top of her head with flowers entwined throughout.

Another man followed her out. He appeared to be about thirty with dark hair and dark eyes. He wore clothing similar to the other gentleman's.

The newcomers came before Rema and Darmik. One of the

Telmena soldiers said, "His Royal Highness, King Metek, and Her Royal Highness, Queen Cora." The king and queen bowed. "And their son, Prince Jem." The prince bowed.

Darmik stepped forward. "It's good to see you, cousin," he said to Metek. "I'd like to introduce my wife, Empress Rema; my son, Prince Savenek; and my daughter, Princess Allyssa. I'm sure you've already met Prince Odar of Fren."

The informal way Darmik spoke surprised Allyssa. However, he must be doing it for a reason. She needed to make sure she played along. Obviously, the Telmena royal family was dressed in their best, trying to exude wealth.

"Father," Allyssa said, "you forgot to say I'm engaged to Odar."

"Ah, yes," Darmik said with a smile. "But I'm sure they already knew that since they're here for your wedding."

Beaming, Allyssa gazed up at Odar. His face was neutral as if he couldn't care less. Yes, they all played their parts exceedingly well.

"We are hosting a ball tonight to welcome all our esteemed guests," Rema said. "But before then, we are asking that our royal visitors meet in the Great Hall. I think it wise that we introduce everyone. What do you think, Your Highness?"

The king nodded. "That is a good idea. Are we the last to arrive?"

"Yes," Darmik answered. "Every royal family from the mainland is now here."

"Excellent." The king exchanged a brief look with his son.

Allyssa knew her parents and Savenek all caught the gesture. However, they just smiled and pretended as if everyone at the castle were the best of friends.

Darmik didn't want either Savenek or Allyssa needlessly wandering around the castle with Telmena there. Since the meeting between all the kingdoms didn't start for another hour, Allyssa went to her bedchamber to wait.

Mayra knocked and came in. "Want some company?"

Allyssa hugged her dearest friend. "Yes." It felt like they hadn't had any time together lately.

"Have you heard the news?" Mayra asked.

There was constant news, so Allyssa wasn't sure to what Mayra was referring.

"Madelin returned. She just arrived with her parents."

"Audek and Vesha are here?" They rarely came to court.

Mayra nodded and sat on the sofa.

"Is Vesha still a great healer?" Allyssa asked, taking a seat next to her friend.

"She is. Your mother said she wanted Vesha here as a precautionary measure."

Probably in case someone was exposed to the poison. Or to even help complete the antidote for it.

"Will you be at the ball this evening?" Allyssa asked.

"Yes. Your father wants me to remain close to the Telmena family so I can eavesdrop on their conversations."

Allyssa didn't like her friend taking on these dangerous assignments. "If you're there, won't the Apethaga family recognize you?" And if they did, wouldn't they make sure the Telmenas didn't say anything around her?

"I'm going in disguise." She played with the edge of her sleeve. "Savenek is helping me prepare." The corners of her lips rose ever so slightly as she fought a smile.

Allyssa rolled her eyes. "I'm sure he is."

Now Mayra did smile. "Savenek is conceited."

"Yes, he is."

"He's stubborn."

"Most definitely."

"He's skilled with a sword."

Allyssa had only seen him shoot a bow and arrow and throw

daggers. He'd excelled at both, so she could only assume he knew how to handle a sword.

"He's pretty much perfect. At least, perfect for me." Mayra stood.

Allyssa had never seen her friend in love before. It was strange to have her brother and best friend smitten with each other. She supposed that meant they would always be in her life in some capacity.

"I need to go and prepare," Mayra said as she headed to the door. "Odar will be here shortly to escort you to the meeting." When she reached the door, she paused. "Go over to your bookshelf and knock three times." She exited the room without further explanation.

Allyssa jumped up from the sofa. The last time the bookshelf had opened, Kerdan visited her. Of course, it could just be Savenek wanting to talk without their parents knowing. Either way, she went over to the bookshelf and knocked as Mayra had instructed. A moment later, it swung open and Kerdan entered. She threw her arms around him, holding him tightly.

"I know I shouldn't be here," he whispered into her hair, "but I had to see you."

She breathed in the smell of him. "I'm so glad you're here." She didn't want to let go.

"We need to talk before the meeting." Taking her hand, he led her over to the sofa where they sat next to one another. "There have been a few developments you need to be aware of." His brows were pinched together with worry.

Fear shot through her. "Is everything all right?"

"As soon as you're married to Odar, the Telmena king and queen plan to assassinate Rema, Darmik, and Savenek. The only reason they are going to leave you alive is so you can control the Emperion people for them."

Although the news was shocking, it didn't change their plans.

"The king and queen will be dead before they can kill my family." Because Savenek's plan would work. It just had to.

"I agree." His forehead creased.

She reached out, cupping his cheek and feeling his stubble against her palm. "What is it?" she asked, afraid there was more he was withholding.

"They have to believe you're marrying Odar," he said. "If they suspect anything, they'll kill Rema, Darmik, and Savenek. Then they'll force you to marry Odar."

It wouldn't come to that. She would do everything in her power to make sure things progressed as planned. But she wasn't stupid, and if her time in Russek had taught her anything, it was that nothing ever went as planned. Panic surged through her.

Kerdan leaned his forehead against hers. "Allyssa," he whispered.

She could feel his soft breath caress her skin.

He reached up and slid his hand around the back of her neck, holding her in place. His touch sent a jolt of pleasure through her. "Make sure you're armed at all times. Pretend you hate me." He squeezed her neck infinitesimally. "Make everyone believe you're in love with Odar. Play your part so well that even I believe it."

Her heart squeezed with panic. "I don't want to."

"I know," he murmured, his lips hovering next to hers.

"I love you," she said.

"I know that, too." He kissed her.

She climbed onto his lap, wanting to be as close to him as possible. Wanting him to know how much she loved him.

"I must go," he said. "Before your father finds me in here."

She wrapped her arms around him, hugging him one last time.

"Please be safe," he said. "And if anyone tries to hurt you, don't hesitate to kill him. Because if you don't, I will."

～

Allyssa strode into the Great Hall. The tables had been moved to the center of the room, forming a long rectangle. Most of the kings and queens from the various kingdoms were already assembled. Rema and Darmik had asked the rulers from Fren, Kricok, and Landania to attend not as a courtesy to those kingdoms, but for show. Having six additional people there to voice support for Emperion would help sway the other kingdoms to see things their way.

Allyssa took a seat between Savenek and Odar. Odar's parents were seated on his other side. She smiled coyly at her pretend fiancé, batting her eyelashes and trying to look smitten—but feeling utterly stupid.

Odar scooted closer and whispered, "I'm trying so hard not to laugh right now."

She wanted to punch him. Instead, she stole a kiss at the edge of his lips. He leaned into her, making the kiss last a second longer than it should have. Allyssa forced herself to remain focused on Odar and not seek Kerdan out to discover if he'd been watching her. She didn't even know if he was there since she hadn't allowed herself to look.

Odar reached out and took hold of her hand. As they sat there waiting for Rema and Darmik to arrive, Allyssa tried not to feel guilty for kissing Odar. She'd only done it to make sure everyone bought the lie. A moment later, the empress and emperor entered the room, sitting in the two empty chairs next to Savenek.

"Thank you all for coming," Rema said. "I thought it wise for us to use this unique opportunity to talk to one another." She scanned the room. "Is everyone here?"

"Your Majesty," Savenek said. "We are missing King Kerdan as well as the entire royal family from Telmena."

Relief filled Allyssa. Kerdan hadn't seen her kiss Odar. She discreetly pulled her hand free from Odar's firm grip.

The door swung open, and Kerdan strode in. "Sorry I'm late," he said, not sounding sorry at all. He did, however, sound slightly out of breath. Allyssa wondered what he'd been up to. There was an empty chair next to Conditto and he quickly took his seat, scanning the room. "What's first on our agenda?"

"I'd like to discuss two items," Rema said, "peace and trade. Does anyone else have anything they'd like to add?"

No one did.

"Excellent, then let's begin. The previous events with Russek were very disconcerting. I would like to prevent something like that from happening again."

Everyone agreed.

"I propose we sign a treaty," Rema continued. "The treaty will state that each kingdom will remain within its borders, and no one will overthrow, invade, or takeover another kingdom through force. If a kingdom raises its army against another kingdom, everyone on the mainland will band together to retaliate."

"I agree," Kerdan stated. "I will sign the treaty."

"So will we," King Viscor said. "I've had enough fighting and killing."

The king and queen from Dromien agreed.

"What about Melenia?" King Theon asked. "Who will control that kingdom?"

A good question. Allyssa knew Russek had withdrawn its troops from Melenia. The kingdom was still trying to recover from the mass slaughter that had occurred there.

"Does anyone have any suggestions?" Rema asked.

"I think we should leave Melenia alone to figure it out," Kerdan said. "I'm sure there is someone still alive from the royal family who can rule."

"Say that is the case," Theon said, "they are not here to sign the treaty."

"What if we left a space for the future ruler of Melenia to sign?" Rema suggested. "Then, once he or she claims the throne, we can send a letter inviting them to sign the treaty?"

Everyone but Apethaga agreed.

"King Theon?" Rema said. "Do you agree as well?"

He shifted uncomfortably on his seat, darting his gaze around the room. "Yes," he said finally, "I will agree to those terms."

"Excellent. My scribe will compose the treaty now for us to sign." Rema folded her hands.

Kerdan was about to say something when the door opened and the king and queen from Telmena entered. Allyssa took note that the prince was not with them. She hoped Neco or Nathenek was keeping an eye on him while the royal families met.

King Metek and Queen Cora sat. When the king went to say something, Rema cut him off. "As soon as my scribe is finished, the treaty will be passed around for everyone to read and sign."

"You should not have started without me," King Metek said.

"You shouldn't have been late," Kerdan said, glaring at Metek.

"I won't sign a treaty unless I have a say," Metek said.

"We are simply agreeing to peace," Rema assured him. "We're all willing to stay within our borders."

"That is not acceptable."

Silence descended over the room.

"Why not?" Kerdan demanded.

"I don't answer to you," Metek said.

Rema leaned forward. "It has come to our attention that King Metek believes he should be the emperor of Emperion, am I correct?" Rema asked the king.

"I should be," he replied.

"So you do not seek peace. Rather, you are here to either assassinate me or overthrow me."

The king's eyes narrowed as he stared at Rema. "I am here for the wedding."

"In addition to declaring war against my kingdom." She'd thrown down the gauntlet, laying it all out on the table.

Allyssa had no idea how the king would respond. Everyone in the room seemed to be holding their breath, waiting for him to say something.

It was Kerdan who spoke next. "Why do you think you should rule Emperion?"

"As you are well aware, the previous emperor, Hamen, was my uncle. Rema murdered and overthrew him." The king folded his arms, glaring at no one in particular.

Rema cleared her throat and said, "He was not the true emperor. He did not bear the tattoo marking him as the legitimate ruler."

"I should be ruling Emperion," Metek insisted.

"I can show you documentation that dates back over a century," Rema said. "I'll prove to you, and everyone here, that I am the rightful heir and you hold no claim. Once I've shown you everything, I will insist you sign the treaty and leave us alone."

"I will do no such thing."

"I'm curious," Darmik said, speaking for the first time. "Emperor Hamen was my father. I sit on the Emperion throne. You are my cousin. Why do you think you hold a stronger bid for the throne than me?"

"You murdered your own sister, Jana," the king said. "My niece. I've been aiding her for years since you so callously banned her from Emperion."

Allyssa pursed her lips, trying to keep her temper under control. She wanted to yell at Metek that Jana was a deceitful, lying, murderous wench who got what she deserved. Odar slid his hand onto her thigh, squeezing it. The contact did the trick, and she reined in her temper.

"I am asking you to leave Emperion alone," Darmik said. "Make no claim against the kingdom. Let us have peace."

King Metek turned to King Theon. "Did you agree to this nonsense?"

"We did," Theon said.

Allyssa studied the elder two siblings, Patteon and Conditto. Both had their heads down, so she couldn't see their facial expressions.

"Why?" Metek demanded.

"We do not care to go to war," Theon stated.

"But we had a deal," Metek said, his voice low and furious. "We won't protect you if you back out."

"You can't control the entire mainland," Theon said. "And if we all ban together to take over Emperion and fail, then Emperion will control the entire mainland. By agreeing to this treaty, we are guaranteed to maintain control over Apethaga. Quite frankly, that is enough for me."

The corners of Conditto's lips rose as she fought a smile. Did the woman actually think Kerdan would marry her? Allyssa's temper started to rise again. Apethaga would be sitting pretty thinking they'd keep control over their kingdom plus have their eldest daughter sitting on the Russek throne. It was far better than being under Telmena's thumb.

"I agree," Viscor said. "This treaty is beneficial for us all. It guarantees we keep what we have. We can put our resources into helping our people instead of keeping a large standing army."

As much as Allyssa didn't like Odar's father, she had to hand it to him. Reminding people that he had a large army without actually saying he had a large army was a wise move. And she appreciated the fact he was backing Emperion. Of course, from his point of view, his son was marrying into the Emperion royal family, which would be hugely beneficial for them.

Which meant that someone had to be vying for Savenek. Who had the most to benefit from such a union? As far as she knew, Lareissa of Apethaga was engaged to Jem of Telmena. That was advantageous for those two kingdoms. However, neither Lareissa nor Jem were first in line for the throne. Conditto clearly was still vying for a union with Kerdan. Allyssa was due to marry Odar. They were both first in line for their thrones. She was surprised Jem hadn't made a serious bid for her hand. Or Patteon. Actually, now that she was considering the matter, Patteon should have courted her since they were both first in line. Not that she would have agreed, but it would have made sense.

That still left Savenek. Would Lareissa find him more appealing than Jem? Allyssa almost laughed. Of course she would. However, the contract had already been signed between Lareissa and Jem. Allyssa found all of this very interesting. Although, she had a nagging suspicion she was missing something.

"I won't sign the treaty," Metek said.

The scribe handed the treaty to Rema. Rema read through it before signing her name with a flourish at the bottom. She passed the treaty to Viscor.

"I must say," Rema addressed Metek, "that I am disappointed. I'd hoped to avoid war. However, you are entitled to your opinion. I appreciate you coming here and at least talking with us."

Viscor passed the treaty to Theon, who read through and signed it. When he finished, he passed it to Kerdan. After Kerdan signed it, he passed it to the king from Dromien.

"Thank you all for coming," Darmik said.

Allyssa stood, eager to get out of there. Odar took her arm and escorted her to the exit. She could feel Metek's eyes following her every move. Odar's hand tightened on her. He must have sensed it, too.

CHAPTER 19

Savenek entered the Dining Hall, which was already filled with royalty and members of court. Everyone sat at the tables talking, having a merry time as they ate. Hopefully, the food was safe and hadn't been contaminated with poison. After the meeting—if one could even call it that—Savenek wouldn't put it past King Metek to poison everyone and take control of the entire mainland. The king was crazy enough to do it.

Strolling past courtiers, he smiled and nodded as he made his way to the head table where he took a seat next to his sister. He wished Mayra was here to keep him company. However, she was working on deciphering a letter written by King Metek. After the meeting, the king had stormed back to his room and composed the letter. He gave it to one of his servants to deliver. Since Savenek had a member of the Brotherhood watching the king, the spy followed the servant, who had given the letter to one of the Telmena soldiers. The spy had managed to copy the letter before the soldier destroyed it. When Savenek saw the letter had been written in a way that made no sense to him, he gave it to Mayra to decipher. Mayra said it was written in some sort of code, and she needed time to figure it out. She'd been holed up in his office ever since.

"What's wrong?" Allyssa asked, concern etching her voice. She held a fork in her hand as if eating, but he knew she was just pretending. He was, too. A precautionary measure—just in case the food had been tampered with.

"Nothing." He didn't want to worry her; she already had enough to deal with.

Rema and Darmik entered. They stopped to speak to several people as they made their way to the head table.

Darmik wanted the family to meet in the Royal Chambers after the ball tonight to finalize their plans for assassinating Metek, Cora, and Jem. For once, Rema hadn't tried to stall or insist on more talks. She'd agreed they should move forward—the sooner, the better. Since then, Savenek had been on edge.

"I wonder what Marek is doing here," Allyssa mused. "He told me he'd remain in the corridor with the rest of my guard since my parents had so many sentries present in the room."

Savenek stood, knowing exactly what it meant. "Mayra must have finished deciphering the letter." He casually strolled across the room, making sure to nod and smile to a few of the courtiers along the way.

"Is she done?" Savenek asked Marek.

"She is." He nodded toward the door, and they exited the Dining Hall. They made their way to the corridor where the offices were located. Marek entered Neco's office, holding the door open for Savenek.

Once they were alone, Marek rested his hand on the hilt of his sword. "Mayra was able to decipher the letter. King Metek gave one of his soldiers a direct order to kill the empress, emperor, and the prince."

"But not the princess?" Savenek asked, immediately understanding why they'd want her alive—to secure the throne.

"Correct."

"Have you told my parents yet?" He realized after the fact that he'd called Rema and Darmik his parents. He wondered when he'd started thinking of them that way.

"No. Mayra came to me, asking that I tell you immediately."

"I need to go and speak with them." He felt for the daggers hidden in his sleeves, around his waist, and in his pants. They were all there. "Did the letter say when the assassinations were to take place?" He'd hoped Metek, Cora, and Jem would leave the castle tomorrow. Once they left, he intended to make sure a fatal accident befell them. However, before he could worry about killing them, he had to eliminate the soldier. He ran his hands through his hair. Nathenek was the man for this job. He needed to find him immediately.

"The soldier was instructed to kill you and your parents after the wedding tomorrow."

They had plenty of time then.

"Mayra asked that you be careful," Marek said.

"I will."

"Yes, you will. I won't have my sister worrying needlessly about you."

Savenek headed for the door. "I'll inform my parents. You find Nathenek. Tell him to take care of the soldier. I assume you know who the soldier is?" If not, they could just remove all Telmena soldiers from the grounds. There were only two dozen or so in the barracks.

"Yes, we've identified the soldier who received the letter and he's being watched."

"Excellent." The next twenty-four hours were going to be intense.

SAVENEK ENTERED THE GREAT HALL WHERE THE BALL was being held. Musicians played in one corner while the people meandered around the edges. All the dancing took place in the center of the room. Many were talking about Allyssa and Odar's wedding, which was due to take place tomorrow.

Several people were watching Savenek. He made sure to

smile as he made his way over to Prince Zek. When he'd spoken to his parents a few moments ago, they were adamant he proceed as if nothing had changed and he didn't know about his own assassination. Since he'd spent his entire life in the shadows, it was now hard to be the center of attention. Nathenek was off hunting the Telmena soldier while Savenek attended the ball. It went against his training—being the one here doing nothing while the Brotherhood and Emperion soldiers protected him.

"Prince Savenek," Prince Zek said. "My father wants confirmation that the only kingdom that didn't sign the treaty is Telmena?"

"You are correct." Even at a ball, all anyone wanted to discuss was politics. Did it never end?

"What does Emperion intend to do about it?"

Savenek cocked his head at the man, trying to act puzzled. "Nothing." He shrugged. "We can't force them to do something they don't want to do." He reminded himself to be aloof, noncommittal, and nonthreatening. He felt like a fraud. It was at that moment he realized if he was going to do this—be the prince of Emperion—that he needed to be the prince he wanted to be: strong, reliable, dependable, and a leader. When this threat with Telmena was over, Savenek would talk to Darmik about that. Until then, he could play along.

"You do understand that they will wage war on Emperion, correct? Now that we are part of Emperion, that includes my people."

"Does it?" Savenek said. "Well, I wouldn't worry about it. I'm sure the empress and emperor have everything under control." He forced himself to walk away before he told the guy that the Telmena royal family would be dead soon.

If only Mayra was here so Savenek could dance with her. She would help ease his nerves. He ran his hands through his hair with the realization he was nervous. Was it because he had a family being threatened? That he cared for Rema, Darmik, and Allyssa?

The herald announced Princess Allyssa and Prince Odar. The pair entered the Great Hall, smiling at everyone in attendance. After them, Rema and Darmik entered. Savenek took a moment to closely observe his family. While his sister looked regal in her red dress with her hair done all fancy, the lines around her eyes were tight, her mouth pinched with worry. Rema and Darmik both headed straight for King Metek and Queen Cora. Savenek knew neither of his parents wanted to deal with or speak to the Telmena royals, but they chose to do their duty. He had to respect that.

Music and dancing resumed.

"The last time I spoke to you, you were in a dungeon," Princess Lareissa crooned from behind Savenek.

He forced his body to remain relaxed instead of tensing up at the mere sound of her sultry voice. Plastering a half smile on his face, he regarded her from under hooded eyes and said, "I heard you are engaged to Prince Jem." He nodded at the prince from Telmena and smirked. The guy was at least twice her age.

"We shall see if that happens," she said, lips going from plump and seductive to a tight line.

The contract had already been signed. While he doubted Lareissa wanted to marry Jem, she didn't have much say in the matter. If King Theon wanted his daughter to marry Jem, she would. He tried not to feel sorry for her. "Dance with me." Without giving her a chance to respond, Savenek took her arm and led her to the dance floor. "Too bad you and I couldn't have been matched."

She placed her right hand far too low on his back for comfort. Maybe it was better Mayra wasn't here to see this. Knowing he had a part to play, he left her hand there and continued dancing.

Lareissa smiled seductively at Savenek. "You are second in line behind your sister."

He never got the impression she sought power. Pleasure,

diversion from boredom, and adventure perhaps. But not power. "You're fourth in line now; if you marry Jem, you'll be second in line. So no matter what, you will not sit on the throne. We are alike in that." He spun her around and pulled her to him, resting one hand on the small of her back, which just so happened to be bare.

"If you think I am happy with my status, that I will just sit around being told what to do my entire life, then you don't know me as well as I thought you did." Her eyes flashed with fury.

An idea suddenly occurred to him. If Lareissa wanted a throne, all she had to do was kill Allyssa. Then Savenek would be the crown heir. Suddenly, he feared for his sister's life. Lareissa had access to poison, and he wouldn't put it past her to slip something in Allyssa's food or drink.

"You always were fun," he whispered in her ear. He needed to get Lareissa out of here.

She laughed, the sound deep and sensual. "And you always were a flirt."

The song ended. "Let's go somewhere we can be alone." He started to leave, pulling her along with him.

"I want to stay," she said, refusing to budge.

Thunder boomed through the sky, making the candles flicker. Savenek turned to face her. He slowly leaned in and whispered, "And I want to see you out of that dress." Although, half her body was already exposed, revealing voluptuous breasts and smooth, silky skin.

She trailed a finger over his lips and down his neck. "There will be time for that. Later. For now, dance with me."

Not wanting her to see his hesitation, he wrapped his arms around her, holding her close. As long as he was with Lareissa, she couldn't harm his sister. He just couldn't let her out of his sight until he managed to tie her up somewhere.

Savenek scanned the people around him, wanting to make sure Allyssa was a safe distance away. Three yards to the right, Kerdan was dancing with Conditto, both stiff and rigid with about a foot of space between their bodies. Savenek tried not to laugh. He spotted Allyssa with Odar standing off to the side, near the food table, talking to King Viscor and Queen Lutia. That had to be an awkward conversation for Allyssa, and one he wished he could interrupt. The only consolation was they were a good fifty feet away.

When the music ended, Savenek released Lareissa and they clapped for the musicians. Lareissa started making her way over to the food table. Savenek hurried and caught up to her, wrapping an arm around her waist.

"I'm thirsty," she said, a small pout on her lips. "Get me something to drink."

He had no intention of leaving her side or taking her any closer to Allyssa. Leaning down, he kissed her cheek, his lips lingering there. "Are you sure you don't want to go somewhere we can be alone?" He kept his arm firmly around her waist.

"Maybe later."

He scanned the nearby servants, trying to catch someone's attention. He could have sworn he just saw Mayra, but he lost sight of her in the crowd.

Kerdan stood not far away, his eyebrows drawn together in worry. Kerdan tilted his head to the side, silently questioning Savenek. Savenek didn't know how to convey that Allyssa was in danger without sending Kerdan into a panic. The guy could be a little intense, and now was not the time for a Russek to be parading around, swinging his sword.

Lareissa used Savenek's momentary distraction to wiggle free from his hold. When he moved to grab her again, she quickly stepped away.

"What are you doing?" she said a little louder than necessary. The people closest to them all turned to stare.

"I'm trying to dance with you," Savenek said with a smile, "but you keep slipping away from me."

"That is because I'm going to get something to drink." Challenge shone in her eyes.

It was time to get her out of there. Forcibly if necessary. Unfortunately, her parents were standing close by. Savenek would have to come up with a viable excuse later. For now, she had to go. He reached forward to grab hold of her waist. He intended to use a pressure point to subdue her so he could take her from the room without causing a scene. As he reached for her, Lareissa withdrew a knife, holding it discreetly in her palm. She smirked, daring him to try something.

Not wanting to be impaled with the weapon, he stepped to the side, grabbed her wrist, and squeezed. She dropped the knife, and he placed his boot over it.

"Let me go or I'll scream," Lareissa said.

Savenek was going to make a scene. Oh well. His sister's safety was his first priority. He let go of Lareissa's wrist and reached for her arms, intending to pin them down.

Someone hit Savenek from behind, and he stumbled. "Keep your filthy hands off my sister," Patteon said.

Lareissa withdrew another knife, staring in Allyssa's direction.

"What are you waiting for?" Patteon snarled. "If you want out of your contract, get over there and kill them."

Before Savenek could ask Patteon what he meant, several things happened at once.

Lareissa took a huge step in Allyssa's direction, her arm coming up as she prepared to throw the knife.

As Savenek reached for Lareissa, intuition told him to turn. When he did, he saw Patteon unsheathe his sword.

Time seemed to slow.

Not having a sword of his own, Savenek withdrew a dagger. He aimed it downward, easily deflecting Patteon's sword. Before Savenek even saw it, he knew Patteon was going to have a knife in his other hand. Savenek flipped his dagger around and raised it, prepared to strike Patteon's arm—enough to end the threat without killing the prince.

He spared a glance in Allyssa's direction. Lareissa reached back, about to throw her knife. Savenek withdrew another dagger, quickly aiming it at Lareissa's back. But before he could send it on its way, Kerdan jumped in front of Lareissa. Kerdan reached up, covering each side of Lareissa's head with his huge hands. In one swift motion, he snapped her neck. Her body dropped lifelessly to the floor.

Knowing Allyssa was safe, Savenek turned his attention back to Patteon. Savenek angled his dagger, ready to strike the prince.

"Did that barbarian just kill my sister?" Patteon sounded horrified, his eyes round with disbelief.

"He did. I suggest you put your weapons away before I kill you," Savenek replied.

Patteon snarled. He swung his sword down while reaching up with his knife. Savenek twisted, angled his dagger, and prepared to strike Patteon.

Mayra jumped in front of Patteon's knife as it came plunging down.

"No!" Savenek screamed.

The knife went into Mayra's side.

Eyes widening in shock, she gazed at the knife protruding from her side before crumpling to the floor.

People started screaming and running in complete disorder.

Savenek didn't bother seeking his revenge on Patteon—he knew Kerdan would take care of the worthless prince. All that mattered was Mayra. Savenek dropped to his knees. "Ari." Putting his hands on her shoulders, he frantically searched her face. Her eyes were clear. "Can you hear me?"

"I'm okay," she said. Her voice wasn't as strong as it should be.

Panic surged through him. He knew Patteon hadn't been trying to kill him with his sword—the prince had been trying to scratch Savenek with his knife. Most likely, the knife had been laced with poison. The room seemed to spin around him. He couldn't lose Mayra.

His hands started shaking. "Ari, stay with me." He felt her skin, noting her body was starting to go cold. Intense fear slammed into him. If he didn't do something, she was going to die. "I'm going to remove the knife," he said, more to himself than to her. Ripping off a piece of his tunic, he wrapped it around the sheath of the knife and withdrew it. He tore off another section of his tunic, then pressed the material against the bleeding wound.

Neco was at his side. "What happened?" he demanded, his voice laced with unsuppressed fury.

"Patteon got her with this knife." He handed it to Neco. "I'm positive there's poison on it."

Neco wrapped the fabric around the weapon and slid it in his pocket. "Let's get her to the infirmary."

Savenek stood, scooping Mayra into his arms.

"I'm okay," she said. "It's just a small stab wound."

Savenek stared into Mayra's beautiful eyes. "Why'd you do that? I saw it coming and moved out of the way." She didn't need to be his protector. He was the one who was supposed to make certain no harm came to her.

"I wasn't sure if you saw it. All I could think about was saving you." Her eyes filled with tears.

Savenek kissed her forehead as he headed out of the Great Hall.

"I can't feel my stomach," she whispered.

That was the first sign of the poison. Cursing, he started to jog, bone-deep fear clutching his nerves.

Marek joined him. "Is she all right?"

"Run ahead and get the healer and Vesha. Have a room ready."

Marek's face paled. He nodded and took off, sprinting down the corridor, yelling as he went for people to get out of the way.

Savenek heard Neco and Ellie behind him, but he ignored them and focused on getting Mayra to the healer as soon as possible before it was too late. Mayra grabbed his sleeve, hissing in pain. He felt her body tense.

"It'll be okay," he said. "Just hang in there." Savenek skidded into the infirmary.

"In here," Marek called out, holding open the door to the healer's office.

Savenek entered the room, setting Mayra on the table. He ripped open the side of her dress, revealing the stab wound, the skin already turning black.

The healer and Vesha were in the room, grabbing bowls and setting them on the table next to Mayra.

"Mash these together," the healer said, handing two plants to Vesha. The healer proceeded to mix the contents of another bowl. Then, using her fingers, she placed the goo on the wound. "This will give us some time."

"What do you mean?" Savenek asked. "Time for what?"

"We don't have an antidote yet," the healer revealed.

"Do whatever you did to save me to her."

"I will. But I did several things to save you," the healer said. "I'm not sure which one of them worked."

Vesha shoved the bowl toward the healer. "Here's this. Do you need anything else?"

The healer shook her head.

"Savenek," Vesha said firmly, demanding his attention.

He swung toward the sound of his name, barely comprehending the events that had transpired. This couldn't be happening. Not to Mayra.

"Have you seen the kepper flower?"

"I have." Savenek could picture it perfectly in his mind.

"Describe it to me."

"The flower itself is small, red, and grows on vines."

"How large is the flower?"

"About a half inch in diameter."

"What about the leaves on the vine? How big?"

"An inch."

She ran over to the shelves containing potted plants, ripping off leaves from three of them. "I have an idea." Vesha took a scoop of the paste from the healer and put it in one of the bowls, mixing in the leaves.

Savenek sat on a stool beside Mayra, gripping her hand. "Stay with me, Ari."

She tilted her head to the side, blinking slowly. "I can't feel my legs." Her voice sounded raspy.

The poison was working through her system too quickly. There must have been a potent dose on the knife. Savenek squeezed her hand. "You didn't let me die, and I'm not going to let you die either." He couldn't lose her.

Neco entered the room, his eyes wild. When he saw his daughter lying on the table, he dropped to his knees.

Ellie rushed in. "What can I do to help?" Her eyes were red from crying.

"Use that cloth over there to remove the goo," Vesha said. "I'm going to try this paste and see if it works."

Ellie wiped her eyes with her sleeve and grabbed the cloth, taking the goo off as Vesha instructed.

Allyssa entered the room. "Is Mayra okay?" She sounded out of breath.

Savenek couldn't take his eyes away from Mayra. It was as if looking at her made her stay there with him. If he glanced away or blinked, she could be taken from him. And he couldn't live without her.

Allyssa put a hand on his shoulder, squeezing it.

Mayra's breathing became ragged. "We're losing her!" Savenek ground out. "Do something!"

Neco took Mayra's other hand. "Hang on, baby girl. You're strong. You can survive this."

Vesha slathered a thick greenish-colored paste over the wound.

"I've seen something like this before," Allyssa said, her voice filled with shock. "When I was in Russek, Soma poisoned me like this. Kerdan had something that saved me. He'll know what to do." She stood there, not moving.

"What's the matter?" Neco asked.

"King Theon is demanding Kerdan's execution. He sent his soldiers after him. Mother and Father are trying to stop Theon, but there's only so much they can do. He killed Princess Lareissa."

"Lareissa deserved to die," Savenek whispered.

"I'll help you find Kerdan," Marek said. "I'm certain Theon and his soldiers are no match for him." He sprinted from the room, Allyssa right behind him.

Savenek prayed they got to Kerdan in time.

"Let's try it again," Vesha said. Ellie wiped off the wound, and Vesha slathered the paste on it again.

"Her breathing is stabilizing," Savenek said, hope bubbling in his chest. It wasn't improving, but it wasn't getting worse.

"The black has stopped spreading as well," Vesha said. "I think the paste neutralizes it, but then it becomes contaminated and no longer works. We must constantly change the paste in order to prevent the poison from spreading."

They continued to work on Mayra, reapplying the paste every minute or so.

After what felt like forever, Marek and Allyssa returned with Kerdan, who was carrying a black satchel.

Kerdan slid to his knees, ripping the satchel open. "Soma used a lot of poisons," he said. "Once he cut Allyssa with a knife that had been laced with poison. I used this one to save her." He handed a small glass jar to Vesha.

Vesha took it and opened the lid. A foul smell permeated the air. "Charcoal, rosemary, mint, and something else I can't make out. How much do you use? A drop?"

"No. You need to cover the entire wound."

"Do you have more?" Vesha asked, holding the glass up to the light. It was only about a fourth full.

"No."

"Then let's hope there's enough." Taking a deep breath, she held the container just above Mayra, slowly pouring the liquid directly onto her wound.

Mayra screamed, the sound punching Savenek in the stomach. Her wound started oozing.

"Hold her down," Vesha commanded.

Savenek took one shoulder, Ellie the other, and Neco held her legs.

Vesha poured more on. The wound bubbled and oozed a greenish-black substance. "This is definitely helping," Vesha mused. "It has stopped the spread of the poison."

"It's not improving the skin or wound, though," Ellie said, her voice breaking.

"What does that mean?" Savenek asked. "It's helping, but it's not the antidote we need?"

"Correct," Vesha answered. "It has bought us time to get the antidote." Sighing, she rubbed her face. "What else is in there?" She nodded at the satchel.

"I don't know," Kerdan said. "Most of it was Soma's. There are some poisons, some antidotes. I don't know what everything is, though." He spread the contents out on the floor.

"Allyssa," Vesha said. "Have someone go to Patteon's room to look for an antidote. I can't imagine he would use such a potent poison without having something to counteract it."

Allyssa ran from the room.

"Savenek, go through Kerdan's supplies. Smell everything. You're looking for something that smells like the kepper flower. Chances are the antidote will smell similar to it."

Savenek released Mayra's shoulder, and the healer took over for him.

He squatted on the floor. As Kerdan opened jars, he handed them to Savenek one by one. Savenek sniffed the first one. It was too tart. He recapped it and grabbed the next. They repeated this over and over. The problem was that Savenek didn't remember how the kepper flower smelled—if it even smelled at all. He hoped that if he came to the antidote, something would trigger his memory. He couldn't fail Mayra.

One of the jars had a white, slimy substance, absence of smell. He handed it to Vesha.

She examined it. "No. This won't work. Keep looking."

Instead of questioning her, he continued to smell the jars.

"What about this one?" Kerdan asked. "I used it when Soma poisoned me once. It saved my life."

Savenek handed it to Vesha.

Vesha sniffed it, stuck a finger inside, and then put a drop on the table. She mixed some of the contaminated paste with it. It started to bubble, growing in size. "This may work." Using a spoon, she scooped a small amount and drizzled it onto Mayra's wound.

Savenek stood and watched, praying this worked. He vaguely heard shouting from out in the corridor, but he couldn't take his focus off Mayra. She started thrashing, fighting against those holding her down. Her wound started bubbling, the skin turning an angry shade of red. The bubbles popped and reformed. Vesha applied more of the stuff onto the wound. Mayra's eyes rolled back. Savenek knew she'd fainted, probably from the pain. His heart pounded—he'd never been so afraid in his life.

Kerdan started pacing.

Allyssa returned to the room. "I have someone searching Patteon's bedchamber." Her eyes widened when she took in her unconscious friend.

"Mayra fainted," Savenek explained. His voice came out softer than he'd intended.

Allyssa came over and wrapped her arm around his waist, hugging him. "Mayra's a fighter."

Savenek knew that. Yet, seeing Mayra in pain, stretched on the table because she'd been injured while trying to protect him made him sick.

"Water," Kerdan said suddenly. "We need to flush out her system. When I was suffering from poison, that's what I did."

Allyssa released Savenek, hurrying to grab the jug of water from the side table. She poured a cup full and handed it to Ellie. Neco lifted Mayra's body, tilting her head up. Ellie poured the water into Mayra's mouth. Mayra's eyes opened, and she coughed.

"We need you to drink this, honey," Ellie said.

Mayra started to gulp the water.

Vesha reapplied the medicine. The bubbling was much less intense this time, and Mayra gave no indication it hurt. After a minute, Vesha wiped it off and put the medicine on a third time. It didn't bubble. The black skin around the wound faded to a pale pink.

"I want her to drink this," Vesha said, handing Ellie one of the bowls.

Ellie put the bowl to Mayra's lips, slowly pouring the thick contents into Mayra's mouth. Mayra's eyes watered, but she continued to drink.

When she finished, Vesha once again applied the medicine. "I think she'll be okay."

Brookfel entered the room, his presence overbearing in the small space. "King Kerdan, a word." The two men exited.

Savenek wanted to find out what was going on; however, he couldn't leave Mayra's side.

CHAPTER 20

Allyssa

llyssa watched Kerdan exit the room. Out in the corridor, she heard him talking softly with Brookfel.

"The Russek army is here," Brookfel said. "Everyone is in position."

Allyssa couldn't fathom why the Russek army would be in Emperion. She glanced at Savenek, who stood unnaturally still. He must have also heard what Brookfel said. She went over to him. "Stay here with Mayra. I'll see what's going on."

He nodded. "I'm guessing they're here to help us."

That had to be it. It couldn't possibly be another act of war.

Allyssa turned to leave. Savenek caught her wrist. "Please tell Kerdan thank you. He saved Mayra's life."

"I will." She exited the room, beyond relieved her best friend was going to be okay. Out in the corridor, Brookfel was helping Kerdan put armor on. "What are you doing?"

Kerdan turned to face her. "I sent for my army a few days ago."

"Why?"

"I was afraid something like this might happen," he said. "I just killed a princess from Apethaga. The king wants my head."

"What about Patteon?" She'd seen Kerdan punch the prince, knocking him out.

"I had Emperion soldiers arrest him. I figured Neco and Savenek would want to kill him themselves."

"Why did you kill Lareissa?" Because he'd feared she was trying to kill Savenek? That didn't make any sense. Savenek was more than capable of defending himself.

"She was going to kill you," he said.

Shock rolled through Allyssa. She'd been at the ball alongside Odar with no idea her life was in jeopardy.

"I reacted before I thought through the consequences," Kerdan explained. "I'm sorry."

"So you protected me, and now Apethaga wants you dead?" And Mayra was injured from protecting Savenek. What a mess.

"Yes. King Theon is calling for my execution. Of course, Telmena is siding with him."

"My parents won't let anything happen to you."

He chuckled, and she wondered how he could laugh at a time like this. "It is not your parents' job to protect me," he said. "I am the king of Russek. I killed someone who threatened you. I will deal with the consequences."

This was bad. Allyssa glanced up and down the corridor, seeing Emperion soldiers positioned at both ends. As much as her mother had hoped for a peaceful resolution, it didn't appear there would be one.

"King Theon is trying to incite a war before any explanations can be given," Kerdan said. "I think this was planned between Apethaga and Telmena. These two kingdoms wanted to create chaos and opportunities for members of the royal families to be killed."

Allyssa wondered if they'd sacrificed Lareissa in order to get what they wanted. The thought both sickened and saddened her. Power made people do crazy things. "What can I do to help?" Reaching out, she clutched onto his forearm, the feel of chainmail digging into her palm.

"Stay alive."

Marek exited the room with Savenek in tow. "Now that I know

my sister will live, I need to move Prince Savenek and Princess Allyssa to another location."

"I agree," Kerdan. "They are not safe here."

Allyssa released him, wondering how she wasn't safe in her own castle. Emperion had an entire unit of soldiers stationed on the castle grounds.

Kerdan turned to Brookfel. "I need to ask a favor."

"Anything."

"Stay with Allyssa."

"I'll protect her with my life," Brookfel said, bowing his head.

Kerdan took Allyssa's hands and squeezed them. "I know you don't like this. I know you want to fight." He held her gaze until she nodded. "But I need you to hide. King Theon is demanding retribution. I'm afraid he will kill you to hurt me."

While she wanted to remain with Kerdan and fight those wishing her and her family harm, she took a moment to think things through rationally. She hadn't seen her parents since Lareissa had been killed. They were probably being diplomatic and trying to keep the kings and queens of the visiting kingdoms calm. However, she couldn't be certain. Her number one job was to protect Emperion. And right now, that meant ensuring Emperion had a ruler and an heir. She studied the man before her, knowing he could very well take care of himself. He was a skilled, proficient fighter. "Very well," she said, agreeing to his request.

"I expected more of a fight."

"You wouldn't ask it if it wasn't necessary." He so rarely asked anything of her.

"True."

"What are you going to do?" she asked. Did he intend to kill Theon? Send the Russek army against Apethaga and Telmena?

Kerdan smiled ruefully. "I plan to keep the peace by scaring everyone." With that, he turned and strode away.

Scaring everyone? Allyssa wasn't sure what he meant by that.

However, she was very glad that Kerdan was on her side. Pity the fool who got in his way.

Savenek snorted. "I can't believe I'm going to say this, but I like him."

Marek just shook his head and said, "Let's get you two in the secret passageways."

"No," Brookfel replied. "They will expect that. Let's get out of the castle and hide somewhere they won't think to look."

Allyssa had just the place.

Disguised as female servants, Allyssa, Savenek, Marek, and Brookfel easily made their way out of the castle through the servants' corridors.

Allyssa led the way through the town to the apartment complex where her dear friend had once lived. She raised her hand and knocked on the door. A moment later, Grevik's mother, Serek, opened the door. Allyssa held her finger to her lips before Serek could say anything.

Serek nodded and opened the door wider, admitting their group into her tiny apartment. There was a single room with a sofa and a table for eating. Down a short hallway were two bedchambers only wide enough for a cot and a dresser.

Once the door was closed and locked, Allyssa hugged Serek. "We need to hide here for a little bit."

Serek wore a simple gray dress, her hair pulled into a tight bun. During the day, she worked in a store selling milk and cheese. "Of course, Your Highness."

"Don't use my title or name. No one can know I'm here." Allyssa quickly introduced Savenek, Marek, and Brookfel. The three men removed the dresses they had been wearing and the bonnets covering their heads. Allyssa bit her bottom lip so she wouldn't laugh. The getup had been Brookfel's idea.

Serek made some tea while the rest of them sat on the sofa or the floor.

Allyssa fiddled with a strand of her hair, wondering how long they would be there. What was Kerdan doing with his army? Had any fighting taken place? Were her parents okay?

"Let's play a game of cards," Savenek said. "Otherwise, I'll go mad worrying about Mayra and what's going on back at the castle."

She knew it was difficult for Savenek to remain in hiding instead of being an active participant in the fray. He wasn't the type to sit still. They were alike in that regard.

Serek brought out the tea and a deck of cards.

Allyssa reached forward, picking up the cards and holding them between her hands. This was the same deck she'd used with Grevik.

"Is there any particular reason you're hugging the cards?" Savenek asked.

Allyssa flicked one of the cards at his head. He caught it, flashing her a tired smile.

Brookfel stood and went to the window, peering carefully outside. "Looks like something is going on down there."

"I'll go and find out." Serek grabbed her sweater and left the apartment. Brookfel locked the door after her before resuming watch near the window.

Allyssa dealt the cards, then started a round of Kingsmen with Marek and Savenek. She lost three straight times because she was too occupied with what could be going on outside instead of what cards she held in her hand.

After about twenty minutes, there was a tap at the door, Serek announcing herself in a whisper. Brookfel cracked the door. After confirming she was alone, he let her in.

"There's nothing to worry about," she assured them once she was safely back inside. "The City Guards just announced that the Russek soldiers are here at the request of our great empress and they're working alongside Emperion soldiers to keep the peace."

Allyssa wondered how many Russek soldiers were here. A shiver ran through her at the memory of being held prisoner in the Romek mountains. The brutality of the Russek soldiers had shocked her. The men Kerdan had called here better be controlled and follow his orders. She would not tolerate any harm coming to her people.

Marek threw his cards down. "I'm out. Neither of you is paying attention."

"Sorry," Allyssa said. It had to be close to midnight by now. After setting her cards down, she rubbed her temple. "What do you think is happening at the castle?"

Someone gently knocked on the door. Brookfel held up a finger, telling Serek to wait while he got into position. When he was ready, he nodded. Serek opened the door a few inches, talking softly to a male voice. She turned and mouthed, "Nathenek?"

"Let him in," Marek said.

When she opened the door wider, Nathenek entered.

Allyssa vaguely wondered how he knew they were here. But this was Nathenek. He seemed to know everything.

"All the kingdoms have agreed to a trial," Nathenek said. "Kerdan will state his case, and each kingdom will have one vote. If he's found guilty, he will hang."

"That's ridiculous," Allyssa said, folding her arms. How could Kerdan have agreed to that?

"I agree. However, if it keeps the peace, then we should go along with it." Nathenek motioned for them to stand.

"When is the trial?" Savenek asked as he stood.

"Right now."

Now? "And if he's found guilty?" Allyssa demanded. "Then what?"

Nathenek's grin was feral. "I wouldn't worry about that. I've already helped one royal avoid an execution."

BACK AT THE CASTLE, NATHENEK ESCORTED ALLYSSA, Savenek, Marek, and Brookfel to the Throne Room. They went to the first row, sitting alongside Rema and Darmik.

All the royal families from the mainland were present. Soldiers lined the walls. No one spoke.

The doors slammed open, making Allyssa jump. Two Emperion soldiers escorted Kerdan to the front of the room. He wore an emerald tunic with the royal crest of Russek on the front. The tunic appeared bulkier than usual, and Allyssa wondered if he had chainmail on underneath. He didn't even glance her way as he strode up the dais and turned to face the royal families. His wrists had been tied together in front of his body.

Rema stood. She still wore the dress she'd had on earlier at the ball. Even though she looked regal, the skin under her eyes was dark, hinting at how tired the empress truly was. "I hereby declare the start of King Kerdan's trial. First, we will hear the accuser's claims. Then, we will hear the king's response. Each kingdom will have one vote. Agreed?" She managed to keep her voice loud, clear, and authoritative.

Everyone agreed.

Allyssa clasped her hands together, her heart pounding. Two of the families would vote against Kerdan—Apethaga and Telmena. Dromien would most likely vote the same as Emperion—for Kerdan. That made it a tie. The deciding factor would be Fren, and Allyssa had no idea how they would vote. Viscor and Lutia could easily side with Telmena, especially since they had a treaty between their kingdoms and Kren was married to Jestina. On the other hand, Allyssa was engaged to Odar. It wouldn't be wise to side against Emperion on this matter.

Odar sat with his parents a couple of rows behind Allyssa. She wanted to turn around to see his face. Would he encourage his parents to spare Kerdan for her sake? Or would he tell them to vote against him? How selfish was he? Eliminating Kerdan meant Allyssa was free to marry. But Odar had to know she would never forgive him for voting against the man she loved.

Savenek placed his hand over her fidgeting ones. "It'll be okay," he whispered. "I promise." He released her.

Theon stood and addressed the royal families. "The facts are simple. King Kerdan snapped my daughter's neck, killing her. He is guilty, and I want his death for her death."

Considering the man had just lost his daughter, he didn't appear the least bit grief stricken. In fact, he seemed too calm and collected. Had he not cared for his youngest child? Perhaps the reality of the situation had not yet hit him.

Theon sat next to his wife. Her eyes were red, and she held a handkerchief. Conditto was sitting next to her mother, her face devoid of all emotion, making her appear cold and calculating.

"What do you have to say in your defense?" Rema asked Kerdan.

A flair of panic shot through Allyssa. What if Rema didn't approve of Kerdan? This would be a way for her to easily get rid of him. Would her mother do that to Allyssa? Maybe Kerdan killing Lareissa had scared Rema so much that she wouldn't allow Allyssa to marry him.

Kerdan took a step forward on the dais, the soldiers guarding him remaining where they were, about a foot behind him. "All he says is true," Kerdan replied, his deep voice cutting through the room. "However, it was a justified killing."

"Killing is never justified," Theon said, jumping to his feet. "You're a murderer."

"Ironic coming from a man who tried to have me killed," Savenek said under his breath.

"What proof do you have her death was justified?" Rema asked.

Savenek cleared his throat. "May I speak? I have evidence."

"You may," Rema said, taking her seat.

Allyssa was thrilled Savenek was willing to speak on Kerdan's behalf. She knew her brother had his reservations about him.

Savenek stood, facing those present. "I first met Princess Lareissa a few seasons ago. She was a beautiful, vivacious woman. However, she is dead because she tried to assassinate Princess Allyssa. I was standing near her. I witnessed her take out a knife and point it at my sister, with the intention of throwing it into my unarmed and unaware sister's back."

"My daughter would never try to kill someone," King Theon stated.

"I also want to bring charges against Prince Patteon," Savenek said. "The reason King Kerdan had to step in to stop Lareissa was because Prince Patteon was trying to assassinate me."

"My son did no such thing," King Theon declared.

"My son's bodyguard would beg to differ," Rema said coldly. "Neco, bring in the bodyguard."

Neco entered the room with Mayra, who looked half dead. Her hair was in disarray, her skin pasty white, and she had several blankets wrapped around her shaking body. Neco had an arm around her waist, keeping her upright. They stopped before the dais, slowly pivoting toward the gathered assembly.

"All he says is true," Mayra said, her pained, breathy voice barely heard throughout the room. "I saw Princess Lareissa take out a knife, aiming it in Princess Allyssa's direction. When Prince Savenek tried to stop Princess Lareissa, Prince Patteon withdrew his own sword and knife, attempting to kill Prince Savenek. I threw my body in front of the blade to save the prince's life."

"What evidence do you have?" Theon demanded. "This is a conspiracy!"

"I have the knife Prince Patteon used," Neco said. He removed a pouch from his waist and untied it, withdrawing a small knife covered with dried blood. "I won't touch the blade because it is laced with a poison produced in Apethaga."

"Convenient you should have the blade and know about the poison," Theon spat.

"I am stating the facts." Neco put the knife back in the pouch. "Anything else?" he asked Rema.

She shook her head. "You may go."

Neco wrapped his arm around Mayra, supporting most of her weight as they made their slow progression back down the aisle to the door. Those gathered watched, a few appearing sympathetic toward the injured woman.

"What motive did my son and daughter have to kill either Princess Allyssa or Prince Savenek?" Theon demanded.

Allyssa glanced at the row behind Theon. Metek, Cora, and Jem sat next to one another. Metek had a slight smile hovering about his lips.

Savenek once again stood. "Lareissa had several motives."

Theon's glare focused on Savenek. "I can't believe anything you say. You came to my kingdom pretending to be an ambassador when you were the prince. You're a liar!"

Ignoring him, Savenek addressed the royal families. "Lareissa told me she wouldn't marry me unless I was the crown heir. Motive number one—by killing Allyssa, she could be assured I was first in line for the throne. At which time, Lareissa could marry me, securing her future as the next empress of Emperion."

A low murmur rippled through the room.

"Motive number two—if she killed Allyssa, Odar would be free to marry someone else. Since Odar is the crown heir of Fren, Lareissa would be the future queen of Fren if she married him. As you can see, killing Allyssa would have greatly benefitted a fourth born child who had ambitions of ruling a kingdom."

"Liar," Theon roared. "My daughter was pleased to be marrying Prince Jem of Apethaga."

"Motive number three," Savenek continued as if Theon hadn't spoken. "Prince Jem is twice Princess Lareissa's age. I overhead Prince Patteon tell his sister that if she wanted out of her contract, she needed to get over there and kill...*them*." Savenek paused there, a shadow of confusion washing over his face. He looked at Patteon. "Did you mean King Viscor and Queen Lutia? Was Lareissa supposed to assassinate the king and queen of Fren?"

"This is an outrage," Theon bellowed.

"Or did you intend for Princess Lareissa to be killed?" Savenek said. "Did you set her up for something impossible in order to try to destroy Emperion? To get back at me?"

Theon's face turned red, his eyes widening.

"That's it, isn't it?" Savenek said. "You wanted me to step in and kill her, not King Kerdan."

Neither Apethaga nor Telmena knew Kerdan cared for Allyssa, so neither kingdom had factored him into their plans.

"It's time for a vote," Rema said. "All those who find King Kerdan guilty for killing Princess Lareissa, have one representative from your kingdom raise his or her hand."

Theon and Metek raised their hands.

"All those who find Kerdan not guilty, raise your hand."

Rema, Viscor, and the king from Drenton raised their hands.

"King Kerdan has been found innocent of the charges brought against him," Rema said. "Release him."

Metek started laughing, the sound hysterical. "How do you always bloody get your way?" he said, pointing at Rema. "You're a parasite. How can you not want King Kerdan dead? After all, he kept your daughter holed up in his room while she was in Russek. Of all people, I thought you would want him gone."

Rema went very still. Allyssa wanted to hide under the seat. How could Metek have publicly humiliated her like this? Now when she married Kerdan, people would assume it was because her virtue had been compromised.

"That is a bold accusation you're making," Darmik said.

"It's not an accusation," Metek said. "It is a fact."

"How do you know?" Darmik asked. His voice became deadly calm, sending a chill through Allyssa.

"I know because I've been orchestrating everything. I've been trying to take down Emperion for quite some time. Yet, you bloody well keep coming out on top. It is infuriating." Metek moved into the aisle, his right hand holding a dagger.

"By orchestrating everything," Darmik said, moving to block Metek's path, "do you mean helping Jana?"

Rema and Allyssa slid down the bench, away from the aisle, trying to put distance between themselves and Metek. Allyssa lost track of Savenek—she didn't see him anywhere.

"Yes." Metek smiled, the act transforming his face into something twisted and vicious. "I provided the funds for Jana to escape to Russek; I helped her lure the king into marrying her; and I had Russek troops sent into Emperion. I even made sure they kidnapped Allyssa. I was certain that would be your undoing. Somehow, Allyssa not only survived, but she also got Kerdan to help her escape. It seems I can no longer pull the strings. It is time for me to take care of your family once and for all."

Darmik unsheathed his sword. "Stay where you are." The soldiers around the edge of the room also had their swords at the ready, moving to surround the Telmena royal family.

Allyssa glanced at Kerdan. He was in the process of untying his bindings.

"Have your men stand down," Metek ordered.

"Not a chance," Darmik said.

Metek shook his head. "Fool. Have you ever wondered who taught Soma to be so well versed in the art of poison? Have you ever considered how he became an assassin? No? Well, let me enlighten you. My son, Jem." He held his hand out to the side, pointing at the prince.

Jem smiled. He had something in his mouth. Upon closer inspection, Allyssa realized it was a blowdart. And it was pointed right at Rema.

Jem fell to the side, a dagger protruding from his neck. Metek suddenly dropped to the ground, a dagger in his chest. Cora screamed and stood. A knife flew through the air, striking her in the throat.

Stunned, Allyssa searched the room until she found Savenek. He stood there calmly, eyes narrowed, scanning the room. He'd just killed three people in less than five seconds. She blinked. *Bloody hell.*

Neither Darmik, Kerdan, Neco, nor Nathenek had even had time to react.

"I guess he isn't an aloof prince after all," Viscor said.

"Is everyone all right?" Rema demanded. "Did Jem manage to strike anyone before he was neutralized?"

"I think everyone is okay," Darmik said, coming to stand beside his wife. It was a challenge to see if anyone would blame Savenek for killing the Telmena royals.

Allyssa's heart pounded as the realization of what had just happened sunk in.

Kerdan went over to Jem's body, squatting beside it. He plucked the blowdart from the dead man's mouth and stood. "It's loaded with poison. There are four darts in here. I'm guessing he planned to kill the empress, emperor, and the twins."

If Savenek had hesitated, Rema could be dead. He'd saved them all. Allyssa ran over to her brother, hugging him.

"I can honestly say I'm glad you're on my side," Viscor stated. He stood, his wife and Odar joining him. "I've had enough chaos for one night. We're retiring."

IN THE LIBRARY, ALLYSSA SAT IN HER FAVORITE ALCOVE, staring outside at the early morning light shining through the clouds. She curled her feet under her legs on the bench.

"I thought I'd find you in here," Savenek said, sliding onto the seat across from her.

"How's Mayra?" After everything that had happened last night,

Neco took Mayra back to his family's private wing. Allyssa hadn't had a chance to talk to Mayra or Marek about everything.

"She's doing much better." He ran his hands through his hair, making it even messier than it was before.

Allyssa smiled at her twin. "I'm glad to hear that. I still can't believe she jumped in front of a blade for you."

He smirked. "True love."

She gazed back outside as the warmth from the sun hitting the ground caused mist to rise. "What are we going to do about Apethaga?" While they'd managed to kill Metek, Cora, and Jem from Telmena, they hadn't solved their problems with Apethaga.

"*We* aren't going to do a thing."

His answer was too confident. She raised her eyebrows, awaiting an explanation. There was no way Neco or Savenek would just let Patteon walk away after he'd almost killed Mayra.

Leaning over the table, he whispered, "Emperion soldiers are escorting them out of our kingdom as we speak. Once they reach Apethaga, the Apethaga soldiers will lead the royal carriage straight to a field of keppers. The royal family will be dead before they know what's happened."

Shock rolled through her. "Who will rule Apethaga?"

"The working class has elected a man to lead the kingdom. They are tired of being forced to work in the mines, pay high taxes, and cater to the rich. As soon as the royal family left to come here for the wedding, an uprising began. I had members of the Brotherhood meet with the workers to help arrange everything. The man who will be ruling Apethaga has the people's best interest at heart." He reclined back, a smug expression on his face.

Her brother had been busy. The possibility of peace throughout the entire mainland made her content. Everything seemed to be working out.

She stared at brother.

"What?" he asked.

"I can't believe how quickly you killed those people."

He shrugged.

"You saved our lives."

"The second I saw him put the blowdart to his lips, I reacted. In that moment, I realized how much I love this family. I couldn't bear to lose it."

Even though Allyssa had only known Savenek for a brief time, she felt a connection to him that she didn't have with anyone else. "I want you to know how much I love you. I'm glad to have my brother home and a part of this family."

He flashed her a smile, hands fidgeting, which was unlike him. Was he nervous about something? "What is it?" she asked.

"I need to…talk to you."

"You can talk to me about anything." Well, almost anything. There were some things she didn't want to discuss with her brother. Like Kerdan.

He sighed. "I know I gave you a hard time about Kerdan."

Oh lovely. The one thing she didn't want to discuss with him was what he wanted to talk about. She bit back her retort, waiting for him to continue. The least she could do was hear him out.

"You must understand that I viewed Russek as the enemy. I assumed Kerdan was Russek. Does that make any sense?"

Unfortunately, it did. "The Russek army is brutal. Especially when the person leading the army has no morals." But Drenton was dead, and things were different now.

"That's my point," Savenek said. He propped his elbows on the table. "Kerdan is a good man." He rubbed his face. "While he can be a little…"

"Unrefined?"

He smiled wryly. "…coarse, he has his priorities right. He obviously cares for you."

Allyssa already knew all this. "What are you trying to say?"

"That I approve."

He approved? Of Kerdan? It certainly took Savenek long

enough to come around.

"Not that you need it, but I know *Father* said you had to get it. So I hereby give you my blessing to marry Kerdan."

Reaching across the table, Allyssa threw her arms around Savenek's neck, hugging him. "Thank you."

"Don't you have a wedding to get ready for?" he asked. "After all, everyone expects a royal wedding today. I think it's only fair to give them one."

ALLYSSA STOOD IN FRONT OF THE MIRROR IN HER bedchamber, admiring her dress. The white fabric was embroidered with gold stitching around the bust and the sleeves. The silky material was form fitting and swayed as she moved. Her hair hung around her shoulders in soft waves. A gold crown sat atop her head.

"You look stunning," Rema said as she came into the room.

"I can't believe I'm getting married today." Or that she'd just come from one of the most awkward meetings in her life. After her conversation with Savenek in the library, she'd gone to see Odar and his parents. She'd let Odar explain that he and Allyssa never signed a marriage contract—well, a new one. He went on to tell them how he'd faked his engagement with Allyssa in order to end the threat with Telmena. Neither Viscor nor Lutia said a single word until Odar was done speaking. Then Viscor had the nerve to say he was glad his firstborn son wasn't marrying Allyssa because she would have stifled Odar.

He'd even had the audacity to say women weren't meant to hold such powerful positions. Allyssa had to bite her tongue at that comment. Then Lutia agreed with her husband, adding that it was a blessing since Allyssa's virtue had been called into question. Lutia didn't want her precious son marrying a whore. Allyssa had sat there quietly until they were done speaking. Then Odar had escorted her back to the Royal Wing without a word. She thanked the stars she wasn't marrying Odar. His parents would have been terrible in-laws.

"I remember the day I married your father," Rema said. "We had just defeated King Barjon and Prince Lennek. The ceremony was held in the half-ruined castle where my parents had lived. It was one of the happiest days of my life." She was dressed in a beautiful gold gown.

"Was that after you'd removed Hamen from the throne in Emperion?" Allyssa asked, turning to face her mother.

"It was." Rema went over to the sofa and sat, patting the spot next to her.

Allyssa joined her. "What is it?"

"I need to discuss something with you, and I want you to be completely honest with me." Rema gathered Allyssa's hands and held them firmly.

"Of course." She had no idea what her mother intended to say.

Rema's brows drew together. She went to speak several times but stopped herself.

"What is it?" Allyssa asked, worried her mother had bad news to deliver.

"When you were in Russek, were you harmed or forced to do something against your will?" Rema's eyes welled with tears. "I'm referring to things that are intimate and meant to be shared between a man and his wife."

Allyssa felt her face flush. When Metek had callously thrown the accusation out there that she'd been holed up in Kerdan's bedchamber, she'd known there would be repercussions. "No. I was not harmed that way at all." She'd already gone over this with her father when they were in Russek at Duke Womek's estate.

Rema but her bottom lip. "Very well. What about not being forced?"

"I don't understand." What was her mother getting at?

"Your father explained to me that when you were removed

from the dungeon, Soma wanted to kill you, but Kerdan wanted you alive since he thought you'd make a valuable ally. In order to protect you, Kerdan kept you in his bedchamber where Soma couldn't get his hands on you." She took a deep breath, letting it out slowly. "What I want to know is if you fell in love with Kerdan under those strenuous circumstances, and if something intimate happened between the two of you while you were there." Rema squeezed Allyssa's hands as she waited for her to respond.

Oh. Not that it was any of Rema's business, but Allyssa understood what her mother needed to know. "My virtue has not been compromised in any way, willingly or otherwise."

Rema's shoulders fell. "I feared he had some hold over you because of what you'd been through. I am glad that is not the case."

Allyssa should have done this sooner. It was time to tell her mother everything that happened in Russek. Starting with Soma kidnapping her and Odar, she explained how they'd escaped only to be recaptured, how Soma had poisoned them, about being tossed in the dungeon, and what she'd endured while there. Allyssa let it all out, telling her mother how scared and hurt she'd been. How all she could think about was saving the people of Emperion.

Tears slid down Rema's cheeks as Allyssa spoke. However, Allyssa forged on, not leaving any details out. She talked about being in Kerdan's bedchamber, Soma trying to kill her, Kerdan saving her, Eliza kidnapping her. She then went on to explain how she and Odar tried to assassinate the royal family, what it was like watching Shelene die, and how it felt to kill Soma. Then she described her harrowing escape to Fren and how Kerdan had aided them. She finished with what had happened in Fren with Odar and his parents, what it felt like to have her engagement severed, and seeing Kerdan on the way back to Emperion.

Allyssa didn't know how long she talked. Rema never once interrupted or asked any questions. Allyssa even told her what it was like living with Nathenek, about going into Russek, and being a part of Jana's assassination. And through it all, she tried to explain how she'd gotten to know and respect Kerdan. How that friendship turned into something more.

"I can't even begin to tell you how sorry I am you had to go through and endure all of that," Rema said, still clutching Allyssa's hands. "However, I know it has helped shape you into the strong woman sitting before me today. I'd feared you didn't truly know Kerdan or what you were getting yourself into. However, I can see now that you know your mind and are capable of making your own decisions." Rema released Allyssa's hands, then wiped the tears from her cheeks. "Thank you for sharing that with me." She hugged Allyssa tightly. "While you do not need my approval to marry Kerdan, I give it to you. I also give you my support." She kissed Allyssa on the cheek. "I love you."

"I love you too, Mother."

Darmik knocked on the doorframe. "Is Allyssa ready?"

"She is," Rema answered. "Let's go."

Allyssa clutched Darmik's arm as they stood before the doors to the Throne Room. Madelin set a gold cape on Allyssa's shoulders, holding it there while Mayra secured it in place.

"Perfect," Mayra said as she took a step back and examined Allyssa from head to toe. "Wait until Kerdan sees you." She smirked.

It was good to see Mayra happy and moving about so well.

"I'm standing right here," Darmik chided them. "I expect those comments from Madelin, not you Mayra."

Mayra's face went bright red. "Sorry, Your Majesty."

"I'm just teasing you," he replied.

Madelin swept in front of Allyssa and said, "I'm going to have to find my own Russek brute to bring to his knees."

"Madelin," Allyssa and Mayra said in unison.

"What?" she asked innocently.

"Case in point," Darmik said.

The doors swung open.

"Saved by the doors, Your Majesty," Madelin said. She winked and picked up her basket of petals. "I'm ready."

Mayra and Madelin began walking down the aisle, tossing rose petals as they went. Allyssa was beyond thankful her two best friends were there to celebrate this day with her.

The music changed. "That's our cue," Darmik said. He patted his daughter's hand and they took a step forward, entering the Throne Room.

Everyone stood and turned to catch a glimpse of Allyssa as she glided alongside her father, one arm linked with his, her other hand holding a bouquet of flowers. She couldn't believe how many people were there to witness their marriage.

Instead of smiling at the people as she passed by, all she could do was stare at the man standing at the end of the aisle—her future husband.

Kerdan was mighty fierce and handsome in his black pants with a dark green tunic. A large silver crown with emeralds adorned his head. And, in typical Russek fashion, a fur cape had been draped over his shoulders. Allyssa couldn't help but smile. His companions—Brookfel, Hurit, and Larek—stood to his left.

As Allyssa approached the dais, she saw Rema seated in the front row, Savenek to her left. Next to them sat Neco, Marek, and Ellie. In the second row, Allyssa spotted Odar sitting with his parents. On the other side of the aisle, Duke Womek, Kerdan's uncle, was seated. Vesha, Audek, Nathenek, and Serek were there as well. So many people she loved and cared for were here to celebrate this day. It warmed her heart.

Allyssa and Darmik stopped at the end of the aisle. Mayra and Madelin moved to Kerdan's right. Directly ahead, an elderly gentleman stood on the dais holding a gold box that contained the wedding rings. He would perform the ceremony.

"Welcome," the man said, his voice gravely from old age. "My name is Mako, and I am honored to be here from Greenwood Island to celebrate this monumental day."

Allyssa recognized his name—Mako was the man who'd saved Rema when she was only a baby and aided her in retaking her kingdom. He had to be in his seventies by now. She was honored he'd traveled so far to be here for her wedding.

"Who gives this woman to this man?" Mako asked.

"I do," Darmik said, his voice loud and clear. He squeezed Allyssa's arm.

"Then step forward," Mako said.

Allyssa turned to her father.

He kissed her cheek. "I couldn't have picked a better man for you." Darmik's eyes were glassy as he released Allyssa and joined Rema and Savenek.

Allyssa handed her bouquet to Mayra before taking her place at Kerdan's side. They both faced Mako.

"We are gathered here today to celebrate the union of these two individuals, Princess Allyssa of Emperion and King Kerdan of Russek."

Kerdan took Allyssa's hand, holding it tightly. She wished his mother was alive to see the man he'd become, to see him getting married, and to see him happy.

"Please turn toward one another."

Allyssa faced Kerdan, and her breath caught. He was gazing at her, his eyes intense and determined, radiating pure love and joy. It was the most beautiful thing she'd ever seen. Reaching out, she took hold of his other hand.

"King Kerdan, do you take this woman to be your wife?"

"I do."

"Do you promise to love, protect, honor, and cherish her for the rest of your life?"

"I do."

"Princess Allyssa, do you take this man to be your husband?"

"I do."

"Do you promise to love, protect, honor, and cherish him for the rest of your life?"

Kerdan smiled at her, a devilish twinkle to his eyes.

"I do," she said without hesitation, a grin spreading across her lips.

"It's time for the rings," Mako said, opening the box.

Allyssa and Kerdan reached inside, each pulling out a gold band. Allyssa slid the band she held onto Kerdan's finger. He, in turn, slid the other onto hers, placing it next to the ring he'd already given her—his mother's wedding ring.

"I hereby pronounce you husband and wife. You may kiss the bride."

As Kerdan leaned down, Allyssa stood on her tiptoes, meeting him halfway. Kerdan pressed his warm lips against hers. She wanted to devour him at once, but everyone started clapping, reminding her they had an audience.

Kerdan moved his lips to her ear and whispered, "There will be time for that later tonight."

"There better be," she replied.

He chuckled as they turned to present themselves to the people in the room. Rema was smiling with tears in her eyes, Darmik's arm wrapped around her. Savenek nodded at Allyssa and winked, as if he knew what Kerdan had just said to her.

"May I present to you King Kerdan and his wife, Princess Allyssa."

They'd decided she would be crowned queen of Russek when she was actually in that kingdom and his subjects could be there to witness the ceremony.

Kerdan took her hand. Together, they made their way down the aisle as everyone clapped and cheered.

Allyssa couldn't believe she was married. To Kerdan. She

couldn't stop smiling.

Out in the hallway, he kissed her. "I just realized I can do that whenever I want."

Russek and Emperion soldiers surrounded them as they made their way to Darmik's office. Allyssa instructed the soldiers to remain in the corridor as she and Kerdan stepped inside, closing the door.

Kerdan wrapped his arms around her, his mouth once again finding Allyssa's. She didn't think she would ever get sick of him kissing her like this. His kisses had the same passion he exhibited when fighting, and Allyssa quite enjoyed it.

Darmik entered a moment later with Rema and Savenek.

Kerdan released Allyssa, then shook hands with Darmik.

Rema hugged her daughter. "Congratulations."

"I'm so happy."

"I can tell just by looking at you."

"We need to sign the contract," Darmik said. "My scribe has prepared three copies. Your man, Brookfel, has already read through the contract to verify everything is as it should be."

Allyssa sat next to Kerdan at Darmik's desk, each signing several pages that detailed how Emperion and Russek would handle their affairs. It had been decided Allyssa would travel to Russek with Kerdan, where she would be crowned queen. The couple planned to reside in Russek for a year. Once the year was up, Allyssa and Kerdan would visit Emperion. The contract detailed how Allyssa would be the empress when she turned thirty. At that time, Kerdan would become emperor, ruling alongside Allyssa. If anything happened to Allyssa, Kerdan would lose his title and the line would shift to Savenek. The contract also stated that Emperion and Russek would merge their two kingdoms together. However, it would be a gradual process.

Once the paperwork was signed, Allyssa stood, eager to head to the Dining Hall where supper and dancing were to take place. It was time to celebrate.

CHAPTER 21

Allyssa

Sitting at the head table next to her husband, Allyssa marveled at the fact she was married. Kerdan reached for her hand under the table, squeezing it. Would he always be so reserved in public? Probably. Just one of his many masks.

"Stop looking at me like that," he said under his breath.

"Like what?" she teased. Even though he'd been careful to keep his feelings and emotions reined in, she hadn't.

"Like I'm the main course." His eyes revealed a hint of laughter.

"Oh, I'm sorry." She pretended to be affronted. "I thought you were dessert."

He full-on laughed, causing several people to look his way. Allyssa hadn't heard him laugh like that before. The sound sent a thrill of pleasure through her—she'd not only been the cause of that laughter, but it also revealed how happy he was that his mask had slipped.

"Spare me," Savenek groaned. "No wait, I have a better idea." The twinkle in his eyes hinted at mischief. Before Allyssa could ask what he meant, he stood and raised his goblet. "If I could have your attention." Everyone stopped talking. "I'd like to make a toast to my sister and her husband."

At hearing the word *husband*, Allyssa couldn't help but smile.

When Savenek turned the full force of his gaze on her, she knew he would try to embarrass her.

"When I first met Kerdan, I thought there was no way my twin sister was going to marry him. I mean, he's from Russek." He paused and everyone in the room laughed, including Rema and Darmik. Savenek forged on, "But after I spent some time with them together, I realized my sister actually loved the brute." He said it as if he couldn't fathom the idea of anyone liking Kerdan. Everyone chuckled. "That's when I came to realize they are perfect for each other. Allyssa needs someone who treats her as an equal instead of idolizing her because of her position as the crown princess of Emperion. Kerdan just needs someone who can teach him some manners." Everyone burst out laughing. Savenek had the crowd rapt with attention, hanging on his every word. He was very good at playing the part of the prince. "Please join me in raising your drink to salute these two lucky people who've managed to find love. Congratulations, Allyssa and Kerdan. May you be filled with many blessings, happiness, health, richness, and some babies because let's face it, you need to produce some heirs!"

Everyone stomped on the floor and clapped in agreement.

Laughing, Allyssa grinned at Kerdan before kissing him soundly. The cheering became even louder.

"Dance with me, wife."

"I would love to."

They made their way to the center of the room where the dancing was to take place. The musicians started playing a slow tune. Kerdan wrapped his arms around Allyssa, holding her tightly against him. She rested her head on his chest, feeling perfectly content.

When the song ended, Savenek approached. "May I?"

Kerdan kissed Allyssa's cheek and released her.

"I can't believe you're going to leave me," Savenek said as he took Allyssa's hand and started dancing with her. "I don't understand why you *want* to go to Russek. You better not let them turn you into a fur-wearing wench who is blunt and speaks without thinking."

She whacked his shoulder, and he pretended to be hurt. "Even though you can be annoying, I am going to miss you." She wished they had more time to get to know one another better. However, Kerdan needed her with him in Russek. Since she'd trained her entire life on how to rule a kingdom, she was more than prepared to help Kerdan get Russek back on track. While the work ahead of her would be difficult, she welcomed the challenge. As for returning to the castle in Clovek, she would worry about facing those demons later. For now, she would enjoy her wedding day.

The song ended, and everyone applauded the musicians. Odar approached. "May I have this dance?"

"You may."

He gently took her hand, placing his palm on her back and making sure to keep a respectable distance. "I want to congratulate you on your marriage."

"Thank you." She couldn't believe how much she and Odar been through together. "I hope that we can remain friends."

"I'd like that." He kept his focus above her head instead of her eyes.

"Thank you for everything you've done to help me and Emperion." With their marriage contract severed, he didn't owe her anything and could have easily let Emperion fend for itself. However, he'd chosen to step in and to do the right thing.

"I'm happy to help you in any way I can. Especially after all I put you through. It was the least I could do." His voice sounded almost pained, and Allyssa realized how sorry he was for all that had happened between them.

Not knowing what else to say, she asked, "Do you plan to return home tomorrow?"

"Yes." He finally met her gaze, his eyes sad. "I can't stay here now that you're married. It's too hard."

Her heart squeezed.

Odar continued, "I'll be traveling with my parents to make sure they're on the same page as me."

Wanting to keep the conversation on a neutral topic, she said, "And what page is that?"

"I want them to understand that we are returning to Fren, where we will remain. I want to make sure we are back to being an isolated kingdom. I also need to make sure my brother is comfortable in his new position and doesn't require any assistance from my parents. I want to keep Fren and Telmena separate."

"I think that's wise."

"And it will keep me busy. I need to be busy right now."

It felt as if he'd reached in her chest and squeezed her heart. Why did he have the ability to do that to her? She rolled her shoulders back, standing tall and refusing to acknowledge what he'd said.

When the song ended, Kerdan came over. "I'm ready to retire and be alone with my wife."

Odar's face paled. "Of course. Congratulations on your marriage. I wish both of you nothing but happiness." He bowed and left, melting into the crowd.

"Ready?" Kerdan asked, his deep voice sending a wave of pleasure through Allyssa.

"I am." A smile spread across her face. She was finally able to be alone with Kerdan whenever she wanted.

Since Allyssa and Kerdan were the center of attention, there would be no sneaking out of the room unnoticed. Taking a deep breath, she went to the head table and lifted her arm. Everyone quieted down.

"Thank you for coming and sharing this special day with us. Please stay as long as you like. King Kerdan and I are retiring for the night." Allyssa felt her face warm with all the statement implied. Instead of ducking her head, she made sure to stand tall as she glided from the room, Kerdan at her side. She refused to look at Mayra, Madelin, Marek, or Savenek as she exited.

Once in the hallway, guards escorted the couple to a room that had been prepared for them in the royal wing of the castle. When they reached it, Kerdan opened the door and Allyssa stepped inside. Their guards were ordered to remain in the corridor for the duration of the night.

Allyssa surveyed the room. It was about twice the size of her bedchamber. An enormous canopied bed stood against one wall, a large stone hearth with a fire already roaring was across from it. There was a rug with sofas and chairs in one section, a dressing closet in another.

Fidgeting with her sleeve, Allyssa waited.

Kerdan closed the door. He stepped farther into the room and removed his cape. "May I?" he asked, pointing at hers.

She nodded.

He reached forward, unclasping the hooks on her shoulders. The cape fell to the ground. She left it there, her focus on Kerdan.

"So," he said.

"So," she replied.

"Do you want to talk? Or..." He reached forward, talking hold of her hips and yanking her body toward his.

"I like the *or* option."

"I was hoping you'd say that." He leaned down and nibbled on her ear. "Do you remember the first time I brought you to my room? You thought it was for this reason although, at the time, the thought hadn't even crossed my mind. And now that's all that crosses my mind." He blew into her ear sending a jolt of pleasure through her.

She remembered that day. How scared she'd been.

He kissed her neck and reached behind her, untying the laces of her dress. The bodice loosened, but he didn't remove it. Instead, his hands slid up her arms.

"Are you okay?" he asked.

There was something she wanted to tell him, but wasn't sure how to.

"What is it?" His hands rested on her shoulders.

She reached up, touching her arm just below his hand.

"Is that where the wood was impaled into you?" he asked.

"There's a hideous scar." Even though it had healed, the skin that had been stitched together was raised and jagged. It looked awful, and she made sure to always have it covered.

"Do you know what made me fall in love with you?"

"I believe you said it had something to do with me attempting to fight your soldiers that day in Russek." The day she'd been plucked from the dungeon and thrown at King Drenton's feet.

Kerdan chuckled. "Yes, that was quite a sight to behold." He stepped back and put a finger under her chin, tilting her head up so she had to look in his eyes. "I fell in love with you because of who you are and the scars you bear."

"What does that mean?"

"When I first met you, you'd been tortured and interrogated."

She refused to relive the memories of being hit with the cane and having her fingernails ripped out.

"Even though you'd suffered greatly, you still were feistier and fiercer than anyone I'd ever encountered before. You'd been through so much but instead of letting it ruin you, it made you stronger. And you shined like a star in the sky, bright and strong and beautiful."

Tears welled in her eyes. She had no idea he'd viewed her like that. Lifting her arm, she cupped his face with her palm. "I love you."

THE NEXT MORNING, ALLYSSA AWOKE SNUGGLED against Kerdan. He was lying on his back, shirtless. She pushed herself up, watching him sleep. He looked so peaceful and content. So unlike the man she'd first met in Russek. She trailed her finger along his cheek and jaw, feeling the stubble of his face against her skin.

His eyes fluttered open.

"Sorry," she said. "I didn't mean to wake you."

He reached up, his fingers curling around her wrist, and he pulled her on top of him. "Morning, wife."

She kissed him, reveling in the feel of his body below hers.

Someone knocked on the door.

"Go away!" Kerdan yelled. "I'm busy," he mumbled as he kissed Allyssa.

"I would if I could," Brookfel replied. "But I have a message from Russek that needs your immediate attention." A second later, he added, "Your Highness."

"I see Emperion is rubbing off on him," Allyssa said as she moved aside so Kerdan could get out of bed.

Grabbing a robe, he went over to the door and opened it a couple of inches. He returned a moment later, reading a letter.

"Is everything okay?" she asked.

"Yes. Several of the dukes are requesting a meeting. They want to know why a substantial portion of the army was called to Emperion." He sat on the edge of the bed, running his hand over his face. "I hate to say this, but I need to return home. I can't afford to be away any longer."

She sat up. "I understand. I'll have a few necessities packed. The rest can be shipped to Russek later."

"Are you sure you want to come with me? You can stay here for a couple more weeks. Spend some more time with your brother."

"Are you trying to get rid of me already?"

"No. I just don't want to take you away from your family."

She shook her head. Didn't he understand? "You are my family. I go where you go." The sheet fell from her body as she rose to kiss him.

It had been decided Mayra would stay in Emperion—a decision Allyssa wholly agreed with. It would be cruel to both Mayra and Savenek if Allyssa insisted her lady-in-waiting went to Russek with her. Thankfully, Madelin was eager to go, insisting on being introduced to eligible Russek men. She intended to find her own Kerdan. Allyssa just rolled her eyes. Never a dull moment with Madelin around.

The issue of Allyssa's royal guard was another matter entirely. Kerdan thought his own men should serve as her guard, Darmik wanted Nathenek to accompany her, and Marek insisted on going. After much debate and negotiation, and no one backing down, they settled on all three options.

Needing a break from the well-meaning but overbearing men, Allyssa headed to the courtyard where she found Mayra. The two of them strolled about, enjoying the warm sun.

Allyssa wondered how long it would be until she returned. "I'm going to miss you."

"The castle won't be the same without you here," Mayra said. "But don't worry, I'm sure Savenek will keep everyone on their toes."

"And you're going to be working with him." Allyssa nudged her friend's shoulder. Mayra had said very little about her relationship with Savenek.

"Promise that if you need me, you'll send word. I'll come to Russek immediately."

Allyssa linked her arm with her friend's. "I will as long as you promise to write to me. Let me know how you are and what you're doing."

"Deal. But you have to write to me as well. I want to hear all about married life."

Allyssa's face turned red as she remembered everything she and Kerdan did last night.

"Are you blushing?" Mayra asked incredulously. "Usually I'm the one with the red face, not you!"

"I must admit that so far, I am enjoying married life." She couldn't contain her smile.

"I bet you are," Mayra said, nudging her friend. "Speaking of your husband, there he is."

Allyssa looked across the courtyard at the archway Kerdan and Savenek had just entered through. The meeting about her royal guard must finally be over. "I still can't believe you jumped in front of a blade for my brother."

"Love makes you do reckless things."

"It does indeed." Allyssa went over and slid her arm around Kerdan's waist.

He kissed the top of her head. "Are you ready to learn the ways of the Russek people?" he asked her.

"I am." She'd already packed for the journey. Mayra would take care of sending the rest of Allyssa's things along in a couple of weeks. Not that Allyssa needed her Emperion dresses since it was so cold in Russek. She'd have to have several outfits made to accommodate the climate. However, she did want some of her books, jewelry, and knickknacks.

"Since we're not leaving until tomorrow morning, we have some time. Would you like to spar with me?" Kerdan asked.

"That sounds like fun," she replied.

"When you say *spar*," Mayra asked, "do you literally mean *spar*? Or is this bedroom talk for something I really don't want to know about?"

Kerdan burst out laughing.

Allyssa's eyes bulged. "Mayra!"

"What?" she asked innocently.

"That's my sister," Savenek said. "Please don't bring any of those images to mind." He stalked away, shaking his head.

Mayra chuckled and went after him.

"I meant sparring," Kerdan said, still smiling. "I want to make sure you maintain your training."

"I know." She stared into his warm brown eyes and tried to keep a straight face as she said, "But people will expect an heir, so we'll have to make sure we're working on that as well."

"Woman." He glanced around the courtyard. Their guards were several feet away and no courtiers were present. "You have no idea what you do to me." He playfully shoved her against the nearby wall, pinning her to it with his arms on either side of her head.

She didn't wait to find out what he planned to do. She threw her arms around his neck and kissed him.

CHAPTER 22

"Wait up," Mayra said. "I can't walk that fast." While she was moving around quite well, the side of her stomach under her dress was covered with a thick bandage to prevent infection from the healing knife wound.

Savenek immediately slowed his pace. "My apologies." His only thought had been getting away from Kerdan and Allyssa before they started kissing. He did not need to see his sister engaged in a public display of affection.

When they could no longer see the newlyweds, Savenek found a bench facing one of the water fountains. He plopped down on it.

"What's on your mind?" Mayra asked, taking a seat next to him.

How did she know he was upset? "Nothing." Mayra didn't need to hear his problems. It wasn't like he was a woman who had to talk about every little thing.

"Fine. Don't tell me." She started to stand.

He grabbed her hand, pulling her back down on the bench. "Don't go." Truth be told, he needed a friend right now.

"Then tell me what's bothering you."

"I'm happy Nathenek is going with Allyssa." And he was. Having Nathenek in Russek with Allyssa meant she would be taken care of, and Savenek wouldn't have to worry about his sister.

"But?"

But Nathenek was his father, not Allyssa's. If he said that out loud, he'd sound like a pansy. "I'm just surprised he is leaving Emperion."

"And by leaving Emperion you mean leaving you?" she asked, cutting to the heart of the matter.

"Yes." Maybe Nathenek was doing it on purpose. By leaving the castle, he was making sure Savenek continued to form a bond with Darmik, his birth father. A part of Savenek even thought Nathenek might be doing it as a favor to Rema. Even though he didn't think Nathenek liked her romantically, Nathenek definitely was insanely loyal and protective. Savenek supposed it was sort of like a sibling relationship. Running his hands through his hair, he tried to make sense of everything.

"I'm glad he's going," Mayra said. "I don't want my brother in Russek without someone he can trust."

Savenek agreed. It made sense Nathenek was going, but it didn't change his jumbled emotions. "You know," he said, looking sidelong at Mayra, "Marek and Nathenek are going to wreak havoc."

"Oh, I know." She smiled.

"And Allyssa will probably be right there in the thick of it with them."

"Yes." She sounded wistful.

"Are you sad you're not going with her?" he asked.

"A little. I'll miss my best friend. However, I'm excited to be here with you."

Watching the water cascade down the water fountain, he tried to imagine what the future held. He'd be running the Brotherhood, working alongside Mayra. "We need to clarify a few things," he said, sitting up straight.

Her eyebrows pulled together. "Like what?"

"Under no circumstances are to you jump in front of another blade for me."

"I couldn't let Patteon stab you. You're the prince." Her cheeks turned a shade darker, the corners of her lips pulling into a devilish smirk.

"And you're the woman I love. I can't have you fighting my battles for me." Regardless of how attractive it was to see Mayra wielding a sword.

She tilted her head back, gazing up at the sky. "What if I told you I didn't do it for you?"

"Then who'd you do it for?" he asked.

A tendril of her hair blew in the wind, taunting him. He slid his hands under his thighs, so he wouldn't reach out and play with it. That was all he needed—Neco walking up the second he touched Mayra. Neco would probably chop off Savenek's hand.

"I did it for me." She gazed at him. "I couldn't imagine my life without you. I didn't think. I saw the blade and acted."

He scooted a tad closer to her until their sides were only an inch apart. "I've never felt such terror as I did when that knife plunged into your side. When you collapsed and said you couldn't feel your legs...I've never felt so helpless." The panic he'd experienced that night came rushing back. "I can't imagine living without you. The thought of you dying, especially on my account, is too much to take."

"Then you know how I felt," she said. "And if the tables had been turned, you wouldn't have hesitated to do the same for me even though your life is infinitely more valuable than mine."

"I disagree with you on that second part. My life holds no value without you in it."

"Who knew you could be so romantic?" she teased. Mayra lifted the chain around her neck, pulling out the key he'd carved for her. She had been wearing it under the neckline of her dresses.

Satisfied she'd been wearing it this entire time, he stretched out his legs before him, crossing them at his ankles. "At least we can be hopeless romantics together. That is, when we're not busy with our spies, assassins, and running the kingdom."

She laughed, the sound echoing through the courtyard and sounding like the most wonderful thing he'd ever heard.

EVEN THOUGH SAVENEK HADN'T BEEN REUNITED WITH his twin sister for very long, he felt like he'd gotten to know her during their brief time together. He stood at the bottom of the laundry chute, waiting for her.

Sure enough, a few minutes later, she came barreling out of the chute. "How'd you know?" she asked as she stood and straightened her clothes.

"It's your last night in Lakeside. Where else would you be?"

She smiled. "Kerdan was a little worried when he caught me sneaking out of our room and back to my old bedchamber. But then he realized what I was doing, and he just shook his head and went back to sleep."

"He probably has one of his men watching you."

"I'm sure he does." She nodded at the laundry room door and they exited, making their way through the castle and off the grounds.

As they walked through Lakeside, the frigid wind whipped around Savenek, making him shiver. He wouldn't say he missed the sandy blandness of Emperor's City, but he did miss being warm. "What do you want to do on your last night here? Go to a tavern? Catch some heathens? Just walk around?"

Allyssa glanced up and down the street before grabbing his sleeve and yanking him into a narrow alleyway. She continued about thirty paces until she came to a ladder attached to the side of the building on the right. Allyssa scaled it, Savenek right behind her, wondering what she was up to.

When he reached the top, he found Allyssa stretched out on the flat portion of the roof, staring up at the stars. Savenek positioned himself next to her. Somehow, the stars seemed brighter tonight. He breathed in the smell of baking bread and thought about his aunt and uncle back in Emperor's City. Did they know who he was now? When he visited them, would they treat him any differently? "I miss the smell of the ocean," he admitted.

"I'm going to miss this. There isn't a town in Clovek. It's just a castle with estates and small villages surrounding it."

That was probably better. She wouldn't get into as much trouble if there wasn't a town for her to sneak out and explore. However, Savenek had no doubt she'd still find something to do that would try Kerdan's patience. "Are you excited about going to Russek?" he asked, wondering if the man who'd tortured her was still in Clovek. How would Allyssa handle seeing him again? How would she deal with being back in the castle that held so many bad memories? Would she be okay? At least she'd have Marek and Nathenek there. But still.

"I'm excited to see Russek through Kerdan's eyes."

Which meant that she was excited to be going with Kerdan, yet nervous to be back at the castle where she'd been held captive. He'd have to keep in contact with Nathenek and Marek to make sure she was doing okay. "Please be careful in Russek. There will be people who want Kerdan's throne." And they wouldn't hesitate to go through Allyssa to get it.

"I will." She turned her head so she was looking at Savenek. "Please promise you'll look after Mother and Father."

"I will."

They stayed there, on the rooftop, staring up at the stars in the sky. Brother and sister. Twins. Prince and princess. Friends.

SAVENEK STILL COULDN'T BELIEVE ALLYSSA WAS leaving. Everything seemed to be happening so quickly. He'd thought he'd have more time with her. He'd thought she'd stay here. He hadn't realized how sad he'd be to see her go.

Everyone from the castle came to see Allyssa off. Savenek stood with Rema and Darmik, waiting for Allyssa to exit so they could say their goodbyes. Mayra was busy with Marek, Neco, and Ellie. They were hugging Marek. Kerdan was busy giving orders to his soldiers, getting everyone into position. There would be no carriages for this journey—only horses.

Nathenek came over. "Can I have a word with Savenek before I leave?"

"Of course." Savenek walked with him a few steps away from Rema and Darmik so they could be alone.

"I'm sorry I didn't tell you about your parents sooner," Nathenek said.

"It's okay." He'd had enough time to get over the shock.

"You had a right to know."

Savenek agreed. However, everything had worked out. "Thank you for raising me and being my dad."

Nathenek nodded. "My life would have been lonely without you. Raising you has been my greatest honor and accomplishment."

Savenek didn't need Nathenek getting all emotional on him now. The last thing he wanted to do was cry in front of so many people. "I'll miss you."

Nathenek put his hands on Savenek's shoulders and looked him in the eyes. "Try not to get into too much trouble while I'm gone."

Savenek couldn't help but smile. "I'll try. But I can't make any promises." He hugged the man who'd acted like his father, raised him like a father, but who wasn't his father.

Nathenek released him and headed over to one of the horses, mounting. He never was one for affection.

Allyssa finally exited the castle, Madelin right behind her complaining about riding on a horse for such a long distance.

"Then don't come if all you're going to do is complain," Allyssa snapped.

Madelin opened her mouth to reply, but Vesha and Audek stepped in front of her, demanding her attention. After Madelin said farewell to her parents, she mounted the horse next to Nathenek's.

Allyssa went straight to Mayra, hugging her. The two friends stayed that way for several minutes. Finally, Allyssa released her and came over to Savenek. "Please watch over Mother and Father," she said. "I'm expecting you to keep Emperion running while I'm gone."

"You can count on me," he replied. "Just don't stay away too long."

"I won't. This is home. I love Emperion."

Savenek hugged his twin sister, thankful for the time they'd had together. As much as he hated that she'd been kidnapped, at least a few good things came from it. Allyssa had met Kerdan. And when everyone thought she'd been killed, Savenek had been crowned prince, which allowed him to meet his parents and his sister. Although he'd loved his life in the Brotherhood, he preferred this life, this family, this happiness. He glanced over at Mayra, who stood watching him. He blew her a kiss and wiggled his eyebrows. Her face turned bright red.

Allyssa released Savenek, approaching Rema and Darmik. Rema started crying as she wrapped her arms around Allyssa, squeezing her. Savenek suspected Darmik was barely holding it together.

Kerdan came over and stood before Darmik. "I promise to take care of your daughter."

"You better," Darmik replied. "Because if anything happens to her, I'm holding you personally responsible. I'll have no qualms about killing you."

Savenek knew his father was half-joking and half-serious. He felt the same way. If anything happened to Allyssa, Savenek would personally seek revenge.

Kerdan hesitated a moment before hugging Rema. He

whispered something in her ear, but Savenek couldn't hear what he said. Kerdan released her and mounted his horse.

"I love you," Allyssa said, kissing Rema's cheek and then hugging Darmik one last time. "And I love you." Allyssa wrapped her arms around Savenek.

He patted her back. "I'll come visit in a season or two."

"You better." After she released him, she mounted the horse beside Kerdan's.

The Russek army moved into formation around their king and future queen. Kerdan raised his arm, giving the signal to move out.

Savenek stood on the steps of the Emperion castle, watching them ride away.

CHAPTER 23

Allyssa

*A*llyssa refused to look back at her family. It would be too hard watching them fade away. Instead, she kept her focus forward, on the path ahead.

"Are you okay?" Kerdan asked.

She smiled at her husband. "As long as I'm with you, I'm always okay."

He grinned one of his rare smiles, lighting up his face.

The last time, she'd been taken to Russek against her will. This time, she looked forward to going and spending time there, seeing where Kerdan grew up, his favorite spots to hunt, and where he trained with his men. She looked forward to helping the Russek people have better lives through trade, farming, and lower taxes. She'd spent most her life learning how to rule a kingdom. Now she would be by Kerdan's side helping him, working together, and making a difference.

There would be peace.

They traveled a little over a fortnight before they reached the castle in Clovek. The dark fortress rose out of the snowy mountains like a beast—just as she remembered. Instead of going across the dangerous bridge as she did last time, they went around to the back where the stables were located.

A stable boy ran over and took her horse. Kerdan helped her

dismount. Her back was a little sore from being in the saddle for so long.

They went in through an entrance in the side of the mountain. When they came to the main part of the castle, it was warm and bright, vastly different from the last time Allyssa was here. All the torches were lit, instead of every fourth one. Servants were out and about, cleaning and bringing in supplies.

"What's going on?" she asked.

"They are preparing for you," Kerdan replied. "Everyone is excited that you are here. They've been expecting you." He led her to the Throne Room.

The last time she'd been in this room, she'd been dragged here before Jana. This time, she entered of her own free will. Two polished chairs stood on the dais, banners of the royal family's crest hung from the ceiling. The place felt alive and new. She looked at Kerdan, her brows pulling together in question.

"The castle has been cleaned from top to bottom. You won't find a trace of Jana or her children here. This is your home now, and we all want you to feel safe and welcome here."

"Thank you."

There were a few courtiers milling about.

Kerdan sat on his throne chair, pointing at the other one. Allyssa sat, watching as people started coming into the room. After a few minutes, the place was packed with courtiers, soldiers, and servants.

Kerdan stood and addressed his people. "Thank you for coming. I am pleased to introduce my wife, Crown Princess Allyssa of Emperion. It is time to crown her Queen of Russek."

Allyssa stood, not prepared for the ceremony to take place right now. She'd been on a horse for days and needed a bath. And she was wearing pants and a tunic—not an outfit befitting of a queen.

Kerdan leaned toward her and mumbled, "You must remember, we don't have Emperion's silly rules and traditions."

This was going to take some getting used to.

Allyssa stared out at the crowd of eager faces, all there to witness the ceremony. She smiled at her future subjects, already feeling a connection to them.

"Welcome home, wife," Kerdan said loud enough for everyone in the room to hear.

The people cheered and stomped on the floor, declaring their approval.

Laughing, Allyssa reached out and took hold of Kerdan's hand, squeezing it. Her husband, her king, her best friend. Together, as equals, they would rule the people of Russek and Emperion.

EPILOGUE

*A*llyssa sat on the bed, exhausted. She was covered in sweat, her body weak from the events that had just transpired.

The baby screamed, arms and legs reaching out in every direction.

Allyssa glanced at Kerdan. His eyes were transfixed on the baby.

The healer holding the infant smiled. "Congratulations. It's a girl."

"A girl," Allyssa repeated, amazed. She had a baby girl.

"Here you go, Your Highness." The healer wrapped the infant in a blanket, then handed the bundle to Allyssa.

Allyssa took the baby, staring at her beautiful, perfect face. "She has your nose," she said to Kerdan.

"And she has your eyes," he replied, reaching out and stroking the side of the infant's face. "She's going to be one fierce little thing."

"Of that I have no doubt."

THE END

ACKNOWLEDGMENTS

Writing a book is an enormous undertaking. I am blessed to have a wonderful husband and three kids who know and understand my obsession with reading and writing. Thank you for allowing me to do something I'm passionate about and encouraging me every step of the way.

I'd also like to thank Leah, Allyssa, Jan, Stacie, Hannah, and Carol for reading through this book and providing feedback. I couldn't have written this one without your valuable input.

I want to thank Sarah for our writing meetings. When I came to the point in my novel where things weren't coming together, you reminded me that everyone needs to have a motivation for what they do. When you said that, everything clicked together and the story solidified. I can't thank you enough!

I also want to thank Cynthia for editing this one. The story was a beast to tackle and you did an amazing job polishing it for me. Thank you!

Last, but not least, I need to thank all of my readers. When I first started out as a writer, I had no idea my stories would touch other people's lives. To receive your fan mail and messages saying how much you love my stories truly warms my heart and keeps me going. Thank you!

ABOUT THE AUTHOR

Jennifer Anne Davis graduated from the University of San Diego with a degree in English and a teaching credential. She is currently a full-time writer. Jennifer is the winner of the Kindle Book Awards: Young Adult Novel (2018), winner of the San Diego Book Awards Best Published Young Adult Novel (2013), a finalist in the Next Generation Indie Book Awards: Young Adult (2014), and a finalist in the USA Best Book Awards: Young Adult (2014).

Visit Jennifer online at:
www.JenniferAnneDavis.com